GOODBYE, MS. CHIPS

Also in the Ellie Haskell Series

by Dorothy Cannell

The Thin Woman

The Widow's Club

Mum's the Word

Femmes Fatal

How to Murder Your Mother-in-Law

How to Murder the Man of Your Dreams

The Spring Cleaning Murders

The Trouble with Harriet

Bridesmaids Revisited

The Importance of Being Ernestine

Withering Heights

GOODBYE, MS. CHIPS

Dorothy Cannell

ST. MARTIN'S MINOTAUR
New York

This is a work of fiction. All of the characters, organizations, and events portrayed in this novel are either products of the author's imagination or are used fictitiously.

 For information, address St. Martin's Press, 175 Fifth Avenue, New York, N.Y. 10010.

www.minotaurbooks.com

Library of Congress Cataloging-in-Publication Data

Cannell, Dorothy,
Goodbye, Ms. Chips : an Ellie Haskell mystery / Dorothy Cannell. — 1st ed.
p. cm.
ISBN-13: 978-0-312-34338-5
ISBN-10: 0-312-34338-8
1. Haskell, Ellie (Fictitious character)—Fiction. 2. Women interior decorators—Fiction. 3. Boarding schools—Fiction. 4. England—Fiction. I. Title.

PS3553.A499G66 2008
813'.54—dc22

2007051827

First Edition: April 2008

10 9 8 7 6 5 4 3 2 1

For Mariah Moore, who likes dogs and cats; Von-she, who likes basketball; and Olivia, who likes being the baby sister. With love from Granna.

ACKNOWLEDGMENTS

To my friend Barbara Cansfield White, who graciously loaned me her computer so I could finish the manuscript.

GOODBYE, MS. CHIPS

1

"Ellie, the headmistress wants to see you."

Words to strike terror in the heart of any inmate of St. Roberta's boarding school for girls who has failed to turn in her Latin prep, left out London when drawing a map of England, or—worse yet—prowled the ruins of the medieval convent at dead of night. Naturally I shuddered, even though I was now a grown woman and the speaker was my dear friend Dorcas Critchley, who had arrived unexpectedly a half hour before.

The school I had attended as a pupil was now her place of employment. Upon the retirement of Ms. Chips at the end of the previous school year, Dorcas had assumed the post of games mistress and now had the dubious pleasure of chivying a bunch of girls in bottle-green shorts and mustard-yellow shirts to victory on the playing field. My being a St. Roberta's old girl was a coincidence, and Dorcas had very sensibly not asked me for a personal reference. Ms. Chips, who undoubtedly still had the headmistress's ear, could not be expected to remember me with enthusiasm, given that the only ball I had ever managed to lob in lacrosse had whacked her squarely on the nose—breaking it, so Matron had informed me icily, in at least three places.

Haunted by this memory and its outcome, I now sought solace from my surroundings. It was a sunny Saturday afternoon early in June, and Dorcas and I sat in white wicker chairs on the back lawn of my home, Merlin's Court. Its fantastical castle turrets poked cheerfully into the pure blue sky, daring a dark cloud to show a malignant face. The miniature moat collected only sanguine shadows. The garden's gently sloping lawns were shaded by beech trees and interspersed with flower beds bursting with riotous color. The air was perfumed with roses. Indoors were my wonderful husband, Ben, and our three adorable children. Given this heaping helping of life's bounty, only an ingrate would not respond to Dorcas's astonishing announcement with an interested smile.

"Why on earth would Mrs. Battle want to see me?" I endeavored to sound cheerfully intrigued. "Surely it can't be to find out why I never joined the Old Girls' Association."

"Nothing to fear in that regard, Ellie," Dorcas reassured me.

"Oh, goodie!"

"Am here as her emissary. Something nasty occurred at old Roberta's. Shocking business! Threatens blight on our outstanding reputation. Ghastly for Mrs. Battle! Blasted all to pieces, as you might expect! Hands trembled the other day when mounting the dais to take assembly."

"To everything there is a season." The words hopped out of my mouth. Dorcas raised an inquiring eyebrow, and I looked at the table between our chairs, but no pot of tea and plate of biscuits had magically appeared to put me in a better frame of mind. "Sorry," I said. "I was remembering how I quivered and quaked when the Battle-ax caught me wearing my uniform cardigan back to front, for a change."

"Frightfully sorry to put you in a spot. Should have remem-

bered your saying you don't have fond memories of school."
Dorcas's gaze faltered. Some people might consider her plain, with her thin face, sharp features, and short ginger hair clipped back from her brow. But I wouldn't have changed a thing about her, from the serviceable tweed jacket and slacks to the argyle socks. My mind went back ten years to our first meeting, shortly after Ben and I had inherited Merlin's Court from an elderly relative of mine. Our good fortune had not gone down well with members of the family who had hoped to find themselves on easy street when the old man finally pegged it. Sadly, we were forced to the lamentable conclusion that one of them wanted us out of the house—and into the graveyard. But Dorcas had been there for us every step of the way until the villain was unmasked and the danger removed. Over the course of the following years she had been a frequent much-loved visitor, always spending Christmas and Easter with us. Knowing a warm welcome awaited her, she also enjoyed making impromptu visits such as this one. I was horrified at the thought of hurting her feelings.

"I'm the one who should be sorry. I've been behaving like an insensitive wretch." I leaned toward her. "This business, whatever it is, has you seriously upset. I thought you weren't your usual chirpy self when you arrived, and now I can see shadows under your eyes. You haven't been sleeping properly."

"Perfectly fit, never better. Can still skim the high bar and land upright."

"Forget the brave front." I wagged a finger at her. "What evil stalks the hallowed halls of St. Roberta's?"

"Don't know how to break it to you." My friend reached into her trouser pocket for a handkerchief the size of a small tablecloth.

"Just say it, Dorcas, dear."

"A sports cup has been stolen from the trophy case in the assembly hall."

"Is that all? I was afraid a bunch of first formers, fed up with shepherd's pie, had murdered the cook."

"Ellie, it was the Loverly Cup!"

I thought she was stammering. "The lovely . . . ?"

"Loverly. Awarded annually by Lady Loverly of the Hall at Upper Swan-Upping to the winner of the area schools' lacrosse championship match. For the past nine years, St. Roberta's has won it handily. Sadly, not in the cards this time. Disappointing season." Dorcas sucked in a breath and blew tremulously into the handkerchief. "Blame myself. Failed to rouse the old fighting school spirit. Offered to resign."

Preferable, I thought fondly, to donning a kimono and falling on her lacrosse stick. What she needed at this moment was a strong cup of tea, but alas, the wrought-iron table remained bare. I decided against nipping into the house and brewing a pot in favor of offering immediate comfort.

"Dorcas, it sounds like a schoolgirl prank to me."

"That's what Mrs. Battle is hoping. But worried stiff the matter could turn out to be more serious."

"Such as?"

"Evil plot to ruin St. Roberta's stainless reputation."

Masterminded, I supposed, by a shadowy figure with an eye patch and a hollow cough who would prove to be the recently dismissed French mistress. "When was the cup taken?"

"This past Monday."

A vital question loomed. "How long before it must be handed over to the new lacrosse champions?"

"End of the month. Last week of term."

"I gather the Battle-ax is against involving the authorities?"

"Can't say I blame her. Police cars screeching down the drive, sirens wailing?" Dorcas paled visibly. "No keeping *that* hullabaloo from the Board of Governors and the parents. Could be the end of good old Roberta's."

Although this seemed to me to be going overboard, I made

soothing noises in the manner of a brook attempting to calm the troubled sea. Had she been a different sort, Dorcas would have whacked me or at least told me to stuff the platitudes.

"Hard enough these days to keep any school going without a scandal. Mrs. Battle brightened when I reported your great success as private investigator."

An unpleasant apprehension seized me. "You said she wanted to meet with me, but this sounds as though more than a nip in and out of her office will be entailed. To unmask the Cup Culprit, I'd have to stay at or near school for days on end—possibly weeks!" My mind shut down at the horror of it.

"Asking a lot of you, I know."

I reminded myself sternly that I was supposedly a grown-up—wife, mother, part-time interior designer. I remembered my parents had sold their souls to their bank manager, unhappily named Mr. Shark, in return for an overdraft the size of the national debt in order to pay my school fees. My courage still failed me. "Dorcas, I don't think I'm up to this."

She misunderstood me. "Know you think yourself an amateur. Modest, always have been; one of the things I admire most. But if anyone can solve the mystery, it's you."

Ignobly I sought an out. "Thank you, Dorcas, but I don't handle cases on my own. I usually work in tandem with Mrs. Malloy."

Even as I spoke these words, a woman with jet-black hair highlighted by two inches of white roots crossed the courtyard at last, carrying a tea tray. Here was my trusty household helper and partner in the sleuthing business. It must be added that she made an imposing figure. Her generous contours were presently displayed to full advantage in a forest-green taffeta dress. Glittering brooches planted here and there suggested she was descended from the czars of Russia. Hopefully she'd never be forced to flee a revolution, her high heels being unsuited to successful escape down a dark alley. I worried about the tea tray; one misstep and there would go a perfectly good teapot and assorted crockery, to say nothing of the cucumber sandwiches and jam tarts.

Dorcas likewise perceived the possibility of imminent disaster. Leaping to her feet as if in response to a starting pistol, she had the tray on a table before I could blink.

"Well, that was good of you, Miss Critchley!" Mrs. Malloy landed in a chair. Her rouged face cracked as she produced a purple-lipsticked smile. "For a minute I thought I was back to me old rugby days, about to be tackled to the ground by sixteen stone of solid muscle."

Bless the woman! Being a romantic she is given to these flights of fancy, and doubtless the scene continued to play out in her mind. The team captain would announce between gasping breaths that he was in actual fact the deposed king of Ruritania; if she didn't think him too bold, he would sweep her off to his flat after the match and deflower her at his leisure.

Dorcas took the cup of tea I passed her and apologized to Mrs. Malloy for startling her. "Sorry! Not thinking clearly. Lot on my mind, I'm afraid." My heart ached, she looked so despondent. She gave much and asked little in return. Would it really kill me to help her out in her hour of need? Biting into a sandwich, I attempted to garner strength.

"It's me that is sorry, Miss C," protested Mrs. Malloy magnanimously. "I could see the moment you arrived this afternoon as you was down in the dumps. It worried me sufficient that I couldn't concentrate on me dusting or work up the enthusiasm to sort out the toy cupboard. What that good woman needs, I said to Mr. Haskell, is a decent cup of tea. And with himself playing Monopoly with the children like he does most Saturday afternoons, I got the kettle going and nipped to it."

"Good of you, Mrs. Malloy. Can't say how much I appreciate. . . ." Out came the handkerchief, with noisy results.

I wasn't equally impressed with Mrs. M's slavish devotion to duty. When last I'd seen her, she'd been on the drawing room sofa with her feet up, reading *The Lamentable Affair at Latchings* while the dust and toy cupboard went unlamented. This, however, was not the moment to play the heavy-handed employer. Much good it would have done me anyway. From the start of our relationship, it has been unclear whether Mrs. Malloy or I rule the roost in domestic matters. Not that it matters. She is above all things a staunch ally when the chips are down.

"Dorcas is here on her headmistress's behalf," I explained. "The Battle-ax wants to see me."

"Forget to finish the fourth form, Mrs. H?"

I smiled dutifully at this quip. "Mrs. Battle was indeed at the helm when I was at St. Roberta's, though I doubt she would remember me without some nudging. No, a sports cup has been stolen. The hope is that I . . . we," I added quickly, "can recover it before its loss has to be made public." I went on to explain that it was soon to be handed on to another school. Meanwhile, Dorcas sat in sad contemplation of her argyle socks.

"Is it very valuable, this cup?" The thrilled expression on Mrs. Malloy's face suggested she was indulging her imagination again. Did she picture a goblet studded with jewels sufficient to ransom Richard the Lionhearted from the bunch of miffed Turks or whoever had locked him up in a moldering stronghold? A just fate, I had always thought, for a man who had gone jaunting off to the Crusades, leaving his brother John to tick off the barons and make life difficult for Robin Hood. "Gold?" breathed Mrs. Malloy.

"Silver cup," replied Dorcas, "but bound to be valuable. Work of Hester Bateman."

"Who?"

"The queen of eighteenth-century silversmiths. A friend of mine paid a hundred pounds for one teaspoon with her hallmark." Having demolished more than my share of sandwiches in a desperate attempt at building up my defenses, I was feeling a smidge more cheerful. "Lady Loverly doesn't stint with her trophy giving."

"Lady who?" Mrs. Malloy held out her teacup for a refill.

"Loverly. A woman, if I remember correctly, who wore horrific hats and seemed to have twice the usual number of teeth. Middle-aged, which would make her elderly now, after nearly twenty years. Goodness! It's amazing to think it's been that long. I left St. Roberta's when I was fifteen. None of its girls could have been happier to go home and burn that hideous uniform than I!"

"What then, Mrs. H? Parents get you a governess?"

"Art school."

Dorcas continued to study her argyle socks. I could tell from her hunched posture that, sympathetic as she generally was to my feelings, she was shocked by my lack of loyalty to St. Roberta's. It came to me then, with an anguished pang, that I could not bring myself to tell her why I was so averse to returning there. A woman of her unfaltering integrity could not but condemn my failure to have spoken out and saved a fellow schoolgirl from unjust disciplinary action when I knew her to be innocent of the charge against her.

It seemed to me that the bright-blue sky paled as I turned my gaze away from Dorcas and Mrs. Malloy. Pretty, immensely popular, thoroughly nice Philippa Boswell had been stripped of the captainship of the lacrosse team and told that she would not be named head girl at the start of the new school year as had been anticipated. The entire school was stunned, the pupils disbelieving. But the accusation—of absenting herself from the school building without leave to conduct an assignation beyond the grounds with a member of the male species—had stood. The Board of Governors, with the bulldoggish Mr. Bumbleton at the helm, congratulated themselves that an example had been made; my heart had broken for Philippa—but in silence.

She left St. Roberta's at the end of that summer term, announcing that she had decided not to return for the sixth form. One class behind her, I exited when she did, having persuaded my parents to let me attend a local art school. I'd kept my dark secret ever since, even from Ben. Not because he would have recoiled in horror and taken to sleeping in the guest bedroom, but because the thought of my confessional words making ugly contact with the air made my heart hammer and beads of sweat form on my brow. It was no consolation that Philippa could not have known I might have spoken up to spare her the shame and disappointment she had endured.

I now drew a ragged breath and listened to Mrs. Malloy.

"Does this Lady Loverly know the cup is missing?" she was asking Dorcas.

"Bound to. Got a goddaughter in the fourth form: Carolyn Fisher-Jones. Wouldn't be cricket to expect the girl to keep mum. Sensible fourteen-year-old. Good deal of poise for her age. Would look at home on a decent horse. Classmate and close chums this term with Matron's great-niece, Gillian Parker. Matie's been in a real tizz about this business. Worried about how it will go down with Ms. Chips." Dorcas re-produced the handkerchief. "Fast friends since their own schooldays at Billbury Academy in Devon."

"Chips?" Mrs. Malloy refilled our teacups. "Is that a nickname? Tip of the hat to the beloved schoolmaster in—?"

"In the tenderly tearful *Goodbye, Mr. Chips*?" I had loved both the book and the movie. "It's her own name. Not even an abbreviation. Dorcas"—I turned to her—"what has been her reaction to the cup's disappearance?"

"Haven't heard, but bound to have taken it on the chin. That sort of woman."

Mrs. Malloy reached for the last cucumber sandwich. "I thought she'd retired and you'd taken her place, Miss Critchley."

"Right enough," responded Dorcas, "but still around. Does

dorm duty if needed. Bought a house nearby in Upper Swan-Upping."

"Blimey! Is that where the school is?" Mrs. M raised a painted eyebrow.

"Mile or so distant. St. Roberta's is on the far edge of Lower Swan-Upping before open country takes over. Bridle paths, lovers' lanes, woodlands, fields. Not surprising Ms. Chips chose to stay in the area. Keen hiker. Matron worries she overdoes it. Not the outdoorsy type herself. Bad experience. Got lost on the moors as a girl."

"Always best to get right away when making a new start," opined Mrs. Malloy. "Like I just said to Mr. Haskell when he had to sell off a bunch of hotels to pay Tam for landing on Park Place, it don't do to cling to the past. Shake the dice and move on. So he did and collected two hundred pounds for passing Go."

"Wonderful!" I said. "Just so long as he doesn't have to sell Merlin's Court when he lands on Mayfair. Which he will do, there being a dreadful inevitability when one is losing at Monopoly. Our children can be pretty ruthless. Miss Chips is fortunate not to be at their mercy. I can't see her being content if forced to move very far from St. Roberta's. It's a good thing that property in country areas tends to be more reasonably priced than in the cities."

"Not the case with Lower and Upper Swan-Upping." Dorcas shook her head, causing a noncompliant strand of hair to escape onto her brow. "Even Cygnet's Way, once a strip of laborers'cottages, has gone up-market, so I've been told."

"It's the fault of them bloody commuters!" Mrs. Malloy's sympathetic outrage refracted off the faux emeralds and rubies on her storefront bosom.

I nodded agreement. "Someone, preferably the government, should put a spoke in their wheels. The cheek of people thinking they can have it both ways! Working in London or Birmingham and going home to a picture-postcard cottage enlivened by children named Buttercup and Daisy after the congenial cows in the adjoining pasture." Turning to Dorcas, I said I remembered Cygnet's Way as a dismal little street.

"Wouldn't know it now, Ellie. Bumbleton and Sons, the builders, bought the houses, did them up, and then sold the lot for a huge profit. Blow for Matron! Had been hoping to buy the one she'd leased over the years to live in during the hols."

"Is that where Ms. Chips bought?" I asked.

"No. Purchased a house on the green. Tudor. Named The Laurels or Fir Trees—something of the sort. Didn't need to worry about price. Came into a handsome legacy last year. Being a thundering good sport, she also financed a new gymnasium for St. Roberta's. Bumbleton's got that job too. Old chap's on the Board of Governors." Dorcas was again compelled to reach for the handkerchief. "Better woman than Marilyn Chips never invoked the old sporting spirit."

I was stunned that Ms. Chips had a first name. Who would have thought! "That must have been some legacy." My attempt to brighten the mood succeeded with Mrs. Malloy. It was her frequently voiced opinion that there is nothing in life more romantic than coming into bundles of money, especially if doing so means cutting out others hoping to scoop the lot after years of buttering up the doddering old benefactor. Something I can say I didn't do with Uncle Merlin. Not that Mrs. M would have held it against me. For Mrs. M, true life should always merge with fiction. Noting the gleam in her eyes, I could tell she was increasingly enthusiastic about the prospect of a sojourn at St. Roberta's. In her mind it would be a storybook school complete with illustrations. A place where the girls were not as bothered with getting an education as in the formation of secret societies, with all the attendant excitement of midnight feasts, whispered passwords, and the thrilling discovery that the fourth-form mistress is the ringleader of an international smuggling ring. To her credit

Mrs. Malloy contained her emotions, merely asking if Ms. Chips's legacy had been unexpected.

"Bolt from the blue. According to Matey, had planned to live off her pension." Dorcas emerged from her handkerchief. "Makes this cup business especially sad, bang up against Chippie's shining moment. Gala evening planned to celebrate the new gymnasium: fruit punch, sausages on sticks, that sort of thing. All arrangements made. Cards sent out. Board of Governors, parents, old girls, local notables invited."

"This event takes place when?" I asked.

"Twenty-eighth of June. Same day the Loverly Cup passes on." Dorcas spoke with a brave attempt at calm.

"No time then to be lost in recovering it." Mrs. Malloy glittered with energy. "When does the headmistress want to see Mrs. H?"

"Tomorrow morning if possible." Dorcas blinked an apologetic look my way.

"I'd drive back with you?" My hand searched for a jam tart.

"Know it puts you in a spot, working out arrangements for the children and setting aside current work."

"That's manageable," I replied, in hollow accents. No escape hatch here. Ben, who owns a French bistro named Abigail's in the village, could delegate as necessary to my cousin Freddy, who works for him, and so be home with Tam, Abbey, and Rose when they weren't in school. Being the husband he is, he wouldn't make a moan about not being able to crack on with the cookery book he is writing. As for myself, I had no interior design commissions on the verge of completion. A check of my calendar, which might lead to few phone calls, would be the only requirement in freeing me up for the next couple of weeks. "Where would I stay?"

Dorcas explained about a house on the grounds that fifty years ago had been occupied by the school chaplain and his family. After that, it had been left to the invasion of mold and decay until Miss Chips came into her legacy. In addition to her beneficence with the gymnasium, she had fulfilled a longtime aspiration of refurbishing the house as a retreat for old girls, ones who needed a temporary escape from the pressures of their lives: divorce, loss of a job. . . . I'd have to come up with a cover to explain my arrival. Dorcas made a couple of suggestions that floated past me.

Some dickey birds had settled in the minstrel's gallery of the closest beech tree and were singing their little hearts out, as befitted their brown choir robes. I'm not much of a judge—in fact, Mr. Middleton, who had taught music at St. Roberta's, had informed me I had a tin ear—nevertheless, I doubted there was a nightingale in that feathery lineup. The performance struck me as sadly mediocre. I was pretty sure that at least two sparrows were off-key, and the bigger one hit a seriously sour note seconds before the sun slunk behind a sudden cloud. My heart went out to the loyal little band of family and friends gathered in the audience with their hearts in their throats and bright little smiles on their beaks, hoping against ardent hope that Percy would get through "O Sole Mio" without being bitten to death by the bird to his left. A portentous little bully if ever I saw one.

I had been horribly bullied my first year at St. Roberta's by a girl in my class named Rosemary Martin, who had a singing voice that drowned out the chirpers and a Roman nose that, in all fairness, she couldn't help. Mr. Middleton had assigned solo parts to her either because she really was good or because otherwise she would have had him fed to the lions.

Now, in a determined effort at more positive thinking, I focused on my father's words of consolation when I'd told him what Mr. Middleton had said about me. "Better a tin ear," quoth Daddy, with a customary flourish, "than a tin cup." Words of wisdom to cling to in my present situation. Dorcas hadn't asked me to sit on a pavement and beg for change from impervious pedestrians. From the sound of the renovated Chaplain's House, its accommodations would more than pass muster. I might even find myself enjoying the company of other old girls who might be staying there.

A sideways glance at Mrs. Malloy showed she was looking as glum as all get out.

"What's wrong?" I asked her.

"Tomorrow's no good for me. Like I've been telling you all week, me sister Melody's coming to stay for a few days, bringing her new husband to show him off. I can't just bunk off and leave them to it, can I?"

"Probably not," I said. "And you've been dying to see the wedding photos."

"She's me only sister. It wouldn't do not to take an interest."

"It was a delightful wedding," I informed Dorcas.

"Jolly ho!" she enthused kindly.

It had been lovely. Unfortunately, Melody could never have been a Grecian urn and at age sixty was ever less likely to be rhapsodized by poets, but she had radiated a joy that made her frizzy hair and dumpy figure enviable, while the bridegroom had beamed with love and pride.

"That cherry suit I helped her pick out was just right," said Mrs. Malloy. "Left to herself, she might have decided to wear white, and that would have been a terrible mistake for a woman of her age. She would have looked like the spook bride in *The Sexton's Secret*, Mrs. H!"

I remembered vividly that particular scene in the book: a ghoulish figure drifting down the aisle . . . gown yellowed and spotted with age, reeking of mildew and death . . . a garland of crumbling rosebuds . . . the organist who displayed a flair for the mournful . . . effigies on the wall that turned a paler shade of marble as their eye sockets searched the gloom for shadows that had life in them. When reading those lines I had recalled the legend of the Gray Nun, whose wraith was said to haunt the ruined convent at the edge of St. Roberta's grounds. My one midnight excursion into the crypt with a couple of my classmates had produced no sight of her, but that might have been because she didn't consider a bunch of giggling fourteen-year-olds a worthy audience for fleshless hand wringing and pitiful moans.

"Of course I want to do right by Melody."

Mrs. Malloy still sounded seriously put out. In addition to her disappointment at not being able to accompany Dorcas and me to Lower Swan-Upping, she might have been remembering that as Melody's bridesmaid she had not looked her best in dusty pink, a color she despised.

"I had intended on giving her and the new hubby me own room with the comfy double bed." Sticking her nose in the air, she risked having it pecked off by Percy, the musical sparrow, or another passing dickey bird. "But on second thought, if I was to put them in the box room that has the single with the thin mattress, they could get to thinking as how they was imposing by staying as long as they planned, and take themselves off." Catching Dorcas's eye, she looked momentarily abashed; then her purple mouth set in a mulish line, indicating that her heart had hardened. "If you ask me, Miss C, it's not natural for a newly married couple to stay with relations. You'd think with both of them waiting so long to tie the knot they'd want to focus on taking the instruction booklet to bed with them every night to see if they couldn't get top marks. What if they're not getting the hang of things because Melody's too shy? Or she thinks Bill should try them pills some men need to take and I'm roped in to listening to their bedroom problems?"

"Difficult." Dorcas's complexion rivaled her red hair.

"Like Mrs. H will tell you, it's not in me nature to enjoy mixing in other people's business." Mrs. Malloy laid out this whopper without the hint of a blush. "Besides, I wouldn't want little Ariel Hopkins thinking I wasn't bothered about seeing her."

The mention of this name gave me a jolt. My horror at the

thought of returning to St. Roberta's and being forced to confront the episode involving Philippa Boswell had made me forget that Ariel had for the past year been a student at the school. Her father was Ben's cousin Tom Hopkins, and the family lived in Milton Moor, making them acquaintances of Melody. The opportunity to spend a few days with the Hopkinses had been a bonus for me in driving Mrs. Malloy to her sister's wedding. Ariel, who had been home for half term, was fourteen.

"Bright girl," said Dorcas. "Plenty of spirit."

But had Ariel wholeheartedly embraced life at St. Roberta's? I wondered. She was a prickly little person, apt to scorn popularity for the sake of it or because she preferred to bury her nose in a book featuring life at its more exciting. One could never tell which way she would jump next, although I doubted it would be into my arms on seeing me. She liked me, and would endeavor to ferret out the reason for my taking up temporary residence at the Chaplain's House, but displays of affection violated the offhand manner she took pains to present.

"I wish you could come," I told Mrs. Malloy with a pang, "but even it weren't too late to put the newlyweds off for another time, doing so would not be kind."

"I suppose not. Although"—her eyes brightened—"what if I was to borrow Tobias Mousecatchky and take him down to my house and pretend he was a stray I'd taken in? Melody was saying just yesterday on the phone as how Bill has a proper aversion to cats and can't be around them without screaming. And of course," she continued, with a self-righteous puffing of the chest, "that wouldn't be fair to the neighbors. Old Mrs. Flagg next door has high blood pressure and don't always remember to take her medicine. A nasty shock like that could kill her. I can't see a nice man like Bill taking the risk."

"Sorry," I said. "Tobias is getting up in years and doesn't adjust well to change. He prefers being home with his pipe and slippers—or communing with familiar surroundings," I was forced to add, spying my beloved feline wending his way across the lawn in dreamy contemplation of a butterfly that, being all beauty and no wit, had settled within easy paw-dabbing distance on a hydrangea bush.

Luckily, Tobias was distracted by the nosy eruption of the children through the kitchen door. Tam and Rose both dark like Ben, Abbey with her elfin fair curls, they came hurtling toward us, laughter spilling around them, one of those ordinary moments that will later be pulled out of the treasure box of memories many times over. It wasn't any trick of sunlight that turned the garden into an enchanted glade. It was the love I saw on Dorcas's face when she looked at my children.

"We'll leave for St. Roberta's early tomorrow morning," I told her with a real smile. Mrs. Malloy's pout was equally genuine, but she would recover from her disappointment when her sister and brother-in-law arrived.

The butterfly turned into a gauzy winged fairy and flitted away as Tobias joined the rest of us in going into the house. No further danger in the garden and none for me in responding to the headmistress's summons. The mystery of the missing Loverly Cup did not amount to evil on a grand scale. No diabolical force was at work in the old school, merely some childish silliness. This thought almost cheered me into facing the prospect of an excursion into my past with less foreboding than might have been anticipated.

What I failed to remember was that one of my reasons for being hopeless at lacrosse was that I had always failed to see the ball when it was coming full at me.

2

The source of the children's exuberance sprang from the three of them having ganged up against their father and ruined him at Monopoly. Mercilessly they had stripped him of houses and hotels, failed to remind him to collect two hundred pounds when he passed Go, and helped each other out with under-the-table loans. After getting out of jail for the third time and immediately landing on the Water Works, Ben had pounded his forehead with his fists and agreed snarlishly to file for bankruptcy. His misery had been music to their unfilial ears. Rose, who, according to Tam and Abbey, had been laughing the hardest, had threatened to put him back in jail if he didn't stop growling.

There was some talk as we sat down for dinner that it might be necessary to sell Merlin's Court to pay for the legal advice Ben had received from Diddle, Swindle & Kashownli. Mrs. Malloy said it was all very sad, but she had no sympathy for people who got in over their heads, thinking they was better than other people because they'd won second place in a beauty contest. She remembered that it was when her second—maybe her third—husband was caught dipping into the Community Chest that she decided to divorce him. Ben assumed a suitably shifty expression; after consuming a second helping of Apple Charlotte, Mrs. Malloy took herself off to make the last-minute preparations for Melody and Bill's visit. Dorcas was more helpful. She advised Ben and me to relax in the drawing room while we still owned the furniture, adding that she would take the children outdoors for a game of tag before bedtime.

As I had expected, Ben made no fuss about my abandoning him at short notice to take off for St. Roberta's. He thought the filching of the Loverly Cup mildly amusing rather than sinister. At the school he had attended in a rough neighborhood of London, a caper of that sort would not have raised an eyebrow. No boarding school for my husband. Unlike my parents, his weren't the sort to have crossed their fingers and hoped like the dickens they could repay a bank overdraft that would have sunk a ship. My in-laws would have made the sensible assumption that there would be a seven-year blight on fruit and vegetables. They'd lose their greengrocer's shop and would one day come home to find a man in a dark coat and a hat tipped over his nose camped in their sitting room. He'd have a gun in his hand and would ask in an adenoidal voice if they'd mind very much having their legs broken. 'Cause if they didn't make good on the loan by Friday, the boss was likely to remember that his mother had always liked his brother best and turn irritable.

A provident couple, Ben's parents had done well by their one offspring in their own way. Ben might not have been born with a silver rattle in his fist, but he hadn't been hard done by in other ways. Mother Nature had been more than kind. Even as a schoolboy he must have been a heart-stopper. When we first met I thought him the handsomest man I'd ever laid eyes on. The intervening years had only enhanced his attractiveness, increasing the strength and sensitivity of his face along with an easy confidence of manner that came from life's experience. I looked into his blue-green eyes and loved the warmth and tenderness I saw in them.

"A penny for your thoughts, sweetheart?" Ben threaded gentle fingers through my hair.

"If it weren't for Dorcas I wouldn't go. St. Roberta's does not have me by the heartstrings, but it will be nice to see Ariel." I returned his kiss and curled up even closer to him on the sofa. "Poor Mrs. Malloy! She pretended that her reason for minding being left behind is she's afraid the cup thief will decide to do away with me if I snoop too closely."

"Somehow I'm not worried you'll be coshed on the head as you join in singing the school song, whatever you think of your voice."

"Don't tell me it thrills you to the core, or I'll never believe anything you say again. Mrs. Malloy is dying to go to boarding school. The concept, if you've read the storybooks, sounds enormous fun. When I lent her *Head Girl at the Manor School* she couldn't put it down, and she's been an addict ever since. . . ." My voice petered out.

"What's wrong?" Ben cupped my face tenderly with his hand.

"Nothing, really. I was just remembering a girl named Philippa Boswell. She was a year ahead of me. Her older sister had been head girl a few years before and it was expected that Philippa would follow suit, but she got in hot water—was unjustly accused of something she didn't do"—my head was beginning to throb—"and that was the end of that."

"Tough on the kid, but I don't suppose she died of a broken heart."

"No. I heard she became a waitress."

"Hardly a fate worse than death!" He grinned at me.

"In one of those seedy backstreet places where the male patrons think a good tip is a pinch on the bottom. London—or it may have been Liverpool. According to my source, her parents disowned her."

"An exaggeration, surely."

"I'm not so sure. I saw Mama and Papa on a couple of speech days, and they both looked as though they were under doctor's orders not to smile. They twitched every time their older daughter—Veronica, I think, was her name—shifted a foot without asking permission. She looked nice and was attractive in a sensible tweedy sort of way. But Philippa was so lovely and full of laughter, everyone else seemed to fade a little when she was present. And always so nice to people, even girls she didn't know well—like me. She had a boyfriend, a young medical student whose father was the local doctor."

"Did he ditch her when she became a waitress?"

"It was off before she left school. The last I heard—which was ages ago—Papa was saying that if Philippa didn't get a proper job he'd march her off to a convent."

"Can't blame the Vatican if it liked the sound of that."

"And I sympathize," I said. "Recruiting these days can't be easy. It's not like the good old Middle Ages, when parents would toss an unmarriageable daughter through the convent door with less thought than dropping coins in the collection plate." Again I recalled the legend of the Gray Nun. "It puts the church in a pickle, having to rely on true vocations, doesn't it?"

"Back to the boyfriend." Ben drew me closer. "Did he shy away from a girl who'd blotted her school copybook?"

"Philippa was the one who broke things off."

"By the way, what was she accused off?"

"Absenting herself from school property without permission."

"To meet said boyfriend."

"That was the story." Knowing me as he did, Ben must have gleaned from the terseness of my reply that I didn't want to enlarge on this. Indeed, I regretted having mentioned Philippa Boswell. Faced with returning to St. Roberta's, I'd thought it advisable to try facing down my demons ahead of time, but the familiar sick feeling had returned full force.

"The Gray Nun was hurled through the convent gates by her ireful parents in the sixteenth century," I murmured into his shoulder.

"Who?"

"All the St. Roberta's pupils were steeped in the legend of the Gray Nun."

"A local girl?"

"A novice who, despite being dragged by the hair into the convent, subsequently defended it with her life. Her ghost is said to haunt the ruins on the edge of the grounds."

"Highly romantic. I can see the appeal to impressionable schoolgirls." Ben continued stroking my hair. "Remind me to lock away any books on the lives of the saints when Abbey and Rose reach that age. I don't think I could bear saying goodbye to them forever at the convent gate."

"I won't forget."

"No need to choke up, sweetheart!"

He was right, I told myself, but I was picturing Philippa playing the part of the Gray Nun in the outdoor summer pageant. She'd been really good, gliding across the lawn with an ethereal grace and fixed stare that seemed to melt into transparency. It was happening again: the suffocating lump in my throat, the feeling that I would never again be able to get enough air in my lungs. Surprisingly, I had not yet broken out in a cold sweat. Progress of sorts, but I'd pushed things far enough. Time to put the mental screen back around her. Mistake. That was the worst possible image, conjuring up as it did the dividers placed around hospital beds when a patient is dangerously ill.

Not that there had been anything seriously wrong with Philippa the afternoon of my silent involvement long ago. Her ailment had been a headache. She had been sent to Matron, given an aspirin, and told to lie down on one of the beds in the sick bay—known as the San. And there she had stayed, left alone when Matron bustled out. I knew this for certain, having an excellent view of the entire room from the window of my secret hideaway. Not once had Philippa got up, let alone crept through the French doors that opened onto the grounds and made off to meet her boyfriend as she was soon after accused of doing. Mine was the voice that could have put things right for her. Instead, in cowardly fashion I had thought of what was at stake for me and squeezed my mind shut. Just as I did now when I heard the murmur of Ben's voice against my cheek asking if I were awake.

"Yes." The word came out quite easily. "But I rather fancy an early night."

"Any particular reason?" I could hear the laughter in his voice.

It must say something about my hardened disposition that I was able to dismiss all unpleasant memories of my school days at St. Roberta's as Ben and I made love that evening to the rapturous accompaniment of the Royal Philharmonic Orchestra. We turned on the radio, but we could have made music just as well on our own. The soaring notes transported me to a glorious place on the outskirts of consciousness. Had I wasted time thinking, I might have made the excuse that this grown-up behavior provided necessary reassurance that I was a mature woman capable of confronting my schoolgirl demons.

Rising early the next morning, I packed a small suitcase and took a brisk shower. Dressed in a fern-green linen suit that I hoped Mrs. Battle would be unable to fault, I studied myself in the bedroom mirror. Ben came up behind me and kissed my neck. Perhaps it was the lovely aftermath of intimacy that gave my skin a glow and added an extra shine to my hair as I wound it into a chignon. I know it was the reason my gray eyes sparkled.

"You look wonderful," he said, as I turned into his arms.

"Presentable."

"Modesty becomes you." His mouth closed over mine. He hadn't yet shaved, and the prickle of dark stubble intensified his bedroom-bandit appeal. Unfortunately, the day called. We could hear the children bounding down the stairs and Dorcas's voice rising above theirs, calling for order. Time to get breakfast organized. Ben saw to the porridge and bacon and eggs while I made a pot of coffee and wrote down phone numbers that he might need while I was gone, along with a short list of reminders of activities and appointments.

"Don't let Tam talk you out of taking him to the dentist on Thursday," I was saying, as I got into the front passenger seat of Dorcas's lime-green Volkswagen Beetle, "and be sure Abbey and Rose send thank-you notes for the dresses your parents sent them."

"Relax! If we can't manage, I'll call on one of my four hundred other wives." Having stowed my suitcase along with Dorcas's overnight bag in the rear, he gave me a kiss through the window and stepped back alongside the children.

"Mum, you're not going to Mars!" Tam called out consolingly.

"Or into a dark and horrible dungeon," Abbey contributed.

"But I expect they'll make you eat the school lunches, and they're yuck!" Rose hopped gleefully from one foot to the other.

"Thanks for all the cheering up!" I laughed and waved to a chorus of "Goodbye, Mum! Goodbye, Dorcas. We love you!" The car bounced to life as if startled out of a heavy sleep. Momentarily confused, it shot backward, but Dorcas wouldn't let it take the blame.

"Sorry, Ellie, wrong gear. Always get emotional when leaving here. Second home and all that. Family!" She dabbed at her eyes with the back of her hand before steering cautiously down the drive. She gave the cottage just inside the wrought-iron gates, home to my cousin Freddy, a tearily sentimental glance before heading out onto the coast road that would take us into

Chitterton Fells, through the towns of Pebble Beach and Brynhaven, and thence onto the motorway. The journey to Lower Swan-Upping should have taken three hours at most, but Dorcas believed in always giving other motorists a sporting chance to pass her, even if this meant moving into a lay-by to be completely fair. As a result we failed to make the best time, something I didn't mind in the least.

That morning she was wearing a sweater in a particularly virulent shade of mustard, but what bothered me about her appearance was how worried she looked the couple of times I brought up Ms. Chips's name.

"Dorcas, dear," I finally said, "I can imagine the difficulties involved in taking over the post of a longtime games mistress who had a tremendous record of success with the lacrosse team. A period of readjustment on the part of the players would seem inevitable. But there's no saying that even had Ms. Chips been at the helm this year, St. Roberta's would have won the championship again and got to keep the Loverly Cup."

"Kind of you to say, but sure I could have done more to uphold past glory."

"What else has you so upset?" I asked.

Her hands tightened on the steering wheel. "Afraid suspicion regarding Loverly Cup will veer in the wrong direction. Always people eager to point the finger at a convenient scapegoat. A life destroyed, often the most vulnerable party . . . reputation ruined." Dorcas choked up. "Doesn't bear thinking about."

I thought of the false accusation against Philippa Boswell.

"Spent a sleepless night, Ellie. Not the bed: great mattress. Thing is: believe if this beastly business isn't cleared up soon, there could be the most awful tragedy. Silly of me, but can't shake feeling of impending doom."

Laying a hand on her arm, I said, "Ellie Haskell to the rescue." It would have been pointless to press her to tell me who it was she feared might be blamed for taking the Loverly Cup. She'd be afraid of influencing me for or against. My sympathy, and finally my curiosity, was aroused. Could there be more going on at St. Roberta's than schoolgirl mischief? I found myself wishing that Mrs. Malloy were with us. For her there would be no emotional involvement, making for clearer insights than were possible for Dorcas or even myself.

The miles lumbered by. Dorcas described the splendors of the new gymnasium. "Twice the size of the old one, Ellie. Vaulted ceiling. Superb climbing equipment. Great lighting. Mr. Bumbleton, on Board of Governors, went all out to please."

"Is he as much of a pompous ass as ever?"

"Haven't had any dealings with him. Man can't help looking like an overstuffed cushion."

Dorcas kept her eyes on the road. We were passing through Tingwell, a shifty-eyed town with glimpses of dark passageways and barred windows on many of the buildings. The place was made even more depressing by the sight of vagrants shuffling out of doorways to approach pedestrians.

"Hate to think of anyone living that sort of life, Ellie! Somebody's once near-and-dear."

"It's awful for all concerned: wanting to help without being an enabler if there's a question of drink or drugs. What agonies of mind some people face."

She took a hand off the wheel to grip mine. A few miles farther on, we stopped at a roadside café for lunch. The hard chairs and weak coffee providing no incentive to linger, we soon pressed on. Within a very short time the scenery changed, becoming less urban and more delightful by the moment, softly pastoral with gentle hills rising beyond fields of grazing sheep and idly stepping horses with the sun on their backs. A bronze and sun-gold brook bubbled over tiger-eye rocks, and a willow dipped its lengthy tendrils into the water in the manner of a reincarnated Greek nymph. Wildflowers embroidered the hedgerows. Summer, I thought, was at home here. And suddenly I realized we had reached the vicinity in which I would be planted, for the next few days at least.

We entered a traffic circle and took the exit marked LOWER AND UPPER SWAN-UPPING. Memory was stirring. There was the Green Swan to our right, a public house of the Tudor period. My parents had taken me to lunch there on one of their visits. We'd sat at an umbrella-shaded table in the shrubbery-surrounded garden. I'd had two glasses of wonderfully fizzy ginger beer while Mother and Daddy had sipped cider from champagne glasses and toyed with candy cigarettes bought from the little sweetshop across the road. Life for them had always been something of an amusing play, with themselves as both actors and audience. Dressing for their parts constituted a big slice of their amusement.

That day Mother had been in her tragedy-queen role, wearing a stark black dress, shadowy picture hat, and sunglasses. Daddy had sported a striped waistcoat and jauntily tipped straw boater. They had adored each other and me. And despite the fact that their love for me seemed at times peripheral, I wouldn't have exchanged them for any parents on earth.

They hadn't sent me to St. Roberta's to get me out of the way; they had succumbed to my pleading that I be allowed to go to boarding school. This had followed my devouring *Cilia of Chilterns' Edge* by Mabel Esther Allen. Had I been expelled and packed off home, Mother would in all likelihood have inhaled deeply of one of the candy cigarettes while Daddy resorted to throwing himself down on the chaise longue and begging for the smelling salts. But I knew they wouldn't have carried on about the wasted expense and the bank loan from Mr. Shark, let alone the disappointment and sorrow of having spawned an only child with an ungrateful tooth, or however it goes. They would have rallied after a couple of theatrical sighs to concede that life had been rather dull of late and that a good part of a daughter's reason for being was to perk up the excitement once in a while. A visit to the fish-and-chip shop would have been considered a wise way of proceeding. And that, more or less, would have been that.

A row of creamy stone cottages came into view. I remembered the one with the thatched roof and the wisteria around the door. My friend Susan Brodstock's grandparents had lived there, and I'd been invited to tea several times. For the first time since Dorcas had dropped her bombshell and the prospect of this trip had become a reality, I acknowledged that my three years at St. Roberta's had not been one long stretch of unremitting misery. I had done well in art and history, made happy use of the excellent library, and in addition to Susan had another friend named Ann Gamble.

When the three of us learned that a clique of the more popular girls, including the bullying Rosemary Martin, had formed a secret society, we instituted one of our own, calling ourselves the Triangle. We liked the name because we thought it combined simplicity with the sinister. Our object had not been to instill terror in others, only in ourselves. It was to fulfill this thrilling prospect that we had crept out of our dorm one night and made our way out onto the grounds by way of a rear door. Delighted with our daring, we had crossed the lawn to a twisty flight of centuries-old stone steps named the Dribbly Drop, cut into the steep embankment. Even on the driest, sunniest day, it looked dark and slick—a wrenched ankle, or worse, waiting to happen.

We made it down the steps safely that night and thence across the pathway to the ruined convent separated from the main road by a pathway known as Lilypad Lane. All that remained of the building aboveground was the roofless refectory, with steps even more precarious than the Dribbly Drop leading down to the crypt. We decided to wait before descending them. Our tremulous courage required a boost. Seated on the remnants of a stone bench against a fragmented section of wall of the refectory, we ate the chocolate biscuits and fish-paste sandwiches we had saved from that afternoon's tea. Ann also contributed some Licorice Allsorts; they were fuzzy with pocket lint, which Susan meticulously picked off. My contribution was a bottle of watered-down still lemonade.

As midnight feasts went, this one was enormous fun, although the three of us did admit to being horribly disappointed when, after an hour of reacting to every shift of moonlight, we failed to catch a glimpse—not even the vestige of a veil—of the Gray Nun. Once a carefree maypole-dancing girl, her life had taken a bleak turn on the day she ran off to wed a man not of her parents' choice. Having followed in enraged pursuit, they dragged her by the scruff of her ruff back down the church aisle while explaining in ragged gasps that she would begin her novitiate that day. Was it any wonder that, knowing her beauty was doomed to fade with every cloistered hour, she never much cared whether her wimple was straight or crooked?

Perhaps it was a mercy she did not languish long in the shadows of the cloister. The dratted Reformation intervened, and she met her end at the hand of her would-be husband. He had arrived, looking handsome as ever, clanking his sword and stomping his spurred boots, to denude the convent of its treasures, because Henry VIII had decided that if anyone should wantonly enjoy them it was he. After all, what was the point of being king if you couldn't put the pope off his mead and potatoes? The Gray Nun, her plucky spirit renewed, had declined to tell the former light of her life where the lady abbess had hidden the gold chalice and other sacred objects from the chapel.

She had fled to the crypt, where the erstwhile bridegroom caught up with her and drew her into his arms before running her through with his blade. Hell hath no fury like a man in tights and a doublet. It was said her initials were engraved on the hilt of his sword, along with a forget-me-not. Inevitably, the legend asserted that the imprint of this flower was seen from time to time on the crypt floor where her blood had spattered.

Susan was the one to confess that even the Licorice Allsorts hadn't made her more enthusiastic about going down to the crypt. It would have been different if there'd been the smallest chance of our finding the chalice, but the stories of failed searches were legion. If it had ever been hidden there, it was long gone. We told each other we didn't regret our escapade and were bitterly disappointed that the Gray Nun had not put in an appearance. The chill night air, coupled with increasing sleepiness, was driving us back to our beds. Truth be told, I was not only scared but terrified, not of an unearthly apparition finally drifting our way with the offer of a clammy embrace but because I was belatedly considering the awful consequences should our nocturnal escapade be discovered.

Typically, I had acted first and thought last. In an agony of frustration, I heard Susan moan that she had dropped her watch, which she had taken off in order to peer more intently at the dial. When she got up to look on the ground, we noticed a separation in the stone bench large enough for a Thermos to have fallen through. Susan dug around inside and, tearing up with relief, found her watch. "I couldn't have gone back without it," she said. "Mummy and Daddy warned me I wouldn't get another if I lost this one."

She wasn't the only one trembling with relief and nerves. The omniscient face of the moon put me quakingly in mind of Mrs. Battle as we scrambled back up the Dribbly Drop; her countenance could also be cold as marble when the situation merited it. I considered myself lucky for days afterward that there was no summons to her office. The pity was I didn't learn my lesson.

Now was no time for a wallow! I resolutely shoved aside the memory of my later entirely independent transgression as Dorcas approached the village green with its wooden benches shaded by fringed canopies of beech and chestnut trees. The circle of houses, set back from hedged gardens, presented a harmonious appearance despite a mix of whitewashed exteriors with brown or pale-rose brick facades, along with a variety of roof styles from sharply pitched to low forehead ones. Old-fashioned wooden or iron gates gave entry to pathways leading to front doors painted mostly green, white, or black, but with an occasional blue one added. Flowers bloomed in crowded cheer, the whole softened by a golden wash of sunlight, creating an effect similar to a filmlike hazy flashback to an earlier point of reference: the idyllic scene before tragedy rips apart the fabric of lives steeped in the traditions of afternoon tea, croquet on the back lawn, and harmless flirtations with the curate.

I thought of the monotonous rows of houses we had passed on the outskirts of Tingwell and of my difficulty in imagining anything pleasurably exciting ever happening in them. These had the reverse effect upon me. I found it inconceivable that one anguished hour had ever been spent within any of these walls. Minor problems, yes! A comb getting sucked up by the Hoover, a near trip over the dog, a misplaced Liberty scarf. But no deaths, seething hatreds, or unanswered dreams!

I was about to express this to Dorcas when she said that the two semidetached houses directly across the green were occupied by Ms. Chips and Mr. Middleton.

"His is on the left, Ellie. Green front door. Lives there with his unmarried sister. Wife died—ten years ago or more, according to the grapevine. It was him told Chippy before her retirement that next door would be up for sale."

"Did they get on sufficiently well through the years for that to be a good idea?" I had just asked, when the genteel calm was shattered by the savage roar of a motorcycle swerving past us. I caught a flash of the male rider's blond hair and black leather jacket as he cut a swath around an old gentleman with a stick before shuddering to a halt within inches of a girl in the all-too-familiar St. Roberta's uniform of bottle-green blazer and mustard-yellow shirt. In my day we had worn Panama hats in summer, a bit old-fashioned even then. If this girl had been wearing one, it would doubtless have sailed off her head as she stepped desperately back, tripped, and broke her fall with her hands.

She was still crouched on the ground like a mesmerized rabbit when Dorcas stopped the car.

"He almost ran her down," I said furiously, as we climbed out. "I'm for giving him a piece of our minds to chew on."

"Right ho! Fellow shouldn't be allowed out on roller skates, let alone a motorbike." It could have been Colonel Mustard marching alongside me, not that Dorcas needed a military mustache to bristle with the best of them. The young man stood straddling the motorcycle. The girl was scrambling to her feet as we crossed a corner of the green to reach them. Neither glanced our way; I saw them as an image sharply delineated within their surroundings, framed by but not included in the golden haze. His profile was sculptured, hers roundly childlike.

"Who is she?" I asked Dorcas softly, when we were a few yards away.

"Gillian Parker, Matron's grand-niece."

"Recognize him?"

"Lady Loverly's grandson, Aiden." She probably would have expounded on this had our attention not been caught by the girl.

"That's a lie! I'm not a thief!" She spoke in little more than a whisper, but Dorcas and I were now close by, and her palpable fear made the words reverberate in my mind during the hours and days to come.

3

Beastly scare for you, Gillian." Dorcas touched her gently on the arm and received a frightened nod in return. I put her age at fourteen or fifteen; she was pretty in a muted way with wavy brown hair and hazel eyes. Seeing she needed a moment to draw breath, I held off on snarling at Aiden Loverly.

The old gentleman had made it onto the green and was now seated on a bench under one of the old spreading trees. A gate opened and a small boy in a red jersey pedaled his tricycle with fierce concentration along the pavement. An unseen dog barked and a ginger cat leaped up into an apple tree the size of a young oak in the garden of the house Dorcas had said belonged to Ms. Chips. I bent to pick up the brown leather satchel lying on the ground, and Gillian took it from me, her eyes staring blankly.

"It's my sheet music." She might have been speaking in a foreign language she didn't understand but had been ordered to recite. "Mr. Middleton told me, if I didn't get on with 'Für Elise,' he'd help me with it this afternoon."

"Still gives private singing and piano lessons at the school several times a week, even though he retired as full-time music master," Dorcas murmured to me.

"I had permission from Mrs. Battle to come to his house today." Gillian winced as she shifted the satchel to her arm.

"No problem there," Dorcas assured her.

Noticing the girl's hands I exclaimed, "You've really scraped them!"

"So you have, Gilly!" Aiden Loverly's upper-crust voice matched mine in concern, but there was something about his laconic pose and the wry lift of his eyebrows that caused me to doubt his sincerity.

Viewed close up, he was an Adonis, golden tan, eyes a dark gray, shoulder-length blond hair lifting like a silk banner in the breeze. I don't often make snap judgments—well, not more than once or twice a day—but I did so now. This young man was not only reckless but cruel. Even if he had reason to suspect that Gillian had taken the Loverly Cup and was upset on his grandmother's behalf, there was no excuse for scaring her half to death. Had Mrs. Malloy been with us, she'd have itched to put a fist in his face.

"You could have seriously injured or even killed her if you'd hit her at the speed you were going!" I glared at him furiously.

"Should be ashamed!" Dorcas placed a protective arm around Gillian's rigid shoulders. The old gentleman on the bench was looking our way, as if wondering what the modern world was coming to.

"Did I cause bodily harm?" Aiden Loverly responded in the manner of one gently addressing a pair of dimwitted children. "I can stop this thing on a button. All she had to do was stand still. Gilly's not cross with me; she knows I'd never hurt a good little girl, which is what she claims to be." To me the threat behind the words was obvious, but I couldn't tell if Dorcas sensed it. She's wonderful, but if she has a fault it's an unwillingness to see the worst in people. Getting through the next few days without Mrs. Malloy's stark skepticism would have its drawbacks.

Gillian's pallor had increased, and she said, still in a wooden voice, that she hadn't been looking where she was going.

"Wouldn't have mattered." Dorcas clapped the girl on the back, unwittingly causing her knees to buckle. "Mr. Loverly drives at shocking speed. Should apologize and promise more decorous behavior in future."

"He doesn't need to," Gillian protested faintly.

"Nice girl," said Aiden Loverly, eyeing Dorcas as if she were an insect meticulously pinned to a board. "You're Ms. Chips's replacement. Haven't done too well for the lacrosse team this season, have you? No holding onto Granny's cup after nine glorious years. And now it has disappeared. What will befall the culprit when unmasked? Will she be dragged down to the crypt and left to molder, a skeleton to scare forthcoming generations of St. Rob's girls?" He laughed—a charming sound, blithe as a minuet played upon a harpsichord—but my dear friend didn't smile in return. She stood, thin and plain, diminished, her hair sticking out and up from a face that was all eyes and orange brows. Squished. Gillian's face had been pale before; now she was chalk white.

"Oh, dear!" Aiden Loverly, still straddling the motorcycle, traced a manicured finger along the gleaming handlebars. "Was it my mentioning the crypt that has made the roses fade from your cheeks, Gilly? I'd forgotten that you schoolgirls are convinced the convent ruins are haunted by the Gray Nun. But of course a sensible girl like you wouldn't go seeking her out at dead of night. The consequences could be quite terrifying if you should happen upon vengeance lurking in the shrubbery."

"Yes." Gillian swayed, and Dorcas came back to life to get a grip on her.

"Please don't let us keep you chatting, Mr. Loverly," I said icily. "We need to get Gillian into Mr. Middleton's house and those hands seen to—"

"Here he is." Dorcas nodded in the direction of a man who had just emerged from the front door to stand peering around him, as if sizing up the weather or hoping for inspiration—from Beethoven or Mozart would be my guess. He looked exactly as I remembered him. Medium height, medium build, medium coloring. Although, if anything, he appeared younger than I had thought him all those years ago. To the young, anyone approaching early middle age looks ancient. I put him now in his early to middle sixties.

Gillian unlatched the green painted gate that matched his front door and stumbled toward him. "Mr. Middleton, I've come to ask for help with 'Für Elise.'" She was clutching not only at her satchel but at the assurance of what was safe and secure, distancing herself from Aiden Loverly by more than the steps she took away from him.

"Yes, my dear, quite right," said Mr. Middleton, "although I'm sure you're managing beautifully on your own. My sister is next door having a chat with Ms. Chips, but I will fetch her back. She always enjoys hearing you play. Confidence is all you lack. One day you will be famous and I shall tell everyone who will listen that I taught you. Don't shake your head, child; I am not being kind, merely truthful." A nearby laugh caused him to look away from Gillian. "Ah, Mr. Loverly," he continued, just as gently. "Are you also here to see me?"

"Just buzzing around the area like the bumbling bumblebee." The reply was steeped in honey. It was also a lie. I knew as if I had witnessed it that he'd either spotted Gillian walking from St. Roberta's or had known ahead of time that she would be coming this way and had followed in order to corner her, before she could streak for safety with the speed of the ginger cat that had minutes earlier gone up Ms. Chips's apple tree.

"A lovely day to be out and about, but shouldn't you be getting back to the Hall?" Mr. Middleton pushed back the sleeve of his navy-blue cardigan to look at his watch. "I know from long acquaintance that Lady Loverly is punctilious about sitting down to afternoon tea at three o'clock, which leaves you barely ten minutes. Doesn't do to keep your grandmother waiting, my boy. Forgive my interference, but I'd buzz home if I were you."

"I'll do that, even though Mrs. Brown has one of her migraines and any refreshment will be a catch-as-catch-can affair. See you, Gilly." A negligent wave and, with a cataclysmic earth-moving roar, the motorcycle shot around the green and out onto the road in the opposite direction to St. Roberta's. Before the sky could get back on tilt or the trees stop grabbing at each other, for emotional if not physical support, Mr. Middleton addressed Dorcas.

"Poor Mrs. Brown. Her ladyship's housekeeper does suffer from headaches. Apologies, Miss Critchley, for ignoring you and this other lady. I see your car parked across the way."

"On route to the school. Saw Mr. Loverly come within an inch of running Gillian down." Dorcas jabbed the recalcitrant strand of hair back into place with its clip. The improvement to her appearance wasn't huge, but she was filling back out from a flattened insect to a three-dimensional figure. "This is my friend Ellie Haskell. Attended St. Roberta's. Back to stay at the Chaplain's House for a few days."

"It was Ellie Simons," I said. "But it's been twenty years, and I'm sure you won't remember me."

"I think I do." His eyes studied me reflectively. "Couldn't sing a note but helped paint the scenery for *Pirates of Penzance*. Some good art pieces up at the Hall that I'm sure Lady Loverly would be glad to show you if you have the time to visit. She enjoys company. Can't be easy having a grandson who"—Mr. Middleton paused to glance at Ms. Chips's tree—"delays her tea. Now, shall we all go inside?" He began leading the way down the short path, but Gillian stopped him with a timid touch on his arm.

"But Mr. Middleton, isn't that Harpsichord in the apple tree?"

"Yes, foolish creature! I saw her from the window bolting up; that's why I came out. But she'll have to languish. Time to attend to your scrapes and bruises."

"You can't leave her up there!" It was a tug this time on his sleeve, and I saw that Gillian's pale face looked ready to disintegrate.

"Won't she come down when she's ready? My cat Tobias is a great one for acting as though he's lost his nerve and is sending out an SOS, but the moment I head inside, down he shoots after me." The moment the words were out of my mouth, I realized how smugly unhelpful I sounded. "No two animals are alike," I amended feebly.

"Weak ankles, perhaps." The words shot out of Dorcas's mouth like a ball lobbed from a lacrosse stick, like the one with which I had demolished Miss Chips's nose.

"Ankles?" Mr. Middleton appeared understandably nonplussed.

"Known plenty of girls who could shin up a rope with no problem but couldn't get down to save their lives, just hung there like flags in the wind. Afraid of a hard landing and wrenching one or both."

Gillian twisted her hands. "Do cats have ankles?"

"Technically speaking, I suppose they do," I said, despite remembering that I hadn't done outstandingly well in Anatomy, one of a couple of subjects taught by Mrs. Battle. In fact, I seemed to recall I had come in bottom each and every term. Despite her staunch desire that life provide a fair playing field for man and beast alike, uncertainty was now written on Dorcas's face. I could hear Mrs. Malloy's voice inside my head saying, *Bees have knees, don't they?* and decided it was just as well she wasn't present or we'd all be up a tree forever.

"Harpsichord's problem," began Mr. Middleton, only to be interrupted by an anguished meow, "is one of uncomplicated funk."

A ginger face peered through the leaves. Perhaps I didn't experience a rush of boundless affection for Harpsichord because the name reminded me of Aiden Loverly's nastily tinkling laugh. That aside, we were looking up at a craven feline if ever I'd seen one. Further mewing made it clear her loyalty would be to the closest extended hand, in return for which government secrets would be handed over. Not a cat to have in one's corner when the chips were down. Then again, neither was Tobias. His price for turning me over to enemy agents would have been the vague promise of having a brand of salmon named for him after his death.

"Anyone would think the silly cat had dropped by parachute from the sky," said Mr. Middleton, his thoughts apparently running in sync with mine.

Gillian managed a shaky laugh. "But she's so scared."

"I'll take you inside and come back for the ladder. Third time this week, but nothing else to do, I suppose."

"Please don't waste time; I can go into the house on my own," whispered Gillian.

"Got an idea, Mr. Middleton," proffered Dorcas. "Ellie and I can accompany her. See to a bit of first aid."

"If the two of you wouldn't mind." He smiled. It was a very nice, kind smile and I experienced regret that I hadn't harbored warmer feelings toward him, due to his having detected my singing off-key in his class, with the result that I'd turned into a goldfish whenever there were hymns at church.

"Delighted to be of use." Dorcas squared her shoulders, and for a split second I wondered if she intended to toss Gillian over her back.

"You'll find antiseptic ointment and gauze in the downstairs cloakroom. Won't be long. I keep the ladder at the side of the house, as opposed to forever getting it out of the shed."

Harpsichord meowed something that from its aggrieved sound could have been a threat to cut Mr. Middleton out of her will if he didn't get moving. Dorcas shepherded Gillian and me onto the doorstep, through the front door, and into a good-sized hall. The staircase went straight up on the right, its russet-colored carpet going well with the dark banisters and amber wall paint. My impression was of a solidly built house, circa 1940s with some Victorian touches, such as the rose-patterned chamber-pot-shaped ceiling light and ornate plasterwork. An open doorway to our left revealed a living room whose focal point was a grand piano, in a corner by French doors that presumably led into the back garden.

Gillian set aside her satchel and sat down on the bottom step, hugging her knees. She announced with pathetically determined cheerfulness that she had a cat of her own at home.

"A ginger one like Harpsichord?" I guessed.

"His name is Carrots. My little sister Sarah has a rabbit named Lettuce."

"It's odd about Harpsichord. I thought ginger cats were always male."

"She's an exception."

The resident voice inside my head said it was fatal to make assumptions about anything. Mrs. Malloy is given to tossing out these pearls of wisdom, which I should take to heart but usually don't.

Dorcas had marched off down the hall to peer behind a couple of doors, in search of the cloakroom. "Aha!" I heard her say, in the manner of a Columbus bouncing his rowing boat onto a beach to behold a row of bikini-clad beauties holding up a sign stating AMERICA THIS WAY.

"How long have you been at St. Roberta's?" I sat down across from Gillian on an oak bench with a tapestry cushion.

"This is my first year." She made it sound an eternity. I told myself that lots of girls suffered from abysmal homesickness. Her distress over Harpsichord's plight probably resulted from missing her cat, along with her parents and the little sister she had mentioned. But what if, despite her whispered assertion to Aiden Loverly that she wasn't a thief, Gillian had taken the Loverly Cup?

My thoughts were cut off by Dorcas, who came back down the hall to say she had located cotton wool and a tube of antiseptic ointment in the cloakroom and would see to Gillian's injuries.

"But they're nothing!"

"Just scrapes," Dorcas agreed bracingly. "But need to clean them up or Matron will have my hide."

"No, she won't! She's always telling me I make too much fuss about everything and will end up with people thinking"—Gillian's voice cracked—"that I exaggerate or even invent things to get attention."

"Matron's from the old school." Dorcas drew Gillian up from the stairs and looked at me as I also got to my feet. "Stiff upper lip and all that."

"I remember," I said, rising from my bench.

"Of course . . . You said you were at St. Roberta's. Matron's my Aunt Wilma, great-aunt actually." A sob broke through the words as Gillian backed against the wall. "Oh, I wish she'd never said she could get me in at reduced fees and talked Mum and Dad into sending me. I hate it! Hate it! And whatever she says, I'm not the only one who has caught glimpses of the Gray Nun from the dorm windows in the middle of the night." With that she made a dash down the hall, and the cloakroom door slammed shut.

"Poor child!" Dorcas patted her pockets like a man from the golden tobacco age in search of his pipe. "I've been worried about her, particularly this past week."

"Tell me later, dear," I forced myself to say. "Go and calm her down."

"Right ho! Clearly Gillian needs to talk. Hope I can get her to open up. Wouldn't want to put a flannel in it." Dorcas bravely resisted using the hanky she found in her hand. "Hard age, fourteen. Intense. Small problems magnified out of all proportion. Worse when worrying over end-of-term exams. See what I can do."

"Do you think it would it be terrible cheek if I used the upstairs loo?" It had been a while since we stopped for lunch, and I was bordering on desperate.

"Good grief, no! Not that sort, the Middletons. Sister Ruth has a heart of gold. One of those nurturing souls!"

Dorcas disappeared and I marched upstairs like the grand old Duke of York with ten thousand men behind him. Luckily, I found the necessary door. There is nothing like being within imminent reach of a WC to make one feel nurtured without help from anyone. This one had an old-fashioned pull chain, which my children would have loved to yank till it came off in their hands. I smiled, thinking of them as I went back onto the landing. It was a broad space with paneled oak doors and a handsome brass urn on the table under the window that overlooked the apple tree. No sign of Mr. Middleton or Harpsichord.

Turning, I noticed a small arched niche displaying a bronze bust of Mozart in the wall across from the staircase. The house had some nice details, I thought, as I made my descent. Altogether, there was a solid feel to the place that might provide solace to Gillian with or without the music lessons. But had her problems reached a point requiring serious intervention, or had Aiden Loverly fabricated his accusation for the joy of watching a timid girl squirm?

Neither Gillian nor Dorcas was in the hall when I descended the stairs, but a woman's voice reached me from the back of the house where the kitchen door was ajar. "We'll talk more of this Aiden Loverly business later, Clive. What Gillian needs immediately is a cup of tea. Marilyn and I were just sitting down to one when Brian Roberts arrived with the cardigan she'd left at the surgery on Friday. It was such a warm afternoon, she took it off and forgot it. No, nothing wrong, just a routine visit. Marilyn told me Brian likes to keep an eye on her blood pressure, even though the tablets she takes seem to be doing the trick. What a gem that man is, as well as being a wonderful doctor. You know Marilyn, Clive. She is much more concerned with Mrs. Brown's headaches than her own dizzy spells when she stands or sits up suddenly. But I'm worried that this could result in a fall and she'll break a bone. Thank goodness for Brian. I'm sure that cardigan was an excuse to make a house call."

"I'll never forget how helpful his father was to me when I was going through my bad time." That was Mr. Middleton speaking.

"I'd love to see Brian find the right woman and get married. . . . Do you think I should nip outside and ask him to come and take a look at Gillian? If I can catch him, that is; he was in the back garden admiring Marilyn's rhubarb when I left. I know you said the child wasn't really hurt, but this nervy business has me worried. People are too quick to say all adolescents are emotional and shrug it off. Not that I think Wilma Johnson would do that in her role as matron, but family is different, isn't it?"

"The whole world is family to you, Ruth." Mr. Middleton's voice carried affection.

I missed what else was said between brother and sister because Dorcas and Gillian emerged from the cloakroom. The girl looked better. Her face was less strained and she had tidied her hair.

"Is Mr. Middleton back with Harpsichord?" she asked me.

Before I could answer, he came into the hall with the cat tucked under his arm. "All patched up, Gillian?" He smiled at her.

"Yes, thank you."

"Nasty scrape on her left knee." Shoulders squared, arms to her sides, Dorcas might have been delivering a report to a senior medical consultant with an entire alphabet of letters after his name. "Applied a good squirt of ointment but decided against a bandage. Best left to the open air was my thinking, but stand ready to be corrected. Can't claim to be Florence Nightingale."

"Dr. Roberts may think you too modest. He was next door visiting Ms. Chips. Ruth was there too and left abruptly when she looked out the front-room window and saw me descending the apple tree. She's gone back to ask if they'd care to come in for a cup of tea and a slice of the walnut cake she made this morning. May I hope, Miss Critchley, that you and your friend will join us?"

The word *cake* always brings out the best in me. I liked Mr. Middleton more and more. After adding my thanks, I was moved to stretch out a hand to Harpsichord. A mistake! I was counting my fingers to make sure she hadn't helped herself to any of them when we assembled in the living room. In addition to the grand piano, there were bookcases on either side of the fireplace with its Victorian overmantel, a sofa of a russet similar to the stair carpet, and a number of comfortable armchairs, their solid shapes softened by embroidered linen cushions. The room nicely blended the masculine and the feminine and was large enough not to be dwarfed by the piano with its display of photographs.

Mr. Middleton saw me glancing that way, said from his chair that they were of his wife, and encouraged me to take a closer look.

"Thank you," I said, crossing the room.

"She was a concert violinist." Easing himself up, he joined me at the piano. What does one say when presented with an unknown image? There's the difficulty of being sufficiently complimentary without sounding fulsome. Especially awkward if one finds oneself looking nose to frame—without benefit of a fond eye—at someone without any redeeming features. Fortunately there was no such problem here. When Mr. Middleton handed me the largest of the photographs, I was able to say, simply and sincerely, "She's lovely."

"Her name was Anya. That was taken on our silver wedding anniversary."

"I can see the happiness." In addition to the softly curling dark hair and beautiful eyes, there was warmth and laughter.

"She was forty-seven. Two weeks later she was killed by a hit-and-run driver when she was walking our dog two streets away."

"What a tragedy." There was a catch in my throat. "Was the culprit apprehended?"

"Never." Mr. Middleton took the photo from me and gently placed it back on the piano.

"No one came forward with information?"

"Mr. Soames, the old gentleman who was out on the green, had also been out walking his dog and gave a statement to the police saying he was sure the driver was a woman, but he didn't get even the beginning of the license number, let alone the make or color of the vehicle. He's not into cars, never having owned one. And though it was summer, the light was poor at ten in the evening."

"No suspects?"

"The person best known for driving when he shouldn't was the late Sir Henry—her ladyship's husband—but he was in the clear, being three sheets to the wind at the White Dog. The landlord said he never staggered farther than the Gentlemen's all evening."

"Nevertheless"—Dorcas pulled out her hanky for an emotional blow—"you'd think someone had to know something."

"People hesitate to step forward for fear of involvement." Mr. Middleton took the photo from me and gently replaced it on the piano. "Or because they're loath to turn in a friend or family member."

"It would take courage," I said.

"Can't go through life being a coward." Dorcas always sounds her gruffest when her tender heart is touched.

Gillian sat gripping the arms of her chair, her face a pale blur against the room's warm colors. "It must have been terrible for you, Mr. Middleton," she whispered.

"I don't know if it would have been harder or easier if we'd had children. We both wanted them. Friends rallied round." He picked up Harpsichord before she could leap onto the piano. "The staff from St. Roberta's were especially kind, particularly Marilyn Chips. She couldn't do enough."

"Not something you forget." Dorcas made noisy use of the handkerchief.

"And then, above and beyond all else, there was dear Ruth. When she realized how bad things were with me, she gave up her job and her flat in Harrow and moved here. The original idea was for her get a place of her own when the time was right, but we settled down well together and made it permanent."

His pause stretched into silence until Harpsichord got away from him and pranced across the piano keys. Despite her name, it was clear she was not musically gifted, or such was my opinion. Apparently Dorcas heard the horrible jangle of sound differently.

"Ah! Beethoven's Fifth, that bit where Death comes knocking. Oh, I say! Hoof in my mouth again. Didn't think! Should have done! Your beloved wife, Mr. Middleton!" Face turning a deep russet to match the sofa, she would have floundered on had Gillian not scrambled to her feet and hurried over to the piano. Seating herself on the stool, she began to play. Immediately, all else was stillness; even Harpsichord turned motionless in Mr. Middleton's arms.

As I've said, I can't sing in tune. Nor did I ever learn to play a musical instrument. My parents gently discouraged the idea after someone gave me a whistle. Nevertheless, I know the exquisite when I hear it. The air was filled with rapture, floating into the sunshine, then ebbing back to some deep quiet where one wanted to follow and have everything revealed.

"She's still a child!" I finally whispered.

Mr. Middleton smiled. "Don't worry; I doubt she knows we're in the room. She has gone inside the music. I wish so much that Anya could have heard her. Already she is beyond me.

All I can provide is encouragement. Amazingly, she's insecure about her abilities. Also, she worries about the expense of furthering her studies. Her family is not well off. St. Roberta's would have been out of the question but for Matron's pull."

"A scholarship to a music college?" I suggested.

"I've been looking into it." Mr. Middleton stood stroking Harpsichord.

At that moment, a middle-aged woman entered through a door to the side of the French windows with their view of the small but pretty back garden. Unless she had wandered into the house by mistake or to help herself to the family silver, she had to be his sister Ruth. I got the impression of a comfortably roomy figure and a face as pleasant as the voice I had heard coming from the kitchen when I was hovering in the hall.

"Marilyn will be over in a minute; she's getting an overnight bag ready. She's doing dorm duty tonight at the school, filling in for that attractive Mrs. Frenton, who I'm pleased to hear has a date this evening. But look who I was able to bring," she proclaimed cheerfully. Close behind her came a tall, ruggedly good-looking man in his late thirties to early forties, carrying a heavily loaded tea tray.

Dorcas got smartly to her feet, but Gillian did not look up. Her fingers continued to ripple across the keyboard, and her eyes remained closed while her expression shifted from dreamy to intent.

"I hesitated to interrupt," said the man softly. He had a deep voice. "It seemed on a par with slashing a painting at the Tate."

"But you see it's just as I told you." Ruth smiled at him. "Our Gillian is lost to all but her music. It's a wonderful escape," she added, in a more sober murmur, "for those blessed with finding the door."

"Let me set this down on the coffee table." Mr. Middleton took the tray. "Brian, do you know Miss Critchley?"

"I regret I haven't had the pleasure."

Dorcas rose smartly to her feet, looking as if she were about to salute. That's the way shyness takes her at such moments. Flinging out a hand, she took the one extended to her in a masterful grip.

"Brian Roberts." His whimper, if any, was swept away with the music.

"Our local doctor." Ruth was now smiling at me.

"Yes," I said, feeling myself drifting. It had dawned on me who he was: son of the previous GP, in medical school when Philippa Boswell was in the lower sixth form—her boyfriend, the one she had been accused of sneaking out to meet in Lilypad Lane. I found myself shaking hands with Ruth, saying something about being pleased to be back in the area and what a warm, inviting house she and Mr. Middleton shared.

"Thank you. Bumbletons were the builders. It's a very old firm, dating back to the middle of the nineteenth century. One of their special touches was the addition of niches. There's one on the landing upstairs." Before I could say I had seen it, she continued. "And the Chaplain's House has several of them. I suppose they were originally included to suit the architecture of the time and became a tradition."

"I like niches," I told her, "and I love your house."

"That's nice to hear." Her smile became a beam. "Most of the furnishings are handed down from our parents. They were the sort who thought a home should look established. Fortunately, Anya liked a homey look. She was such an easygoing person. None of the temperament that might have been expected from a woman who traveled the world as a first violinist."

"Just been hearing about her. Sounds a gem!" Dorcas again reached into her pocket for the handkerchief.

There was a general movement to be seated. Abruptly, Gillian stopped playing and came to join the circle around the coffee table, huddling—it seemed to me—away from the outpouring of praise that greeted her. Ruth poured from the handsome silver teapot and her brother handed around the cups and saucers, along with plates to hold the sensibly sized ham sandwiches and even more generous wedges of cake that were quickly proffered.

"This is splendid, Ruth," said the doctor, "and more than welcome, seeing I skipped lunch."

"In addition to breakfast, if I know you." A laugh colored her voice and lighted up the brown eyes that must have matched her curly hair when she was younger.

"I've been rather rushed off my feet these past few days. Half of both Lower and Upper Swan-Upping are coming down with one thing or another. How's it going at St. Roberta's?" he asked Gillian while helping himself to another sandwich. "Matron not being kept too busy in the sick bay?"

"I don't think so." The girl hadn't eaten anything or sipped her tea.

"And yourself?" He was sizing her up in a casual manner. "Not slacking off on second helpings of wonderful school food?"

"No." This said over the general ripple of laughter. She finally took a determined bite of her sandwich. Was he reflecting behind his thoughtful gray eyes that it might be a good idea to have a talk with her great-aunt about getting to the root of her unhappiness? Had that been Ruth Middleton's hope in fetching him over here? My thoughts wandered off down their own path. How long was it since Dr. Brian Roberts had last thought of Philippa Boswell? My romantic—some might say *mindless*—meandering was cut short when I heard what sounded like the back door opening, and footsteps accompanied a voice in announcing another visitor.

"Any tea left in the pot?" It was cheerfully said, and everyone in the room beamed in response, except for Gillian—although she did smile faintly—and, of course, my cowardly self, who felt my face congeal as I burrowed back in my chair.

"I'm pouring you a cup, Marilyn." Ruth's hands moved efficiently, happily, among the contents of the tray as the two men got to their feet and Dorcas sat smartly to attention, while I stared fixedly at the woman stepping past the piano with a smoothness of motion that could equally be called grace. What was I thinking? This was recognizably Ms. Chips of haunted memory. Not that I had recalled her entirely accurately. The image I'd held in my mind had been of a beanpole of a woman with a severely plain face. In reality she was about five-foot-seven, with a slim figure that, if not curvy, did not go straight up and down. Her hair, which appeared more ash blond than gray, was confined now, as it had been all those years ago, in a French pleat. At the time I had thought the style pinched her face into grim authority, but I now saw it not only suited her but added a timeless elegance to her quiet good looks.

The mind plays such tricks. As with Mr. Middleton, I must have thought Ms. Chips older than she really was twenty-odd years before—sixty, at least, which was what she must be now. I found myself getting to my feet, along with Gillian and the two men. She was an adult, a teacher; it wouldn't be right to remain planted on my bottom. I could feel myself flushing as I extended a hand, amid a whir of voices that sounded like a fan turned up too high, said who I was, felt the firm grip, heard the acknowledgment, and sat dizzily down in a seat across from her. She accepted a teacup and saucer from Ruth but declined the walnut cake, adding in a laughing voice that she knew she wouldn't be able to stop at one slice; such restraint couldn't be expected of anyone. I saw she was smiling at Gillian and was surprised to realize what beautiful eyes she had. They were an unusual dark gray-green, but it was their expression that drew me; it was compassionate and pensive as she took in the girl's face.

Amid the flow of conversation, she asked me if I had just arrived at Swan-Upping and remarked upon the delightful weather we were having, but she neither made inquiries into where I was in my life nor offered a wish that I would enjoy my visit. I sat feeling perplexed by this, while she and Dorcas exchanged pleasantries, until it came to me that of course she would not pose any leading questions or suggest that I was here to enjoy myself. As a temporary occupant of the Chaplain's House, I supposedly was seeking refuge from a major problem in my life. Feeling all the more awkward for being a fraud, I seized a pause in the general conversation to congratulate her upon the upcoming ceremony honoring the new gymnasium. Her fair skin flushed.

It was Ruth who said, "Dear Marilyn, don't I keep telling you that the price of doing a good deed is a certain amount of grateful attention? Mrs. Battle and the Board of Governors have not arranged the event to punish you. And you don't need me to remind you how the pupils adore an end-of-term celebration."

Ms. Chips smiled at her before turning to me. "My friends know me for what I am, which is the most terrible stick-in-the-mud."

"Nothing of the kind!" Dorcas protested. "Frightfully good sport. Can never thank you enough for helping me settle in."

"And here you are," said Mr. Middleton in his kindly way, "doing dorm duty for Diane Frenton this evening instead of attending the concert in the park as planned."

"I'm pleased to do it. She's a dear girl and was dreadfully cut up over her divorce. By all accounts she did everything she could to keep the marriage going. I'm happy to hear she has a date for this evening."

"You would be, dear," said Ruth in a gentle voice. "You are such a romantic. Always have been, always will be."

I sat listening in bemusement. How odd to discover that Ms. Chips bore so little resemblance to the woman I'd tried not to think about through the years. I found myself studying her nose. It didn't look as though it had been broken in three places. It was in fact a remarkably nice nose: *patrician* might be the word. Dorcas caught my eye. She was quite right, it was time for us to be leaving, but we would have to wait a moment because the conversation had turned to Lady Loverly's housekeeper, Mrs. Brown, and her bad headaches. Perhaps remembering Aiden Loverly's mention of one of those headaches, Gillian got up, after a low-voiced aside to Mr. Middleton, went to the piano, and leafed through some sheet music.

"I know you can't say anything about what causes her pain," Ruth said to the doctor, "but I can't help wondering—knowing her from church and the sewing circle as I do—if the cause isn't stress. Not the ordinary everyday sort but from a much deeper source. She's such a bottled-up woman. Try as I will I can't get close to her, but I have the feeling it could really help if she opened up to someone. Perhaps a psychiatrist, but"—Ruth looked into the doctor's eyes and continued as if in response—"Mrs. Brown wouldn't, I can see that. What she needs is a sympathetic listener, and I know just the person for the job." She was smiling impishly at Marilyn when the room was jolted to the alert by the sound of a phone.

"That'll be my cell." The doctor reached apologetically into his jacket pocket.

"Never a moment's peace for the committed," said Mr. Middleton, as Harpsichord leaped out of nowhere onto his lap and began purring angelically. It would have been so easy to believe that I had been wrong about the cat and that she had a heart as well as eyes of gold.

4

Dorcas and I received a gratifyingly warm send-off from the Middletons. Walking with us to the gate, brother and sister each voiced the hope that we would return during my stay. They also said they'd drive Gillian back to St. Roberta's in a couple of hours. I was glad of this, as it put paid to the possibility of her encountering Aiden Loverly on the way. This might have been on their minds too, or perhaps they would have insisted on taking her anyway.

Dorcas and I talked briefly about Ms. Chips and whether she yet knew about the missing Loverly Cup. Then my thoughts strayed elsewhere as we drove around the green and along the leafy road to St. Roberta's.

"He struck me as the sensitive sort of man who'd never get over losing the girl he loved." The words slipped out—the result, as my young friend Ariel Hopkins, now an inmate of St. Roberta's, would have known, of reading too many romantic novels. The sort where true love is torn asunder and nothing can bring about a happy resolution, unless the author shows mercy and, close to the end, does some jiggling around as to what really transpired to cause the rift.

"Talking about Mr. Middleton?" Dorcas braked for a rabbit hopping across the road.

"No," I said. Dorcas could have reasonably pointed out that Anya Middleton, tragically young as she had been to die, couldn't be called a girl, having recently celebrated her silver wedding. But Dorcas, unlike Mrs. Malloy, was not inclined to nitpick. "I meant Dr. Roberts."

"Pleasant chap. Never thought about his love life."

Neither would I, if it hadn't been for Philippa Boswell. I had to flounder for an explanation. "It struck me there has to be a reason why a good-looking man of his age hasn't been snapped up along ago."

"Not the marrying kind?"

Eager to get off the subject before digging myself deeper into Dr. Roberts's personal life, I agreed. It was Dorcas who changed the subject.

"Really liked Ruth Middleton, Ellie."

"Same here. That was a bang-up tea she provided."

"Genuine article. Like to get to know her better. Have one thing in common for starters—both of us go by Miss rather than Ms. Always thought women's lib got that one wrong. Much more sensible to come up with a form of address to differentiate between single and married *men*. Time the male sex made some adjustments. Must say I was surprised to discover Chippy goes by Ms. Chips. Old-fashioned sort; would have expected her to stick to her generational guns."

"It doesn't mean she's ashamed of being single."

"True enough! Each to his own. Good thing is, women today can be proud of going it solo. Chest out, chin up!" Dorcas stopped for another rabbit, which had ignored the level crossing we'd just passed. Did they have their own boarding school, perhaps the Beatrix Potter Academy, in the area?

"About Gillian," I said. The car stalled, and in starting it up again—clearly against its will, given the irritable grunts—we took off past a small post office and general store.

"Heard what she said, Ellie, to Aiden Loverly. Hate to say it but have been worrying."

"That it was she who took the cup?"

"Been clear all along she's not settled as well as might be hoped, and there's a worrisome change in her this week: not good at words, but she's haunted . . . bleak. Carolyn Fisher-Jones said Gillian seemed fine last weekend. The two of them stayed at the Hall. Carolyn, being Lady Loverly's goddaughter, goes regularly and occasionally takes a friend along. Aiden Loverly arrived for a visit teatime on Sunday. Didn't seem to take to Gillian."

"Well, that could explain her being more down in the dumps than usual. Girls at that age take rejection by handsome young men as evidence that they are horribly unattractive and will never have a boyfriend. But it doesn't explain how Aiden zeroed in on Gillian as the cup thief."

Oh, go on with you! Mrs. Malloy's voice hooted inside my head. *He could have heard her tell Carolyn what she was plotting. At the time he'd maybe think it was a case of talking big; then, when word got back that the cup had been nicked, he'd be rip-roaring furious with the kid.*

"Do you think Carolyn might be involved if Gillian did take it?" I asked Dorcas.

"Wouldn't think so. Devoted to her godmother. But never can tell. Friendships are fiercely important at that age."

I well remembered. At fourteen I had crept out to the ruined convent at dead of night with Susan and Ann because loyalty to the Triangle was all important.

"I wonder why Aiden waited until today to confront Gillian," I said.

"Imagine he went back to Tingwell for the week."

"Is that where he lives? It looked such a grotty town."

"Has a shop there. Antiques, paintings, curios . . . that sort of thing."

"I don't want it to be Gillian," I stated flatly. "Any other suspects spring to mind?"

"Not mine." Dorcas shook her head vigorously.

"Meaning?" I was glad to note the car kept on track.

"Mrs. Rushbridge says culprit has to be a first former. Tend to feel big for their boots after ascending to senior school. All that impish bravado bubbling up."

"Who's Mrs. Rushbridge?"

"Home Skills teacher. Been suffering with her teeth lately, poor woman."

"Then perhaps we shouldn't rely on her opinion. If I were sucking on cloves to ease the agony I'd probably loathe and distrust all eleven- and twelve-year-olds."

We had entered a shady avenue. A squirrel scampered up a tree, but of rabbits there was no sign. Not much of a thrill for them here in attempting to make it from one side to the other without ending up as prepackaged stew. Ours was the only vehicle moving in either direction, and we were traveling at thirty miles below the speed limit, which meant a rolling stone could have gone faster and gathered moss at the same time. A peep at Dorcas's profile showed her deep in thought.

"Thing is, Ellie, can't see Gillian as a girl who'd upset her family by stealing."

"She sounded fond of them, from the way she talked," I agreed. "And then there's Mr. Middleton. However much she may detest being a pupil at St. Roberta's, it's clear that she values him not only as a music teacher but as a shoulder to lean on. But that still leaves Aiden Loverly's hostility and her response."

Mrs. Malloy's voice, having taken up permanent residence inside my head, told me not to go all soft on the girl because I was missing my own children. *For all you know, Mrs. H, she's a real little cheat.*

"About Ms. Chips," I said. "Do you think she will be dreadfully upset about the cup's disappearance when she gets wind of it? If she hasn't done so already."

"Bound to feel it deeply. Terrible breach of school honor."

"Is she much at the school these days?"

"Fair bit. As special old friend of Matie, she likes to keep in touch. Not the first time she's done dorm duty this week."

"She looked very well. Although when I was standing in the hall, I did overhear Ruth Middleton and her brother mention that she has high blood pressure."

"Not uncommon as we get older. Easy to treat these days, I gather."

"Retirement must have been a huge adjustment for her."

"Hard on anyone to leave a lifelong job, Ellie, but, for someone like Chippy, St. Roberta's is more than a workplace, it's home and family."

I placed a hand on her arm. "Dear Dorcas, you have Merlin's Court, Ben, me, and the children and don't you ever forget it. Ms. Chips strikes me as the sort to take life as it comes."

"Matey fusses she'll become depressed, if she isn't already."

"Surely Dr. Roberts would know about it and be providing help if that were the case, and Ruth Middleton wouldn't be suggesting she help Mrs. Brown with her problems." Unless—I leaned back in my seat—Ms. Chips is the sort who would be ashamed to admit to weakness and would battle on alone . . . until something cracked inside. Fast on the heels of this thought came the memory of a particularly thrilling book from my childhood, *The Case of the Missing Hockey Stick.* The only way for Felicity of the fourth form to clear her good name had been to discover the identity of the true villainess, who turned out to be—shocker of all shockers—the much-admired games mistress, Miss Something-or-Other. So unsettling was this jolt to my system that I missed Dorcas's reply. What if it was Ms. Chips who had taken the Loverly Cup—her cup—because she could not tolerate seeing it handed over to a rival school? Distorted thinking, paranoia—we've all heard or read stories of real-life people whose emotional problems escalate to the tragic. I knew I was fabricating fantasy, but at that moment I stopped thinking of the theft as something silly that I wouldn't have given two hoots about except for Dorcas's sake. I was seized by a determination to get to the bottom of the matter.

We had reached the brick pillars marking the entrance to St. Roberta's. My reasons for not wanting to return came flooding back. Part of that disinclination was my breaking Ms. Chips's nose and my loathing of lacrosse, but I could no longer continue to hold that against her.

"Ah, here we are," announced Dorcas, taking the car at a crawl down the sweeping drive, bordered by stately trees. A smile brightened her pale face. Being a woman of deep attachments she had, despite her short tenure, already given her heart and unfaltering loyalty to this place.

All hard feelings on my part aside, the building *was* beautiful, cousin of sorts to the manor house that promises admittance by a deferential butler, bowing footmen, and housemaids keeping fit by bobbing curtsies at every opportunity. King Charles spaniels on velvet cushions having their portraits painted by a descendent of Landseer. Fourteen-course meals being prepared in the nether regions. Drawing rooms inhabited by Britain's best if not brightest, discoursing about what was being said in *The Tatler* regarding hems going up or down that season or how long it would take for French to be considered a dead language.

Yes, a lovely building! But, unpleasantly to my mind, an imposter. It had been built in the 1950s after its Victorian predecessor was demolished. The air of antiquity had been sneakily acquired by the use of old brick graced with Virginia creeper, latticed windows, and an abundance of chimney pots that nostalgically recalled the days when small boys got to be chimney sweeps, so much more fun than all the hair-raising rides Disney now has to offer.

Dorcas stopped the car on the curved expanse of brick paving before the imposing entrance. I was about to get out—prematurely, it turned out.

"Thought you'd want to see the old place up close before we park. Has to be an emotional moment; no shame in having a blubber. Bawled my head off the first time I returned to my old school. Memories of jolly old times came flooding back: Miss Pinky telling me my essay on why I wanted to be the sixth-form netball captain had brought tears to her eyes. Would offer you my hanky but it's been used a lot today."

"Did you get to be captain?"

"Wasn't to be. Broke my ankle at the start of term. Thought at the time my life was ruined but, shoulders back, have to go on. Can't dwell on life's disappointments. Not alone in them. Similar thing happened to Matron as a girl. Out hiking on Dartmoor, got trapped in a dense fog, was out in the open overnight, came down with pneumonia, and missed taking her A levels."

"Who told you, Matron herself?"

"Can't remember. Things get bandied about in a closed community. Not saying, of course, aren't secrets that get to be kept."

"Let's hope the identity of the person who took the Loverly Cup won't be one of them." My voice came out sounding mechanical rather than heartfelt. I was staring up at those gleaming window eyes, all of them looking deep into my soul, searching out my schoolgirl sins, and savoring my desire to flee back to my grown-up world where people such as my husband and children liked me. The car windows were open and a breeze whispered in my ear: *That's because the poor dupes don't know the wicked, cowardly you—the schoolgirl who embarked on a course of deception.* Where was Mrs. Malloy when it would have been comforting to hear her pipe up in my defense? Probably taking a nap, I thought wretchedly.

"Want to talk some more?" inquired Dorcas kindly.

What could I say? Would it brighten her day when she was already concerned about the mystery of the missing cup to be informed that I was a person hearing voices and, even more disturbing, fretting when they were silent? Better for me to remark on the lovely vista to be perceived by twisting my head around so that I was looking away from the school building, its lawn sparingly ornamented with trees spread out like a vast green counterpane fringed around the edges with honeysuckle and privet sloping gently down to a shadowy glimpse of the convent ruins. From this vantage point, I could see neither the Dribbly Drop nor Lilypad Lane, where Philippa was said to have kept her assignation with Brian Roberts.

The Chaplain's House stood well down to the right, reduced in size and importance by distance. There seemed something apologetic about the way it hovered behind its low brick wall. I found myself recalling Uriah Heep and his "Ever so 'umble, Mr. Copperfield." Would I be the only one staying there, or were others of my fellows already in temporary residence? If so, who? And what would be their reasons for seeking a retreat from their everyday lives? It was something I had failed to ask Dorcas and she hadn't thought to tell me. Now the moment was lost because a girl came around the side of the school building, head down, fair hair brushing her shoulders.

"That's Carolyn Fisher-Jones. Hope she's not down in the dumps worrying about Gillian." Dorcas started up the car, sending it bucking into reverse before we were catapulted around the left side of the building into the parking area.

"Small wonder, if she's had a phone call from her godmother's loathsome grandson, describing how he almost rode the girl down with his motorcycle." I ground out the words. "How I'd love him to be the thief himself, trying to put the blame elsewhere. He's perfectly cast as the villain of the piece."

Dorcas's response was muffled by more grinding of the gears.

I'm not the best parker, but she—dear woman—is worse. The next minute or two incorporated several panicky nosedives and rocketing retreats between two cars that strove valiantly not to look frightened. I kept expecting them to collapse from fear into heaving heaps, which we would have to surreptitiously shovel over a hedge for the dustman to collect next Sunday. Then again, would it be so dreadful if a policeman complete with helmet and truncheon popped out of nowhere and I, nobly denying any involvement on Dorcas's part, was hauled away and ordered never again to set foot within a hundred miles of St. Roberta's?

My head was cleared by the final jolt, and I seized the moment to reach into my bag for my compact mirror. It was a pretty thing—engine-turned silver and jade-green enamel—but what really counted was that it had belonged to my mother and she had given it to me on my seventeenth birthday, only a month before she died. Just holding it when I was anxious or unsure of myself helped me feel better . . . calmer . . . more resolute. Within minutes of setting eyes on Aiden Loverly, I had sized him up as my favorite kind of suspect: spoiled, ruthless, and utterly cocksure that he could get away with murder . . . or in this case, a sports cup. But above the desire to bring him to justice there was another pull—my need to know more about what was going on in the lives of Gillian and Ms. Chips. Finally the car was stationary, if infringing on the personal space of the Honda to its left. I gave my head a shake and, on legs that trembled only infinitesimally, joined Dorcas in stepping out onto concrete that I hoped would do us the kindness of staying in place until we were safely inside St. Roberta's.

"Feel the most frightful fool. Hit the bull's-eye on a dartboard nine times out of ten but can't park to save my life."

I had been wondering how well Ariel Hopkins knew either Gillian or Carolyn, but refocused to say encouragingly, "Rubbish, you did a bang-up job!"

Aware that this term was not comforting, seeing how narrowly it missed being the truth, I got out of the car and was about to follow her toward the building when were both jolted by a bellowing roar. A man was racing across the lawn in pursuit of two girls—one carrying the other on her back, a fair head pressed against a dark one. There was a sense of panic about them, heightened by the occasional stumble. I realized we were about to face a collision, unless it could be averted by Dorcas. Stepping forward in the nick of time, she placed a hand on the girl doing the carrying and brought her to a halt. Instantly the man was also there. Seen close up, he appeared a surly fellow in late middle age, a short sparse figure with small eyes peering darkly through narrowed lids and yellowed teeth biting down on lips stretched into a scowl.

"Hold on! What's happening here?" Dorcas surveyed the threesome, but it was the man she addressed.

"I caught sight of the pair of 'em from the toolshed where I was doing some tidying up." He grunted. "Making from the Dribbly Drop they was, skipping about and giggling like a pair of six-year-olds instead of acting their age." From the look of them, both girls were about twelve. The one doing the carrying looked solidly strong; the one being piggybacked displayed skinny arms and legs.

"Miriam and Shirley, isn't it?" Dorcas cocked an orange eyebrow. "Surprised at you both. Usually so well behaved. Those steps are out of bounds because they are dangerous. Easy to take a spill going down."

"It was coming up that Shirley tripped," said the sturdy girl. "We knew we shouldn't have gone down, but we'd got the idea that the Loverly Cup might be hidden in the ruins. The stone bench just inside the refectory has a wide crack down it that would be the perfect place. But oh, Miss Critchley, we didn't get that far because when we came down the last step and stood on the path we had the biggest fright. We saw someone crouched inside the ruins with this shawl thing on her head and a horrible old dress that looked like it was falling apart."

"Miss Critchley, you can accuse us of lying, but we swear it was the Gray Nun!" The other girl spoke from around her neck. "It was hard to make her out because she was wrapped up in shadows and it was so quick. When we heard Mr. Mossop shouting, we turned to come back up. And then I fell and twisted my ankle, so Miriam told me to get on her back; luckily I'm pretty light. We thought if she ran fast we could get inside before he caught us and got us into huge trouble."

"These legs is old, not useless." The man's glower struck me as malevolent, but then I do tend to dramatize a situation, and he couldn't be faulted for wanting to prevent an accident.

"Shouldn't have gone down the Dribbly Drop, whatever the reason." Dorcas reddened, as is her wont when called upon to be stern.

"Accident waiting to happen is them steps," Mr. Mossop said, with grim relish.

"Thanks awfully for looking out for their safety," Dorcas was saying, when a short woman wearing a dark woolen sweater and pleated skirt unsuited to the heat of the day came through a door in the building and hurried toward us, anxiety evident in her clasped hands and darting eyes.

"There's the missus," said Mr. Mossop. "Even of a Sunday afternoon she finds reason to be in the school pushing a broom. Says if I'm at the toolshed what's to keep her in the cottage? I've tried explaining to her that there's a difference between me having a quiet hour to meself and her slaving away to no purpose when she could be watching the telly. Can't sit still for a minute, that woman." He stood scratching behind his ear, his lower lip thrust out as the woman reached us.

"Hello there, Mrs. Mossop!" Dorcas hailed her heartily. "Please accompany these two girls to Matron's office and explain that Shirley tripped when out of the grounds and hurt her ankle."

"I'll do that, miss." The woman ducked her head before turning to lead the girls toward the main door of the school. The man remained standing for a few moments before taking himself off with a shrug and a grunt in the opposite direction, presumably to return either to the toolshed or his cottage, which Dorcas informed me were both located behind a grove of trees about fifty yards up from the Chaplain's House.

"So now you've met the school's caretaker and his sad little wife. Afraid to say yes, and afraid to say no, that's Mrs. Mossop. But a worker in a million! Building gleams. Spit and polish. She has helpers, of course, but she sees nothing is missed."

Dorcas took my arm as we turned and made for a side door that gave entrance to the area of the building with flats for the staff members who lived in. These, she explained, were in the majority. The larger quarters were provided to those who were married, whether or not they had families. As should be expected, the exception was Mrs. Battle, whose widowhood predated her arrival on the scene as headmistress. I listened and nodded while thinking of Miriam and Shirley and their suspicion regarding the Loverly Cup and the stone bench in the refectory ruins. I remembered Susan dropping her watch down that gap during our own nocturnal visit. There would indeed have been room for a much larger object.

We were in a square lobby painted a rich hunter green with several handsome landscapes adorning the walls and golden parquet flooring that gave onto an ornately carved staircase, carpeted with a richly hued Turkish runner. It might have been the side entrance of a lovingly maintained manor house. On reaching the floor above, Dorcas led the way along a wainscoted corridor with stained-glass windows and ceiling-hung lanterns. There were more paintings, mostly portraits of women from different eras, dating possibly from the 1930s to the present day. I guessed these to be old girls who, given their handsome attire and faintly smug smiles, had made good.

"My flat." Dorcas pointed at a door in passing.

"Nicely in the middle," I said, seconds before she turned a corner.

"Battle stations!" she announced brightly. Taking this to mean the doorbell she was now pressing would fetch forth Mrs. Battle, I fixed a smile on my face and started mentally reciting my nine times tables while trying to remember when the Gold Coast had been renamed Ghana. Before I could fail in either of these attempts it was too late to start testing my memory of French beyond *ouvre la porte*. The woman who greeted us did so with a smile, but I had little hope that I would be sitting on her knee and calling her "my dear old Battle-ax" anytime soon.

5

Do come in." Mrs. Battle stepped aside to enable us to do so. "Good of you, Miss Critchley, to fetch Mrs. Haskell."

She must now have been in her fifties, a tall woman—a good five-foot-ten to my five-six—an unfair advantage that I tried nobly to convince myself was not intentional. A long bony hand was extended, to be heartily wrung by Dorcas, who had every right to make up in brute strength for being the shortest, and meekly clasped by myself. There followed the usual series of polite greetings, which drifted along with us down the short hall into a large living room.

My tremulous gaze took in the square floor, square windows, and ceiling, and I tried to convince myself I would soon feel as comfortable as a square peg in a square hole. Nothing was reminiscent of the manor house here. The furnishings were contemporary and minimalist in the extreme. The first words that registered with me came from Dorcas, who declined to take a seat on the grounds that she would instead return to the car and take my luggage along to the Chaplain's House.

"We could do that later." I twitched an eye at her, having never mastered a proper wink.

"I think Miss Critchley wants to give us a moment alone in which to discuss what I hope you can accomplish while giving up your undoubtedly valuable time, Mrs. Haskell, to help sort out this little trouble in which St. Roberta's finds itself."

Mrs. Battle's smile was of the sort that comes from practicing as frequently as possible in front of a mirror, the equivalent of religiously using dental floss, tiresome though it might be. I found myself regretting not having faced this interview in her office. Before I could come to terms with this emotion, the room was empty of Dorcas, thereby losing its one charm. That she had promised to return for me within the hour was a reed to which I would cling till my fingers disintegrated.

Seated in a chair with a rigidly flat bottom, ramrod back, and square arms, I decided all the furnishings had been chosen with discomfort in mind, a wise choice if one doesn't want visitors to linger. Mrs. Battle excused herself, saying she would fetch a pot of tea from the kitchenette. I thanked her and made up my mind to decline biscuits should she bring them. It would hardly do to get off on the wrong foot by appearing undisciplined.

While she was gone I studied the decor, the barest essentials of desk, coffee table, and chairs, no photos and no ornaments. Where did the woman keep her life, in a drawer? I was longing with the warm glow of nostalgia for the Middletons' comfortably inviting house when Mrs. Battle returned with a tea tray. She did bring biscuits, two narrow rectangular ones on a square beige plate.

The whole room was beige. Perhaps—I was always eager to grasp where hope was not—she believed the innocuous color scheme flattered her looks.

Some hope! Mrs. Malloy's voice almost took the lid off my head. *Woman's got a face like the back of a bus!*

This—ill-put though it might be—was the unvarnished truth. Much as I hate to say it, Mrs. Battle would have needed one of the contestants to die on the runway not to come in last in a beauty pageant. Her dark hair was all right on its own, but in combination with hooded eyes, a sallow complexion, and jutting pitted nose it completed her crowlike appearance. Given those negatives, I noted—when she straightened up after setting the tea tray on the coffee table—that what she lost on the roundabouts she gained on the swings. Her slim figure, minus any helpful contribution from her navy skirt and cardigan, was superb, added to which her legs were long and shapely. Photographed from the neck down, she would have made Marilyn Monroe weep. That's life, I thought, accepting the teacup handed to me; none of us gets it all. I have always considered my feet my one true beauty and, coming in second, my ears. Ben says—

"I hope your husband did not object to your responding to this rather peremptory summons." Mrs. Battle sat across from me.

"Not at all." I repositioned myself in an attempt to emulate her superior posture. "He was only too delighted to think I might be of help to you in this troubling situation."

"How kind. What is his name?"

"Ben."

"Short for Benjamin?"

"Bentley." Were we working on English as a foreign language?

"Interesting." She crossed her ankles and I followed suit—too quickly—knocking off a shoe.

"You have children?"

"Three. Two girls and a boy."

"Ah!"

"They thought it most exciting that I was going back to

school." My cup rattled in my saucer as I squirmed my foot back into my shoe, not helped by hearing Mrs. Malloy ordering me to tell the old bugger to get down to the matter of the Loverly Cup.

"Do help yourself to a biscuit, Mrs. Haskell."

It was a highly tempting offer, which I was forced to decline. Were I to reach for the plate, I would inevitably drop my tea and lose my other shoe. In a pathetic attempt at making up for what she might view as rank disobedience—to be punished by my not being allowed to visit the sweetshop—I requested that she call me Ellie.

"Certainly." Mrs. Battle took a restrained sip of tea that to my flurried state of mind epitomized her entire character: conservative, reflective, disciplined. In a moment I would break under the pressure of this constrained small talk and start singing the national anthem or reciting "Hiawatha." She was studying me intently—suspiciously might be a better word—from those dark hooded eyes. "I regret to say . . . Ellie . . . that I don't recall seeing much of you during your time as a pupil."

This was the moment to say Oh, whoops! That isn't surprising because I've suddenly realized I'm at the wrong school. The St. Roberta's I attended was in the Outer—far, far Outer—Hebrides, and if you wouldn't be horribly offended, Mrs. Battle, I won't stay to finish my cup of tea but scoot off in hopes of catching the next Bonnie Prince Charlie ferry so as not to be late for evensong in the chapel.

A happy thought but best scotched. Mrs. Battle's eagle gaze informed me that she had long experience with prevaricators and my time would be better spent suggesting to the pope that I teach him his catechism than in trying to get a pack of nonsense past her. Counting myself lucky she hadn't slapped my hand with a ruler for not paying attention in class—or rather, her flat—I accepted that I was stuck in an uncomfortable chair until she granted me permission to slink away.

"I was only here for three years."

"Yes." She wasn't about to admit that she didn't remember me from Adam—or, rather, Eve.

"I wasn't memorable. Not remarkably good in any subject."

"Now we mustn't take the discouraged view." Her tone was for the first time kindly; suggesting that she saw me as a student who needed to be persuaded there was still time for improvement were I to pull up my socks. "What about sports? Perhaps that was where you excelled?"

"No, I was hopeless at any sort of game." Memory having taken me by the throat, I took a swig of tea to steady my nerves. "But I did like drawing."

"That's something, isn't it?" She was in the process of smiling when her face darkened. "You weren't the one who drew that nude—extremely rude—portrait of Mr. Bumbleton, chairman of the Board of Governors, on the refectory wall?"

"Certainly not." The very suggestion accomplished some stiffening of my spine. "My interest at that time was in drawing flowers."

"A great pity the artist did not include a bunch of them where most desperately needed. Mrs. Bumbleton, who most unfortunately happened to be visiting the school that day, took particular exception to the portrait's not having been done to scale."

"Oh, dear!"

"I'm sorry if I offended you, Ellie." As if by way of atonement Mrs. Battle handed me the plate of biscuits, and I, after the barest hesitation, took one. "You weren't in my Greek class?" She made it into a casual question.

"Afraid not. Greek would have been . . . Greek to me." I saw no point in jogging her memory by saying I had been happy to remain securely third from the bottom in Anatomy.

She permitted herself the narrowest of smiles. "But you did take A levels?"

"Not at St. Roberta's. I left here before studying for them and did them later at art school." Noting from Mrs. Battle's dubious expression that to her mind this made them null and void, I decided it was high time I faced her woman to woman. The biscuit, tiny as it was, had helped enormously. "Shall we talk about the Loverly Cup and how I can help in locating it?" I said, with a briskness I thought deserving of congratulation from Mrs. Malloy, but she remained uncannily silent.

"Miss Critchley spoke highly of your success as a private detective. I understand she is a close friend of yours and would under those circumstances be partial, but we find ourselves in desperate straits."

"I'll do my very best."

"No more can be expected of one of our girls, whether she is taking her end-of-term exams or being asked, as you are, to preserve the luster of St. Roberta's good name." Mrs. Battle inclined her head in my general direction. "As Miss Critchley will have told you, the cup's disappearance, while seriously disturbing at any time, couldn't have come at a worse one for the school."

"She explained it has to be passed on shortly to another school and that failure to do so could put a blight on the ceremonial presentation of the new gymnasium."

"Mr. Bumbleton, should he get wind of the situation, is sure to be seriously displeased. He might urge the other members of the board to insist upon my resignation, unless"—her lips tightened—"I can see my way to pacifying him, which is unlikely, given that he is the sort of man who believes he rules the world. He has a granddaughter here, but I am not unduly concerned that she will go to him with the story. Naturally I did not suggest to the girls that they keep the matter secret from their parents and family members. That would have been unconscionable. But I do believe they understand the difference between discretion and disloyalty." Meeting her eyes, I was convinced they did.

"Mrs. Battle." I had given up crossing my ankles and keeping my elbows off the arms of my chair. "Who informed you that the Loverly Cup was gone?"

She picked up her teacup. "I received the news from Mrs. Mossop, one of our cleaners. It's her job to keep the glass front of the trophy cabinet shining and to dust inside every few weeks. It was last Monday at about two in the afternoon when she glanced at the case in passing and saw the empty space. She stumbled into my office in tears."

"Does she have her own key?"

"I have the only two, a spare kept here in my flat and the other in the top drawer of my office desk. Mrs. Mossop asks me for one when needed and has never failed to return it promptly. She's a dithery woman in many ways, but conscientious; there is no possibility of her having taken the cup. I had to send for her husband, who is the general handyman, to take her home, such was the state she was in! She had been cleaning inside the case at half past one or thereabouts."

"Might she have left the door unlocked or even open?"

"She assured me she did not." Mrs. Battle stared me full in the face. "I will not allow that poor, befuddled woman to be blamed." A lesser mortal might have pounded her fist, but her vehemence came across just as fiercely, and I experienced my first flicker of liking for old Battle-ax.

"When did you announce the theft to the school?" I helped myself to the remaining biscuit because it looked in desperate need of human contact.

"The following day—which was Tuesday—I summoned students and staff to the assembly hall before the start of morning classes. After informing them of what had happened, I issued a forceful appeal for the guilty party to bring the Loverly Cup to my office before final bell that afternoon."

"Without result."

"Regrettably, no one came forward." Mrs. Battle reached for the biscuit that wasn't there. "A search of classroom desks and dormitories was not considered; as you will know, St. Roberta's has always adhered to the honor system. Added to which, some of the parents would undoubtedly object if word were to leak out in future."

"I'm sure." Mustn't ruffle the little darlings' feathers.

"I did send for Carolyn Fisher-Jones and her friend, Matron's great-niece Gillian Parker, not because I suspected them but because the situation affected them more closely than the other students—Carolyn being Lady Loverly's goddaughter and Gillian a frequent visitor with her at her ladyship's home. I told them I did not expect them to withhold the information from her but not to dramatize it."

"Weren't you worried that Lady Loverly might say something to Mr. Bumbleton or the other members of the Board of Governors?"

"Her ladyship cannot tolerate Mr. Bumbleton or his *cronies*, as she terms them. She resigned from the board for that reason."

"How did the two girls react when you talked with them?"

"Carolyn was clearly saddened but calm. A very steady girl."

"Gillian?"

"An entirely different type. The early reports, when she joined us at the beginning of the year, were that she was decidedly reserved. She was not a good mixer but wandered around on her own, until Carolyn befriended her. I was pleased about that—in contrast to Ms. Chips, who surprisingly voiced a concern about clinging vines."

That seemed to me rather hard. "Is Ms. Chips often at the school?"

"Fairly frequently. She comes over to assist when we need a substitute for dorm duty. In fact she is filling in this evening. Being the sensible woman she is, she doesn't make unnecessary visits, but we are always glad to see her." Mrs. Battle's voice revealed an unexpected hint of warmth. "Marilyn has always given much and asked little. It is distressing to think that she may not be able fully to enjoy the presentation of the new gymnasium. Gillian, who takes piano lessons from Mr. Middleton, is to play for the occasion, a selection of pieces by Beethoven. And she will accompany a classmate of hers, Elizabeth Anderson, who has been chosen to sing the school song."

"That sounds wonderful."

"Mr. Middleton believes Gillian has a great future ahead of her. One must hope she finally settles in at St. Roberta's. It's not unusual for some of the new girls to suffer from homesickness. She did seem to gain her footing as the term went on. It may have helped that she was invited to the Hall by Lady Loverly. She and Carolyn were there last weekend. Matron must appreciate the kindness."

"Do you think Gillian may have taken the cup?" It had to be asked.

Mrs. Battle got to her feet. "The thought did cross my mind; she was a bundle of nerves when I talked to her and Carolyn about it. She had that badly frightened look that sometimes results from guilt. I hoped it wasn't her; it would be such a blow for Matron, who's been delighted to be able to provide her with the opportunity to attend St. Roberta's. The Board of Governors sometimes waives the fees for girls with a family member on the staff. And in Gillian's case there is the added factor of being musically gifted. No, Ellie"—Mrs. Battle began to pace—"I very much hope for her sake and Matron's that Gillian isn't the one. And I don't believe it would be in character; she's far too timid—afraid of her own shadow, poor girl. It is a great blessing that Mr. Middleton's sister takes a kindly interest in her. Lady Loverly has been very good by having her to stay with Carolyn, but I think Gillian may have found life at the Hall intimidating."

"It sounds rather grand."

"If I didn't believe St. Roberta's might prove the making of her, I would suggest to Matron that she be sent home."

"Mrs. Battle, did you expect the Loverly Cup to be speedily returned?"

"I was hopeful, strongly so, but as that day passed and then the next, I began to fear that if some action was not taken we would be destined never to discover who pulled this stunt, as was the case with the dreadful depiction of Mr. Bumbleton on the refectory wall. The good thing there was that a fresh coat of paint took care of all but the affront to his dignity. The Loverly Cup is a different matter. A Hester Bateman piece: one of a kind, so I understand. We can find a substitute, I imagine. Indeed, we will have to do so if necessary, but I very much hope it will not be the case. Lady Loverly has long been a great friend of the school, and she's already suffered enough disappointments in her life; her husband was a constant worry until his death from a lifetime of drink."

"Is her ladyship likely to turn nasty if the cup isn't returned?"

Mrs. Battle smiled thinly. "She is one of those people who like to think of themselves as larger-than-life characters, but she has a practical side. Makes wonderful apple pies for the summer fete. Used to darn her husband's socks. I doubt she'll drag a dagger off the wall and threaten to kill herself after withdrawing all financial contributions." Mrs. Battle continued to pace, something she did rather well, given her fantastic figure. Had she been wearing a veil over her face she'd have had men leaping through windows in droves. "Whatever Lady Loverly's reaction, Ellie, the story is bound to leak out further once she knows of it, one likely source being her grandson."

"Aiden Loverly?"

"You've heard of him?" She did not pause for an answer. "Miss Critchley has certainly done a good job of bringing you on board with who's who in Swan-Upping. A highly capable woman—not entirely her fault that we didn't do well this lacrosse season."

"I'm sure of that."

"We lost our best players; they were all in last year's sixth form. It takes time to rebuild. I barely know young Mr. Loverly, but according to some he has a malicious tongue and an undue sense of his own importance—although it must be admitted he seems to be making a success of his art business. It wouldn't be surprising if he resented his grandmother's financial gifts to the school, seeing them as cutting into his inheritance. His father, now deceased, was an only son and so is he, making him her ladyship's primary heir, one assumes. I must confess I wince at the thought of his holding forth at the White Dog about what a great comeuppance it is to St. Roberta's to be made to look such poor losers at lacrosse." Mrs. Battle's eyes narrowed, and I found myself in total sympathy with her. At all costs Aiden Loverly must be prevented from gloating, whether or not he turned out to be responsible for the situation.

"Does he visit his grandmother frequently?"

"In spurts, from what I hear. At the Hall last weekend and back again this one, according to Mrs. Rushbridge, who teaches our Home Skills class. Whether he'd be as devoted if his grandmother were a woman in reduced circumstances living in a cottage is another matter." Sarcasm dripped from every word. "Her ladyship said as much to me; she's no fool. And I do believe she'd try to prevent his stirring up the current situation. It's not only the school's reputation I'm thinking about, Ellie. Ms. Chips is also in the forefront of my mind. We owe her a great debt, not only for her years of devoted and productive service but because of her enormous generosity in providing the new gymnasium."

"Dorcas—Miss Critchley—told me that Ms. Chips came into an inheritance." I dangled the sentence hopefully.

"From her former husband."

"She was married?" I cupped my chin before it could hit the floor.

"Years ago, when she was very young, just down from university, and only briefly. His family disliked the match and persuaded him into a divorce before the ink was dry on the wedding register."

"Why?" Shades of the Gray Nun, only in her case the evil parents had stopped the marriage at the altar.

"Her mother and grandmother had both suffered from severe mental illness. Tragically, in those days there was a tendency to think, in terms of insanity in the family, that any children would be at risk from birth on." Mrs. Battle actually looked misty-eyed, and I further warmed to her. "The young man, some relation to the Loverly family and the Fisher-Joneses, caved in, but it would seem he felt sufficient remorse to remember Ms. Chips substantially in his will, when he died a couple of years ago."

I had to ask the question. "Mrs. Battle, have you seen any recent signs that Ms. Chips may have been having a bout with depression as a result of the disappointing lacrosse season?"

"None at all. Matron said something to me on the subject, and I told her we all have our up days and down. The thing is not to obsess about it."

"The Loverly Cup must be recovered before the celebration of the new gymnasium," I said, with grim determination.

"I feel sure, Ellie, you will put your heart and brains into sorting out this unpleasant business." Mrs. Battle paid me this compliment without flourish or fuss; indeed, her manner conveyed that I should not take it as permission to run in the hallways, shout at the top of my lungs, or otherwise comport myself in a manner unbefitting the decorum expected of a St. Roberta's old girl.

"I'll get started promptly." My teacup was empty, the hope of a further biscuit nonexistent. It was clear my immediate future would not be a picnic in any sense of the word. "Have the staff been informed of my reason for being here?"

"I have spoken with them and you are free to question any of them, including Mr. and Mrs. Mossop and the other janitorial help. As for the girls, I thought it best not to get them stirred up by telling them a private investigator has been brought in, which is not to say you may not confide in some of them if you think it would be helpful."

"I'll have to consider my avenues of inquiry," I said, in my best professional manner, having received a mental elbow in the ribs from Mrs. Malloy.

"I understand, but I do rely on your discretion. In the interest of preventing too big a stir, I think it wise not to mention your real reason for being here to the old girls currently staying at the Chaplain's House. I hope you won't mind making up an excuse?" A note of embarrassment entered her voice, understandably so, given that prevarication of any sort violated St. Roberta's honor code. Before I could respond, she was temporarily saved by the bell—or, rather, the ringing of the telephone on the desk.

While she was speaking into the receiver, I racked my brains to come up with a plausible reason for seeking retreat at the Chaplain's House. I absolutely refused to tempt fate by making up something dreadful such as a death in the family. Perhaps I could say I was hiding out after having cosmetic surgery, but that would require punching myself in the face to provide the necessary puffiness and bruising—and that seemed to be asking a bit much even of one determined on giving back to St. Roberta's. Besides, the automatic suspicion would be that Ben had hit me. I was contemplating the sad thought that one or more of the other women might have sought sanctuary from an abusive spouse or partner when Mrs. Battle put the phone down.

"That was Miss Critchley, Ellie. She regrets she has been detained but is sending Ariel Hopkins to escort you to the Chaplain's House. I understand you are related to her."

"She's my husband's cousin's daughter."

"A new girl this year: intelligent and, more importantly, dogged. A terrier after the bone of life. Young Ariel will go far, whatever her chosen course." A shrewd gleam showed in Mrs. Battle's dark eyes. "Perhaps she can be your inside source, Ellie, in the quest for the elusive truth that threatens St. Roberta's." The doorbell rang. "Ah, that will be her now." Mrs. Battle headed down the hall, but the voice that responded to hers did not come from Ariel or any other schoolgirl. It was a deep rumble with snorting overtones.

"How nice to see you, Mr. Bumbleton. But unfortunately this is not a convenient time."

"You break my heart, Mrs. Battle. But this is important."

Did he want to borrow a book?

"A serious matter."

"I am not alone. A meeting with one of our old girls." Mrs. Battle returned in a sweep of movement that splendidly registered condescension. So might God look if interrupted by St. Peter in bumbling search of the golden gate's admission forms. "Ellie"—she inclined her head in my direction—"may I present William Bumbleton, member of our Board of Governors and head of the building firm that just completed our new gymnasium."

A fleshy hand engulfed mine. He was a stout red-faced man with thinning hair, combed carefully over a balding pate, and pale watery eyes that took in my appearance before dismissing me as an object of interest. It was on Mrs. Battle that those eyes lingered. Was he about to confront her with his awareness that the Loverly Cup had gone astray?

"Mr. Bumbleton and his firm are also responsible for the revitalization of Cygnet's Way," said Mrs. Battle, as if proffering a half-filled cup of lukewarm tea.

"Miss Critchley mentioned that." I beamed enthusiastically.

"We pride ourselves on the quality of our structures." His moist-looking lips puffed into a gloat and his stomach expanded in time with the accordion wheezing of his breath. "The Cygnet homes are roomy enough for families, cozy enough for two."

"Delightful, no doubt." Mrs. Battle did not wave him to a chair, but someone had to depart and I decided it should be me, a sentiment heightened when Mr. Bumbleton informed the room at large that he was a busy man and could only spare a limited amount of time to discuss a distressing report he had just received from China.

6

After suggesting to Mrs. Battle that I wait for Ariel downstairs at the entrance to the staff flats, I gratefully accepted her nod of dismissal. Mr. Bumbleton's words of regret at my departure rang with insincerity. All was becoming clear, I thought: it was a case straight from one of my boarding-school storybooks. The headmistress's secret life had been uncovered. She was being blackmailed by a stone-hearted villain who'd discovered that she had been handing over state secrets to China. Her code name was Sly Sally and she had disposed of the Loverly Cup because hidden in its false bottom was a list of her counterpart agents. What Mr. Bumbleton would require in return for his silence I did not ponder deeply. I was too busy picturing myself being received at Buckingham Palace by a trumpeting of the Guards before being presented with a medal by Her Majesty, along with a gift card to Marks & Spencer, honoring my service to the nation. Mrs. Malloy, of course, would be horribly jealous and say some very cutting things about people hogging the limelight and how she could have solved the case sitting home watching the telly and eating a bag of crisps.

"Hello, Ellie," said Ariel Hopkins.

I hadn't realized I'd exited the outside door but there I was, back on terra firma and looking into the face of reason.

"Hello, Ariel," I responded, in the same matter-of-fact manner. She was not a girl who went in for starry-eyed smiles or exclamations of delight on meeting. Hugs and kisses smacked to her of sloppy sentiment, only to be permitted in the most extreme circumstances. As I did not expect to expire in the next fifteen minutes or embark on my first solo mission to the moon, this wasn't one of them. The last time I'd seen her, she had worn her sandy hair in two stiff plaits; now it was woven into a tight coronet jammed on top of her head. The result, coupled with her round spectacles and prim mouth, was a governessy look.

"Just what are you up to?" she demanded, as if catching me nipping out the nursery window in my underwear.

"I was talking to Mrs. Battle until Mr. Bumbleton of the Board of Governors showed up, wanting to talk to her—about China, of all things."

"That's his granddaughter. She's twelve and horribly full of herself." Ariel rolled her eyes behind her glasses. "Most of the school thinks she needs taking down a peg. But what I want to know, Mrs. Sherlock, is if you're here on official business."

"I've no idea what you're talking about."

Taking her arm, I steered her away from the building. There was no one else about. In my day, St. Roberta's had adhered to a strict respect for the Sabbath. Quiet activities such as reading and sedate strolls in the grounds were encouraged, but there were no green-and-yellow-uniformed strollers this afternoon. Had that activity been restricted until the Loverly Cup was returned? It seemed to me, given Mrs. Battle's steel hand on the helm—secret life or no—highly likely. She was a woman who knew how to bring pressure to bear.

"Ha!" Ariel peeked up at me. "Exactly as I thought!"

"Meaning?"

"That you're not here because your doctor said your only hope of recovering from a rare, usually fatal, disease was a respite in a warmer climate."

"The weather here is glorious. I shall wallow in the sun and savor the balmy breeze." The trick I'd learned with Ariel was not to succumb to her curiosity without putting up at least a parody of resistance. To do so was to allow her to walk all over me the way she did with her stepmother, Betty, and sometimes her father.

"Oh, Ellie!" She succumbed to a giggle. "You're so annoying. I suppose you think I'm going to beg to be told why you're really here."

"Absolutely not. I know you to be far too strong-minded." We were crossing the green counterpane lawn in the general direction of the Chaplain's House. A butterfly drifted by like a scrap of multicolored silk blown off a sewing table in the Home Skills room.

"Don't you want to go round the back of the school and take a look at the playing fields?" she asked, in a voice that suggested she would have given her plaits a toss if she had still been wearing them loose. She knew full well from former discussions that sport of any kind was anathema to me.

"I hate playing fields," I said unnecessarily, and received a sharp look in return. "Whatever promises are made they will never be even." Lengthening my stride, I asked quickly after her father and Betty.

"Oh, they're all right, I suppose. One of the few good things about being sent to this place is that they're having to learn to fend for themselves without my constant supervision."

"Sent? I thought it was your idea. In fact, I distinctly remember explaining forcefully, as I snatched a copy of *Millie at Mayhem Manor* from your grasp, that real life at a real boarding school is not a series of one thrilling adventure after another. One of the great regrets of my life is giving you that book. I should have sent you a tome on the joys of staying at home catering to the whims of aging parents." I expected her to state bitterly, as she had done in the past, that Betty wasn't her mother, but either she had given up seeing herself in the bleak guise of pitiful stepchild, destined to kneel on stone floors slopping water around with a scrubbing brush, or she was thinking about how better to wheedle information out of me.

"Well, I don't have to tell you there has been mayhem this term; otherwise we both know you'd be at home with Ben and the children," she responded smugly. "And I must say I've found the sense of restrained panic a nice change from algebra, which is not and never will be of the least interest to me. Who cares if A=B+C when we don't have a clue who they are and what they have been up to when D wasn't looking? Come on, Ellie; do tell what you know about the Loverly—"

"Isn't it truly a lovely day?" I paused to glance around and, as a reward for my appreciation of Mother Nature's offering of gentian-blue skies and lambs'-wool clouds, narrowly missed stumbling over a rut in the otherwise rutless lawn. Fortunately, there was a bench at hand, onto which I was able to topple in graceless fashion. It was within a few yards of the walled garden encircling the Chaplain's House, which I was in no desperate hurry to enter. Sharing a dorm with a bunch of old girls might be interesting, but what if one or more of them had been a prefect and still horribly prissy or bossy and unable to suppress the urge to tell me to stay clear of the walls, raise my hand when asking to be excused, and—worst of all—not reach for the biggest, gooiest cake on the plate?

"Ellie"—Ariel heaved a pained sigh—"kindly do not treat me like a child. You're here to try and recover the Loverly Cup."

"Is that so?"

"Why isn't Mrs. Malloy with you?" The bottle-green skirt

and mustard-yellow shirt suited Ariel's coloring better than most. She sat down beside me with a bounce that gave no deference to the brass plate on the back of the bench, inscribed with the name of the donor and the information that she had been head girl in 1956–1957. Did she still reflect on those days of glory? I wondered. Did she still relish the memory of leading a crocodile of girls into the refectory for a midday dinner of shepherd's pie and rice pudding?

"Mrs. Malloy?" I echoed. "The timing wasn't good for her. She's entertaining her sister and the new husband for a few days."

Ariel was acquainted with the former Melody Tabby and Police Sergeant Walters. All the residents of the Yorkshire village of Milton Moor knew one another. It was located in the vicinity of the Brontë parsonage at Haworth in Yorkshire. Since moving there a year or so previously, after Tom and Betty won a ton of money in the lottery, Ariel's enthusiasm for novels steeped in dark doings and tortured longings had become what she called, in her loftiest manner, her enduring passion. Her vocabulary, already advanced, came to include words such as *visage* or even *physiognomy*, to be tossed off when she felt a description of the paperboy required more dramatic impact.

This was very trying for Tom and Betty, who were the sort who called a face a face and would have preferred to get their exercise taking an amble down to the pub rather than being forced to race for the dictionary every five minutes. For this I shouldered a good portion of the blame, having mentioned the first time I met Ariel—purely by way of finding something to say other than Isn't it warm for March?—that I loved the sort of books where the butler descends the stairs with a fluttering candle held aloft and announces in a sepulchral voice to the waiting throng of jittery housemaids that her ladyship has succumbed to her nighttime cup of cocoa and consequently won't be going riding in the morning.

To that lapse of judgment I had later committed the indiscretion of letting slip to Ariel that I also was an avid enthusiast of boarding-school books for girls, as was Mrs. Malloy, when she could sneak one away from me and feign a sudden devotion to dusting the attic. That being said, I did not hold myself entirely responsible for Ariel's decision that life at St. Roberta's would be preferable to a good day school.

"You've guessed it." I leaned my head back to capture more shade from a copper beech that could have been a close relative of the one at Merlin's Court. "Dorcas told Mrs. Battle that I'd done some amateur sleuthing and was sent to fetch me."

Ariel was not one to be easily won over when believing some callous personage had ruthlessly toyed with her sensibilities. She sat, arms folded, lips pursed, putting me forcibly in mind of my children when they decided they'd had just about enough of mothers for one day and would very much like to take away my teddy bear and send me to bed without my tea.

"Mrs. Battle doesn't object to your assisting me in the investigation."

"Oh, really!" Ariel didn't yawn in my face; Betty—once the bane of Ariel's existence, along with Tom when he took sleepy note of life around him—had instilled certain proprieties. She studied the copper beech as if counting its leaves and multiplying that sum by the number of tiles on the Chaplain House roof. "Can a mere girl of fourteen be of much help to an established private detective?"

"Oh, come off it," I said. "You know you're a whiz at ferreting out the villain before the end of the book. It's good to have Mrs. Battle's seal of approval, but I'd planned on our joining forces from the beginning."

"Thanks for forcing me to grovel." Ariel kept her nose in the air, daring a blackbird to mistake her for the maid hanging out the clothes. "You're desperate because Mrs. Malloy isn't with you."

"She said the worst part of being stuck at home entertaining the newlyweds was not getting to confer with you about the case."

"Did she?" The pale face brightened to a pretty pink. Ariel held Mrs. M in high esteem. "Isn't it rotten?"—forsaking her sense of injury—"I bet she felt horribly left out, seeing you drive off with Miss Critchley. You don't suppose she'll throttle her sister and brother-in-law in their sleep and come rushing after you?"

"She's already here—has been all day—inside my head, piping up with words of advice or criticism every five minutes."

Ariel sat very still, studying my physiognomy intently.

"What is it?" I asked.

"You look sad."

"I feel sorry for Ms. Chips. The theft has to be hard on her." I sat forward on the bench, forgetting my desire for shade. The image of Ms. Chips as I remembered her—striding across the playing fields, a sergeant major rallying the troops—refused to reduce in size to a broken nose.

Ariel gave me one of her sharp looks. "You're keeping something back, but I'll get it out of you later. We're friends, aren't we, despite our different levels of maturity?" Her expression made clear which of us had the disadvantage there. "Did Miss Critchley tell you that Ms. Chips paid for the new gymnasium out of an inheritance she received from the man she was married to for only a few weeks—or days—when his parents put the nix on it because they discovered there was insanity in her family?"

"It sounds like something from the Victorian era," I said, "but none the less tragic. Mrs. Battle told me that Lady Loverly is in some way connected to the man's family. I wonder if his name was Chips?"

"I asked Carolyn Fisher-Jones about that—she's her ladyship's goddaughter—and she said that Ms. Chips reverted to her maiden name. It had struck me as interesting, Ellie, that a woman of her era didn't go by Miss. Oh, I know she wasn't born in the nineteenth century, but you know what I mean; it was one of those little anomalies that you kick around with your toes when algebra class goes on into next week."

"Miss Critchley was also surprised."

"But Chippy, as lots of the girls call her, wasn't a Miss *or* a Mrs.; she was something in between, so I suppose when the term Ms. entered the vernacular it seemed exactly right for a woman torn from her bridegroom's arms ere they could send thank-you cards for the toaster ovens and tea sets." Ariel's sigh was dramatic but, given her hidden softness, heartfelt.

"It's easy to condemn the man's parents for interfering and him for failing to stand up to them, Ariel, but the times have to be taken into account. In those days, my mother told me, people were even afraid to admit having cancer in the family because of the perceived stigma."

"Do you think he left her the money out of guilt?"

"Probably."

"Or because he continued to hold her enshrined in his heart as the only woman he ever loved?"

"Real life doesn't work that way, Ariel. Very likely he married again, was extremely happy, and had an armload of children."

"He didn't. Well, I'm not sure about the marriage part, but Carolyn did say there weren't any children. Lady Loverly thought, with there being no descendents, that she would figure prominently in the will. Again, I got that from Carolyn, who was also distantly related to him."

"Poor Aiden Loverly," I mused, "done out of an additional inheritance. I didn't take to him at all." In response to Ariel's surprised look, I explained about his coming within inches of running Gillian Parker down with his motorcycle.

"He sounds loathsome, all right; even his good looks can't make up for that. I pity the girl he marries; she's in for a nasty shock when the scales fall from her eyes. I'm never going to take the risk of getting married." She sat up straighter on the bench and scowled straight ahead at the Chaplain's House. "Oh, I know, Ellie, you're one of the lucky ones. Ben is a dear as well as heroically handsome. And Dad and Betty seem to be doing better in the romance department."

"That's good."

"Not"—folding her hands primly—"that I wouldn't prefer to think of them as being married in name only. There are certain behaviors that are okay—I see that now I'm older—but for other people, not one's own parents." Ariel conveyed the strength of this conviction with a shudder. "As for myself, I would prefer to become a nun."

"Don't say that!" I tried not to smile. "You're romanticizing that old legend. It's similar to Ms. Chips's story. You're feeling sympathy for a ghost."

"Don't pretend to be a spoilsport." Ariel raised her chin. "It's a thrilling story."

What either of us would have said next was cut off by a voice behind us. We turned to see two people crossing the lawn some yards away. If the man had not been shouting, we wouldn't have been able to hear what he said.

"You listen to me, woman, and listen good. Just let me bloody well get wind that that sister of yours has been within a mile of here, and I'll have you out on your ear so fast you'll be living with her in a cardboard box in Tingwell before the door slams on you."

"Ted"—the female voice came to us shrill with panic—"I told you I'd never—"

"That's the Mossops," Ariel said, without turning her head, and we heard no more. Had they spied us sitting on the bench or was the conversation over? "He's a surly customer. Want to bet she's sorry she didn't become a nun instead of marrying him? Carolyn says Mrs. Battle only keeps him on because Mrs. Mossop is worth her weight in gold."

When I looked around, there was no sight of the couple. "It sounds as though Carolyn is a prime source of information."

"She's been at St. Roberta's from junior school up." Ariel stared at the sky. "Don't be too shocked, Ellie, but since coming here and learning of the Gray Nun's heroic path to glory, I have seriously been considering the possibility of entering the cloistered life."

"You might not like being a nun," I cautioned. "You don't get to sit around with a plate of baked beans on your lap reading one book after another. There's a fly in the ointment called the rule of obedience. Forget poverty and chastity! You'd have to do what you were told for the rest of your, I hope, extremely"—I extended the word—"long life."

"Not if I get to be Mother Superior." Ariel gave her head a toss, without dislodging the braided coronet. I thought about telling her taking the veil would necessitate having most of her hair cut off, but I wasn't sure it was true in this day and age, with the modern garb. Clutching at straws, I said that the habit wasn't nearly as romantic as it used to be.

"Although I'm sure you won't mind that," I added mendaciously. "It'll just be like wearing your school uniform forever, only not perhaps in colors that suit you so well. Navy or black, when shapeless, can drain the life out of anyone."

"But I'd get to carry a rosary."

"And spend long lovely hours in church. It's a pity you didn't like going on Sundays when I last saw you, but—"

"That was only to let Dad and Betty know they can't rule my life. But of course I haven't made a final decision."

"Plenty of time." Perhaps it was time I went into the Chaplain's House and acquainted myself with its sofas and chairs.

"Well, I haven't completely made up my mind." Ariel shifted to give me more than my share of the bench. "Maybe I'll become a great novelist instead of a nun. What I think I'd like would be to write one truly magnificent book, like Emily Brontë did in *Wuthering Heights* and Harper Lee in *To Kill a Mockingbird*. Then when I'd got that out of the way I could spend my time thinking up stories without the bother of having to write them down. Of course, I'd want to be independent while learning my craft; otherwise I'd have Dad and Betty on my back, telling me I should be working toward a proper career. I'll be a waitress, eavesdropping for the sake of research while I pass the soup."

"There was a girl one year ahead of me who became a waitress." I stared off into space, but Ariel's antenna had shot up and she was eyeing me keenly.

"Why the sad voice, Ellie? Did she die or something awful?"

"No."

"What was her name?"

"Philippa Boswell. Ariel, I should go in and meet the other residents of the Chaplain's House before I am an old girl in every sense."

"Not so fast." She drew me back as I made to get up. "And don't try to fool me that you're dying for a nap. We haven't talked about how to start accumulating a list of suspects in the Case of the Mysterious Disappearance of the Loverly Cup."

"We will, but not till tomorrow. First I need to sift through what I've learned so far." To my surprise, Ariel did not press me to say more. Instead, she tilted her head from one side to the other, sizing me up from both angles.

"Ellie," she finally said, with unaccustomed gentleness, "you can't fool me. My eyes bore deep into your tortured soul. I know there's a reason you aren't embracing the opportunity to again be Ellie Haskell, private investigator."

"Of course I want to get at the truth." I defended myself. "But I'm not much in the mood for digging into other people's sorrows."

"At least this time there hasn't been a murder."

I was vaguely relieved when she didn't add the word *yet*. "No, but there's Ms. Chips, likely to be denied her shining moment; Mr. Middleton, whose adored wife died in a traffic accident; and Gillian Parker, who struck me as deeply troubled about something."

"Carolyn's very worried about her. That's what led to our

getting to know each other better—Carolyn and I, that is. She needed someone to talk to about Gillian, and I am blessed in being a sympathetic listener."

I recalled the tremulous voice denying to Aiden that she was a thief and recounted that part of the story to Ariel.

"Perhaps when he met her at the Hall last weekend, Ellie, she struck him as the nervy sort, and if he heard that the Loverly Cup had gone missing he might have decided she'd be the sort to pull such a crazy stunt."

"Mrs. Battle told me she'd informed Carolyn that she was not obliged to keep the matter from Lady Loverly and said the same to Gillian, who having been a guest at the house might feel uncomfortable staying silent if she were to meet her ladyship."

"Well, I can't see Gillian feeling honor bound to spill the beans, and Carolyn would hate being the one to upset her godmother."

I heard myself saying that Philippa Boswell was the sort of girl who was liked and respected because she never stirred up trouble. Ariel eyed me sharply before responding.

"Carolyn thinks Matron is the cause of Gillian's depression."

"Why's that?"

"Because Gillian didn't want to come to St. Roberta's. Her parents thought it absolutely wonderful of Great-aunt Wilma to provide the wonderful opportunity. Carolyn says some people just love being saints even if other people get martyred in the process."

"It's one point of view."

"Not that Carolyn believes Matron is anything close to a saint. Quite the reverse! She thinks the woman is positively evil."

"Why?" I hadn't been overwhelmingly fond of Matron, particularly after she informed me in a voice dripping acid that I had broken Ms. Chips's nose in three places, but *evil*? That was a stretch.

"Her interference in Gillian's once-happy life. . . ." Ariel paused to stare up at the tree behind our bench, either to admire the effect of sunlight shimmering through its leaves or to heighten the dramatic impact of her words. "Lady Loverly told Carolyn that it was Matron who wrecked Ms. Chips's chance of married bliss—the supposed friend who spilled the beans to the groom's parents about mental health problems in the bride's family."

"Surely," I protested, "she didn't do so on purpose or Ms. Chips wouldn't have continued the friendship. Stories repeated at second or third hand get distorted. Or someone has the facts wrong in the first place."

"I'm not saying Carolyn is right about Matron being evil. *Bossy and bustling* is the way I would describe her. Likes to think of herself as Florence Nightingale, I expect, but that's not a crime, is it?"

"Perhaps you could bring Carolyn to talk to me," I said. "But not a word yet to her or any of the other girls about why I'm really here. I have to proceed cautiously—Mrs. Battle's instructions. Only the staff is currently in the know."

"There's no need to swear me to silence." Ariel had her nose in the air. "I'm completely trustworthy."

"I know that."

"Then why won't you tell me what makes you hate being back at St. Roberta's?"

"Whatever put that idea in your head?"

"Ellie, I can see a dark cloud hanging over you."

I believed her. From our first meeting, Ariel and I had shared an unlikely rapport, given the differences in our ages. Mrs. Malloy, who has also read too many novels steeped in the uncanny, would have said this was because we had known each other in a previous life, making the connection already there, just waiting to be renewed. My reasoning was more prosaic. Ariel reminded me of how I had been at her age: uncertain and inclined to be on the defensive. At times too old, at others too young, in comparison to my contemporaries. Where I had been overly plump, she agonized over being skinny. Confiding in her now would be like speaking out loud to myself. Suddenly I knew there was no putting off the evil hour; this was the time and place to open the book titled *Wickedest Girl at St. Roberta's.*

"It all began with my being utterly hopeless at games, especially lacrosse." I dragged my gaze away from the Chaplain's House, where I had glimpsed a shadow at one of the downstairs windows. "When I was in the lower fifth, our practice time was on Friday afternoons—which should have made it bearable, I suppose, because there was the weekend just ahead."

"That would make you fifteen." Ariel sat glued to her seat.

"That's right. Lacrosse all afternoon, from after lunch until the final bell. Sometimes I felt I couldn't bear another minute of pretending I was enjoying myself. It hadn't been so bad when we first started learning and just ran up and down practicing cradling without the ball in our nets. But dodging around, panicking that I wouldn't catch it if it came my way or that I'd get clobbered in the face, was close to unbearable. And then came the awful day when Ms. Chips told me it might be helpful if I went off on my own and worked on my toss."

"What was so bad about that?"

"She didn't get far enough away fast enough. I raised my lacrosse stick—tentatively, I may add—and my arm must have jerked the wrong way because the ball took off and broke her nose."

"No!" Ariel opened her eyes wide behind the spectacles. "Was she furious?"

"Not verbally. She couldn't speak. Rosemary Martin, who always treated me with the utmost scorn, suggested I drop dead while she fetched Matron. And a good many of the other girls were furious. Ms. Chips was extremely popular. Rosemary had a mad crush on her. Even my friend Susan Brodstock was angry with me."

"Did Susan turn on you?"

"She told me I wasn't safe to be let out of a cat basket, but no. The incident didn't ruin our friendship." I smiled at Ariel, while noticing another watchful shadow, this time at an upstairs window of the Chaplain's House. "When I went and apologized to Ms. Chips the next day, she had a big pad of gauze strapped on her nose, but she said it wasn't as bad as Matron had told me. Not broken in three places."

"Only one?"

"It's no joking matter, even at this late date." I pulled a face. "Really, she was awfully nice about it, saying these things happened and it hadn't been such a great nose to begin with."

"Well, then, I can't see why you've agonized. It's not like she dropped dead three days later from a blood clot or went unconscious when driving her car and killed someone else." Ariel shook her head at me. "Honestly, Ellie, I was expecting you to tell me something that, even though you've kept it bravely hidden through the years, ruined your life."

"Not mine," I said, feeling my throat tighten.

"Then whose?"

"I'm getting to that. On the day I apologized to Ms. Chips, I asked if I could switch from lacrosse to hockey and she agreed, saying I might be better suited to a game that took place on the ground, not in the air."

"Why hadn't you made that choice at the beginning?"

"Because my parents had increased their bank overdraft to buy me a lacrosse stick, and for the first year we practiced cradling without a ball. By the time the horrid object was added, I was stuck. We didn't get to change our minds midstream, not unless there were special circumstances."

"As in the case of Ms. Chips's nose." Ariel nodded encouragement. "Well, how did you get on with hockey?"

"I didn't."

"Now I *am* perplexed."

"I was supposed to start the following Friday. But I never went."

"What?" Her eyes widened dramatically.

"The beginning of my downward spiral into a life of deceit. I suppose Ms. Chips told Mrs. Worthing, who was young and pretty with a permanent spring in her step, to expect me on the hockey field, but I squeezed that thought out of my mind."

"Now, let me get this straight," said Ariel. "Are you saying you didn't show up on that particular Friday"—eyes now the size of a soup plate—"or for the entire term?"

"Actually, I absented myself for the rest of the year."

"Ellie!"

"Yes, I know! It was a dreadfully underhanded and wicked thing to do."

"You silly." Ariel beamed at me fondly like a proud parent. "I think it was wonderfully brave! I'm so impressed! But how did you get away with it?"

7

"This is a cautionary tale," I reminded Ariel, "not an encouragement to follow in my faltering footsteps."

"Sorry. It was just so astonishing to think of you being that naughty." She folded her hands and assumed a meek expression. "Do go on."

The setting was wrong for a confession: the sky innocent as a baby's eyes, the breeze a soothing touch, the ivy greening on the Chaplain's House a mantle of virtue. There should have been a rebuking rumble of thunder, a massing of dark clouds representing the state of my soul, and lashings of cleansing rain.

"I suppose I got away with it for several reasons. It's possible that Ms. Chips wasn't her usual efficient self, on account of the nose, and forgot to tell Mrs. Worthing to expect me. Or Mrs. Worthing forgot. Or neither woman could conceive of any girl wanting to get out of games and the privilege of being picked last by a team leader. I had gone into midday dinner, dreading the looks I would get when I couldn't remember which hockey side I was on and directed the ball to the enemy. To hover impotently would be the safe course. But some leaping enthusiast was bound to yell at me to do something—anything—and I would stick out a mesmerized arm or a quivering foot at precisely the wrong moment, with the result that I'd find myself surrounded by a mob, drowning in a roar of voices shouting, *She's the one who almost killed Ms. Chips!* It was too much. I couldn't face my rice pudding."

"Maybe if it had been treacle tart, the whole course of your life would have been different," mused Ariel.

"There's no point in dwelling on what might have been." I leaned wanly back on the bench. "Grabbing up the book I had brought with me, I slid out of the refectory and raced up the stairs to the second floor. I needed a bolt-hole, a place to sit quietly and gather my rattling bones together. My first thought was my dormitory cubicle; I'd pull the curtain and huddle. Then I decided that was out; Rosemary Martin was dorm prefect that year and she enjoyed doing spot checks, hoping to catch someone, preferably me, in the act of eating a bar of chocolate retrieved from under the mattress."

"It's still the same. We aren't allowed to eat in the dorm either. And to think"—Ariel sighed gustily—"that the most exciting thing for me when Dad and Betty won the lottery was the prospect of being able to buy tons of sweets. The girls still hide them, though, just where you did. And there's always someone with the munchies conducting a search."

"You can lead a horse to water, but you can't make it swim."

"That sounds like one of Mrs. Malloy's sayings."

"I told you she's been in my head all day." My sigh was picked up by the breeze.

"So where did you hide out, Ellie?"

"I remembered the small mending room at the end of the corridor, the one used by the woman who came in twice a week to repair the bed linens, neither day being a Friday. No one was around to see me go in. When I closed the door, it was just me and the sewing machine and a comfy old armchair under the window. I meant to sit down only for five or ten minutes, but I decided that reading a few pages of my book might settle my nerves."

"I know the room you're talking about." Ariel nodded vigorously. "Carolyn showed it to me. She said it's where Gillian goes when she's feeling miserable. I guess despairing minds think alike, to quote our Mrs. Malloy."

"Don't tell me she's moved in on you too!" I laughed, then sobered. "I don't imagine I was the first or that Gillian will be the last to use that mending room as a refuge. Something has to be done to help that poor girl."

"We'll put our minds to it."

"For starters, I should try to ferret out what Aiden Loverly was accusing her of stealing."

"First, go on with your story."

"The book did calm me down. Within moments, I was lost in the adventures of a girl escaping East Berlin with her parents in the hope of reaching an aunt in America who had a ballet school, so lost, I never heard the bell for the start of afternoon class. When I finally came to the surface, Tatiana was in New York, and a stunned look at my watch showed it was almost time for hockey to be over. To show up at that point without a decent excuse would surely not have gone down well with Mrs. Worthing, pleasantly skippy as she was! So after some panicky reflection, I decided to stay put until it was time to go to tea."

"Weren't you scared stiff of being hunted down and sent to Mrs. Battle?" Ariel searched my face for signs of residual terror.

"Petrified for the rest of that day and the entire weekend! Susan Brodstock and my other friend, Ann Gamble, wanted to know why I looked so queasy, but I couldn't bring myself to talk to them about it. Splendid as they both were in many ways, they were both horribly sporty and would have been immensely shocked. Luckily, they both played lacrosse, and no one else to whom I was close played hockey. By Sunday night I was beginning to breathe easier, until it suddenly occurred to me that the powers that be were taking their time deciding what to do with me."

"Anything said the following week?" Ariel was perched on the edge of the bench.

"Not a word. When Friday rolled around again I was all set to do my duty for good old St. Roberta's—until it became time to go and change into my gym clothes. Whereupon I realized that not only had I not come up with an excuse as to why I was presenting myself on this belated date, I simply couldn't face an afternoon of unmitigated torture. That Tatiana had faced far worse was no incentive, especially when I now had in hand the sequel to her adventures. Budding ballerinas are made from finer molds than clodhoppers. It was back to the mending room for me."

"How did you feel that time?"

"More nervous than the first, heart pounding every time I thought I heard someone outside the door, but the hours passed and no one came. And afterward, except for a few heart-clutching moments, I didn't worry so much. The trick was not to think about the awkward side of things. I squeezed my mind shut and went about my everyday life, and the next Friday was easier—better than that, it was fun. There were fourteen books in the Tatiana series, and my great hope was that she would meet up again with the mysterious boy who had also been a stowaway on *The Ocean Vessel.* The nearing of end of term did bring me back to reality. What would happen when Mrs. Worthing went to mark my report?"

"That has been on the tip of my tongue."

"On the day the reports were handed out I was sick with fear."

"And?"

"It was Ms. Chips's handwriting. She had given me *Very Fair* instead of the usual *Fair* and had even added: *Tries hard.*"

"Yours not to reason why, Ellie!"

"It certainly was a puzzler. And when the next end-of-term report came it was the same, except that she wrote, *Keeps trying.*"

"How spooky!" Ariel looked around as if expecting Ms. Chips to stroll up and offer a belated explanation. "So, after those lucky escapes, what happened to bring life crashing down around your ears?"

"The window in the mending room doesn't overlook the exterior of the building," I heard myself say in a ragged voice. "It gives a view of the San."

Ariel nodded. "Short for sanitarium, delightfully Victorian. That's what we still call it. And I know what you mean about that window. The mending room is on the second floor and the San is on the first, but it goes up two stories, so you can look right down to where the beds are lined up on the wall across from the medicine cupboard. All that white on the walls and the sheets and pillows makes it look dreadfully tubercular. Thank goodness I haven't had so much as a finger ache since coming to St. Roberta's."

"It was the chapel of the old building. The arched oak door with the iron strapwork that opens onto the grounds is original. From the beginning I was careful to stay clear of the single window, in case Matron or one of her patients should look up and catch me. Fortunately it wasn't large or positioned low on the wall, and my reading chair was tucked well into a corner. However"—I took a breath before forging ahead—"sometimes when I reached the end of the chapter or was feeling recklessly nosy I'd duck over to the edge of the window and raise my head just enough to get a peek at who, if anyone, was ill that day. Sometimes all six beds were occupied, along with girls sitting on chairs with thermometers in their mouths or in the process of being bandaged up. On other occasions there was no one there, not even Matron: meetings, perhaps, or the opportunity seized for a chat in the staff common room."

"Are we getting to the bad bit?" Ariel asked, with frank impatience.

"Sorry," I said robotically. "One Friday afternoon toward the end of the school year there was only one girl in the San, Philippa Boswell. She came in shortly after the start-of-class bell. I heard afterward that she claimed to have a rotten headache."

"Claimed?"

"It was decided later, after what followed, that she had pretended illness to get out of going to class."

"To escape taking a test?"

"To meet her boyfriend in Lilypad Lane, that narrow pathway between the convent ruins and the road. A member of the Board of Governors was driving along when he noticed a girl in a St. Roberta's uniform talking to a young man at the bottom of the Dribbly Drop. Sensing something furtive in their manner, he parked his car in a lay-by, but by the time he got out they were gone."

"I'll bet that was Mr. Bumbleton." Ariel curled her lips.

"You're right."

"He looks likes his mission in life is to catch sinners in the act. It was he who got one of the maids sacked early in the term after he claimed she stuck out her tongue at him when he told her to speed up her dusting. No wonder China is such a snot. I expect Philippa and her boyfriend dodged into the ruins to hide in the crypt, and that's why he couldn't find them."

"Probably. Perhaps he would have pursued them with more tally ho if he hadn't been afraid of having a heart attack. Or frantic pursuit may have seemed unnecessary when he discovered the dropped note." I stared into space. "It was to Brian Roberts, who it turned out was taking a weekend break from his medical studies, and signed *Your loving Phil.*"

"What else did it say?"

"According to the school grapevine? That he was her entire world and she hated being parted from him, but they both had to be brave until the time was right. Mr. Bumbleton marched in to see Mrs. Battle and handed her the note, along with the information that the sighting had taken place fifteen minutes earlier, putting it at two o'clock when Philippa was supposedly in the San with her headache. But Matron could not verify that fact because she had been giving a talk on nursing to the lower fourth Home Skills class. There was no one else in the San to say that Philippa hadn't got off the bed and exited by the arched door. She could have known that Matron would be gone for half an hour from having heard about her planned talk. It was all very damning."

"But *you* knew she hadn't left the San." Ariel adjusted her specs for a better look at my face.

"That's it exactly! I'd finished my book and, needing to while away the time, I was crouched at the window the whole time Matron was gone, leaving Philippa alone. A year her junior, I admired her tremendously, so much so I began weaving a story about her. One in which she followed in Tatiana's ballet steps and went to New York, where she was discovered huddled in a dingy doorway by an incredibly handsome young Russian composer who immediately sensed her genius, along with falling madly in love with her. It was a beguiling way of spending the time, but having learned to keep an eye on the time when in the mending room, I glanced frequently at my watch and afterward remembered doing so at two o'clock."

"You didn't speak up in Philippa's defense for fear of getting into trouble, because you were the one who wasn't where she was supposed to be."

"I was too much of a coward."

"What happened to her?"

"The most brutal punishment. . . ."

"She was expelled?"

"Equally dreadful! Mrs. Battle informed her she would not be made head girl, as had been planned, at the start of the following school year."

"Is that all?" Ariel scoffed. "Who'd want the job?"

"If you'd read the boarding-school books—"

"The ones you didn't send me?"

"—you'd know"—I pressed on—"that becoming head girl is the highest aspiration, the giddy dream of all who proudly wear the school uniform."

"That cuts me out. I'd much rather wear a pair of old jeans and a sloppy sweatshirt. And I can't imagine, Ellie, that you ever yearned to walk around like you had a book on your head while still managing to look down your nose at anyone who so much as thought of sliding down the banisters."

"Of course not!" I closed my eyes against the sun. "My giddy dream was to find the jeweled chalice the Gray Nun is said to have hidden when fleeing Henry the Eighth's soldiers, led by her former bridegroom. And if that couldn't be achieved, my second choice was to come in second from the bottom in algebra, which I disliked as much as you do. But Philippa would have made a wonderful head girl. She was both incredibly popular and thoroughly nice."

"Who got the place in her stead?"

"Her closest friend Sally Brodstock—my friend Susan's sister. But I wasn't there during her reign. I left, as did Philippa, at the end of that fateful year. I heard from Susan that Philippa was working as a waitress in a greasy-spoon restaurant in a grim part of town." I could not contain the anguish in my voice."

"London?"

"Or another big city."

"And all these years"—Ariel spoke sternly—"you've blamed yourself for ruining her life, picturing her serving up egg and chips to unshaven men who spit on the floor and want to talk about how they'll never understand why their wives left them."

"Any heart must have gone out of her."

"Did it never occur to you, my noodle friend"—Ariel patted my hand—"that waitressing was a stopgap job for Philippa before embarking on a career? A lot of school-leavers take time out these days before getting down to the grind. The more I think about it, the more I like the idea of being a waitress while I'm working on my novel. I'd learn a lot about human nature while staying humble."

"You're right. I expect I have dramatized the situation. That's what guilt does to me. Philippa is probably married by now and has forgotten all about that business with Brian Roberts."

"Who has?" A startling voice inquired from behind our bench. Wrenching my neck, I turned to see Dorcas, looking—if her breeze-tussled red hair was any indication—as if she had done the run from the school in three seconds flat.

"A girl named Philippa Boswell," Ariel replied for me, as she got to her feet.

"Dr. Roberts was her boyfriend when she was in the upper fifth and he was a first-year medical student," I added.

"Won't you please sit down, Miss Critchley?"

"No, thank you, Ariel. Have to re-energize after being cooped up in the car for so long." Dorcas executed half a dozen jumping jacks before jogging at speed on the spot. Within five seconds, I was winded watching her. Ariel sank back down beside me.

"Miss Critchley, aren't you supposed to warm up first?" she inquired worriedly. "Isn't leaping right in bad for the heart?" She didn't add *for a woman of your age*, but I read her mind.

"Would be if I had high blood pressure like Chippy. Arrived half an hour ago and was just telling me Dr. Roberts gave her some new tablets that do a better job of stopping her dizzy spells when she abruptly changes position. Thinks the world of that man. Must say he seems a pleasant chap!"

The afternoon was still warm, verging on hot, but Dorcas maintained her even breathing while I, starting to puff, told Ariel about meeting the doctor at the Middletons' house and that Gillian had also been present.

"I've never seen Dr. Roberts. Is he still handsome?" she asked.

I was about to say that I'd only glimpsed the young Brian Roberts in passing, and from the opposite side of the side of the road at that, but that I had thought him attractive on meeting him at the Middletons. But Dorcas, still dancing on the spot as if about to embark on an Olympic race, answered ahead of me.

"Good-looking in a rugged, manly sort of way. Nice eyes, though never in the same league as Aiden Loverly. Old adage—handsome is as handsome does—fits that young man to a T. Surprised to hear Chippy speak up for him just now. Said whatever else he may be, unlike his grandfather, he has stayed away from the drink and is devoted to his grandmother. And works very hard at his art and antiques business."

Ariel resettled her glasses on her nose, the better to give this some thought. "Then maybe he isn't so bad after all. Everyone says Ms. Chips is always strictly fair."

"She's here for her dorm duty already?" I patted the bench but Dorcas kept to her feet.

"Was returning from the Chaplain's House after depositing your luggage"—gesturing toward the building with stone and Virginia creeper walls—"when I spotted Chippy stepping out of a taxi in the parking lot. Told me she'd been to the Hall. Wanted a word with the housekeeper, either to see if the woman's headache was better or leave a note for her. Turned out both she and her ladyship were lying down. Found Aiden Loverly on the point of leaving. He blamed the headache on there having been an upset earlier. His grandmother unable to find a brooch, one her husband bought on their honeymoon. Not in the jewelry case where it should be, and she couldn't remember when she'd seen it last. Not too worked up about it, said she'd probably left it pinned on a dress or jacket. Reasonable woman, from what I've heard. It was the housekeeper who went into a state, which led to her being incapacitated."

I absorbed the implications. "Given this new tidbit of information, Aiden could have been accusing Gillian of stealing the brooch, rather than—or in addition to—the Loverly Cup. Remember, she was at the Hall last weekend with Carolyn."

"That shouldn't make her a scapegoat." Ariel flared up. "Maybe the housekeeper took the brooch and was consumed by guilt or panic when Lady Loverly realized it was missing. Or the culprit could have been another member of the household help. For that matter, Carolyn could have taken it, although that's stupid."

"It was Carolyn whom Chippy had come to see," Dorcas went on. "Didn't get anything out of her. Said the girl clammed up but wasn't rude, that's not her way—"

"Which suggests she may suspect someone she doesn't want to believe involved." I felt my heart sink. There had been something about Gillian in addition to her musical gift that had really touched me.

"Invited Chippy to my flat for a cup of tea. Informed me Matie had told her about the Loverly Cup, thought it best coming from her rather than another member of the staff. Surprised me by saying felt sorrier for whoever took it than anyone else."

I glanced sideways at Ariel, knowing she would understand that this conversation was not to go beyond the bench.

"Spoke about the ceremonial opening of the new gymnasium without a quiver in her voice." Dorcas produced the handkerchief to dab at her eyes. "Said Mrs. Battle will find a replacement for the cup if necessary and in every way handle the situation with grace and honesty. Has her dress picked out but says she won't attempt to make a speech, though Matron said she should. But for all her brave assurances, bound to be the most frightful blight if the Loverly Cup isn't recovered." Choking up completely, Dorcas disappeared behind the handkerchief, unable to continue.

Ariel, head lowered, sat fiercely polishing her spectacles. "We'll get it back, won't we, Ellie?" Her voice was gruff.

"At least we'll give our all." I was about to ask Dorcas where she had put my luggage, when the Chaplain's House door opened and an imperious voice called out, "Who are you, police conducting a stakeout? You've been sitting there forever."

"Oh, cripes!" Ariel giggled in my ear. "Who's that? The Ogre's mother in *Jack the Giant Killer*?"

"Shush!" I mouthed back, thinking she might well be right. The voice emanated from a tall, massively built woman. "I'm Ellie Haskell, a new resident." I offered this tidbit in the hope that she wouldn't reel me in with a mighty arm and swallow me whole.

"Friend of mine." Dorcas clapped me on the shoulder, causing my already trembling knees to buckle.

"Same here!" Ariel continued giggling.

"How nice and chummy! If you haven't decided by now whether or not to put your money together and buy that bench, you should make up your minds."

"We're enjoying the sunshine," I offered apologetically.

"Sunstroke's more like it. Are you bringing your entourage in with you? If so, don't expect much by way of dinner. We're having pizza and it's a small one."

"No, just myself!" Feeling as though I were being ripped from their protective arms, I told Dorcas and Ariel that I would see them later—if not that evening, certainly tomorrow.

"Make sure she doesn't serve you for pudding," Ariel warned me in a whisper.

"Rubbish!" Dorcas took her arm. "Ellie's going to have a thumping good time chatting about the old days."

Deciding no good would come of delaying the evil moment, I gave them a final wave and opened the iron gate in the low brick wall surrounding the house. My feet kindly took charge, marching me down the path dividing the rectangular lawn with its flower-bed borders—mainly filled with marigolds of the same vivid yellow as the school shirts. To my left was a tree, scraggly and almost leafless, bending low to the ground as if an arthritic back prevented it from straightening up to the height of its youth. Poor thing, I thought. Did it tremble in fear of an ax falling the next time a scrap of firewood was needed? Was there a lingering hope of seeing yet another spring, or would a few more days of blue skies and sunshine be enough? Perhaps the sweet possibility that a bird—an unassuming sparrow, perchance—would ignore sturdier trees to perch upon its weary boughs and chirp a final lullaby?

"There's no point standing staring. It won't grow any taller and neither will you." There was now something horribly familiar about the voice. It couldn't belong . . . ? I turned toward the door, knowing there was no escaping the brutal truth. I was looking into eyes of the nemesis of my schooldays at St. Roberta's.

"Oh, God! It's Ellie Simons!" Rosemary Martin growled. "Well, come on in. You can't expect me to keep this door open forever."

8

What ill wind blew you in?" Rosemary demanded, as I stepped over the threshold.

"Thanks for the warm welcome." I smiled, attempting to appear amused. In contrast to my schoolmate's scowl, the hall in which we stood could not have been more welcoming or charming. The walls were whitewashed pine, the doors and banisters my favorite sage green, and to further lift my spirits fragrant yellow roses brimmed a vase in a niche to my left. I remembered that Ruth Middleton had told me to expect such architectural embellishments. The coat cupboard and the mirror above it looked as though they had been rescued from a thrift shop and lovingly restored. Such old-world touches complemented the oak stair tread that would creak with every step.

"I meant"—she spoke slowly, to enable my dim brain to absorb the words—"what are you escaping from at home that necessitates your visit?"

"Oh, this and that," I replied vaguely, hoping she would take this as a desire not to discuss the matter further because I found it upsetting. I still had to think up a reason for my presence, none having yet popped into my head.

"There *is* a home, I suppose?"

"Yes, fortunately. I haven't been reduced to living on the streets." My laugh sounded hollow, my breathing too loud.

"Still living with Mummy and Daddy?"

"Husband and three children."

"My God!" she continued, looking down at me from her superior height. "I would have bet on it when we were in school that you'd never marry. But I have to say your looks have improved. You've lost the fat and that goggle-eyed look."

I was temped to say it was harder to lose a Roman nose, and her eyes were still too close together. But enjoying myself wasn't part of the mission; I consoled myself with remarking cheerfully that she hadn't changed a bit, which was in the main true. The same old bully. She had been a powerfully built girl, towering above everyone else. The hair was different. At school she had worn it in thick plaits; now it was cut in a bob—a stylish one, I had to admit—and the color was the same: a rich polished brown.

"I appreciated Dorcas—Miss Critchley—bringing my luggage along while I was catching up with Ariel on how her family is doing." It would not have done to say I had been with Mrs. Battle.

"Lucky you! Your own personal porter, no less!" she said with a mocking laugh. "I didn't see her. I've been out most of the day, stuck visiting an acquaintance who's fallen on hard times and is now living in Tingwell, a scurvy town crammed with shops that have to be bolted down at night and wretched houses all exactly the same. I hear Lady Loverly's grandson has an art shop there. Imagine a member of that family being reduced to living among the lowlifes. He must have got on the old girl's wrong side. With his purported looks and charm, it must have been something serious. Who could he have killed, do you think?"

"No idea. I passed through Tingwell on the way here. It did look depressing."

"Unless one is into drugs. Dealers on every other corner apparently." Rosemary hunched a massive shoulder. "As for your luggage, there wouldn't have been a problem even if there was no one around to let Miss Crutchley in. The door is never locked."

"Critchley," I corrected, only to be ignored.

"And as you'll see for yourself, there's nothing worth stealing."

"Where will I be sleeping?" I asked, as she led me into a good-sized sitting room decorated in the same soft colors as the hall. The sage green was repeated, along with yellow and rose on the chintz curtains and sofa. Several armchairs in buttery twill provided further cushiony seating. Striped pink and cream lampshades adorned brass table lamps, and two more niches displayed prints of botanicals on gold-leafed easels. A bookcase, drinks table, and bureau gleamed with age-old patinas, but the coffee table was sensibly modern with a top that wouldn't react nastily to spills and would look even more sensible with the appearance of a teapot and plate of buttered crumpets.

"Don't look so petrified." Rosemary sank into a chair and stretched out surprisingly shapely legs. "You aren't back to sleeping in a dorm. There are four bedrooms—not counting the ones in the attic—so we're all able to have rooms."

"All?" I echoed. "How many are we?"

"I've been here for nearly two weeks and Tosca came a couple of days later; she's having a lie-down—calls it meditating, but whenever I go up to get her she's sacked out, not sitting cross-legged with her fingers steepled while she chants or hums or whatever they do. . . . And now there's you," Rosemary continued, looking none too thrilled. "You get one of the two rooms at the left of the stairs. And there's someone else expected either today or tomorrow." She reached out a hand for the filled glass on the table by her chair. "I haven't bothered finding out who she is. Last names change." She looked up at me while sipping her drink. "It still boggles my mind to think you found a husband."

Mission Loverly Cup be damned! I wasn't taking any more of this. "Were you born this rude," I asked sweetly, "or is it an acquired skill?"

"Oh, my! Haven't you come into your own!" She showed no sign of discomfiture. "Help yourself to a gin and tonic if you fancy one." She waved at the table, on which stood several bottles and an assortment of glasses. It was an invitation not to be refused if I were to get through the rest of the afternoon and evening without grinding my teeth down to the gums.

"What about you?" I lifted the lid of the ice bucket and dropped a solitary cube in my glass.

"Meaning?"

"Are *you* married, Rosemary?"

"Didn't you notice my rings?" She extended a large hand. "But perhaps you're not into jewelry. Gerald had them designed in Paris. He grew up spending oodles of time there. His parents saw the importance of travel as part of a child's education. We do the same for our Nichola and Sheridan. Last summer we spent two glorious months on the French Riviera. We had a little trouble persuading Nanny that she wouldn't have to eat snails at every meal, but luckily she came round. Traveling without her would have been a nightmare. Do your children have a nanny, Ellie?"

Staving off the desire to say that actually we had two—an inside one and an outside one—I added a good slosh of gin and a mere trickle of tonic to the ice cube in my glass and went and sat in the chair across from her. "Somehow we've managed without. By the way, Rosemary, what is your married name?"

"Still Martin."

"A lot of women are keeping their maiden names these days."

"You and your quaint way of talking. Maiden name, my foot! That term went out with the milk cart, thank God!"

I noticed a platter of assorted cheeses, pâté, and grapes on the sideboard, along with some canapé-sized plates, and helped myself enthusiastically. "We live in a village; we're a bit out of touch." Had my children been present, one of them would have asked why she kept taking the Lord's name in vain. My mother-in-law, a strict Roman Catholic, has preached sermons to them on the subject, and our unworldly vicar at St. Anselm would also have taken a dim view.

"Gerald's last name is also Martin."

"A relative?" It was an explanation. Having grown up with her, he might be inured to her nasty nature.

"Pure coincidence. We were introduced at a friend's coming-out."

"How nice. That must still take some courage."

Her face turned a most unbecoming purple. "Millie Bellingham isn't gay. Her parents had a wonderful bash for her at their hunting lodge when she turned eighteen."

"Sorry! I misunderstood."

"No, you didn't!" She banged down her glass. "You took the chance to needle me because of those letters I wrote to Ms. Chips, and everyone gabbed about after some beastly snitch spread the word that she'd torn them up and told me to stop."

"It wasn't me; I know nothing about any letters, thus no dig intended. Ms. Chips may have thought you could be better occupied writing to your parents."

"I'll never forget the way she talked to me."

"Was she nasty?"

"Kind . . . compassionate!" Rosemary gave an empty laugh. "She said it was all part of growing up—hormones—a stage lots of girls went through and nothing to be ashamed about, but I needed to focus my energies on enjoying being a schoolgirl. I have never been so humiliated in my life."

"Teachers can't risk encouraging a crush."

"These jolly hockey-sticks women! The new one—your friend, whatever her name is!—no life outside of the school. Small wonder if they're inclined to be dotty."

"What are you getting at?"

Rosemary shrugged. "Rumor has it there was insanity in Ms. Chips's family."

My face flushed with anger. "Even if true, that's a hateful thing to repeat."

She had the grace to look embarrassed. "I wasn't serious. A large number of my acquaintances see a psychiatrist on a regular basis. Gerald and I move in very sophisticated circles."

"How nice."

"We're fortunate in being extremely well placed. He's an architect with a top-notch firm; an absolutely marvelous job that enables us to travel a lot. Fortunately, the nanny is wonderful. Our friends say"—leaning back in her chair—"that Gerald and I have the perfect marriage. In addition to common interests, our love life is perfect."

"Congratulations!" Taking a deep sip of gin, I felt the room reel.

"We make love three times a week—four, if Gerald isn't playing golf on Sunday afternoon. What does your husband do?" Again, to give her some credit, she made an attempt to sound mildly interested.

"Do?"

"As in job?"

"Oh! He's a chef."

"Fast food?"

I tightened the grip on my smile.

"Just kidding. I wasn't making a dig about the way you loved to eat at school. What's his name?" She picked up her glass, waving it at me.

"Ben. Short for Bentley. He has a bistro in Chitterton Fells."

"Didn't aim for London or one of the big cities?"

"He's quaint that way! In his copious free time he also writes cookery books."

"Under his own name?"

"He thought of Julia Child, but that was already taken."

"God, aren't we witty?" Rosemary got to her feet, poured herself another drink, but ignored the canapés. "However successful he may be—and I don't doubt from the glow in your eyes that he is—I wouldn't have heard of him. I haven't opened a cookery book in years. We have a super housekeeper-cook who never serves the same thing twice."

"That bad." My voice was steeped in sympathy. "Speaking of food, you mentioned pizza?"

Rosemary had turned to glower at me when footsteps sounded on the stairs. "Here comes Tosca. I decided to wait for her before opening the box and putting it in the oven. It's one of the supposedly gourmet ones with artichokes and portobello mushrooms, so perhaps it won't feel so primitive not having someone to serve dinner."

"Hello." A sleepy voice from the hall preceded an attractive woman with spiky black hair and equally dark eyes who stood in the doorway. Getting to my feet, I decided she would always make something of an entrance. Not necessarily by design, but because the immediate impression was of a vivid personality in tandem with exotic good looks. She crossed into the room, stretching her arms above her head, her figure—voluptuous in the right places—displayed to great advantage by a red velour pantsuit.

"That was some sleep. I half woke up around one o'clock, Rosemary, when I heard you come back." She settled cross-legged on the sofa, dangling wrists loaded with thin gold bracelets.

"Your imagination at work; I didn't get back until gone three."

"If you say so, darling!" There was the suggestion of a foreign accent. "I am Tosca Flitmouse," continued the bird of paradise from her perch; amused eyes met mine.

"Ellie Haskell. She was in my class." Rosemary got in ahead of me as she sat back down with her drink. Rather than continuing to stand like a lone soldier, I followed suit.

"So now we are three! One more the merrier!"

"Be a pet and stop gushing." Rosemary closed her eyes. "I was beginning to hope I could get to like you."

"It's nice to meet you, Tosca." I refused to rein in my enthusiasm; she might prove an ally during the long days ahead. Also, she added vibrancy to the fading afternoon.

"Flitmouse is the same as when I was at school. I am not married; too busy looking for myself and not finding. It is a silly name, yes? My great-grandfather chose it when fleeing the Russians—or perhaps it was the Turks. They were confusing times and the family chose not to talk too much of the old days. Too many of them. . . ." She drew a finger across her throat.

"How dreadful!" I could hear the thunder of Cossack horses, see the silver slash of sabers.

"Since then we have been nomads, the scared little mice that flit. As I say, a silly name but no worse perhaps than Chips."

"Tosca has nasty memories of Ms. Chips," interposed Rosemary, "most unjustly in my opinion, seeing the woman came to her rescue in the *nick*"—emphasizing the word—"of time."

I looked from one face to the other, and suddenly the name Tosca Flitmouse seemed familiar. Ah, it came to me! She was the foreign student who had gone up to London on a Saturday shopping trip with Ms. Chips and had been stopped by the store detective when going out the door of a shop called the Liberty Bodice. Brought back inside and taken to the general manager's office, she was found to have stolen items in her coat pockets. Small personal items, sometimes referred to as unmentionables.

She wasn't charged because Ms. Chips said the *mistake* sprang from a misunderstanding. She claimed to have told Tosca that anything she bought would be charged to St. Roberta's account, and the girl had assumed that she, Ms. Chips, had taken care of the purchases. A child in a new country, struggling with a foreign language and so on. However thin this may have sounded, the matter was dropped, but unfortunately word leaked out and several London newspapers printed the story, under banners such as SCHOOLGIRL NICKS KNICKERS and THE CASE OF THE PURLOINED PANTIES. Needless to say, Mrs. Battle was not nearly as amused as the rest of the school.

"You were two classes behind Rosemary and me," I said.

"I did not want Ms. Chips to speak up to save me." Tosca tied her legs into even more complicated yoga knots. "I wished to be hauled off to prison by a policeman in a helmet. My parents would have flown in from Geneva to get me out. And if I did not get expelled, as was my hope, they would be furious anyway and take me away from this oh, so stupid school with the boring rules and the bad food. I would have been back with my Dutch governess, Mevrouw Van Winkler, who closes her eyes and lets me do just as I like."

"So that's why you took the knickers?" I wished Ariel were present to hear this; it was a tale equal to the adventures of *The Naughtiest Girl at Northwood*. Hard on the heels of this thought came another. Had the Loverly Cup been stolen by someone hoping to be expelled from St. Roberta's?

"Let's not make light of your behavior, Tosca," said Rosemary righteously. "Nichola and Sheridan knew better as tiny tots than to take so much as a sweet without asking."

"How nice for you and the husband who is so good in bed. You are glad you married him instead of pining away for Ms. Chips?" said Tosca cheerfully as Rosemary, turning purple, choked on her drink. "That is good, because I can never—if I live to be an old woman—forgive her for ruining my life. And if you were with her still in love, I should blame you too. To be stuck here at St. Roberta's until I am eighteen; it was unbearable."

"I was not in—"

"You say so in your letters. The grape seeds do not lie."

"A schoolgirl crush." Despite my lack of enthusiasm for Rosemary, I had to feel sorry for her now.

"Gerald is not only the perfect lover, husband, and father, he is a collector of Flemish wines and has an expert's knowledge of goat cheese!"

"Speaking of cheese," I said hastily, "I've enjoyed the Camembert and Brie enormously, but how about that pizza?"

'Is it tofu?" Tosca inquired hopefully.

"No, but perhaps it will taste like it," Rosemary said nastily. "Frozen pizza, however gourmet it claims to be, almost always does. Gerald won't have it in the house. Of course, there's no need, given our housekeeper-cook is Cordon Bleu trained—"

"At least"—I got to my feet—"it's quick and easy. Shall I pop it in the oven?"

"If I could have a small salad." Tosca lay back on the sofa, folded her hands on her middle, and raised her legs, toes pointed before bringing them back over her head, to hold the position for the count of ten.

"What does she think this is, the Ritz?" Rosemary followed me, heavy-footed, into the kitchen behind the sitting room. It was minuscule, to say the least. Barely enough room, as the old saying goes, to swing a cat without knocking down everything breakable in sight. The yellow tiled floor was about the same size as the window above the sink and the crisp white walls did little to enlarge the space, jutting out as they did with a hodgepodge of cupboards that looked as though they'd been made by girls in Home Skills class. I pitied the maids of bygone days cooking for the chaplains—who, it had to be hoped, were all bachelors and never entertained.

Rosemary pointed laconically to the tiny refrigerator, which could easily have been mistaken for a bread bin. While I removed the pizza from the freezer compartment, she stood in the way, glowering down her Roman nose.

"I suppose I should view you as a breath of fresh air," she said begrudgingly. "You can see how impossible Tosca is."

"The three of us must make an effort to get along." I turned on the oven before opening up a couple of cupboard doors in search of a metal tray. This found, I removed cardboard and plastic wrap and eyed the anemic circle of pastry. It needed something—several somethings.

"I wish I had your kindly disposition." She sounded as though she might mean it.

"Just trying to be practical."

"I don't know why she can't sound English after living in the country as long as she has." Rosemary backed away from me to lean up against the old-fashioned draining board next to the sink. "Talk about affected! All that yoga and meditating! Want to know why she's here?"

"Perhaps she'll tell me." I opened a tin of pineapple chunks that had turned up in another cupboard, drained and added them, along with some slivers of ham from the fridge, to make the pizza a little more appetizing and filling.

"You won't need to hold your breath!" Rosemary assigned herself more square footage by spreading her arms out along the counter. "There's nothing she likes better than yapping on about herself and her antecedent, the Grand Duke of whoever it was. The trouble is, she does still have connections: a cousin who's married to a lord and another one going places in the Swiss government."

"Why is that a problem?" The pizza in the oven, I searched the fridge for the makings of the salad Tosca had requested.

Rosemary evinced increasing irritation. "It makes it impossible to snub her as effectively as I would wish. There could come a time when knowing her, and being on reasonably good terms, might prove useful."

"If you or Gerald got arrested in Switzerland or wanted to arrange an aristocratic marriage for one of your children?" I couldn't resist.

"Living in a tiny village, charming as it may be, you wouldn't understand. It's different in our social sphere. Knowing the right people is frightfully important if one does not wish to be left holding the cheese straws while the rest of the world parties."

Cheese! There was that word again. I abandoned the lettuce and cucumbers to their glass bowl and checked on the pizza. Whether or not it would taste like tofu, it smelled appetizing and was browning nicely.

"That's what Tosca is escaping from." Rosemary inched sideways to allow me to hunt for plates and cutlery. "She can't deal with cocktail parties and black-tie suppers after the opera right now."

"Yes, I imagine they get harrowing." I discovered a bottle of salad dressing lurking behind some tinned peas.

"She's trying to give up smoking. I suppose she has to be given points for that."

"It wouldn't seem to go with yoga."

"You'd think that would have sunk in before she got up to a couple of packets a day. Apparently, most of her friends smoke. Why these people can't be shipped off to a leper colony, I don't know. But I suppose we have to hope Tosca succeeds by isolating herself here."

"I don't suppose it's easy to stop."

You don't smoke?" She sounded as though she wouldn't have put it past me, along with going around without a bra or eating with my mouth open.

"No."

"You still haven't given your reason for seeking asylum."

"It's not easy to put into words." This was true, seeing I still hadn't come up with any ideas. "You first, while I get the pizza out of the oven."

"Nothing terribly dramatic." Rosemary provided some assistance by adding paper serviettes to the stack of plates and cutlery. "Gerald thought I was showing signs of exhaustion and had a word with our doctor, who suggested I get away for a few weeks' rest." Her back still to me, she got out salt and pepper shakers. "I've always had a tendency to push myself too hard, on the go from morning till night, organizing the household help, bringing in flowers from the greenhouse, arranging them in vases, making sure. . . ." Her voice wound on, to be interrupted by Mrs. Malloy, saying inside my head, *Making sure Hubby's toilet paper is hung just as he likes it.*

"Would you please shut up?" I'd almost dropped the pizza.

"What did you say?" Rosemary rounded on me.

"Would you please close the oven door?"

"Oh, I suppose so!" She banged it to, rattling the racks and causing the kettle to give a little hop on its burner. "Now, where was I?"—elbowing me out of her way—"Oh, yes! I was explaining how I came to be on the brink of collapse ferrying Nichola and Sheridan back and forth from after-school classes. She takes ballet and tap on Mondays, Wednesdays, and Fridays before going on to her flute and cello lessons, and he has soccer practice every day except Tuesday and Thursdays, when he has harp and violin. After dinner each night, it's riding for both of them. Nichola is shaping up well at dressage—her teacher thinks there's a possibility of the Olympics—and Sheridan takes jumps well in advance of his age."

"Which is?"

"Just turned nine, and Nichola won't be seven until next April."

Precious little prodigies! Mrs. Malloy chipped in.

"On Saturdays they both have chess club, drama, and gymnastics."

"Goodness! No wonder you were ready for a rest, Rosemary. How about my bringing you breakfast in bed?" I regretted this offer the moment it popped out of my mouth; having a lie-in might make this visit slightly more pleasant.

Before Rosemary could answer, Tosca stuck her head around the doorway. "No room for me, I think. Is there maybe some fruit . . . an apple or an orange perhaps?" She provided a much-needed brightness to the cramped kitchen and her smile was engaging, or so I thought.

"Sorry, the pantry and fridge are closed." Rosemary picked up the bowl of salad and returned to the sitting room, leaving me to follow with everything else. Having seated ourselves on chairs at the oval walnut table in the corner across from the fireplace, we surveyed the meager feast. A vase of flowers got shifted sideways. Plates were passed and the salt and pepper requested without any false festivity. Tosca soon gave up toying with her knife and fork. She hadn't helped herself to so much as a slice of cucumber from the salad she had requested, a fact that Rosemary did not allow to pass unobserved.

"There's no need to starve for thinking of all the starving millions."

"Mealtimes are the worst." Tosca made a valiant attempt at a laugh. "No cigarette afterward with my coffee. It is too much sometimes to bear without going crazy."

"It must be hard," I sympathized. "I can't imagine having to give up something I really enjoy, such as crusty bread and butter, but I'm sure you're right to persevere."

"I have not the choice," she replied soberly. "There is, you see, more. I have been a very silly girl. I lose a lot of money at the casino. I borrow to pay back from some men who are easy to make smile when I pinch their cheeks and chuck them under the chins, but who can also look very cross."

"Oh, my God!" Rosemary gasped. "Are you talking about the mob? Can we expect the doors to be kicked in when they come after you?"

"It is not that bad!" Tosca waved an airy hand. "There's still time before I have to pay up, and my father he has promised to give me the money if I give up smoking for three months. He says he will give me the blood test himself. So cruel!"

"There's no point in whining!" Rosemary reached for a second slice of pizza. "Thank goodness I've never had time for such vices."

"What sadness! All the interesting people get into the hot water. I see Aiden Loverly in town and he tells me he borrows from the same people as I when he gambles too high, but somehow he comes straight before they have to break his arms and legs."

Rosemary closed her eyes. "In addition to all the running around I do for Nichola and Sheridan, there's Laurence to be taken to his swimming lessons."

"Who?" Was there a child I had missed?

"Her dog," said Tosca, wilting on her chair.

"Laurence is a Portuguese Water Dog. We had him imported at great expense."

Along with a crate of wine and a selection of goat cheeses? I wondered. "And you take him for swimming lessons?"

"Every Sunday morning after church."

"At the public baths?" Tosca roused herself to inquire.

"Don't be ridiculous!"

'Course not, intruded Mrs. Malloy. *The furry love will do his practice at the country club.*

"What does he like more, the Australian crawl or the backstroke?" Tosca's impish grin reappeared.

"Aren't you funny?" Rosemary pushed her plate away.

I liked the idea of the backstroke. An image formed of Laurence, inverted, going down the length of the pool, arms—or, strictly speaking, front legs—flailing at top speed as he zipped past the competition to win the heat. For surely he would already be entering local competitions, if not yet national ones. Did the hope of an Olympic medal gleam in his future? A pity cats hate water; it would have been good to have aspirations for Tobias. The thought of him made me long for home. What would Ben and the children be doing at this minute?

"Ellie, do you have a dog?" Tosca waved two fingers as if they held a cigarette, inhaling deeply the imaginary wisps of smoke.

"Our cat won't allow it. He claims to be allergic."

"You two!" Rosemary snorted. "I've never met people quite so odd!"

"My in-laws have a dog—a little one, mostly poodle." I pictured Sweetie descending gingerly into the water, testing the temperature with her toes. The public swimming pool for her, and a pink rubber bathing cap with a strap under her furry chin. When she got going it would be the breaststroke, head above water in the accepted British style for elderly ladies, brown eyes popping, back legs forgetting what they were supposed to do. Hoping desperately for the reward of a nice cup of tea and a sit-down after staggering back up the steps.

The look Rosemary gave me suggested she had a good idea of what was going on inside my head. "Well, it's not surprising," she said bitingly.

"What isn't?"

"That you're the way you are. Your parents were an odd enough pair." She turned to Tosca. "I remember seeing her with them, sitting outside the pub having drinks. The mother was wearing an outfit that looked as though it had come out of Lady Loverly's attic. The most enormous hat with a veil and some sort of Edwardian garment! If that weren't enough to knock one's eyes out, there was the father's attire. He was wearing a boater and a claret velvet smoking jacket. Can you picture it?"

"They were larger than life and absolutely wonderful," I said coldly.

"I adore artsy people." Tosca stubbed out the imaginary cigarette while I choked on my pizza.

"Wasn't there an equally eccentric aunt?" Rosemary continued blithely. "Mutton dressed up as lamb, decked out to the nines, with far too much makeup and frightfully common to boot?"

"I don't have any aunts, common or otherwise." I would have thrown my pizza at her if I hadn't already eaten it.

"Look, don't get huffy, I was only twanging your strings." Rosemary went on the defensive. "Not all my relatives are wonderful, or the sort to reach out if I were in difficulties." She drew a breath. "Are we going to let this salad go to waste?"

Not if I stuffed it down her throat, I was thinking, when an inspiration occurred to me. I had determined that I couldn't bring myself to pretend I had come to the Chaplain's House in search of a rest after nursing an ailing family member. It would seem like tempting fate. But an imaginary aunt? That was not at all the same thing as the children, Ben, or his parents.

"Oh!" I beamed a smile at Rosemary. "You must have been thinking of"—I sought inspiration and found it in the vase of flowers on the table—"Petal. Dear . . . dearest Petal! She's not a real aunt. A friend of my mother's, and indeed quite eccentric. How interesting that you should remember her! Last year when her lumbago worsened and her eyesight started to fail . . . coupled with her inviting the milkman in for a chat and not letting him leave until she had sold him raffle tickets . . . the long and the short of it is, Ben and I decided she should move in with us and the children."

"Does she smoke?" asked Tosca hopefully.

"No, but she does like her nip of gin—needs it, I should say, for medicinal reasons—but when she falls down I have trouble getting her up without help. And of course Ben can't always be there. Last week my doctor talked to me, just as yours did with you, Rosemary, and said I had to get away for a break."

"Who's taking care of the old girl while you're gone?"

"The vicar's wife has agreed to keep an eye on her," I improvised rapidly. "Petal wouldn't stand for a nurse; she's got this idea that they all want to put old people away in their sleep. Not that she's really old." It was surprising how fond I'd grown of Petal in the last couple of minutes, causing me to feel sad about limiting her remaining number of years. "She's only in her sixties and still quite spry . . . sometimes for minutes on end," I hastened to add, "especially when a man visits. We end up hiding them in the hall wardrobe."

"You must live in a madhouse!" Rosemary expostulated as Tosca got up from her chair, staring rather wildly at us.

'Did you hear that?"

"What?" I asked, scrambling up in my turn.

"Someone is moving about upstairs."

"You're imagining things," scoffed Rosemary. "This is an old house; it creaks."

"I tell you—" Tosca headed across the room and into the hall.

"There's no talking to some people! This giving up smoking has driven her round the bend!" Grumbling, Rosemary joined me in pursuit, providing a bulwark when I backed up in amazement.

"It is as I said!" Tosca pointed a finger at the staircase, where a woman of similar age to our own stood halfway down. She was pretty, with honey-brown hair a shade lighter than her eyes. Maybe five-foot-four, with a figure that showed to advantage even in a shapeless navy blue sweater and blue jeans.

"Hello!" she said. "Sorry if I startled you. I arrived at one-thirty this afternoon after a long journey and on finding a bedroom that didn't appear to be occupied lay down and slept until a couple of minutes ago. I'm Phil Boswell, by the way."

"Philippa?" I took a couple of unsteady steps forward, and

from the surprised look in her eyes I knew my voice must have sounded odd.

"Yes, but everyone calls me Phil these days."

"I said I heard someone come in at that time!" Tosca glowed in triumph. "You don't smoke, by any chance?"

9

I sat on the bed, staring around the room where Dorcas had deposited my luggage. It would have taken a picky guest to find fault with my surroundings. Snowy white bedcovers contrasted crisply with teal painted walls, which color was repeated in the stripes of the slipcovered easy chair and the curtains at the two windows. A sleek ebony-stained wardrobe invited the emptying of suitcases, and a sea-green glass jug on the dressing table contained an artful arrangement of leafy twigs. If there was a chamber pot under the bed, it would remain there gathering dust. The Chaplain's House possessed two bathrooms complete with all mod cons, one of them directly across from my door. Another amenity was the telephone, in an alcove on the landing.

On coming upstairs shortly before ten, I'd phoned home and found refuge in Ben's voice. I apologized for not getting in touch sooner, explaining that it had been a long day and giving him the nuts and bolts of it, not focusing on any one aspect other than to stress that it had been wonderful to see Ariel.

"How's she settling down?" he'd asked.

"She's making friends," I reassured him.

"Not being treated as a curiosity on account of her family winning the lottery?"

"If so, she didn't mention it. But I doubt that's a problem." I stared up at the large round plastic clock on the wall above the telephone table; it didn't go with the rest of the house. "Most of the girls at St. Roberta's come from money. One of the women staying at the Chaplain's House—she was a couple of years behind me—is connected to foreign royalty, and another lives in considerable style, from the sound of it." Before I could bring up the addition of Philippa Boswell, I heard the children clamoring to speak to me. Ben allotted them each two minutes before telling them it was time to scarper upstairs. Knowing he would want to see this accomplished without too much bouncing on the beds, I said a quick good night.

Now, as I hung a few items of clothing in the hospitable-looking wardrobe and put others away in the chest of drawers, I decided there wouldn't have been much to say about Philippa, other than my surprise—too limp a word, make that shock—at seeing her standing on the stairs. She had made a pleasant addition to our group, cheerfully eating cold pizza and a good deal of the salad, but she provided very little information about her life other than to say when pressed hard by Rosemary that she was unmarried and had never stuck with any job very long. Something new always seemed to beckon. Most recently she'd been a veterinary assistant. She was fond of animals, particularly cats. Being presently at loose ends, she'd decided the Chaplain's House would be an ideal place for a period of contemplation.

"How did you hear about it?" Rosemary had demanded, with all the rudeness at her command.

"From Ms. Chips. We've corresponded off and on over the years, and she is so happy about fixing up this place and offering it as a temporary refuge." Philippa was even more attractive than in her schooldays and seemed equally nice.

When Rosemary said it was a shame she wasn't more settled, Tosca entered the fray.

"I do not see what is wrong in not wanting to be chained to an office chair or the kitchen sink."

To stave off an ensuing squabble, I brought up the missing Loverly Cup and how Mrs. Battle must be champing at the bit to see it returned.

Now, having finished my unpacking, I stowed my suitcase and overnight bag on the wardrobe floor, drew the curtains, got undressed, and stepped into my thin cotton wrap. Its pink print did no justice to the tasteful ambience of the room. Telling myself I looked like someone's invalid aunt, I gathered up what was needed by way of soap and lotion and headed across the hall.

While soaking in the claw-foot bath I thought about Petal, whom I had invented so convincingly she was beginning to seem real. More real, in a way, than Philippa, whom I had trouble accepting as being truly here, rather than an image conjured up by my overwrought conscience. A question loomed as I toweled myself. Should I tell her that I knew she had not left the San to meet Brian Roberts on that fateful Friday? Or would I be easing my guilt at the expense of her current peace of mind? It was one thing to tell myself that fate had brought her here for a purpose, but wasn't it arrogant to assume that I was the cosmic force?

My musings were interrupted by the telephone ringing in its alcove. Probably Gerald phoning up Rosemary or one of Tosca's friends out partying and indifferent to the concept that less sophisticated people turn in earlier. I took my time wiping down the bath and leaving everything neat before returning to my room. Plenty of time for whoever had received the call to conclude a conversation and hang up. Equally likely was the possibility of a phone downstairs, although Rosemary had only mentioned the one up here.

My nightdress was no more glamorous than the pink wrap, there having seemed no point in bringing anything frilly, but I was glad to pull it over my head and get into bed, leaving the table-side lamp on for the moment. I thought about reading the book I had brought with me but wasn't all that eager to read someone else's adventures when there was so much to sort out in my own life. For the moment, I stared at the teal and ruby feathers of the painted birds on the breakfast set on the bedside table. Did they ever yearn to fly away and get lost in some remote jungle?

This brought me back to what Rosemary had said about my parents. She was a difficult woman but somehow pathetic, with her boasting about Gerald and the children and, let him not be forgotten, Laurence the aquatic dog. I could see him in a pair of swimming trunks—red ones with little brown bones on the fabric—poised on the diving board, paws above his head, before executing a triple back somersault to the admiration of all who witnessed it. Was I already dreaming? Probably still awake since I was aware that the mattress was comfy and the pillow plump; but I could feel a yawn stretching my face and decided it might be well to turn off the lamp. I was wondering fuzzily if that clock above the telephone table had been hung there to cover an unsightly crack in the wall when I heard a tapping at one of the windows.

Sitting up with a back-snapping thrust, I stared at the window to my left. There it came again, timid still but more imperative. A loose drainpipe, I told myself sensibly. The Gray Nun wouldn't have tapped; she would have materialized, unless—I got reluctantly to my feet—she was feeling tired or poorly and therefore not up to passing through walls or windows. Who was I to assume that ghosts didn't have their off days? Telling myself I would make more sense if I were fully asleep, I drew back the curtains, not seriously expecting to see anything. Silly optimistic me! I beheld a face looking back at me.

"Hold on!" I stifled my alarm in order to wrestle with the latch and shove up the sash. It was impossible to move in anything other than slow motion. My hands shook and I was in terror of my bedroom door being flung open. But finally my visitor climbed over the sill, to survey me with a diabolical smile.

"Hello, Ellie!" said Ariel, as if we were meeting at the breakfast table and she would next ask me to pass the cornflakes.

"Whatever are you doing here?" I dragged the curtains shut without bothering to close the window. She wouldn't be staying long if I had anything to say about it!

"I couldn't sleep; I was dying to talk to you." She sat down on the bed and patted it invitingly for me to join her, a gesture I ignored.

"You look like a cat burglar in those dark jeans and sweater."

"I don't have a balaclava or I'd have put that on too," she replied.

"Did you arrive by ladder?" I demanded, forgetting to keep my voice low. Hopefully the rest of the house was asleep, but it would be foolish to count on it.

Ariel giggled happily. "Oh, I suppose there's one in Mr. Mossop's shed, but I didn't bother to look. I came up the drainpipe. Don't look so panicked! I was in no danger of falling. The Virginia creeper is really tough; it gave me a great handhold."

"I don't believe this! And do lower your voice!"

"What I find hard to believe"—she rested her coronet of braids on the pillow—"is that before I came to St. Roberta's I couldn't even climb a rope all the way up. Miss Critchley was so sweet and encouraging, saying it was just one tiny pull at a time. I'll never be able to thank her enough for teaching me."

"I'll have a few words of my own for her!"

"Please, Ellie, don't be cross. I had the most frightful scare on the way here." Ariel pressed a hand to her forehead in appropriate damsel-in-distress fashion. "I suppose it could have been my imagination, but I'm sure I saw the Gray Nun gliding into the bushes by Mr. Mossop's garden shed."

"How extremely distressing," I said unsympathetically. "What if one of the girls in your dorm wakes up to find you missing and raises the alarm?"

"They won't; they all sleep like logs. But just in case, I paved the way by mentioning casually that when I was at home I had a problem with sleepwalking and was surprised that it hadn't happened once since I came to St. Roberta's."

"And they should do nothing if they woke up to find you gone?"

"Well, I explained that I could die of shock if pounced upon and dragged back, so it was enormously safer for me to return under my own steam."

"What if a member of the staff should see you out and about?"

"Same story." Ariel grinned impishly. "Don't tell me you never crept out at dead of night on an adventure of your own when you were at St. Roberta's?"

She had me there! "Once. And it was a case of never again. My friends Ann Gamble and Susan Brodstock and I went down to the convent ruins."

"Goodness! That *was* brave!" Ariel sat up and hugged her knees.

"Stupid is the word."

"Did something terrifying happen?"

"Susan dropped her watch down a cavity in the stone bench we were sitting on."

"Is that all? No sign of the Gray Nun?"

"Not a wisp of her veil." Why was I engaging in silly conversation when it was imperative that Ariel return to her dorm as speedily as possible? I'd have to accompany her, I realized; to let her slink back on her own was not an option, even though the possibility of a midnight strangler on the loose was remote.

"Speaking of schoolgirl pranks," she said more seriously, "I've been thinking about Philippa Boswell."

"She's here!" I was the one forgetting to whisper.

"Whatever do you mean?" Her eyes became the size of her spectacles.

"She arrived this afternoon. That makes four of us."

"Along with you and the Ogress and . . . ?"

"Tosca Flitmouse."

"What a name! But tell me about Philippa." Ariel oozed empathy. "How are you coping with the shock of seeing her again?"

"Fine."

"Are you sure about that?" Ariel adjusted her specs the better to size me up.

"She goes by the name of Phil these days."

"Have you had a chance to talk?"

"You mean confess to keeping quiet instead of speaking up for her?" My voice quivered. "I haven't been alone with her, and I'm not sure it would be the right thing to do."

"Well, there's no rush, is there?" Ariel shifted her feet when I went to sit down on the bed. "I've been thinking about that day, Ellie, and the mystery of the girl who was in two places at once. Either Mr. Bumbleton, esteemed member of the Board of Governors, fabricated his sighting of Philippa and the boyfriend—"

"There was the note, remember?"

"Dropped at another time, perhaps in another place. But amusing as it would be to make him the villain of the piece, out to ruin poor Philippa because her mother wouldn't marry him or her father humiliated him in a fencing match, it's far more likely that Philippa sent another girl in her place." Ariel eyed me closely. "You must have realized that's what happened."

"Of course! And it explains why Philippa didn't defend herself. I just never dwelt on anything other than the part I played."

"It also explains the note, Ellie. Why the need for one if she had gone herself?"

"There is that."

"The courier would have had to be a close friend, willing to take the risk." Ariel rested her chin on her knees. "Or someone who wanted Brian Roberts for herself. After Miss Critchley and I left you, I went to the library and found one boarding-school book. It's called *False Friend at Falcon Abbey* and is about this head girl who doesn't realize her best friend is horribly jealous of her popularity and out to bring her down. It brought tears to my eyes."

"I'm sure it's a heartbreaker." I couldn't continue allowing myself to be distracted; the longer Ariel was gone from the dorm, I told her, the greater the chance that she would be missed. We would have to risk exiting the house by way of the stairs and front door because there was no way that I, who had never learned to climb a rope, was going to grab hold of a drainpipe. A jump off a cliff with the possibility of hitting water a hundred feet below would have been preferable.

"Didn't you say that your friend Susan's sister was best chums with Philippa?" Ariel asked as I stood up.

"Yes. Her name was Sally, and she became head girl the following year."

"Aha!"

"Ariel, I really don't think I can talk to Philippa about any of this."

"Perhaps she'll bring it up."

"I don't think so. She gave the impression of not wanting to talk other than superficially about herself."

"Well, I don't see how you can stand not knowing what really happened that day. In a book everything would be explained."

"This isn't—" I got no further. There was a sound at the window, a scrambling reminiscent of the moment before Ariel made her entry. Before we had finished gaping at each other, a leg extended over the sill and the curtains were pushed aside.

"Ahoy there!" sounded a familiar voice.

"Dorcas?" I shot across the room to let her all the way in. "What is this, the Mad Hatter's tea party?"

"I can think of something even better!" Ariel exclaimed. "How about a midnight feast, Miss Critchley? In the story I'm reading, several of the girls have met in the tower room at Falcon Abbey. I'd just reached the part when they hear ominous footsteps—"

"Shush!" I darted a frantic look at her. "Someone's outside on the landing!"

"Now?"

"Quick! Under the bedclothes, Ariel! Dorcas, behind the curtains!"

Without waiting to see if they did as told, I reached the door just as it opened a couple of inches.

"Ellie?" It was Rosemary's Roman nose inserted into the gap, which I did not allow to widen. "Are you having an interesting conversation with yourself? I could hear you through the wall. It woke me up."

"I think you must have been having a bad dream. It's the pizza." I raised my voice over the hiccuping sounds coming from the bed. "You know the old saying that eating cheese at night gives people nightmares."

"I suppose it must have been that; I've a lot on my mind with Gerald . . . having to cope on his own. Are you wearing a transparent nightgown or nothing at all?"

"Why?"

"There has to be some reason you're not opening the door."

"Sorry, just rather keen to get back to bed."

"You haven't taken your teeth out or your wig off?"

"I only need to do either once a month." More sounds from the bed. Dorcas at least was behaving herself.

"What's that sound? Do you have the hiccups, Ellie?"

"Yes, the pizza gave them to me. I'd better get a drink of water. Talk to you in the morning."

"All right." I heard her move away—three steps by my count, but it was too good to be true; she was back again before I could summon the composure to close the door. "There was a phone call for you. Aren't some of us popular?" I detected resentment in her voice.

"Who?"

"Mrs. Battle. I told her you were having a bath. A deep one, from the sound of all that running water."

"Sorry." I hadn't thought to ask whether it was rationed.

"Anyway, she apologized for calling late, said she's a night owl and forgets that others turn in early; also, her reason for telephoning had just come up. Mrs. Rushbridge can't take her Home Skills class tomorrow morning at ten, and Mrs. Battle wondered if you'd fill in with a talk about interior design."

"Oh!"

"I gather you're an expert at choosing lightbulbs and such."

"It's my job."

"I suppose it beats selling knickers at the Liberty Bodice." Rosemary followed this observation with a yawn. "Thank God I don't have to work, Gerald wouldn't hear of it. Anyway, if you don't get back to the Battle-ax saying it's not on, she'll send a girl down at nine-thirty to escort you to the Home Skills room."

"Thanks." I closed the door and stood with my back against it.

"Goodness," said Ariel, emerging from the bedclothes, "I had it right about the Ogress! How do you stand her?"

"Can't always pick and choose our companions." Dorcas had come out from behind the curtains; the backdrop of teal caused her red hair to stand out in sharp relief. It was also sticking up in tufts. "Close one, that, Ellie. Good thing the walls in these places are a foot thick. Otherwise not so easy to convince her she dreamed our voices."

"What brought you here?" I whispered.

"Drainpipe."

"Same as me. And you won't believe how fast I shinned up, Miss Critchley!" Ariel said, in a voice bursting with pride.

"Got those calf muscles working and the old heave-ho with the hands in rhythm? Good show!" Dorcas beamed at her before recollecting that as a member of St. Roberta's staff she ought not to applaud a girl for taking off from her dorm, however admirable the ensuing gymnastic exploits. "Won't report you this time, Ariel, but mustn't bunk off again. Mrs. Battle would have kittens! Came out myself for a late-night constitutional. Couldn't sleep for thinking about the Loverly Cup. Saw you heading across the grounds, knew you by those plaits on your head—"

"You do think they look nice?" The wretched girl patted her coronet.

"Another interruption and I'll yank them off," I informed her.

"Sorry! I was forgetting the Ogress. I'm hungry." She attempted to look wistful. "I don't suppose you have any chocolate?"

She sounded like Tosca in hope of a cigarette. I cut my glare short. "You were saying, Dorcas?"

"Followed Ariel and saw her go in through the window. Waited outside, thinking you might be discussing private family matters. Thought I saw movement down by the Dribbly Drop, but must have been my imagination giving me the jitters. Decided I'd better come in before the hounds started baying."

"You see?" Ariel exclaimed triumphantly. "There *was* something out there cloaked in shadow. We both saw it!"

Ignoring her, I addressed Dorcas. "I was going to take her back, but now you're here I'll gratefully allow you to do the honors." I shifted my young friend off the bed and nudged her forward. "With my luck, I'll be the one reported by Rosemary to Mrs. Battle for disobeying curfew."

"On our way." Dorcas raised a hand in salute and then hesitated. "Wouldn't be a bad idea, Ellie, for you to have a chat with Matron. Not just to find out what's going on with Gillian; get her impressions of the other girls. See if she's noticed anything different about anyone since the cup disappeared. Someone looking off-color or bursting into tears for no apparent reason—that sort of thing."

"Dear Dorcas"—my heart brimmed with affection—"you believe everyone has a conscience as active as your own."

"Not entirely an old softie. Doubt if that unpleasant young man Aiden Loverly would hesitate to murder his grandmother, or anyone else who got in his way. Now, out that window, Ariel. Get a good hold and full speed ahead. Can't come to any harm, ground's soft."

"Do both be careful," I instructed nervously, and stood watching until they were both safely down.

"Oh, and don't forget me, Ellie, and the help I can be," Ariel called back up. "Why don't you ask Mrs. Battle if you can take Carolyn and me out to lunch and see what she can spill? I think we have to take her into our confidence."

"Okay, but go!" I continued to stare after her and Dorcas until they faded into shadows and finally disappeared from sight. After securing the window against any other visitors and turning off the light, I climbed into bed but lay awake for fear of being startled into heart-thudding alertness by the shrill ringing of the telephone or a pounding on my door.

The day's events drifted through my mind, becoming woollier and more disconnected with the passing minutes, until only stray thoughts remained. One of them was wondering if Ms. Chips harbored the hope of being reunited with her bridegroom when she too passed into the next world. Someone must tell her it wasn't safe to walk alone at night; Aiden Loverly dressed as the Gray Nun might force her off the road, spinning them both into oblivion. . . .

Morning comes too soon for those haven't enjoyed their allotted shut-eye and aren't early birds under normal circumstances. I opened my eyes to the thought that I should struggle downstairs to help Ben with the children's breakfast, and afterward, if Mrs. Malloy did not decide to be horridly punctual, there'd be a few moments of blissful alone time with him, before he departed for Abigail's or disappeared into the study to work on his book. It was dismal to sit up, stare at the teal walls, and realize that I was at the Chaplain's House. Nothing on earth would tempt me to sit on *Rosemary's* lap while I sipped my desperately needed first cup of tea. It was past eight o'clock, making it necessary to get a move on if I wanted to be ready when collected by the girl Mrs. Battle was sending to escort me to the Home Skills room.

As luck would have it, there was no sign of Rosemary ten minutes later, when I entered the sitting room wearing a sage-green dress topped with a matching cotton cardigan, my attempt to look cool and competent should the class prove unruly.

"Good morning." Phil, wearing the same jeans and sweater as yesterday, turned to look at me with a smile on her heart-shaped face; she had a green and yellow eggbeater in her hands. For a moment I thought she was going to tell me it was for sale at a reduced price because the paint was worn and there was some rust. "Wouldn't you know?" She laughed. "The school colors! A bit antique, but that's what the present bunch must think we are, right up there with Mrs. Battle and Ms. Chips."

"Probably." I knew I must sound stilted, but exchanging chitchat with her the previous evening hadn't removed my discomfort in her presence. My conscience was still killing me. "I saw Ms. Chips when I first arrived."

"Did you? I liked her enormously. Being lacrosse captain, I was around her a lot."

"It must have been awful when that position was taken away from you." Instantly I could have kicked myself. She must think me hateful for verging on the subject of her disgrace.

"What?" She stood frozen in place, still holding the eggbeater.

Blushing furiously, I sat down on a stool at the handkerchief-sized table next to the back door. "I'm sorry I brought it up, Philippa . . ." My voice petered out miserably.

"Don't worry." She brushed back a lock of honey-brown hair with a hand that trembled noticeably. "Someone was bound to remember that incident."

"It was so unfair, what happened to you." I floundered on like a horse that no amount of yanking on the reins will stop. "Losing out on becoming head girl, being blamed for leaving the San that afternoon."

"We all do stupid things when we're young."

"Yes, but—" I saw the suggestion of tears in her eyes and finally shut up.

"I've never forgiven myself for the way. . . ." She stood spinning the eggbeater's handle. "Rosemary mentioned that Brian Roberts has taken over his father's practice. It's what he always wanted: country living, the cottage with the thatched roof. He never had any interest in theater, opera, or being a man-about-town. It worked out best for both of us. I suppose he's married?"

"I don't think so." I almost asked if she were happy; selfishly I wanted that reassurance, but I bit my lip and inquired instead what she planned to do during her stay.

"Not much." Her smile returned. "I'm resting." She stared at the eggbeater as if wondering how it came to be in her hand. "While I'm here I might as well take the opportunity to learn to cook. Goodness knows, it's about time. My sister is a whiz in the kitchen, in addition to being a highly successful barrister and mother of three. Our parents can't figure out where they went wrong with me."

"I think Dr. Roberts would find you've matured wonderfully if you chance to run into each other." There was no keeping my nose out of other people's business . . . with the exception of that long-ago time, when it had really counted. And why should Philippa care what I thought about anything? It had been obvious the previous night that she did not remember me.

"I thought I'd scramble some eggs. Do you think this antique"—she brandished the beater—"is safe to use?"

"I'd be a bit worried about the rust. Better perhaps to use a fork."

"Will that do it? Just the ordinary kind?"

I got off the stool, opened a drawer, and handed her one. "Here! My husband, Ben, is a chef and he isn't madly keen on gadgets. His food processor is a sharp knife."

She laughed. It was a merry, mischievous sound, but it came through strongly that for the most part she wasn't happy.

Getting out a mixing bowl, I told her that the rule of thumb was one tablespoon of milk for each egg and the idea was to cook them very slowly. While she stirred the contents of the saucepan I filled the kettle for tea and popped slices of bread into a toaster that was as much an antique as the beater. There was barely room to move in the pint-sized kitchen without butting elbows, and I could see now that Rosemary had prevented potential injury by doing little to help with last night's supper. Filled with good resolutions, I determined to focus on her better qualities the moment I discovered them. A glance at my watch showed I had a comfortable fifteen minutes left to eat my share of the scrambled eggs. I was congratulating Philippa on how well they had turned out and enjoying a second cup of tea when Tosca wandered in.

Even with her dark hair tousled and her eyes drowsy with the remnants of sleep she looked fantastic, in a filmy rose peignoir that must have cost a bomb, but I surmised she was not a morning person from her forced smile and the dreary way she hovered at the table without sitting down.

"Hello, you two!" Her voice was dragged from the depths of melancholy.

"There's tea left in the pot," I offered. "Or perhaps you'd prefer coffee?"

"What I need—what I'd kill for—is a cigarette. I've been down on my knees half the night."

"Praying?" Philippa stopped buttering a slice of toast.

"Spoken like the Gray Nun." Tosca grimaced at her. "I suppose it would have made as much sense. But no, I was crawling around in hope of finding a discarded ciggy under the bed or the wardrobe. I was aware it was going to be hard, but never this bad. I'm afraid I'm going to crack."

"It's rough . . ."

"Speaking from experience, Phil?" Rosemary's sneering laugh preceded her into the room. She was wearing a polished cotton dress that crackled with every step and a straw hat that looked like a flying saucer forced into an aborted landing. She was also holding a handbag. Clearly she was going out. But what were the chances she would do so within the next five seconds?

"Have a heart." I rounded on her. "Tosca is suffering. The rest of us should be her support group."

"Oh, for God's sake!" Rosemary shifted the handbag as if preparing to throw it at me. "She's been here almost two weeks. I've heard the first three days can be difficult, but by now she should be well over the craving. What she's looking for is sympathy, and if you and Phil keep feeding into her narcissism, she'll continue to wallow. But that's your lookout. I'm off to get my car from the parking area and have a day's outing."

"Have you ever thought of playing Lady Macbeth?" Philippa stood to gather up the dishes. "No, don't bother answering, it might delay you." Her voice was serene. "Come into the kitchen, Tosca. Between the two of us we may be able to make a cup of coffee." They disappeared, leaving Rosemary to fume at me.

"And you should be getting a move on if you aren't to keep the girl Mrs. Battle sends waiting. You see, there goes the bell!" She marched into the hall with me at her heels and flung open the door as if eager to devour whoever stood there.

"Good morning. I've come for Mrs. Haskell," said Gillian Parker.

10

On our walk across the gently sloping lawn to the school, I was relieved that Gillian seemed in a better frame of mind than the day before. She was reserved and in no way a lively fourteen-year-old, but I detected none of the nervous agitation that had so worried me. Even so, I hoped I could learn more about her from Matron.

It was Gillian who brought up her great-aunt. “Mrs. Haskell, I told Aunt Wilma about seeing you and Miss Critchley when I went for my lesson with Mr. Middleton, and she told me to tell you she hopes you’ll stop in and see her after you have finished the Home Skills class.”

“I’ll do that. Will she be in her office or the staff common room?”

We had drawn level with Mr. Mossop busily clipping grass around the base of a tree. He mumbled something but didn’t look up, and we passed on. I made a mental note to have a word with both husband and wife on the off chance either of them had seen a shifty-eyed someone making off with the Loverly Cup.

"Her office," said Gillian. "Do you remember where it is?"

"Roughly."

"It's around the corner from the main corridor on the left, outside the San." We were now going up the broad steps to the front entrance door. Gillian added hesitantly, before pushing it open, "I wasn't myself yesterday, but that's no excuse. I shouldn't have spoken unkindly about Aunt Wilma. If she's been cross with me, it's because she doesn't want me to get into Mrs. Battle's bad books and be seen as a problem that might end with me being sent home."

"But do you want to stay here?" I said, looking around the reception hall, with its high, partially wainscoted walls, parquet flooring, and broad oak staircase. I turned my eyes back to her. "Not everyone is cut out for boarding school. You shouldn't feel you've failed if it isn't for you."

"Did you like it, Mrs. Haskell?"

"I enjoyed the friends I made." It was a struggle to sound more positive, especially when I had the feeling we were a subject of disapproving interest to the somber-faced men and women represented in the portraits on the staircase wall. All of them, if I remembered correctly, had been members of the Board of Governors. It seemed to me that a fiercely mustached gentleman, his cheeks and waistcoat swelling with importance, looked down at us with a particularly jaundiced eye. One of Mr. Bumbleton's forebears, if I wasn't mistaken. Perhaps even the founder of the architectural firm with a fondness for niches.

Gillian wasn't looking at him or at the companion portraits. "Mrs. Haskell, did you ever think of running away?" The face she raised was calm, but I heard the tightness in her voice and picked my words accordingly.

"I imagine every girl at boarding school does when she is homesick or things go badly. It's easier, I suppose, for the ones who are tremendously popular and clever. I was neither of those things, besides being hopeless at games and sports. But whenever the urge came to escape to the railway and catch a train home, I realized I'd cause my parents a great deal of unnecessary worry when all I had to do was phone and ask them to come and get me."

"But you never did?" She was now looking straight ahead as we crossed the parquet floor to the archway, which opened onto a broad corridor interspersed on both sides with doors, one of which had a sign above it indicating Mrs. Battle's office.

"No. On reflection, the situation never seemed sufficiently desperate. But if it had been, I'm sure I would have got ahold of them, and if it was something I couldn't pour out over the phone, they would have come at once. They were such dears and not particularly flappable."

"But"—Gillian stopped to again look at me—"what if Mrs. Battle had got to them first and told them stories about you that they didn't want to believe but had to—because they could be true?"

"They would have listened to me. Parents—loving ones—do, and everything would have got sorted out." I placed a hand on her arm, but she moved away as Ariel would have done if feeling crowded. Inadequacy swamped me. Gillian desperately needed someone to talk to, but I wasn't the right person. Nor, it would seem, was her great-aunt. I wasn't looking forward to my talk with Matron. Anything I said about the girl might fairly be taken as interference.

We were nearing the end of the corridor when Gillian spoke again. "If you didn't love St. Roberta's, why did you come back, Mrs. Haskell?"

"I've needed a rest after months of taking care of my Aunt Petal, who hasn't been well." This deception made me intensely uncomfortable, but I'd promised Mrs. Battle to keep as much of a lid as possible on my true mission. Still, this couldn't have been worse. Gillian was someone I wanted to trust me, and I was lying through my teeth to her. I felt awful. *And so you should,* intoned Mrs. Malloy in her most righteous voice. *Aunt Petal indeed! How did you come up with that one? If I'd got to choose it would have been something sensible!* I turned down the volume inside my head to listen to Gillian.

"Are the others staying at the Chaplain's House nice? The Ogress who answered the door scared me."

"Have you been speaking to Ariel Hopkins?" I asked, as we turned the corner and headed down a short flight of steps.

"Yes. She's become friends with Carolyn Fisher-Jones, and she told both of us about . . ."

"Rosemary."

"Is that her name? Ariel described her perfectly." It was the first time Gillian had laughed with real spontaneity in my presence.

"Between you and me," I confided, "I couldn't stand her when we were at school together. She was the worst bully. Horribly eager to get people into trouble."

"There's a girl like that in my dorm. Her name's Deirdre Dawson." The brief merriment was gone. "She's unkind, but she doesn't scare me the way . . . some people do."

"Gillian, are you talking about Aiden Loverly?"

"No, he's all right, really."

"What did he accuse you of?" I asked gently. "I heard you tell him you weren't a thief."

"He was teasing me." Her voice trembled on the edge of panic. "Pretending to think I'd taken the Loverly Cup." She was backing away from me, biting down on her lip. "I overreacted, that's all."

"He almost ran you down."

"No, he had his motorcycle under control. Do you like the others staying at the Chaplain's House?" Gillian was now clearly speaking at random. Looking at her, I was convinced that if I said one more word about Aiden Loverly or the cup she would make a dash down the hall.

"There are two others in addition to myself and Rosemary: Tosca Flitmouse and Philippa Boswell. Neither was my age. Tosca was a couple of classes below me and Philippa one above. I think they'll both prove good company."

"Tosca . . . that's a wonderful name." She stood opening and closing her fists.

"Isn't it? I imagine it specially appeals to you, Gillian, with your gift for music." We had paused again at the bottom of the stairs. "She has a fun personality, sort of quirky. Occasionally she gets cranky, but only I think because she's given up smoking, and even when the urge takes over she's amusing."

"What about the other one?"

"Phil Boswell. You'd really like *her*. She told us she recently worked for a vet and loves animals, especially cats."

"Then she has to be nice!"

"She is. You should come down and meet her. Somehow I think the two of you would really hit it off." I drew a breath and smoothed back my hair. Before Gillian could say anything, we saw a woman hurrying down the narrow hall in which we were standing. I'd forgotten about the time, but it had to be almost ten o'clock, making it more than likely that here came Mrs. Rushbridge.

"Ah, there you are, Gillian. And this must be Mrs. Haskell." The words came out in a series of gasps as she drew up in front of us.

"Am I late?" I asked, catching some of her obvious panic.

"Not at all, just in time." She looked down, as if searching for something, before vaguely extending a hand in my direction. "So good of you to fill in for me at such short notice. Going to the dentist is never any fun, is it?"

"I hope it's nothing major."

"I've been having some trouble with one at the back. Been

taking aspirin and applying a warm compress. My own fault for delaying my six-month checkup, but I hate all the poking around and those suction drains in the mouth and the hygienist talking the whole time and seeming to expect answers." She turned to fluster at Gillian. "Hurry along now, dear, the rest of the girls are already in place. Mustn't dilly-dally. Of course, I do need to explain a few things to Mrs. Haskell before I bring her in and introduce her."

"Yes, Mrs. Rushbridge." Gillian took off at speed down the hall.

It hadn't occurred to me that she would be in the—my—Home Skills class, although it should have. It explained why she would be a candidate to fetch me, or had there been more to Mrs. Battle's selection of her? A desire for me to get better acquainted with the girl? I didn't allow myself to consider the reason, should that be the case. Ariel was right. We would have to take Carolyn Fisher-Jones, the girl most closely associated with Gillian, into our confidence.

I concentrated on what Mrs. Rushbridge was saying, which was quite a lot about nothing very much, the gist being that this particular class, made up of those members of the upper fourth who weren't studying art history, were all quite keen on sewing. Most of them were, that is; others preferred to stick things on with glue: sequins on silk cushions—well, not real silk, that would be too expensive, but that sort of look. If I were to talk on fabric design, that might be of interest . . . or what sort of furniture to put in corners . . . really, whatever I chose would do just fine, and of course I mustn't feel I had to fill up every single minute. Her voice went on, scattering words in incomplete sentences punctuated at random with harried exclamations and wild glances at her watch.

The name Rushbridge couldn't have fitted her better. It would have been apparent to a blindfolded person that she was the sort who would appear rushed even when sitting looking out the window, forever crossing bridges before she came to them, always so far ahead of herself that she got behind. I found myself warming to her. She was an average-sized woman who perhaps appeared a little bigger than she was because of the bulky sweater and thickly pleated plaid skirt she was wearing. Both of them were winter items, giving the impression that she had grabbed the first things her hands had touched when reaching into the wardrobe. Here was a woman who saw to the basics and left the rest to nature. Even her graying hair looked in need of a comb. Her rounded face, which should have been jolly, had the appearance of permanent worry and near-constant panic, but the kindness came through in little bursts, like sunshine though an overcast sky.

"Are you sure you're not nervous, dear?" When we finally took off in Gillian's wake, she edged me into the wall with her hurrying walk. "No collywobbles? You only have to say, and I'll put off the dentist till whenever. Perhaps it's not the best time for me to go anyway. As you know, we've all been so upset about the missing Loverly Cup. The other day I read an article in a magazine that said it is ill advisable to have any medical procedure done during times of stress. I'd be tempted to back out of this appointment if I weren't afraid I'd regret it."

"Better not."

"You're right." She cupped a hand a few inches from her cheek. "Ariel Hopkins is in this group. I understand she's some sort of relative of yours. Ah, here we are! And there goes the bell! No need to have fretted that we wouldn't be on time." As the piercing sound subsided, she pushed open the farthest door on our left and sailed in ahead of me.

I had been prepared for a rush of memories on entering a St. Roberta's classroom. There was familiarity in the expanse of white walls and wide windows and the pale wood of the desks and bookcases. But I didn't see myself in any of the girls in the yellow blouses and bottle-green skirts who got to their feet to stand like statues until Mrs. Rushbridge gave them permission to be seated. It came to me that I had felt nothing much on passing Mrs. Battle's office. What emotion I experienced now was the equivalent of returning to a department store that I had once frequented, nothing more.

Time had turned back for me with the arrival of Dorcas at Merlin's Court. On the drive to Lower Swan-Upping, seeing Mr. Middleton again, finding Rosemary—and, most importantly of all, Philippa at the Chaplain's House—the past had crowded in: entire vivid scenes, often disturbing. But here I found myself ejected into an alien present. There was no Susan Brodstock or Ann Gamble eager for a whispered conversation behind our exercise books. My connection to this group of girls, with the exception of Ariel, was as remote as that of a person from one of their history books. And, if their indifferent stares were an indication, someone they expected to be considerably less interesting.

Ariel, seated in the back, eyed me sternly through her spectacles, daring me to embarrass her by tripping as I followed Mrs. Rushbridge onto the elevated platform that held her desk. As it happened, I was the one to save that lady from a spill as she collided with her chair. She made a commendable recovery, letting go of my arm without wrenching it off and turning her one small shriek into a fairly convincing laugh.

"A good thing Miss Critchley didn't have me on her lacrosse team this year!" she joked gamely, facing the class while I hovered offside, afraid to move in case the least vibration sent the pens and pencils skittering off her desk.

"Wouldn't have mattered, the way the rest played," shot back a girl in the front row. Her pretty face was marred by a mean-spirited look. "It was a disgrace and wouldn't have happened if Ms. Chips had still been running the show."

I bridled at this blatant attack on Dorcas, and Mrs. Rushbridge flushed all the way up to her forehead. "That's enough, Deirdre!"

So here was Gillian's bully.

"We shouldn't be bothering about what can't be helped," said a snub-nosed girl with curly red hair. "What matters is getting the Loverly Cup back so it can be handed over to the school that won it this time around."

"That shouldn't be hard if the culprit had the guts to do the right thing, and I think we've all got a pretty good idea who that person is." Deirdre did not turn her head, nor did anyone else, but I saw Gillian grip the sides of her desk, and Carolyn Fisher-Jones—whom I suddenly recognized from my glimpse of her coming out of the building yesterday—bit her lip before looking down.

Mrs. Rushbridge shifted uncomfortably. "If you have any accusations to make, Deirdre, you should talk to Mrs. Battle,"

"Deirdre doesn't know anything," retorted the red-haired girl. "She's just being spiteful, hoping she'll get someone to crack."

"And what's wrong with that?" a voice from the middle piped up. "It's awful the way things are—everyone under suspicion."

"Girls, please!" Mrs. Rushbridge held up both hands. "None of this concerns our guest, whom I have the pleasure of introducing." A nod and a smile in my direction. "This is Mrs. Haskell, and she is one of our old girls. She's staying at the Chaplain's House. Mrs. Battle thought you might benefit from hearing her talk about her experiences as an interior designer. I'm sure she has lots of tips to share about making our homes look pretty. So many of our girls go on to interesting careers, and I think hers has to be both fulfilling and fascinating."

Mrs. Rushbridge waved me forward before making a flying exit, leaving a trail of words in her wake.

Ariel was making eyes at me behind her spectacles; it was time to get on with the task at hand before the girls started throwing spitballs. I heard myself talking, explaining that an interest in art, without sufficient talent to set myself apart from the crowd, had led to my career choice.

"Why couldn't Mrs. Rushbridge have given us the firefighter or the actress?" Deirdre Dawson lolled back in her chair. "Either of those would have been worth hearing."

"Because no one from either of those professions is currently staying at the Chaplain's House." I kept a light rein on my voice.

"Mrs. Battle's secretary said—"

"She may have been thinking of another occasion. There must be a lot of coming and going at the Chaplain's House."

"In spurts," said the redheaded girl, "and then for weeks on end it's empty."

"Except for the Gray Nun nipping in to make herself a cup of tea because there isn't an electric kettle in the convent ruins," someone added.

Carolyn Fisher-Jones raised her hand and at my nod said, "I think yours has to be an exciting job, Mrs. Haskell, and seeing that one day we're all likely to have homes of our own, decorating is something we need to know about." A good-looking girl, with her healthy glow and thick fair hair, and a nice one too, I decided.

"It *is* rewarding to bring all the elements together, including color and fabrics, to make an inviting space."

"My parents always talk about getting furniture that lasts," said a dark serious-eyed girl seated in the row by the windows. "But how can you be sure that what you buy won't fall apart after a few years?"

"People get what they pay for." Deirdre patted a yawn.

I corrected her. "Not always. It helps either to do some research or buy from a reputable establishment that will give your needs and tastes serious consideration."

"That goes without saying." She had now closed her eyes.

"Why don't you sleep," I told her equably, "and let the rest of us make the most of what time is left before the bell rings." Ariel gave me a thumb's-up and even Gillian smiled.

"What if you're someone who gets tired of stuff quickly?" the red-haired girl asked. "Last year I begged my parents to paint my room purple and let me have a shag rug and lots of fluorescent sparkle. Now I'm sick of it."

"Same here!" someone else piped up. "I was mad on red and now it's my least favorite color."

I explained that exploring options was the basis for establishing individual style, and the incorporation of some neutrals during this process helped ground a room so that changes could be worked in without starting from scratch. Paint was cheap, cushions could be given new covers, and curtains be inexpensively replaced with ones made from sheets. It became apparent, from one question following another, that most of the class was becoming interested.

"Even when you begin to see what you might like long-term," I continued, "you don't have to buy a van load of furniture all at once. Make do with what you have, reinvent it, and buy one good piece at a time, chosen because you really love it. Take your time, acquire some knowledge, and never be persuaded by a salesperson—or an interior designer—into purchasing something that doesn't fit with how you want your home to look."

"Some dissatisfied customers, Mrs. Haskell? Is that why you're in retreat at the Chaplain's House?" Deirdre came spitefully back to life. A couple of girls laughed—her sort always has some staunch admirers—but there was a general murmuring of disapproval. Warmed by this encouragement, I continued cheerfully.

"Furniture kept forever should not include a sideboard that cost the earth and now strikes you as better suited to the Chamber of Horrors. Any questions?"

The serious-eyed girl by the window raised her hand. "I've an aunt who likes everything more or less matching, but I think that's rather boring."

"It doesn't have to be," I said, "not if there's enough individuality to liven things up. It all comes down to personal taste."

"Do you agree with the saying that there's no such thing as bad taste?" This came from a girl who hadn't yet spoken.

"No." I was compelled to honesty. "I think that's—"

"Codswallop!" Ariel giggled delightedly. "Dad and Betty have friends who've just had their bedroom done up. It looks like something for a teenager on drugs. They used blindingly bright colors—lime green and citrus yellow with lots of black and purple squiggles on the furniture—and the carpet has ice-cream cones painted all over it. That's the theme, an ice-cream parlor. The wardrobe is done up to look like an ice-cream machine. I've never seen anything so stupidly hideous in my life."

"She's funny!" a girl in front whispered to the one sitting next to her.

This exchange and the glances sent Ariel's way pleased me enormously. Not only had she found her feet at St. Roberta's, I sensed she was popular. The members of the class now started talking about rooms they had seen and hated—everyone except Deirdre, who shrugged.

"There's a knack to mixing and matching to achieve a successful eclectic look. You want pieces that provide their own interest but work together. No one piece should stand out so dramatically that you look at it and think, That's wrong."

"Would you please give us an example?" the redheaded girl asked.

"A pair of life-sized pink plastic flamingoes in a room where the ambience is one of restrained elegance. As in Regency with an artful inclusion of contemporary."

"I think I get it. Anything that stops you dead in your tracks," the serious-eyed girl was saying, when the bell rang.

The time had passed surprisingly quickly. I realized I had enjoyed myself more than I had expected. I thanked the class for listening but did not add the hope that they had learned something. It would suit Deirdre Dawson all too well to tell me what a boring waste of time it had been. As I came down from the platform, several girls came up to thank me, including Carolyn Fisher-Jones.

"That was fun, Mrs. Haskell. Mrs. Battle has said that Ariel and I may go out with you to lunch tomorrow, if that's all right with you."

"I'm looking forward to it." I smiled at her as she followed me to the door, with the rest of the girls behind us. They were changing classrooms, she told me. Their next subject was geography, taught by Mrs. Frenton in a room at the end of the main corridor on the ground floor. Ariel tapped me on the shoulder as we mounted the short flight of steps to reconnect with that area.

"Good job, Ellie! I was scared at the beginning that you'd been struck dumb with stage fright, but you did great and didn't let the awful Deirdre rattle you."

"After that encounter"—I laughed—"I'm beginning to think Rosemary was a peach in her school uniform days."

"Rosemary's the Ogress I was telling you about." Ariel tugged at Carolyn's arm. "You absolutely have to meet her. Oh, and look"—turning her head with its governessy coronet—"here comes Gilly. She has to come too, doesn't she, Ellie?"

"Absolutely."

"Come where?" Gillian joined us as the others flowed past and gave a falsely bright smile. There could be no more putting off my visit to Matron.

"To the Chaplain's House. We'll meet all the inhabitants and find out if they have any wildly entertaining stories about their adventures as schoolgirls." Ariel beamed at her.

"Yes, do come down, all of you," I urged.

"I think I will," said Gillian slowly. "Goodbye for now, Mrs. Haskell." She moved away from the other two. "We do have to hurry, or we'll be late for Mrs. Frenton."

Carolyn looked as though she were about to say something to me, but merely waved before pulling Ariel along with her. Had she remembered that Gillian was not included in the invitation to lunch with me tomorrow and didn't want her feelings hurt at being left out? Yes, a nice girl, Carolyn—who, I sensed, would only talk to me about her friend's problems if I could persuade her that I might be able to help.

Taking the entrance stairway up to the first floor, I went past the biology and chemistry labs, absorbing my surroundings. The feeling of space and light that prevailed throughout the building was in evidence: large windows, pale wood doors, highly polished parquet floor. Pictures on the walls representing the local countryside. Wall-mounted cases displaying the work of former or current students. All spick-and-span and polished.

Matron was not in her office, which was just large enough to escape being poky. From the lack of clutter on her desk and the tops of the filing cabinet, I saw she managed to keep herself well organized. No surprise. I remembered her as a woman who defined orderliness and efficiency. I find such people daunting. When around them I'm inclined to feel indolent and sloppy. Smoothing my hair back and giving my sage-green outfit a tug or two, I told myself—before Mrs. Malloy could do so—not to be a ninny, excused myself as I brushed past the wastepaper basket, and knocked on the door opening from the office into the San.

Surely here I would experience stronger emotions than the Home Skills room had produced. Seeing the white-covered beds and the arched door leading to the outdoors did bring its sharp reminder of Philippa lying still and alone, but even when I looked up at the rectangle of window high on the wall to my right it was the *now* that predominated. Should I confess to Philippa my part in her unjust punishment?

When Matron closed the medicine cupboard door and came toward me, I searched her face for some sign that she would be the sort of great-aunt capable of putting the world to rights for a fourteen-year-old girl.

"Ellie . . . Ellie Haskell?"

"Good morning, Matron."

"Good to see you again after all these years." Her handshake was firm without being crushing, as Dorcas's tend to be. The smile was there, attended by the right display of welcome, but her eyes struck me as hard and the set of her jaw suggested a woman who would not readily accept disagreement. In fact, she was very much the way I remembered her: a sizably built woman in a blue overall. Hair turned from gray to white. A good perm, Mrs. Malloy would have said. An exterior that should have been a cozy complement to her bustling movements but wasn't. I hadn't liked her, and Carolyn Fisher-Jones had gone so far as to describe her as evil. A slanted viewpoint from Gillian's close friend. It could hardly be said that my opinion was unbiased.

"I don't expect you to remember me, Matron," I said, as, at her suggestion, I sat down in one of two chairs with a small white enamel-topped table between them. "Regrettably, I was the girl who broke Ms. Chips's nose with the lacrosse ball."

"These things happen." She adjusted a roll of bandages before seating herself. "I remember the incident and am afraid I was far too hard on you. Here is my chance to apologize." She drew in a breath, and her face and eyes appeared softer, more kindly. "Forgive me at this late stage. I allowed my fondness for Marilyn Chips to get in the way of fairness to you."

"That's understandable."

"Most often she's Chippy, to the staff as well as the girls talking among themselves. My relationship with her is rather different. We've been friends since our own schooldays."

"I'd heard that."

"It is more on her behalf than for any other reason that I am sick at heart over the theft of the Loverly Cup. Breaking the news to her was hard, but I knew if I didn't do it someone else would. It is typical of her that she is troubled over who may have taken it and the repercussions she—and it surely has to be a she—will face."

Hearing the distress in her voice caused me to wonder if I had been too quick in assessing her character. She couldn't help the pebble-brown eyes, decided jaw, and thin lips. I did the same thing with houses, I realized—took a look at the outside and formed an opinion, sight unseen, of what the interior was like. Because the houses in Tingwell had presented dismal fronts I'd found it hard to imagine people living joyfully within their walls. Those surrounding the green here had seemed built for days of endless happiness, but Mr. Middleton had known the grief of his wife's death in his warmly welcoming house, and just next door Ms. Chips was contending with her own worries.

"We've been through a lot together over the years," Matron was saying. "I think it says volumes about the strength of our friendship that it has endured."

I looked at her inquiringly.

"If the bond hadn't been so strong, we'd have given up on each other years ago. The strange thing is we're so different, Marilyn and I—not all that much in common, some would say." She picked up the roll of bandages and moved it from one hand to the other. "Marilyn was always keen on physical activity, while I was more the bookworm. When we were seventeen and in our final year of school, I agreed to go hiking with her on Dartmoor. We got trapped in bad weather overnight, with the result that I came down with pneumonia and was unable to take my A levels."

"What a blow! At that age a setback can seem the end of the world."

"I shouldn't be taking up your time reminiscing when I know, as do the rest of the staff, why you are here. Not that I think I can be of any help to you in your search. But at least let me get you a cup of coffee." Matron went to stand up.

"Thank you, I'm fine." My heart did go out to her. Life can chisel hard lines into a face. "Please, I'd like to hear more."

"What a nice woman you've become!" She set aside the bandage roll. "The devastating part was that my parents couldn't afford to send me back for another year. Night school would have been an option, but a few months later my father died unexpectedly, and as I was the one at home—my sister Gloria being away at teachers training college—I became my mother's emotional support, along with helping out with the household expenses. She couldn't deal with being left alone in the evenings, so there went my chance of going on to university. It didn't help that Marilyn blamed herself for urging me to go on that hike, knowing I wasn't the outdoors type."

"At that age we want so desperately to please our friends."

Matron sat with clamped jaw staring into space. "Salt in the wound, every time she brought it up. I felt she was easing her conscience at my expense."

I looked up at the window high on the wall, and knew I must not allow myself to do the same with Philippa.

"I'd wanted to be a doctor for as long as I could remember. When my mother died a couple of years later, I went in for nursing, second best but as close as I could get to the old dream. And through all the changes Marilyn and I remained friends; she stopped dwelling on the past when I met my future husband, a lab technician at the hospital where I trained. And then she fell in love and got married."

Unbidden came the image of Ms. Chips walking down the aisle carrying her lacrosse stick in lieu of a bouquet.

"His parents hadn't been keen on the match from the word go, and at the reception I committed the terrible indiscretion of telling the mother about Marilyn's family history." Matron again picked up the roll of bandages and squeezed it hard.

"How did that happen?" I hoped nothing in my manner

revealed how appalled I was at hearing her say this, despite already knowing what Carolyn Fisher-Jones had told Ariel.

"The woman collared me and began making some very condescending remarks about Marilyn and I lost my temper, saying she should be delighted to have a daughter-in-law of character, a devoted supporter of her mentally ill mother and grandmother. When I saw the look on her face, I could have bitten off my tongue."

"Did Ms. Chips blame you for her marriage ending before it began?" It seemed to me inevitable, but here were these two women all these years later.

"I didn't see how she could ever forgive me. For all her virtues, Marilyn was one to harbor resentments, and in this case she had every reason. But she was always staunchly fair. When I explained how the conversation had come about, she said she understood and I should not continue to berate myself."

"As she had done about the hiking incident?"

Matron looked at me with those polished stone eyes. "The two situations were very different. In time I recovered from my unhappiness; poor Marilyn never did. That brief love never faded. The ache in her heart was always there. Also, she had wanted children, which was never a priority of mine, although when the chance came to do something for Gillian, my sister Gloria's granddaughter, I was pleased to do so. Marilyn's students helped fill her void; she told me many times that perhaps it was a mistake to make them her substitute offspring, but under the circumstances. . . ."

I sat silent.

"You can see, I'm sure, from what I've told you that only the deepest affection has enabled our friendship to survive. When my husband died and I found myself with very little money, it was Marilyn who recommended me for this post. . . . But back to you, Ellie. I was never more relieved than when Mrs. Battle informed the staff that she was bringing someone in to investigate. That cup needs to be returned. But I agree with Marilyn in wondering at what price."

"Is there nothing that suggests who may have taken it?"

"I take care of the girls when they're not feeling well or are injured; I can't be expected to know them as well as their teachers do." Matron was back to looking steely-faced—on the defensive—angry possibly with herself for believing she had to protect someone at the expense of loyalty to St. Roberta's. I still wasn't sure I liked her—indeed, there was something repellent about the pebble eyes, making it all the more important to give her an unbiased hearing when it came to her great-niece.

"I hate to bring it up, but I've met Gillian and I'm really concerned about her nervous state. Do you think she might be responsible?" Something inside me quivered on meeting those eyes, but Matron's response reminded me I was ever quick to judge. So much for my resolution not to focus on externals!

"I'm the problem, not the Loverly Cup. It's become increasingly clear that I should never have interfered in Gillian's life. As for my reasoning, it seemed sound at the time. She's incredibly gifted musically. Neither her parents nor her grandmother—my sister Gloria—could afford a top-notch education for her, while here was I at St. Roberta's, perfectly placed to lend a hand. But now I'm not sure I haven't made another miscalculation in my well-meaning interference. I've done all the wrong things. I can only hope that the results won't be as disastrous—"

She was not allowed time to finish, but I suspected she would have clammed up anyway. The door to the San was pushed open, and a girl with a makeshift bandage on her right arm was propelled forward by the red-haired girl from the Home Skills class.

"Excuse us, but Wendy felt faint in class and Mrs. Frenton asked me to bring her to you."

"Leave her to me, Elizabeth." Matron was on her feet at once, with an apologetic smile in my direction. "May we continue this conversation at another time, Mrs. Haskell?" It was a dismissal and I departed, like a first former instructed to go and get started on her nature study project.

11

On my way down the main staircase to the reception hall, I consoled myself that getting much more out of Matron concerning Gillian might have been like trying to yank out her teeth with a pair of pliers, gaining her cooperation only after hitting her over the head with a hammer. *And you're supposedly here to solve a crime, not commit one*, Mrs. Malloy informed me snidely.

It was a crying shame she wasn't present to take command of the investigation, but I was remarkably on point in thinking about dentistry, because who should I see as I came down the last step, but Mrs. Rushbridge entering through the outside door?

"Hello!" I greeted her like a long-lost friend. "How did your appointment go?"

She stopped like a car screeching to a halt at a red light. "Mrs. Haskell!" A spiral skid brought her around to face me. "I'm feeling no pain at the moment. The dentist gave me something to numb the area, but he said there's an abscess affecting two teeth and they'll have to come out. He'll take care of that tomorrow. Luckily I don't take classes on Tuesdays, but I'm on dorm duty in the evening."

"Will Mrs. Battle find someone to relieve you?"

"Oh, yes! Or I could ask Mrs. Frenton myself. She's a sweet young woman with time on her hands since the divorce. Such a shame; but someone else—really fine this time—will come along. Such a beautiful face and figure. I can't help thinking it would be nice if she and Dr. Roberts were to fall for each other. He's the school doctor, so they're bound to meet every now and then. My dentist's assistant put the idea in my head. She said she'd seen the two of them talking together after church one Sunday, and wouldn't they make a lovely couple."

"Really?" I tried to sound pleased while thinking about Philippa.

"Mrs. Perkins has been with the dentist for years. She's a nice person and would have a lovely smile if she wasn't missing her front teeth. Not what you'd expect from a person in her job, but it does say a lot about the dentist being an equal-opportunity employer. Even so, as I said to Mrs. Brown in the waiting room, you'd have thought he'd have talked the woman into having that gap fixed."

"Mrs. Brown?"

"Lady Loverly's housekeeper. Just minutes before her name was called she was saying that perhaps Mrs. Perkins had seen too much on the job and was afraid of the injections and the sound of the drill. To which I replied that surely in such cases the patient could be given a general anesthetic, although it wasn't something I'd want after hearing from a nurse friend of mine some of the revelations people make when they're going under or coming out—from what she said, you might just as well leave your tell-all diary lying round for someone to read. And it was really very odd." Mrs. Rushbridge stared at me as if looking for answers. "Mrs. Brown turned the most awful color. I thought she was going to faint, but she got up, very slowly, and left."

"Do you know her well enough to bring it up the next time you see her?"

The members of the Board of Governors scowled down from their portraits. No doubt they thought it cheek that I, a woman who had never banged a gavel in her life, was getting to ask the pertinent questions while they couldn't so much as twiddle their thumbs.

"Not really. Mrs. Brown's a reserved woman. Devoted to her ladyship, from what Elizabeth Anderson, the redheaded girl you may have noticed in this morning's class, told me. Last year Elizabeth visited the Hall quite frequently with Carolyn Fisher-Jones. But that stopped and I wondered why. They're both such nice girls."

Could the reason have something to do with Aiden Loverly? Had he been as rude to Elizabeth as he had been to Gillian?

"Mrs. Mossop might be someone I could ask. She knows Mrs. Brown quite well." Mrs. Rushbridge brightened and sobered between one breath and the next. "Admittedly, her husband's a good worker, but that's never been the be-all and end-all, has it?"

"I suppose not."

"He doesn't allow her a thought of her own. She's got a homeless sister she's not permitted to see. Apparently she's been living on the streets in the worst part of Tingwell." Mrs. Rushbridge lowered her voice. "Drink, that's the poor soul's problem. From what's said, that is, you'd think to hear Mr. Mossop talk he'd never touched a drop in his life, when the truth is he keeps a bottle of whisky in his shed."

Clearly Mrs. Rushbridge's tooth problems weren't making speech unbearable, so I didn't feel bad in seizing the moment to ask if she had any thoughts on the disappearance of the Loverly Cup.

"So distressing." She now looked in pain. "I keep hoping it was an accident . . . that whoever took it out of the display case just wanted to look at it and—hearing someone coming—panicked and made off without putting it back. A number of the girls—a dozen or more, I gather—complained to their teachers of having stomach upsets after lunch last Monday, the day it was taken, and were sent to Matron. I had a couple in my class. If anyone of that group passed the assembly hall and saw the cabinet door open. . . ." She paused significantly.

"Mrs. Battle told me Mrs. Mossop insisted she had relocked it after cleaning inside."

"We all get confused at times, don't we? Not that I'm saying she did forget . . . but I do remember going to my window early that afternoon and seeing her standing talking to someone on the lawn and looking—from the way she was gesticulating—extremely worked up."

"Could you see who the other person was?

"Mrs. Mossop was in front, but I assumed it was her husband."

I said that life at St. Roberta's did not lack interest.

"True enough! Ah, here she comes now."

"Mrs. Mossop?"

"No, dear, Mrs. Frenton. If you'll excuse me, I'll go ask her about taking my dorm duty and inquire about her new puppy. A girl that stunning should have been an actress, don't you think?" Mrs. Rushbridge sped away to corner a young woman at the other end of the entrance hall.

From where I remained, some yards distant, it was evident the blond beauty might have caused even the bad-tempered Mr. Mossop to set aside his pruning shears and fantasize about being fifty again. And this puts the wind up his wife. I was considering Mrs. Battle's reaction to having a femme fatale on staff when her office door opened and out she came.

"Ellie, I was on the phone to Matron and she told me she'd

just been talking to you, so I thought I'd try to catch you on your way out. Do come in." She waved me forward. "I have Mr. Middleton's sister with me. She drove him here for his afternoon classes and would like a word if you have time."

"Of course." I followed her into the office, where Ruth Middleton stood looking every bit as comfortably reassuring as she had yesterday. "Hello." I smiled at her. "How nice to see you again."

"And you. I'd planned on going down to the Chaplain's House to see you, but Mrs. Battle said you had taken over the Home Skills class for Mrs. Rushbridge and might still be on the premises."

"I've told Miss Middleton the real reason for your presence, so there's no reason for you to feel awkward when conversing." The Battle-ax's hooded eyes took in every feature of my face. "I trust you are making some progress in the investigation?" She might have been asking me if I thought there was any likelihood of my passing the advanced physics exam. I strove to look hopeful yet modest while mentally donning my school uniform.

"These things take time." This sounded pitifully lame to my own ears, but before I could hang my head in shame, Ruth Middleton spoke cheerfully.

"I wondered, Ellie, if you'd like to go out for lunch before I come back to collect my brother when his classes are done, which should be"—she glanced at her watch—"in just over an hour."

"I'd love to." My smile must have got into Mrs. Battle's eyes, causing her to blink before adjusting the small clock on her immaculately tidy desk.

"By the way, Ellie, I regret ending our interview abruptly yesterday. Mr. Bumbleton had come to inform me that he'd spoken by phone to his granddaughter, China, and she had informed him that one of the girls had taken a tumble on the Dribbly Drop, which because of its hazardous steps is forbidden territory. I suppose we must be grateful that China would seem not to have mentioned the Loverly Cup." She inclined her head, and taking this as dismissal I looked inquiringly at Ruth.

Moments later she and I headed outside in the direction of the parking area. Her elderly blue car had plush-covered seats that looked comfy enough for a nap, and after my broken night, the temptation was one to which I might easily have succumbed. Having fastened my seat belt, I waited until Ruth had taken off down the drive before speaking.

"Do you think from what you know of her that Lady Loverly will be very upset about the cup?"

"Somehow I don't think so. It's Marilyn's feelings that worry me more. Of all the sports programs, lacrosse meant the most to her, and she'll hate to see it tarnished in any way. If something like this had to happen, any other year would have been better."

"Because of the new gymnasium?"

"It means so much to her. On its own account and because the money came from the man she loved." Ruth drove with a placid competence that would in my judgment characterize most of her activities. "Lady Loverly is a splendid woman, but not the sort to look closely into any unpleasantness. I suppose that's the only way she survived marriage to her alcoholic husband and—shortly after his death—the loss of her son, who'd rarely come home to visit."

"Aiden's father?"

"That's right. And, like Aiden, an only child."

"How sad for her ladyship."

"With so little family, it's hardly surprising she's learned to turn a blind eye to those closest to her. I've done it myself." Ruth turned on her turn indicator. "Every time Clive goes up Ms. Chips's apple tree to bring Harpsichord down, I pretend I'm not petrified he's going to fall. At his age it could be serious, I won't let myself think fatal." We were now out on the main road, passing the Dribbly Drop leading to the convent ruins and

Lilypad Lane. To their rear was the Chaplain's House. Would Phil be on her own or had Rosemary and Tosca returned? The hands of my watch pointed to five minutes past one.

"Do you always drive your brother to work?" I asked Ruth.

"He hasn't been able to get behind the wheel since Anya was killed." She glanced at me, her expression sad. "That may seem odd, with him not being present when she was knocked down—he was fetched to the scene—but that's how it took him. He's an incredibly sensitive man. I suppose it's the musician in him." Her face sobered. Was she thinking of Gillian as well as her brother?

Ruth hesitated, giving Mrs. Malloy the opportunity to get back inside my head: *Spit it out for goodness' sake! You're here to investigate, Mrs. H, not to win a popularity contest.*

"Ask me whatever you like," continued Ruth comfortably. "If I don't want to answer I'll say so. I imagine whatever it is has to do with the Loverly Cup, and Mrs. Battle did give you the go-ahead to talk to me."

"Do you think Gillian might have taken it to sell in order to raise the money to get home?"

"I'll have to think about that." Ruth sounded surprised but not the least outraged.

"This morning she asked me if I had ever thought of running away when I was at St. Roberta's, and the first thought that popped into my head was that any child that unhappy would write or phone their parents and ask to come home, but—"

"Taking action would create a fait accompli. Even if her parents thought it best to send her back, the school wouldn't likely agree." Ruth nodded. "Yes, I do see Gillian thinking along those lines, and she has been particularly unhappy this past week. Clive has mentioned it to me."

"One of the old girls staying at the Chaplain's House tried to get herself expelled by stealing several pairs of knickers from a London store. At that age everything seems so desperate, doesn't it?"

"And the most bizarre actions seem reasonable. Even so, I just can't picture Gillian going through with it. She's not the sort to upset her cat, let alone the rest of her family, and I can't believe she'd risk her musical future." Ruth overtook a car and cut a broad swath around a motorcycle that brought Aiden Loverly back to mind. I still wanted him as the Cup Culprit. I wondered if his poor grandmother knew about the gambling.

"Another thought," I said, "is that whoever took the cup did so to upset Ms. Chips."

"The idea has crossed my mind; Clive's too, for that matter. Who would care more deeply than she about the ensuing embarrassment to St. Roberta's? Not even Mrs. Battle, in our opinion." Ruth drew up outside a whitewashed and timber teashop with ye olde lettering above the door. "I thought we'd eat here if you're agreeable. They do a marvelous Welsh rarebit along with a variety of other things, including fish-and-chips."

"That sounds wonderful."

"I often stop here after dropping Clyde off. It makes a nice change from poached eggs at home."

A bell jangled at our entry. Most of the small tables were taken, but we found one to ourselves by the window and within moments of settling ourselves were approached by a motherly looking waitress who took our orders with the promise that she would be back in a jiffy with a pot of tea.

"You're being so nice, just as you were yesterday," I told Ruth. "I hope I didn't upset you with my talk of Gillian."

"Don't worry. We have to consider the possibility that the cup was taken by someone very unhappy at school or by an otherwise disgruntled party. Someone, perhaps as you suggest, with a grudge against Marilyn." She smiled up at the waitress, who had returned not only with our tea but also with two plates of Welsh rarebit. "Which might seem to put Clive right in the mix."

I stared at her over the bud vase on the table.

"Clive and Marilyn being such good friends, some people

may have expected that Chippy would use part of her inheritance to endow music scholarships for girls such as Gillian. That would certainly have pleased Clive enormously, but he understood. What others may not know is she told him that she had taken care of that in her will. The cost of the new gymnasium was enormous and she had to keep enough to live on; it would be unreasonable to expect her to give everything away during her lifetime. How's the Welsh rarebit?"

"Delicious."

"Our waitress is new here, but I know I've seen her somewhere else. Any room left for a pudding?"

"That coffee and walnut cake in the glass case looks delectable."

"Take my word from experience, it is. Let's each have a slice."

"We could share," I offered, while pouring more tea into our cups.

"No, let's be greedy. Life is short. I used to hope that Clive and Marilyn would get together." Her smile was a little wistful. "But they are both the one-love one-lifetime kind. As for myself, I've been reasonably content to stay single. Moving in with Clive seemed a sacrifice at the time, but I enjoy our life together. And we do have Harpsichord to provide excitement."

We had started talking about the peccadilloes of cats when the motherly waitress returned. She declared the coffee and walnut cake was an excellent choice and was about to head off to fetch it when Ruth stopped her.

"Your face is so familiar."

"I was thinking the same about you." The woman cocked her head. "I've only been here a few days after taking a break from work for a couple of years. Before that, I used be a barmaid at the White Dog. That's the pub on the corner of—"

"I know it." Ruth included me in her pleased expression. "My brother and his wife used to take me there for a meal when I'd come to stay with them for the weekend. But I haven't been back since I moved to the area eight—no, it must be nine years ago."

"Nice living near family. Get on well with your sister-in-law, do you?" The woman sounded as if she had a problem one.

"Sadly, she died."

"Ooh, dear!" This with that look of pleasurable expectancy even nice people get when getting to hear about someone else's tragedy. "What was it, cancer? Or the heart? There never seems to be any getting round those two, does there? Doctors aren't gods, although most of them think they are. You wouldn't believe what they put my old mother through when she went into hospital the last time. She told them it couldn't be hemorrhoids because she'd had them removed."

"It was an accident." Ruth's restless stirring in her seat suggested she wished she'd not embarked on discovering where she and the waitress had previously connected.

"Car?"

"A hit-and-run. She was out for an evening walk."

The speculative eyes widened. "I remember. . . . She was a musician, a violinist; that's right, isn't it? It was the talk of Lower and Upper Swan-Upping and an especially big topic at the White Dog. Everyone kept saying how for ages they'd expected to hear that Sir Henry Loverly had been knocked down, staggering across the parking area after closing. Many a time left to himself, he wouldn't have reached the road. But well ahead of time, on nights no one was willing to drive him home, someone—probably Mr. Lemming that managed the place—would ring over to the Hall and ask her ladyship or the grandson—after he reached driving age and happened to be there—to come and fetch the old guzzler."

"At least we know it wasn't Sir Henry who killed from behind the wheel."

"There is that!" It wasn't clear from the waitress's voice if she felt a silver lining, however thin, rather spoiled things. She went and fetched our cake, which clearly Ruth no longer wanted.

Looking at her watch, she said she still had ample time before returning to the school to pick up her brother, but I said I was ready to leave if she was. We were on our way out when we saw Ms. Chips deep in conversation with a woman seated across from her at the table nearest the door, a woman in her middle to late sixties, with a plain large-featured face and coarse graying hair scraped back into a bun.

"Hello, Marilyn." Ruth took a smiling step toward them. "And how are you, Mrs. Brown? Recovered from your migraine, I hope?"

She might as well have asked if there was a cobra hidden in the serviceable black handbag. The effect was the same: a shrinking deeper inside the beige cardigan.

"We haven't seen each other for a while, and this being such a lovely day we decided to treat ourselves to lunch out." Ms. Chips's smile made up for the fact that Ruth's had been blotted from her face. She said the usual things—hoped we'd enjoyed our meal, to which Ruth replied that we must let them get back to enjoying theirs before it got cold. As they had plates of salad in front of them, this made no sense, and the moment we got outside she eyed me in bewilderment.

"That was Lady Loverly's housekeeper. She's usually quite normal. Always inclined to be glum but not as though she'd like to slide under the table. Being plagued with headaches has to be awful. Easygoing as Lady Loverly seems, it must be hard to be at someone's beck and call, and who knows what other stress she may have in her life."

"Mrs. Rushbridge mentioned sitting next to Mrs. Brown in the dentist's surgery this morning and having her scurry away between one sentence and the next of their conversation."

"I suppose we've all been tempted to make a dash for the door at the thought of the drill. I'm probably worrying unnecessarily, but there was something about that look on her face just now that rather put the wind up me."

We got into the car and headed back to St. Roberta's. On approaching a thatched cottage nestled behind a honeysuckle hedge on a side street, we saw a dark green Jeep parked outside.

"That belongs to Brian Roberts," Ruth said. "He's such a dear man, as dedicated as his father was before him. He'll be making a house call." As she spoke, the front door opened and the doctor came down the path, wearing slacks and a light sports jacket and carrying his doctor's bag.

Stopping the car just short of the gate, Ruth rolled down her window and waved, and he came toward us. His pleasant greeting warmed his rugged features, making him handsome. He asked with interest how I was enjoying my stay at the Chaplain's House, and I said I was settling in nicely, to which he responded that he had met Tosca at the Boots pharmacy counter that morning.

"She told me she's trying to give up smoking." He shifted the bag from one hand to the other. "A very spirited, amusing woman; I enjoyed chatting with her."

"Yes, she seems lots of fun."

"And what a delightful name," said Ruth.

"But is she fond of opera?" Brian Roberts raised an amused eyebrow.

"I don't know." I smiled back at him. "I barely remember her from our schooldays."

"Speaking of people not seen in a while." Brian Roberts maintained his light manner. "Tosca mentioned that one of the other guests newly arrived at the Chaplain's House is Philippa Boswell. How is she?"

"As nice and pretty as ever." I took my cue from his manner, keeping my voice airy.

"That's good to hear." He shifted the bag again, then glanced at his watch. "Glad to have seen you, but I shouldn't be keeping you."

"If you have a minute"—Ruth leaned a little farther out her

window—"we just saw Mrs. Brown having lunch with Marilyn Chips, and I'm a little worried." She explained concisely, but anxiety threaded through her voice.

"I'm glad Marilyn was with her. If anyone can get a troubled person to open up, it's that good woman."

Ruth smiled ruefully as we drove off. "He's right, of course, Marilyn does have the velvet ear. I really have tried with Mrs. Brown, but she always shies away."

"Is Lady Loverly kind to her?" I asked.

"In an absentminded way but with a deep underlying affection, I would say. Her ladyship's clothing and manner can make her seem a bit batty, but she's a warmhearted woman. When Marilyn Chips's marriage ended abruptly so soon after the wedding, her ladyship—who was connected to the groom's family—aligned herself with Marilyn and had her stay at the Hall while she recovered emotionally. That visit lasted a couple of months, and Marilyn has told me the respite was her salvation. It inspired her to suggest to Mrs. Battle that the vacant Chaplain's House be used as a retreat for old girls who needed somewhere to go while sorting themselves out. It's also the reason Lady Loverly can't stand Matron."

"Who told me she spilled the beans to the bridegroom's mother about Ms. Chips's mother and grandmother suffering from mental illness."

Ruth nodded. "And that was that."

We continued talking until suddenly we were back at St. Roberta's and Ruth was parking the car.

"Thank you so much," I said as we got out. "I've really enjoyed this time with you."

"Same here! Let's do it again before you leave, and if at any time I can be of help do give me a ring. Promise?"

"Promise!"

I watched her go into the school and was about to wend my way back to the Chaplain's House when—with my mind on friendships—I had a sudden vivid memory of myself, Susan Brodstock, and Ann Gamble laughing and talking in the junior common room in our free time between end of class and beginning of prep. My head teemed with remembered snippets of delightfully silly conversation. And for the first time since arriving at St. Roberta's I was filled with a glow of nostalgia. Before I knew it, I was mounting the staircase, ignoring the frowning portraits on the wall beside me and moving along a second-floor corridor gleaming with polish and a broad expanse of windows. From behind the common-room door at the end came the murmur of voices.

Turning the handle, I entered a large room painted daffodil yellow. There were pictures on the walls that I remembered: prints of illustrations from *Alice in Wonderland*, *Little Women*, and *The Children of the New Forest*. The scattering of tweedy armchairs also appeared unchanged. But no Susan or Ann was there to share the moment.

My arrival, however, was noted by three girls seated at one of the large round tables dotted around like giant mushrooms. Heads bent toward each other, they had that look of plotting serious mischief that is common to twelve-year-olds—which is what they appeared to be. They rose to their feet as if poked in their backs by Mrs. Battle's ruler.

"Hello. I'm Noreen and these are Jenny and Andrea," said the redhead, who seemed likely to be the leader of any group she was in. Her two companions stared at me with the irritation that comes from being interrupted at the crucial moment of an all-important conversation. I apologized for intruding and urged them to sit back down.

"I'm Ellie Haskell. I didn't think anyone would be here during class time."

"We're taking end-of-term exams this week," piped up Andrea, the fair-haired one, "and as we finished ahead of everyone else, Mrs. Frenton said we could stay here until the next bell rings."

"I suppose we could read," said the dark one, who had to be Jenny and whose straight black brows and surprising dimples brought Ann's image wistfully to mind. "But there's nothing on those bookshelves that isn't too babyish for words or so boring that the only person in our class who'd be interested is the ever-so-clever China Bumbleton." Her pals nodded and giggled agreement. Perhaps sensing they weren't offering me a fully fledged St. Roberta's welcome, Noreen asked if I were one of the old girls staying at the Chaplain's House. And when I acknowledged this, her expression brightened. "Are you the actress?"

"Sorry, I'm afraid there's a misplaced rumor going round. No one that exciting is among us. I'm an interior designer."

"Oh!" The red hair and something in her face reminded me of someone else, one of the girls I had encountered that morning. "You're the one who took Mrs. Rushbridge's Home Skills class this morning. My sister Lizzie said you were really great."

The resemblance clicked into place. "Elizabeth Anderson?"

"Yes. Everyone thinks *she's* so wonderful they can't understand why *I* don't have a halo round my head too. But at least she isn't a smug show-off who thinks everyone else needs taking down a peg like—" She stopped abruptly when the door opened, almost hitting me in the back, and another girl walked around me to march over to the bookcase and pull out a thick volume with a dark cover.

"Thanks for the greeting, China," caroled the other three as one.

"It's class time." She turned to present a solemn, self-important face. "Mrs. Frenton allowed us to leave on trust, and I for one intend to respect that." She wasn't a bad-looking girl, but something about her demeanor suggested that she considered her pudding-basin haircut and thick eyebrows as merit badges, signs she was far too superior to have any interest in her looks.

"Well, bully for you," responded Noreen. "Where are your

manners when it comes to this lady here? Her name's Haskell and she's staying at the Chaplain's House."

"How do you do?" China began leafing through the book she was holding. I was saved from responding by Jenny's rounding on her.

"That was a pretty rotten thing you did, telling your grandfather about Shirley and Miriam on the Dribbly Drop. I expect next you'll be running to tell him that Noreen said it could have been Mrs. Frenton who took the Loverly Cup because she's dating her ladyship's grandson, and he might want to sell it in his antiques shop but knew her ladyship wouldn't let him ask for it back."

"It was a wicked thing to say." China curled her lip. "But of course I'll keep to the code of secrecy on that score. There's a difference between that and Miriam and Shirley's stupidity. A bad fall down the Dribbly Drop and they could have been killed. Grandfather says it's a wonder there hasn't been a fatal accident already. It should be blocked off, but the staff don't want that because it's a shortcut to the bus stop."

"Come on, it's not all that dangerous. Shirley just twisted her ankle, and she could have done that playing lacrosse or hockey. And I hope your grandfather doesn't go blaming Mrs. Battle," Noreen snapped back. "She believes maturity comes from learning to follow the rules."

"I've enjoyed taking a look at the common room again," I said brightly, and added my goodbyes without much hope that anyone was paying attention. A bell began to clang as I started back down the corridor, and on the stairs I got caught up in a march of girls making for the ground floor in an orderly stampede. I was thinking about Aiden Loverly and the luscious Mrs. Frenton as I exited through the front door and saw Ms. Chips crossing the path toward me.

She greeted me pleasantly, and I expected her to continue into the school without further comment, but she stood looking at me with a faintly amused expression in those remarkably beautiful eyes. How ever had I thought her harsh-faced and plain? Suddenly I heard myself babbling that I was the girl who had hit her in the face with a lacrosse ball and broken her nose.

"Well, as you can see it's still here, smack in the middle of my face. But there *is* something I would like to ask you."

"Yes?"

"Where did you go on those Friday afternoons when you weren't at lacrosse or hockey?"

I thought for a minute that my voice had gone into hiding in my feet. "The little sewing room above the San."

"Ah!" A smile flitted across her face. "A perfect retreat for the harassed soul. I've suggested to Mrs. Battle that it be set aside for those times when any girl feels the need to snuggle down on her own for a while. I suppose you read or did some drawing. A better use of your time, I think, than pretending to enjoy something you loathed."

Before I could respond, she remarked that she was doing dorm duty again that night, so Mrs. Rushbridge could get some real sleep despite the troublesome tooth, and moved on.

I watched her enter the school building and decided against returning directly to the Chaplain's House. Instead, I wandered around the grounds, avoiding the playing fields for the rose gardens, where I came upon a bench shaded by a flowering cherry tree. The invitation was irresistible. I sat with the idea of staying put for five or ten minutes, but the air was so fragrantly warm and the twittering of the birds so soothing that I lay back, tucked my hands behind my head and thought about the missing Loverly Cup for all of thirty seconds before sinking into a dead sleep.

I woke to the sound of a heavy buzzing, coupled with the feeling that a swarm of bees was about to descend upon me. When I opened my eyes and struggled first into a sitting position and then to my feet, I found that bottle green and mustard yellow had become the overwhelmingly prominent colors. Girls in uniform skirts and blouses were walking, running, jumping and doing cartwheels with a vigor that struck my groggy state as excessive. Classes were most definitely over for the day. My watch told me I'd slept for over an hour. Hurrying guiltily toward the Chaplain's House, I told myself what I needed was time alone in which to come up with a plan to unmask the Cup Culprit.

Unfortunately, when I opened the front door and stepped into the hall, conversation was flowing from the sitting room. I could have sneaked upstairs, but that would have been rude, and I especially did not want to get on Rosemary's wrong side. Combing a hand through my hair, I opened the door to the sitting room to find her seated in the same chair as on the previous evening. It was now barely four o'clock, but she had a sizable glass of what was undoubtedly gin and tonic in one hand, and a book in the other. Tosca was on the sofa, her arms and legs laced into a cat's cradle. It looked horridly painful, but she was speaking cheerfully.

"It is interesting, what you are reading?"

"It's fast-paced." Rosemary did not lift her eyes.

"And that is good?"

"No! I'd rather it dragged line by dreary line, one excruciatingly boring page after another."

Tosca looked round to where I stood inside the doorway. "You are back, Ellie, to see her at my throat again. It is too bad, don't you agree? I try so hard to get along. In I came after sitting in the garden this afternoon, feeling the best I have been since I gave up smoking. Everything smelled so good. I could taste the earth and the sky. The birds!" Tosca closed her eyes. "How sweetly they sang!"

"Don't they have birds where you come from?" Rosemary lowered the book to eye her nastily.

"Since it is London, yes!"

"Oh, for God's sake! And Ellie, do you have to stand there like Samson holding up the Temple? Either get yourself a drink or sit down!"

"What brought on this sunny mood?" I asked, without budging.

Tosca smiled smugly. "Her husband hasn't phoned. Not once since she got here! She jumps every time there's a ring-ting-a-ling, but it's never for her. Twice for you since I've been back from my drive. A woman, but she wouldn't say who."

"Oh!"

"Probably your personal shopper to say she got the tins of Spam you wanted." Rosemary turned a page. "As for Gerald, I told him not to get in touch except in an emergency. He wasn't happy about it—"

"Doting on the very thought of you as he does!" Tosca undid her legs one foot at a time and stretched her arms above her head.

Rosemary shot up in her chair and flung the book across the room, missing me by inches. "If either of you cares to know why I'm angry as hell"—her voice shook with rage—"it's because somebody has stolen two pairs of my knickers from the drawer I put them in. And don't tell me I've misplaced them!"

I waited for her to say she treasured those knickers.

"Who'd want them?" Tosca asked reasonably.

"You've done it before and were lucky not to get arrested. I expect it's a fetish!"

"But not *your* knickers! I expect they're the sort my great-granny used to wear: stockinet and down to the knees."

"They're silk. Pale blue and purchased in France."

"Don't tell us. They are like gossamer, and you can see right through them. Perhaps for your husband to take his mind off your nose. But me"—Tosca held up her hands imploringly—"I wish not to imagine."

"You're disgusting. I don't believe you're descended from

foreign royalty. No one as uncouth as you could be. I'll bet you live in a slum and eat baked beans out of a tin while watching *East Enders*!"

"I read that the Queen watches that program."

"So you can read? Give me an hour to get over the shock!"

"Where's Phil?" I asked before a body—or two—hurtled my way.

"In the kitchen with some kid."

Ariel? How good it would be to interact with an adult in a child's body, instead of the other way round. I skirted the warring factions. Had I been the sneaking sort I might have considered reporting their behavior to Mrs. Battle. Tosca had been severely provoked. But it would serve Rosemary right to be expelled from the Chaplain's House and sent home in disgrace, to face not only Gerald and the two children but the ghastly consequence, should word leak out, of Laurence the Portuguese Water Dog being banned from swimming competitively in the country club pool.

It wasn't Ariel in the tiny kitchen with Phil. Gillian was sitting on a stool by the sink, holding an apple.

"Hello!" they said together.

"Please, no shouting." I closed the door and leaned against it.

"Let's hope they don't kill each other." Phil's impish smile included Gillian; I was relieved to see the girl had a little more color in her face.

"At the moment I don't think I have it in me to rearrange the furniture to hide the bodies."

"I enjoyed your Home Skills class this morning, Mrs. Haskell. And I thought I'd come and see you like you suggested. I hope it's really all right?"

"You're a sight for sore eyes. Especially with Rosemary and Tosca going at it in the sitting room. Didn't I say you'd enjoy meeting Phil?"

"We've been talking about cats and . . . different things."

"The life of the working girl and its possible hassles," added Phil.

"Perhaps fame and fortune are overrated," I said, and they both eyed me rather sharply, or so it seemed.

"One of my biggest life mistakes," continued Phil, smiling, "was not growing more domesticated, but now I have a sudden urge to learn how to cook. I expect you helped your mother out at home, Gillian. You have the look of a girl who knows her way around a kitchen. People like me who don't know how to hold a tin opener can spot people with that innate ability a mile off."

"I know how to make jam tarts and shortbread, but I'm not really good at dinners yet. Except shepherd's pie; that's easy and I've watched Mummy make it hundreds of times. We always have it on Mondays."

"So did our family. Why don't we search the pantry and the fridge to see what we can round up? I'll do my part by putting on a pinny and handing you things. What about you, Ellie?" Phil looked at me inquiringly.

"You two make a fine team. Isn't there some old saying about too many cooks? I'll go upstairs and read, but it will be my pleasure to sample the results. That is, if you're prepared to share with slackers."

"There's Rosemary and Tosca as well. How many potatoes would that be? And could we use a tin of corned beef for the meat if nothing else presents itself?"

"I don't see why not—Mummy is a great one for improvising. I'd like to stay," said Gillian, "but I have to get back. I only had permission from Mrs. Battle to leave for an hour."

"I'll phone her, if you like, and explain we'll starve down here without your assistance," Phil offered.

The door opened, propelling me into the middle of the kitchen.

"Goodness!" Tosca landed neatly on the one and only chair. "I had to escape before that woman sends me jumping out the window. I would like to pull off her big nose and see how she likes that!"

"Rosemary is very unhappy." Phil had the corned beef in her hands, along with a tin of peas. "I think we need to let part of what she says go over our heads and give her some healing time. That may sound preachy but—"

"You are a nice person, unlike the sinner who is me," quipped Tosca equably. "Ellie"—she crossed her legs in super-advanced yoga technique—"I forgot to tell you Miss Critchley came when I was sitting outside and asked me to tell you she will meet you in the parking area tomorrow at noon, for you to go out for lunch with your little cousin and her friend."

"Thank you." I avoided looking at Gillian, concerned that she would be hurt by not being included, but the purpose of our outing was to try and discover why she was so nervy.

"I hope you enjoyed your day out." Tosca eyed Gillian's apple but did not ask for it. "I had a happy time, especially when I was in Boots, asking the lady at the counter what stop-smoking aids they sold, and who should be standing behind me but a doctor. The loveliest man—very good-looking in a country gentleman way. Like a tree you know will not topple in a storm. We got talking. So nice! And now I have a date for tomorrow night."

"Really?" This was not the moment for me to look at Phil.

"Dinner with the ruggedly handsome doctor. And I think perhaps he can turn my mind off smoking for good. What a good thing I brought with me my naughtiest little black dress!"

The tins of corned beef and peas hit the floor with a dull thud. Before I could finish jumping, the door was shoved open and Rosemary stuck a furious nose into the kitchen. "Two more damn kids have showed up to see you, Ellie: Ariel Hopkins and Carolyn Fisher-Jones, they say. I caught Miss Granny Specs sneaking up the stairs. I expect the other one followed her up and they're still nosing around."

"Ariel wouldn't sneak," I answered hotly. "She'd be looking

for me in my bedroom, expecting me to be holed up with a book." Or more likely trying to think like a detective, I thought, as I headed out in the hall to find the two girls sitting on the bottom stair.

"Sorry," I told them. "Perhaps you'd better come back another time, Rosemary is in a foul mood and out for the blood of English girls."

"Of course," agreed Carolyn. "By the way, Mrs. Haskell, that clock on the landing is wrong."

"Nothing of the sort," bellowed Rosemary from the sitting room. "It's exactly to time."

12

After taking a long hot bath, I phoned Ben before bed. All was going well, he told me cheerfully, but he couldn't remember what day he was supposed to take Tam to the dentist. My pocket calendar was in my handbag, which I hurried to fetch from the bedroom. I am one of those people who can't find the one thing I'm looking for in all those pockets that are supposedly useful for keeping everything organized without digging out everything else. In this case it was my keys, a packet of tissue, my compact mirror, and several pieces of paper that were probably old shopping lists. Having spilled these onto the table by the phone, I finally located the calendar and gave Ben the time of Tam's appointment on Thursday. After a chat with each of the children—who fortunately did not seem to be missing me desperately—I hung up and gathered up the clutter without paying much attention.

Getting into bed, I lay staring at the ceiling long after it was too dark to see more than the shadow of the fluted light fixture.

Thoughts kept crisscrossing each other, most of them regarding Gillian. I hoped she had found a confidante in Phil.

They had served up a really tasty version of shepherd's pie, along with the tinned peas and carrots enlivened by a hint of mint. Ben, who is no cooking snob, would have approved of their enterprise. Even Rosemary begrudgingly conceded it was better than last night's pizza. Tosca had toyed with her portion, pretending at times to smoke her fork. Intermittently I had seen that beleaguered look on Gillian's face and my heart had ached for her.

What fear gripped her? Was Matron worried about her? And if so, how much comfort would she be? The woman wasn't well liked, that much was clear. She appeared hard, and yet didn't her long friendship with Ms. Chips say something positive about her? What was behind the incident of the motorcycle and Gillian? Did Aiden Loverly really suspect her of stealing the Loverly Cup, or had he selected her as a scapegoat because he had seen her as vulnerable on her visits to the Hall?

A snippet of information popped into my head: Dorcas telling me she'd learned from Ms. Chips that Mrs. Brown's migraine might have been caused by Lady Loverly's discovery that a brooch was missing, a brooch received from her husband on their honeymoon. What if Aiden Loverly had stolen it himself? Tosca had indicated that he gambled. Perhaps he was in trouble—as she was—with the loan sharks. I pictured the brooch bursting with diamonds and Aiden craftily feigning outrage at Gillian in front of witnesses. And if he *had* taken the brooch, why not the Loverly Cup, using his girlfriend Mrs. Frenton as his accomplice? In addition to the financial motive, might he not resent the grandmother who had failed to provide a more salubrious setting than Tingwell for his art and antiques business? Perhaps a good part of his merchandise had been sneaked out of the Hall over the years without her ladyship's seeming to notice. But if she were truly fond of that brooch, this might be the time for her to take action.

Turning on my side, I willed myself to sleep. At some point before midnight I dozed off, to wake to the sound of clothes tumbling around in a dryer. Struggling to sit up, I realized that what I was hearing was my heart thudding. I must have had a nightmare; indeed, the vestiges of horror still clung to my mind: someone creeping stealthily up the stairs and along the landing, silence as if the whole house stopped breathing, and then more footsteps to the accompaniment of creaking boards before the sound of a door—the front door—closing. It took several heart-pounding moments to realize I was being a petrified fool. Any one of the other three women in the house could have come up, then gone downstairs for a drink or something to nibble on, and it could as easily have been the sitting room door as the front one.

Settling back down, I dozed off. A shaft of moonlight cut through the gap in the curtains, allowing me to see the bedside clock. I'd slept longer than it seemed because it was now almost two in the morning. I got up to close the curtains, knowing the room needed to be as dark as possible if I was to get back to sleep. The curtains did not want to adjust; I pushed and tugged, with the result that the rod came down in a flurry of fabric. Suddenly I was looking out into the night. There shouldn't have been anything of interest to see in the moonlight, other than the charcoal shapes of trees, but there was. . . . A chill crept down my back. A figure was creeping around the side of the house. It didn't seem likely to be the Gray Nun unless she had given up wearing her habit. I would have welcomed a glimpse of a gauzy veil, but late-night lurkers must be accepted as they are.

It took only moments for me to scramble into the clothes I had set out for the morning, shove my feet into my shoes, and hurry on tiptoe across the landing, down the stairs, and out the front door. No hint of the day's warmth lingered in the air. It was damply cool with a hint of future rain. That was no reason to shiver; I wasn't planning to knit or do crossword puzzles. I should count myself lucky that whoever was out there might provide a break in the case. Suddenly I remembered Shirley and Miriam's reason for breaking the rules and going down the Dribbly Drop. If the person who had taken the Loverly Cup had heard that they thought it might be hidden in the stone bench, she—or he—might be heading for the ruins with the idea of hiding it somewhere safer. Mentally kicking myself for not having already checked out this possible hiding place, I turned the corner of the side of the house under my window.

Real life is not nearly as much fun as reading about an intrepid—if slightly stupid—heroine bent on pre-dawn pursuits. My age was against me. One needs to be no older than nineteen for such adventures. Also, I didn't look the part. I should have been wearing a cloak that billowed behind me, with my hair unraveled from its plait to frame my face in mystery. My progress was slowed when I stubbed my toe on a hidden tree root. Hobbling on, I saw no one and was about to head for the Dribbly Drop when a voice out of nowhere exclaimed fiercely, "You'd scare the life out of anyone, you would!"

There went Mrs. Malloy again. Being used to these mental interruptions by now, I accepted that she had taken up residence in my head; doubtless before long I would be the one told to go because she had squatter's rights. What did scare the life out of me was the pressure of a hand placed on my shoulder. A seriously big shudder moment, this! I opened my mouth to scream, but no sound came out. My voice box must have needed a new battery. Really, I should remember to replace them every six months as per manufacturer's instructions.

"Sometimes you worry me," Mrs. Malloy continued irritably. "Going around in a daze, lost in your own little world! Oh, well"—sounding increasingly huffy—"I guess I shouldn't be surprised at the lack of welcome; it was clear from the start you wanted to hog this case all to yourself. Still, I'd have thought I'd get some sort of welcome after coming all this way. And at a great deal of inconvenience, let me add—seeing as how I had to beg a lift to the station with Mr. Cross down the road—him as always wants something in return and turns awkward when you kick him in the shins, or a bit higher if possible."

I turned slowly, like one of those stiff mechanical figures that revolve under glass domes. This couldn't be happening . . . but it was! There she was in the flesh, wearing one of her taffeta cocktail frocks and a hat she had bought at St. Anselm's Christmas bazaar. A dozen God-fearing pink flamingoes had given their lives for that hat.

"You might try looking pleased to see me, Mrs. H!"

"I am, but you did give me the most awful fright. Why on earth are you wandering around outside the house?"

She heaved a pained sigh. "I was looking for an unlatched window. Being the sensitive sort, I didn't want to go ringing the doorbell at this hour and waking the whole household."

"The front door's never locked because the key can never be found when needed, and no one seems to worry about breaking and entering."

"I'd have thought as that would have changed once the cup was stolen. But never mind that. What about the headmistress? With a name like Battle, I picture her as having a face like the back of a bus."

"Such was your opinion when I was at her flat," I mused and, on seeing her startled look, explained about all the talking she had done in the last couple of days.

"Well, I must say it's good to know I wasn't left behind entirely."

"Not a chance!"

Her damson lips curved in a pleased smile and her iridescent eye shadow gave a much-needed sparkle; that her rouge had faded was no doubt due to the rigors of travel.

"Let's go inside." I preceded her into the hall. "You must be worn out."

'Like I told Melody and her new hubby, it didn't feel right leaving you to risk life and limb while I sat looking at their wedding photos, especially when I wasn't in most of them—not liking to upstage the bride. And much to my surprise, they understood the position perfectly. You could say they couldn't get me out of me own house fast enough. Went on about how they liked the idea of being able to watch what they liked on the telly without feeling they was being pushy. But I wasn't born yesterday. Them two is middle-aged and in love. It's a giddy time in their lives, and there they are at the seaside—aching to run barefoot through the sand without me following behind with the picnic basket." She sighed sentimentally as she ensconced herself in Rosemary's chair and accepted the gin and tonic I handed her. "Let Melody and her Bill be dreamers, Mrs. H. I still like to think of love as being the ever-after sort."

"I wonder if Philippa Boswell feels the same way."

"Who?"

I explained, giving the whole sorry story of my connection to her and the guilt that had consumed me for years. This took time, and when I paused my watch showed it was nearly three in the morning.

"Well, you should've told me," she said kindly. "That way I'd have understood, instead of feeling hurt when you'd have them fits of staring into space instead of asking if I felt up to doing a round with the feather duster after a late night at bingo. And next to me, you should have shared your burden with Mr. H; now's there's a man wouldn't ask his lady love to get up to tricks as would shock the vicar out of his pulpit, like my third husband did till I brought him up short with me fist. Still, what's most important is for you to tell this young woman how you acted the coward and leave it to her whether she wants to hug and make up or clobber you over the head with a frying pan. In the meantime, you'd best fill me in with what else has been going on."

Egged on by Mrs. Malloy's eager and insightful questions, I

poured out all that I could remember of the conversations and accompanying observations of the previous two days. An hour ticked away.

"Seems to me," Mrs. Malloy announced at length, "that this missing Loverly Cup is only a small piece of what's wrong around here. There's another worm in the apple, so to speak. I know that sounds silly, Mrs. H, but I feel it in me bones!"

I was about to say my emotional antennae told me the same thing when the sitting room door was flung open and Rosemary stormed in upon us as if she were still the dorm prefect, righteously determined on catching anyone out of bed in the middle of the night. What a shame for her, if not Mrs. Battle, that she had not been hot on the trail earlier!

"What's all this?" She flung an arm in Mrs. Malloy's direction, popping a button off her bulky quilted dressing gown in the process. "I was roused from the first good night's sleep I've had in ages by the sound of talking. Why is this person here, Ellie? It's against all rules to bring anyone unconnected with St. Roberta's inside these walls."

I hedged. "She arrived very late."

"Or you could say early," inserted Mrs. Malloy brightly. I'd provided a sufficiently detailed description of Rosemary for her to know what she was up against. "Of course it wasn't me plan to show up in the wee hours, but the trains didn't work out like I would have wished. Three changes, with the lav out of order on two of them. There I was standing with me legs crossed till I thought I couldn't take it no more, and me with a weak bladder." This was the first I'd heard of this ailment, and I had to give her points on seeing Rosemary's face.

"I'm not interested in your . . . health problems."

"Tosca and I weren't particularly keen to hear about your missing pale-blue silk knickers," I said, "but hopefully it relieved your mind to talk about them. Now, what were you saying?" I turned to Mrs. Malloy as Rosemary sank into a chair. "I should have asked you sooner about your journey, but in the joy of our reunion that got overlooked."

"Well, the straw that broke the camel's back, so to speak, was when I got to Tingwell—a nasty grubby-looking place from what I saw—and found I'd missed the last bus to bring me the rest of the way. So I crossed the road to this café—a bit nervous-like, in case it was frequented by the wrong sort. But as I was sitting over a nice cup of tea, counting the coppers in me purse to see if I'd enough for a taxi, this nice couple—he was a good deal older than her but not bad-looking for a man of his age. Anyway, the upshot is—"

"It's been long enough coming!" growled Rosemary.

I, on the other hand, inwardly applauded the cozily rambling manner Mrs. Malloy had adopted; it allowed me time to think up a reason for her making the journey to see me in the first place. Regrettably, my mind blinked and went out. I didn't come up with one that would enable me to spend time with her when I was supposedly in retreat from my everyday life.

"Their car had broken down, you see, and with no garage open they'd rung up some friends as live in Lower Swan-Upping to come and get them. They'd soon be along, would Frank and Marge, said Mr. and Mrs. Whatsit, and seeing as how they thought it risky for me get in a taxi—what with Tingwell being the grim place it is—I accepted their kind offer of a lift."

"No objections from Frank and Marge?" Rosemary inquired, with what passed at a pinch for interest.

"Couldn't have been nicer! We had to pass their house on the way to the school, and they asked if I'd like to pop in for a drink. Well, I didn't see how I could refuse, what with them being so kind. And, as tends to happen, one g and t led to another—"

"Rosemary likes gin and tonic," I said encouragingly.

"—and of course it wouldn't have done for Frank to drive under the influence. Besides, he'd fallen asleep, as did the rest of us after a bit. If a dog across the road hadn't started barking, my guess is we'd still be sacked out."

"At least you arrived safely, that's the important thing." I couldn't blame Rosemary for glaring at me. I did sound fatuous, but the moment was at hand and I didn't have an idea how to prevent Mrs. Malloy from being sent packing. "By the way"—I managed to stall a moment longer—"where is your luggage?"

"On the step outside. You didn't notice and I didn't like to ask you to fetch it in when you looked so tired; always thinking of others, that's me." Mrs. Malloy was back to her own self. Rosemary eyed her narrowly.

"I've got it!" she crowed in triumph. "I know who you are now!"

"Kind of you to say so." Mrs. Malloy's haughty nod was worthy of a duchess handed a damp package of sausages by a blushing gawker who wanted to make a gesture but didn't have a bunch of flowers. Disdainful, but mindful of the requirement to be kind to the little people.

"You're the aunt!"

"I'm the what?" Mrs. Malloy's painted eyebrows shot up an inch.

Aha! I thought. Here lay a possibility!

"Ellie's reason for seeking refuge at the Chaplain's House"—Rosemary jabbed a finger in my direction—"having worn herself out tending to your every ache and ailment."

The eyebrows skyrocketed.

I leaped off the couch and skimmed across the room to perch on the arm of Mrs. Malloy's chair. "Now then, Aunt Petal"—gripping her hands—"you know you mustn't upset yourself. It's bad for your lumbago and the vertigo . . . and that twitch the doctor can't explain."

"For God's sake don't remind her of the weak bladder!"

"Please be quiet, Rosemary," I begged. "Can't you see she's in no fit state to be harangued? The journey could have killed her!"

"She looks healthy as a horse to me."

"Petal?" Mrs. Malloy murmured.

"Bewildered, you see." I glowered up at Rosemary's looming figure. "She'll be in no state to return home for days . . . possibly weeks."

"Can't you get it through your thick skull that you've been had?"

"Kindly keep your voice down. Shouting causes her vision to blur, and you'll be the one leading her around by the hand while I'm frantically trying to find Dr. Roberts!"

"She's clearly a malingerer!" Rosemary sucked in a vicious breath.

"That's all part of me illness." Mrs. Malloy slipped valiantly into the role thrust upon her. "Remind me again, Ellie, about how we're related? I'm feeling a little muzzy; it's me corns playing up again."

"You were always such a dear family friend, Mummy said you wouldn't mind if I called you Aunt Petal." I patted her shoulder. "So when you began having your little health problems, I insisted on taking care of you."

"Sounds to me like you've done some complaining to that lamppost standing there!"

"You mustn't think that, dear. It's true I was ready for a teensy rest, but I explained all that before I left and you told me you understood. What went wrong, Aunty? Did Ben forget to bring you breakfast in bed? Did the children become a little too rowdy without me there to explain you need lots of nice peace and quiet?"

"I got to missing you something fierce." Mrs. Malloy choked on a realistic sob.

"My heart bleeds!" Rosemary flung up her hands. "But staying here is out! For starters, Mrs. Battle would never agree to it!"

"Oh, I think she may when I explain the circumstances." The

important one being, I thought, that Mrs. Malloy was my detecting partner. Two heads would be better than one for recovering the Loverly Cup.

Before Rosemary could recover her equilibrium, Tosca appeared in our midst wearing a doleful expression at odds with her lime-green satin negligee and the exotic appeal of her tumbled dark hair and near-black eyes.

"Hello." She eyed Mrs. Malloy hopefully. "You must be a new girl. I don't suppose you smoke?"

"No, but that isn't to say I won't if it's a requirement."

"Oh, Aunt Petal!" I chuckled delightedly. "You're going to be the life and soul of our little group!"

Let Rosemary put that in her pipe and choke on it! "I'm off back to bed," she snapped, "and if any more people show up, tell them to set up camp beds outside. I need my sleep." She left, closing the door behind her with something close to a slam, and moments later Tosca drifted out in her wake.

"What about bed for you?" I suggested to Mrs. Malloy, but she assured me, as so often happened, she was prey to the dreaded second wind.

"Why don't we go down to the ruins now and check out that stone bench those two girls thought could be a hiding place for the cup?"

Feeling wide awake myself and sadly aware that instead of snoozing outdoors that afternoon I should have been on the case, I agreed, and we set off through a light drizzle.

Even on the finest dry day, there was a dangerous-looking gloss to the dark surface of the steps going down the Dribbly Drop. Always the slow trickles of green water, waiting to be lapped up by the gelatinous creatures—part lizard, part jellyfish—that Susan, Ann, and I had been convinced hid, watchful and slyly blinking, in the tufts of grass between the bushes at the top.

"It might be a good idea to take off your shoes," I felt compelled to advise.

"Not on your Nellie! I've been wearing heels this high since I was four."

I decided against arguing. The look she gave me couldn't have been fiercer if I'd suggested she take off all her clothes in the middle of Oxford Circus. But in the interests of saving her from her folly, I went ahead of her, one slow step at a time. Then, half a dozen steps from the bottom, I saw a dark shape huddled on the ground. I knew, of course, that it was a person, but my mind strove to believe it was some other object—perhaps a black plastic bag filled with garden refuse, left there by Mr. Mossop to be collected later when it was quite full. I could feel Mrs. Malloy's hand on my shoulder, her face pressed close to mine as we stood frozen, peering in dreadful disbelief.

I did not feel the ground beneath me as we knelt beside the contorted figure. There was movement, a slow-motion turning from side to back, and we were looking into Ms. Chips's eyes. I felt a faint stirring of hope when she drew a shallow breath and her lips parted. There was more: recognition in the eyes that met mine. "My nose mended, as you saw." The faintest of smiles crossed her face. "But my heart never did. Loved him so dearly . . . grateful for the time we had together." Silence. Then another murmur I couldn't catch.

" 'Will,' " I think that was it, and then 'my' . . . " said Mrs. Malloy," but so hard to hear."

There could be no confirmation or denial of this. Ms. Chips had left us—to be reunited, I could only hope, with the man she had loved and lost so long ago.

13

I didn't stumble out onto the landing and into the bathroom until five past eleven, and that after about three hours of sleep. Even a lot of sloshing with cold water and a snappy brushing of my hair couldn't stir my interest in descending the stairs. Mrs. Malloy had stayed with poor Ms. Chips, while I'd gone and phoned the police. After their arrival and that of the medical people, we endured a brief questioning as to how we had found her when setting out on an early morning walk. They didn't appear to find anything significant in her last words and clearly regarded the event as a tragic accident—which had to be the case, of course. The question was, Why had Ms. Chips been out in the grounds in the early hours of the morning? But even that was not difficult to explain. She had always been an active woman and, upon seeing her dorm charges well settled for the night, might have felt like taking a brief stroll. Or—the sudden thought occurred—what if she had learned from her friend Matron of Miriam and Shirley's reason for going down the

Dribbly Drop and had gone too, as Mrs. Malloy and I had intended, to check out the stone bench?

My need to talk to Ben was strong. I left my bedroom and went to the telephone on its table under the big plastic clock that was so unsuited to the rest of the decor. As I hung up, lucky to catch Ben as he was heading out the door to Abigail's, I noticed my mirror compact on the table, where I must have left it when digging in my handbag for the details of Tam's dental appointment. I then saw that the inappropriate clock had shifted, so that the twelve and six were decidedly off-kilter. Rather than merely straighten it, which might scrape the paint, I lifted it off its nail on the wall and found myself looking into a niche that was larger than the ones in the hall and the sitting room. Why cover it—let alone with something so unsuitable?

The answer was right there in front of me. The Loverly Cup gleamed like boxed starlight. Should I march it straight up to school and hand it over to Mrs. Battle or endeavor first to find who had put it here?

I had replaced the clock and was stepping back when my foot turned, causing me to stumble forward on one knee and brace myself on the floor. No more than an inch from my hand was a thin silver chain. When I picked it up and stood erect, I saw that the little ring in the center held a small flat cat charm. I turned it over. It was engraved with the word, or name, CARROTS.

On legs that felt even woollier than when I'd got out of bed, I went and sat on the top stair. Gillian had told me at the Middletons' that she had a cat named Carrots. Gillian had been at the Chaplain's House yesterday; she might well have gone upstairs before I got back and dropped the charm while making a phone call. But why wouldn't she have used the phone downstairs? Memory came of waking in the night and hearing someone creep across the landing and down the stairs. What if it hadn't been one of the other residents, as I had convinced myself? What if Gillian had slipped out of the dorm, as Ariel had done the previous night, and hidden the cup behind the clock? If so, why the risky urgency? Obviously, wherever she had previously hidden it no longer seemed safe.

I had mentioned out-of-place objects in my talk to the Home Skills class. Gillian had been there. What if she remembered hearing, perhaps from Ruth Middleton, that an inappropriate clock covered the niche on the landing at the Chaplain's House? Ruth had mentioned the niches to me. I pictured Ms. Chips looking at that wall and deciding that, charming though the niche might be, what was needed above the telephone was a clock. Perhaps the plastic one was intended to be temporary and a more suitable replacement had not been found. I could almost hear Ruth explaining this to Gillian. I swallowed hard. Why hadn't Gillian made an excuse to go upstairs yesterday—perhaps to use the bathroom—instead of running the risk of a middle-of-the-night visit? I pictured her face as she had sat talking to Philippa. She had looked happy at that moment. I had to believe that was real and all the rest nonsensical speculation.

Returning to my bedroom, I placed the chain and charm in the side pocket of my handbag before returning my mirror compact to the middle section. Then I went downstairs to find Mrs. Malloy in the kitchen, which was at least two sizes too small for her, making a pot of tea.

"If we're to stay more than a couple of days"—she handed me a slice of toast—"we'll have to get this kitchen enlarged. You can't expect your aunty in her poor state of health"—eyeing me severely—"to be banging elbows into cupboards."

"You're going to get better rapidly." I sat down on the stool and took the cup of tea she handed me. "We'll say we've talked to Dr. Roberts and the advice you've been previously given is all wrong. You need to be more active—get out and about more. How did you sleep, such as it was?" She knew I wasn't yet ready to talk about Ms. Chips.

"All right. How about you?"

"Not bad. I like that Tosca. Nice of her to help me make up the pull-out couch in the study across the hall. And Phil couldn't have been more pleasant when I saw her some fifteen minutes ago. Funny thing is"—she leaned against the cooker with her cup—"I have this feeling that I've seen her somewhere before, but all I can grab on to is a snatch of song from that advert as used to be on the telly for Happy Splash Kiddy Shampoo."

"She does have pretty curly hair."

"Shiny like a child's. Yes, that could be it. Being the romantic you are, Mrs. H, I'm guessing you're wondering if she came down here hoping to connect with the old boyfriend."

"It's been close on twenty years, but she certainly did seem upset when Tosca said she's going out to dinner this evening with Dr. Roberts."

"Understandable nostalgia. I get moony sometimes thinking about me third husband, and he'd have fed me to the lions at the zoo if it would have got him a free ride on the elephant."

"Brian Roberts is the nicest man."

"So was Mr. Machiavelli, I expect, when you met him on a good day." Mrs. Malloy fortified herself with another cup of tea. "A pity, when the other two ladies are so nice, that Rosemary's got to be so unpleasant."

"Phil thinks she's very unhappy."

"And you and me could be a mite kinder, Mrs. H, especially after what's happened." It was finally said. "But as I used to tell my George when he was a little lad, being a churchgoer would be a lot easier if the pews was more comfy. So for now I'll leave it to others to polish their halos—not that I'm saying Phil is a prig. I can see why you said everyone liked her at school."

"It would be wonderful if she could gain Gillian's trust and find out what's making her so unhappy." Having looked at my watch, I scrambled off my stool. "We've got to get moving. Unless Dorcas feels it wouldn't be right to take off for lunch, she's meeting us in the parking area at eleven-thirty and it's gone twenty past."

"This is the first I've heard of it."

"I told you right before we went to bed that Mrs. Battle has given me permission to take Ariel and Carolyn Fisher-Jones to lunch."

"How am I supposed to remember what's said to me when I'm half dead?" Her face flushed under her rouge. "Sorry!"

"Don't feel guilty. You didn't know Ms. Chips. And you don't have to come if you'd rather stay here and bond with Rosemary."

"She's gone out, Tosca's having a lie-in, and Philippa went up to the school to see if she could give Matron a hand with comforting girls who are in shock over what's happened. She's got a way with her, that young woman, and I don't doubt kiddies take to her in a big way. As for me, I'm not going to stay behind twiddling me thumbs when the right question from me could get this Carolyn to tell us something that'll put all the pieces together. It's just as I don't like going out looking unpresentable! Now, where did I put me hat?"

Luckily it wasn't in the sitting room. She conceded, as she picked up her handbag, that it wouldn't be fair to keep Dorcas waiting by going into the study to look for it, especially when she'd come to remember putting her suitcase on top of something pink.

My hope, as we headed out the door, was that those flamingoes had lived happy, fulfilled lives, seeing as death had not done them proud. I was wearing a navy cotton dress that lacked style, but whatever I'd had on could not have lived up to Mrs. Malloy's green and bronze shot-silk ensemble.

"I don't know what you were going on about," I told her, as we went around the side of the school building to where the half dozen cars were parked. "You're far too glam to be seen with the likes of me."

"Kind of you to say, Mrs. H. Like I said to me sister Melody when she came down to breakfast in a nightie that looked like something the cat wouldn't even consider dragging in, we can't all be into haute couture."

"Very true."

"What about Mrs. Battle? Shouldn't we have a quick word with her about me being here?"

"We'll do that on our return." The question of whether or not I should reveal that I'd found the Loverly Cup hung heavily upon me, dulled only by the memory of watching Ms. Chips, the woman I had long thought of as my nemesis, die. But I couldn't keep the information from Mrs. Malloy. I told her about finding the cup hidden in the niche behind the unlikely clock, the discovery of the cat charm and chain on the floor, and my belief that the movements I'd heard on the landing and heading up and downstairs in the middle of the night had not belonged to anyone staying in the house. She would undoubtedly have asked when I intended to report my find to Mrs. Battle, but I'd only just finished when we saw Dorcas coming toward us.

My heart warmed at the sight of the soldierly figure marching our way, a strand of ginger hair escaping from its clip onto her forehead, the freckles sharply in evidence against her pale complexion. No fashion sense, this dear friend—but I wouldn't have changed an inch of her. Understandably, she was astonished at seeing Mrs. Malloy but shook hands with typically warm enthusiasm. The two of them had always rubbed along very nicely, their affection for the children forming a strong bond.

"Dreadful, this business of Ms. Chips." Mrs. Malloy couldn't have sounded kinder.

"Can't take it in yet." Dorcas reached for her handkerchief and gave a resounding blow. "Frightful shock for the school, from Mrs. Battle down to the smallest first former. Heard several of the girls talking about filling a basket with signed lacrosse balls in lieu of flowers. Regret I wasn't blessed to get to know Chippy better. Frightfully good egg! Heart goes out to you and Ellie, being the ones to find her. School's at sixes and sevens. Sensible of Mrs. Battle to relax the class schedule, so the girls can spend more time in the common room talking over their memories and trying to come to grips—" Choking up completely, Dorcas waved a hand. The gesture of someone who had said all there was to be said.

"Are Ariel and Carolyn up to coming out to lunch?" I asked.

"Best thing for them, to get off the premises for a while. Final morning bell about to ring. You'll hear the stampede to the refectory from out here. Always bangers and mash on Tuesdays and Spotted Dick for afters. Generally goes down well."

"I should think so," said Mrs. Malloy approvingly. "Nothing like good old-fashioned grub to warm the cockles. Not but you'll be glad to get away for an hour or so yourself, I'm sure."

Dorcas looked abashed. "Sorry, Ellie! Should be made of sterner stuff, but don't feel up to it. Forgive me if I don't tag along."

"Are you sure it wouldn't help?"

"Always so kind—both of you—but wouldn't do even had things been different. Idea is to get Carolyn to open up about Gillian—and whatever else she knows. Less likely to happen with one of her teachers sitting there."

"You're probably right," I agreed reluctantly.

"Well, Miss Critchley, you make sure you get a good helping of them sausages; especially in times of trouble, it don't do not to take care of yourself. Now, what about transportation?" Mrs. Malloy surveyed the parking area as if expecting a chauffeur complete with cap to materialize three feet away.

"There's a bus stop." I brought her back to reality. "We can reach it by going across Lilypad Lane to the main road. It's only a few yards from the convent ruins."

"Won't hear of it. Take my spare set of keys." Digging into

her pocket, Dorcas handed them over. "Sorry the car's such an old bucket. The thing is to talk to her, jolly her along. Got a heart of gold but inclined to be touchy if you press her too hard. Good-oh! Here come the girls now!"

Ariel came toward us as one accompanying a funeral procession on foot, her sober face exactly right for her coronet of tightly plaited hair and prim spectacles. Carolyn followed sedately. Seen close up, her look of bred-in-the-bone refinement was even more apparent. I pictured the ancestral home with the strict but kindly nanny and the parents that dressed for dinner even when it was just the family, the pony in the paddock, the tennis court, the visits to museums and art galleries. The mother would play the cello and the father collect first editions. A different world from Gillian's. And yet Carolyn had befriended her.

"Mrs. Malloy!" Ariel interrupted the exchange of greetings. "When did you get here? Oh, it *is* good to see you, especially in light of the tragedy! Ellie, did you know she was coming?"

"A middle-of-the-night surprise. Why don't the two of you get in the backseat of Miss Critchley's car and Carolyn can come in front with me?"

Both girls looked at Dorcas, who wished them an enjoyable lunch, saying she would toddle along. My plan was to drive to the café where Ruth and I had eaten on the previous day, although I thought it too cramped and brightly lit for a confidential conversation. On the other hand, with only an hour at our disposal before classes resumed, I didn't want to waste time looking for somewhere more suitable. Fortunately, we came upon a small hotel within a mile of the school that Ariel informed me had a nice restaurant. One of those somber ones with beams and dark wallpaper, just the sort of place for people in mourning.

"Isn't that right, Carolyn?" She leaned forward with a bounce that unnerved the car into stalling halfway up the drive. "You said they served the best roast beef and Yorkshire pudding when Lady Loverly brought you here for your birthday?"

"It does have a good reputation." Carolyn spoke in barely a whisper.

I made a decision. "Girls," I said, "I know you're hurting, but I don't think Ms. Chips would want you to spend this time cast down in gloom. A much better tribute to her would be for us to all try and be cheerful by way of recognizing that life, every minute of it, is too precious to be wasted."

"You're right," murmured both girls in unison.

"Fish is what I've been fancying," said Mrs. Malloy.

"They do an excellent grilled trout." Carolyn's voice had risen to a normal level.

"Then let's waste no time going inside." Parking the car, I nipped out smartly before Mrs. Malloy could say trout would only do if served with herbed butter and baby brussels sprouts. She has her moments of posing as a gourmet. The girls followed, and we entered an austerely lit reception area, to be ushered by an elderly man, whose hunched posture in no way diminished his dignity, into a wainscoted dining room hung with claret velvet draperies. Once seated, we were handed menus the size of fire screens and left to make our selections. One or two of the other diners glanced our way, but no one was within eavesdropping distance. Our meals arrived piping hot and fragrant. I had joined Mrs. Malloy in ordering trout, and the girls each had the roast beef.

"I pity those left to make do with sausage and mash." Ariel spooned horseradish onto her plate. "This is heaven." She looked awkward but forged on. "There's even a harp in that far corner, Carolyn."

"So I see."

"Do you play?" I asked.

"The harp?" Carolyn laid down her fork and tucked back a strand of flaxen hair. "No, but my mother does, along with the cello. I never got on with any musical instrument."

"You've got a lovely voice to make up for that," said Ariel

loyally. "I don't understand why Mr. Middleton picked Elizabeth Anderson to sing the school song at the celebration of the new gymnasium, especially when Gillian will be playing the accompaniment and you're her best friend."

"I'd rather sit and listen, especially when Gillian's at the piano. It's as though she goes somewhere I want to follow."

"Sort of like the Pied Piper?" Mrs. Malloy cocked an eyebrow.

"Yes, but . . . he wasn't nice, was he? And Gillian is," Carolyn replied sadly. "She'd never do anything nasty to anyone, which makes it especially mean of Deirdre to pick on her the way she does."

"Deirdre's the class bully," explained Ariel, who had made excellent inroads into her roast beef and Yorkshire pud.

"She showed her fangs in the Home Skills class," I said.

"I was putting Mrs. Malloy in the picture, Ellie."

"Ta, love." An appreciative nod from that lady. "It's always a handicap not being in on a case from the beginning, but I don't want you thinking Mrs. H is out to hog the limelight, what with St. Roberta's being her old school and Miss Critchley her friend."

Carolyn looked from Mrs. Malloy to me. "I hope you're not upset that Ariel told me you're here because of the Loverly Cup. Although that doesn't seem very important now, does it?"

"Not so much," I agreed. "But you will keep the information to yourself? Mrs. Battle would rather it wasn't generally known among the girls."

"I promise not to breathe a word; but if you suspect Gillian you're wrong. She'd never take anything that didn't belong to her. The girls saying she had to leave her old school because of being caught stealing are just going along with hateful rumors." Carolyn's face flushed. "You did ask me out to lunch because you want to talk about her?"

"I hadn't heard about the rumors. But I think Aiden Loverly must have got wind of them and accused Gillian of moving on to steal the Loverly Cup when he cornered her outside the Middletons' house on Sunday."

"His source could have been his girlfriend, Mrs. Frenton." Ariel cocked her head to one side and assumed a speculative expression. "But she doesn't seem a vicious talebearer. Then again, I didn't want to suspect any of the nice characters of treachery when I read *False Friend at Falcon Abbey*."

"I think I missed that one." Mrs. Malloy sounded aggrieved, perhaps because she was thinking of Ms. Chips.

"From what I've seen of Gillian"—I'd had trouble eating more than a few bites—"it's clear something's troubling her."

"That doesn't mean she's done anything wrong." Carolyn's voice trembled. "She didn't want to come to St. Roberta's. She's not the boarding-school type. The first few weeks were torture for her. She couldn't sleep. That's why her mother mailed her the binky."

"Come again?" Mrs. Malloy looked up sharply.

Ariel took up the tale. "What's left of Gillian's baby shawl, not much more than a scrap. That sneak Deirdre took it from under Gillian's mattress a few days ago and made a huge thing of it, saying there had to be something seriously wrong with a fourteen-year-old who needed such a thing. She said Gillian probably sucked her thumb as well when she thought no one was looking." Ariel was panting, either from fury or too much horseradish.

Carolyn spoke more mildly, but her face flushed. "Deirdre claimed she hadn't singled out Gillian's mattress; she had been conducting a dorm search for the Loverly Cup and anyone who really cared for St. Roberta's would be doing their part looking everywhere they could think of."

"There wasn't any arguing that." Ariel scowled.

"Finding a good hiding place would have been an issue." I avoided Mrs. Malloy's eyes but guessed she was vividly picturing the niche on the landing at the Chaplain's House and the damning evidence of the cat charm with *Carrots* engraved on the back. "Carolyn," I said, "do you know if Aiden Loverly had anything against Gillian, in addition to the rumors about why she left her old school?" Not that rumor alone wouldn't have been sufficient, I was forced to admit to myself.

Carolyn stared down at her hands before meeting my eyes. "It's all nonsense on his part. He phoned me Sunday afternoon, all upset. Apparently, when she was getting ready for church, Lady Loverly looked in her jewelry case for a brooch and couldn't find it. And Aiden remembered that the weekend before, when Gillian came with me to the Hall, he saw her outside Godmother's bedroom door with what he said was a peculiar look on her face. But of course that doesn't mean anything. She goes into a kind of trance when she's thinking about her music, and he probably startled her. If she had been in the bedroom it would be because Godmother had sent her up to get something for her. She is always leaving her glasses or watch upstairs and suddenly wanting them. I told him he shouldn't be so sickeningly suspicious."

"Good for you, Carolyn!" Ariel pushed aside her empty plate. "I expect Lady Loverly forgot to put the brooch back in her jewelry box the last time she wore it."

"That's what I told Aiden." Carolyn bit her lip. "But he wasn't convinced. He said the new maid described Gillian as a sneaky, vengeful kid. Her name's Luanne Wyles. She used to work at the school before Mr. Bumbleton got her sacked for cheek, as he called it. I thought that unfair because she did seem really nice. Godmother says she's a breath of fresh air about the place. Mrs. Brown is splendid though rather gloomy. But I don't understand why Luanne would speak so hatefully of Gillian." Her voice petered out.

Mrs. Malloy waved away the hovering waiter. "Do some of

the girls—like this Deirdre, for instance—resent Gillian because her great-aunt is on staff?"

"I don't see why they would. It's not as though she gets any special treatment. I told Matron about the binky incident, hoping she'd talk to Gillian to make her feel better, and she did just the opposite. I hate that woman!" Vehemence flared in the blue-gray eyes. "She told Gillian earlier in the term that she would break her parents' hearts if she didn't make the most of her opportunities, especially with Mr. Middleton being set on helping her achieve great things in music."

"We can't all be the warm fuzzy sort," said Mrs. Malloy judiciously.

I looked at my watch. It was time to head back to St. Roberta's. The waiter expressed regret when we declined to view the sweets trolley. Ariel said nobly that treacle pudding should be reserved for happier occasions.

"We'll sort things out for Gillian." I spoke with more optimism than confidence.

"That would be wonderful. We need something good to happen, after poor Ms. Chips," responded Carolyn with a determined smile.

"I keep wondering what took her outdoors so early." Ariel sat, chin cupped in her hands, eyes wide behind her spectacles. "I wonder if she caught a fleeting glimpse from her window of the Gray Nun descending the Dribbly Drop and hurried in pursuit. Miriam and Shirley both have sisters in our class, who say they remain adamant that they spotted a ghostly figure on Sunday afternoon before Shirley took her tumble."

"Wonder if them steps is cursed?" There was a quiver of hastily suppressed excitement in Mrs. Malloy's voice, but I didn't get to observe her face because I was rooting through my handbag for my purse in anticipation of paying the bill. Naturally, out came a number of superfluous items, including a couple of pens and my compact mirror. "Don't go leaving that on the table." A beringed finger came pointing my way. "You know how upset you'll be if you go losing it for good one day, seeing as how it was a present from your mum."

"It is elegant." Ariel smiled kindly at me as I looked up. "I think I'll collect compacts when I'm grown up."

"Yours is a Marie Chantal, isn't it?" Carolyn surprised me by saying.

"I'm impressed."

"Is it?" asked Ariel.

"Yes." I turned the compact over. "Here's the signature on the back."

"My godmother has several." Carolyn flushed under Ariel and Mrs. Malloy's admiring looks. "That's how I knew. Thank you very much for lunch, Mrs. Haskell. It was a great treat."

The drive back to the school took next to no time, and we decanted under a glorious blue sky as the bell announced the start of afternoon classes. After heading across the parking area with Carolyn, Ariel turned back to give me an unexpected hug, during which she whispered in my ear.

"Ellie, you do believe Ms. Chips's death was an accident?"

"Of course!" I locked the car door and put the key in my bag. "Why?"

Carolyn, after a momentary hesitation, continued toward the school. Seeing this, Ariel drew back from me and spoke in a normal level voice. "I woke up in the middle of the night; I looked at my watch, and it was four-thirty. Gillian wasn't in her bed, Ellie. She has the one next to mine, and though she'd tried to make it look as if she were there—by rolling up a blanket under the bedclothes—I wasn't fooled, because I tiptoed over to make sure she was sleeping soundly and leaned down really close. I was thinking of making my own escape and coming to see you as I did the other night."

"You think Ms. Chips might also have discovered Gillian's

absence, perhaps spotted her from a window moving about the grounds, and gone hurrying after her?" I was picturing it all too horribly. Gillian hiding when she saw Ms. Chips crossing the lawn from the school and then stealthily moving forward to give the woman a fatal shove when she reached the top of the Dribbly Drop.

Carolyn added a wave to the one she had just given before disappearing through the entrance door.

"I don't believe it," said Mrs. Malloy vehemently. "Without so much as having set eyes on this Gillian, it's clear to me that someone's out to make it look like she's the villain of this piece, either out of sheer spite or to cover up for themselves."

Ariel stood looking uncertain. "Some of the girls are saying she's unbalanced. If that's true, and Ms. Chips surprised her—well, she might have panicked without meaning to kill her. I don't want to think it. . . ."

"But it all seems to fit, don't it?" Mrs. Malloy replied smugly.

"Yes, I see what you mean." Ariel drew in a relieved breath. "I suppose I'd better get after Carolyn, or she might think we're talking about her. This situation could make even the sanest person paranoid!"

"Well, you keep your head on straight. And your eyes and ears open!" Mrs. M called after her as she ran toward the school. I stood wondering if Ms. Chips would one day rival the Gray Nun as a haunting figure created out of hearsay and muddled thinking. Suddenly and quite fiercely, I knew I would do all in my power to save her from that chillingly ridiculous fate.

"I'm right about Gillian's innocence!" Mrs. Malloy took my arm, something she only did when feeling chummily superior. "That dropped chain with the cat charm. It's all too obvious! And that business of the clock. It must have struck someone else as out of place before you ever got sight of it, and that person, after listening to, or may be about, your talk to the Home Skills class, decided you just might take a look behind that clock, and wouldn't it be nice if you was to find the Loverly Cup in the niche and something left behind to show it was Gillian as put it there?"

I said that sounded possible. What I didn't say was that she'd triggered a memory that fitted her theory, but I wasn't ready to accept such a poisonous idea, let alone share it with Mrs. Malloy. I wanted to be wrong and had the feeling she would speedily decide I wasn't.

"I'll be interested to meet Gillian's great-aunt." She let go of my arm to pat her hair in a sudden sharp little breeze. "Sounds stiff and starchy, like the matrons in books. Can't say from what you've told me that I'd want her coming at me with a thermometer."

"Some people don't have the knack of being likable." I had my moments of striving to be fair, and given my concern—make that, my hope—that I was wrong about Gillian's tormenter, this was one of them.

"Don't give me that, Mrs. H. Our job is to look for the worst in people, not search every nook and cranny for redeeming qualities."

"I thought objectivity was the name of the game."

"If that's the case, it's not looking all that good for Miss Gillian, is it?"

I ignored this and said we should march ourselves into the headmistress's office. With this valorous intent in mind we entered the reception hall, where Mrs. Malloy drew up short to stand absorbing the moment, as she put it.

"Hold me arm, Mrs. H! I don't know as I can stay steady on me feet, what with this being me girlhood fantasies come to life. Roxie at St. Roberta's, sounds just right for a storybook!"

"You wouldn't like wearing the uniform," I pointed out.

"I don't know about that! It might be fun to make those stuffy gents' eyes pop." She pointed to the portraits on the staircase wall. "Who are the old goats?"

"Former members of the Board of Governors. And"—I lowered my voice—"I'm sure all of them would strongly disapprove of your posing as my Aunt Petal." I hurried us over to the office door, ignoring her mumblings that she could own to the name without blushing like a geranium.

"Don't you dare talk about how good I was to you, Mrs. H, when you was a nipper, and how it's now your turn to tuck me into bed at night with a cup of cocoa and a bedtime story." She stood breathing down my neck as I knocked on the door.

"Come in," instructed Mrs. Battle.

We entered to find her seated at her desk, where the pencils and notepads had the look of being on their best behavior, along with the telephone, which would only ring when given permission to do so. As for the potted plant under the window, it exhibited such good posture I straightened my spine and watched Mrs. Malloy do likewise. Whether Mrs. Battle noticed our efforts to conduct ourselves appropriately was questionable. It seemed to me there were added lines on her face today and the hooded eyes were those of a sorrowful eagle.

"I do hope we're not interrupting." Reverting to a schoolgirl state, my voice started with a wobble and ended with a squeak. "I know this must be a dreadful day for you."

"But for Marilyn's kindness in taking over Mrs. Rushbridge's dorm duty, it would never have happened." She roused herself to beckon us forward. "I told the authorities, when they raised the question of her being out and about so early, that it did not surprise me to think she would have woken and relished the idea of a stroll." She stared unseeingly into space. "Do you have something to report, Ellie, on the whereabouts of the Loverly Cup? And this will be . . . ?"

"My investigating partner, Mrs. Malloy. She arrived late last night." I couldn't bring myself to tell her I had located the missing trophy.

"Pleased to meet you, ma'am." My cohort stood to attention

on her high heels. "I was able to set aside me other obligations to make meself available." The impression conveyed was that this included deposing an errant monarch and establishing a new state church.

"That is good news." Mrs. Battle stirred in her chair, but I sensed she was adrift somewhere else, perhaps conjugating Greek verbs or whatever else is required of those seeking to find some remove from sorrow.

"Mrs. H was doing her best forging on alone, but like she often says, she can't be the brain as well as the brawn of our operation," said Mrs. Malloy.

No such concession had ever passed my lips.

"If your presence will help speed matters up, I will be most grateful. I have devoted my life to education, but I never had the ability or the desire to win hearts." The dark eyes misted. "What were you saying?" I felt the urge to race around the desk and give her a hug, but rightly or wrongly I resisted.

"May Mrs. Malloy have your permission to stay at the Chaplain's House?"

"Certainly."

"I'm posing as Mrs. H's Aunt Petal," supplied Mrs. Malloy. "A silly name, you might say—"

"Not at all. My late husband used to call me his dewdrop." Would Mrs. Battle regret this astonishing revelation? Perhaps she already had; she signaled dismissal with an inclination of the head.

I closed the door upon exiting and allowed my shoulders to slump.

"Dead bodies stuffed in trunks or the butcher's freezer is bad enough, but things like that woman's sorrowful face is just too hard to bear. Still, it's nice to know she had a private life once upon a time." Mrs. Malloy pursed her butterfly lips. "You don't think she and your nice Mr. Middleton could make a go of it?"

"I wouldn't think so, although perhaps if he were to learn the identity of the hit-and-run driver who killed his wife, it might provide closure, as they say, and let him live his life to the fullest again."

We were interrupted by a march of bottle-green skirts and mustard-yellow shirts descending the staircase. It was an orderly stampede, no jostling or raised voices. The teacher at the rear looked capable of herding a pride of lions across Africa without incident. She nodded in passing, and when the reception hall had returned to its former empty calm, Mrs. Malloy and I decided to take a look at the new gymnasium.

It proved to be magnificent: the vaulted ceilings imposing, the floor a gleaming golden sea of parquet. Ms. Chips and the Bumbleton firm of builders had done St. Roberta's proud. Even so, I refrained from climbing the rib stalls or taking a flying leap over the horse. The trophy case to the left of the entrance drew me to stand gazing through its glass doors at the assortment of prize memorabilia. An empty space on the second shelf called sharp attention to the vanished Loverly Cup, and to my surprise I experienced a spurt of outrage and sympathy for all the girls who had earned the right to see it proudly displayed during previous seasons; for Ms. Chips, who had led them to victory while undoubtedly demanding good sportsmanship; and not least for Dorcas, who, while feeling keenly the disappointment of defeat, believed even more strongly in according one's opponents their moment of triumph.

In the hall outside the gymnasium, Mrs. Malloy and I came upon Matron, and I made the introductions.

"Your partner, you say." Her smile was taut and her hands clenched. "Forgive me if I have trouble focusing. As you must realize, Ellie, this has been one of the most dreadful days of my life. I am in shock. My beloved Marilyn! How will I go on without her? We were in my office, chatting about past times, late into the night. I think she may have had some sort of premonition because she suddenly, quite out of the blue, began telling me that she had just made a new will, leaving her remaining capital to St. Roberta's for scholarships for gifted students. Recommendations to come from their teachers and to be agreed upon by a majority vote of the staff, with no input necessary or desired from the Board of Governors. That won't please Mr. Bumbleton, but it didn't bother Marilyn. She had her own sense of what was right. I must take comfort from our last time together. Indeed, it was well into morning before she left for the last time to check on the girls in the dorm. Forgive me if I'm rambling. Mrs. Battle was in a fog when I spoke to her a half hour ago. I'm not sure she was aware what she was saying from one sentence to the next."

"Yes." Only from behind a veil of fog would Mrs. Battle have revealed that her late husband called her his dewdrop. Poor Matron. I was shocked by her pallor and trembling hands.

"What you need is a good cry in bed with a hot-water bottle," said Mrs. Malloy at her most cozy.

Matron's response was cold, her lips frozen with grief. "I have the girls' distress to deal with. You'd think some had lost their mothers; there'd have been no sense in going on with classes. Dr. Roberts has been in several times, prescribing sedatives where needed, and will be back this evening. Philippa Boswell has been here most of the day, mopping up tears and lending an ear. A frustrated nurse, I'd say, but nice with it."

"She always was," I agreed.

"Dr. Roberts didn't spare her more than a word or two in greeting, although I seem to remember that they were once boyfriend and girlfriend. He couldn't have been kinder to me, knowing as he did of my long and close friendship with Marilyn." Matron squeezed her eyes shut for a moment before continuing. "On a different subject, there is something I need to discuss with you, Ellie. Perhaps I would have brought it up if we hadn't been interrupted yesterday morning."

"We"—Mrs. Malloy emphasized the pronoun—"are here

to listen." I was relieved she didn't add *Matey*. As it was, she was ignored.

"Gillian had a run-in a couple of days ago with a girl in her class named Deirdre, who'd taken it upon herself to go checking under mattresses—"

"We know." I looked at Mrs. Malloy.

"Who told you?"

"Carolyn Fisher-Jones."

"At lunch today," added Mrs. Malloy, in a display of how forthcoming she and I were prepared to be.

"She's a pleasant enough girl, but I'm not sure she's the right friend for my great-niece. Encouraging Gillian to see herself as hard done by defeats the efforts of others to help her move beyond her initial homesickness. Someone more bracing, such as your relative, Ariel Hopkins, Ellie, might be a help rather than a hindrance." Matron's lips tightened. "I have to admit I've reached the point of wondering if I should have put myself out to help Gillian be admitted to St. Roberta's. It's not that I expected an abundance of appreciation, but I certainly didn't count on her making difficulties. Perhaps I should just throw up my hands and concede it would be better all round if she doesn't come back at the start of the new school year. On the other hand"—she drew in a breath and her eyes hardened—"I'm concerned that someone may be intent on making Gillian look unstable."

"Meaning?" My eyebrows shot up in unison with Mrs. Malloy's.

"That business of her security blanket. I admit I lost my temper with her over such childishness, but the point is she told me she always hid it under the mattress on the side that's against the wall and that she walked into the dorm to see this girl Deirdre pull it out from the near side. The reason she flared up and told me this is because I said if she had to have a silly scrap of baby shawl, she could at least have made it more difficult for someone else to get at. It was Carolyn, walking in on our conversation"—Matron bristled with irritation—"who suggested that someone who already knew about the binky—to use Gillian's name for the thing—had moved it where Deirdre was more likely to find it in her dorm search for the Loverly Cup."

"As—from what I saw and heard from her in the Home Skills class—she inevitably would," I said. "But what was to be achieved other than making Gillian a laughingstock? What has you so worried, Matron?"

"My fear," she said, looking suddenly old and tired, "is that the next thing to be discovered under Gillian's mattress will be the Loverly Cup."

I was worried too. I knew, of course, that the Loverly Cup wasn't under Gillian's bed—but was the place where I had actually found it any better?

14

Mrs. Malloy and I were leaving the school building when I told her of my grand plan.

"We'll pay Lady Loverly a visit this evening and see if we can find out if she shares her grandson's suspicions of Gillian's honesty."

"Sorry if I startled you!"

Turning around, I saw the red-haired girl with the snub nose and freckles from the Home Skills class.

"I spotted you from down the hall, Mrs. Haskell, and wanted to catch up with you and this lady to tell you how much I enjoyed your talk on decorating."

"That is kind of you."

"I'm Elizabeth Anderson."

"How nice to meet you properly. This is my friend, Mrs. Malloy, who is also staying at the Chaplain's House for a little while."

"Oh, what fun!" The flash of an engaging smile. "Were you in the same class when you were girls here?"

Nice to know I didn't look my age. The summary piling on of superfluous decades does so much for the female ego.

"Some friendships are made to last." Mrs. Malloy swirled out her skirts. If she didn't take that smirk off her face, our friendship would be in the duck pond.

Elizabeth continued to beam at me. "Thank you again, Mrs. Haskell, for the helpful tips on making a home look nice. It was a lot more fun than sitting through a lesson on how to overhaul the Hoover or having to stick pieces of colored glass on cardboard boxes trying to make them look like jeweled containers."

"The class was fun for me too."

"It's awful to think how quickly things can change. It's so hard to believe about Ms. Chips, I mean. Everyone's wondering what caused her to fall. It seems wrong somehow for an athletic person—one who stayed fit—to die that way. Pamela Erickson from my class said she'd heard Ms. Chips had high blood pressure, so maybe she turned dizzy at the top of the Dribbly Drop. I could see that happening if she'd been running. But why would she run?"

"That's a good question." Mrs. Malloy was wearing her wise-owl face.

"She was the best kind of teacher." Elizabeth's pleasant face puckered. "The kind you can really like while respecting them at the same time. That's why so many of the girls want to do something special for her as a goodbye present. Flowers just don't seem right, so"—she opened her right hand to reveal a lacrosse ball—"we thought we'd get people to sign these and perhaps add a line or two."

"I think that's a wonderful idea," I said.

"Meaningful." Mrs. Malloy nodded. "In my case what I'd like is to have me funeral sermon done by a bingo caller. No missing what *he'd* say at the back of the church. A friend of mine had a bag of the markers tossed at her wedding instead of confetti. Everyone loves a nice bit of sentiment."

"We think Ms. Chips would like our idea. Will you take this with you back to the Chaplain's House"—Elizabeth handed me the lacrosse ball—"and have anyone who wants to sign it?"

"Of course." I put the ball in my handbag.

Elizabeth abruptly changed the subject. "Ariel Hopkins told me she's related to you, Mrs. Haskell. I like her; she's really interesting. We met in the corridor just now and she wants to talk to me in the common room, but I wanted to catch up with you first. But you will understand that I don't want to keep her waiting. Nice meeting you, Mrs. Malloy. 'Bye!"

Elizabeth was gone with a wave, and Mrs. Malloy and I proceeded to the Chaplain's House.

"I bet she's a really nice girl." I smoothed back my hair, which was getting tugged by the breeze.

"A change from some."

"Yes."

"I'm thinking of that Deirdre, Mrs. H, as has been mentioned. Sounds to me like a nasty girl in a boarding-school story, the one out to make life miserable for the main character. But at the end she gets her comeuppance when it's discovered she's been cheating on her exams or—"

"In this case, stolen the Loverly Cup?"

"Well, I've got to say as I wouldn't sob in me hanky if it turned out that way. Something along the lines of Deirdre's parents being world-famous pianists and expecting her to follow in their footsteps, only she can't so much as ping a triangle and then along comes Gillian, who Mr. Middleton thinks is a prodigy and who becomes best friends with Carolyn Fisher-Jones to boot, that used to be Deirdre's best chum. Gillian gets blamed for the theft and turfed out of St. Roberta's by way of revenge. That's the plan."

"It's classic." I was genuinely impressed.

"And up to us to spoil it."

"Yes."

"What's got into your craw, Mrs. H? You sound all huffy and puffy! Missing the hubby and the kids, that's what it is."

"Didn't you see the sun move behind that cloud?" I said, in a feeble attempt at humor. "Can't you tell an omen when it's right above your head? I've got prickles down my spine, beads of sweat on my brow, and a thudding heartbeat. All that's missing is a howling dog and a hovering of ravens in a tree that's about to be struck by lightning. We're moving to some awful climax, as sure as I broke Ms. Chips's nose all those years ago."

"Now I understand." Mrs. Malloy's high heels tip-tapped up the path to the Chaplain's House. "You've got the willies, Mrs. H, at the thought of foisting your company on Lady Loverly when she's in mourning for her friend. The better families always do their mourning up proud, that's one thing you have to say for them. My suggestion is not to phone up and risk being told no. Just show up this evening and stick your foot in the door like a man selling brushes."

"Sounds like a plan," I conceded, as she pushed open the front door. "I remember her as a woman wearing formidable hats."

"There now." Mrs. Malloy might have been speaking to one of my children. "You'll have Ms. Critchley at your side but not sucking up air the way I do on account of me powerful personality. No, don't argue with me. I'm not one to step aside often. But we can't all three of us go like we're the circus come to town. And Ms. Critchley didn't come out for lunch and should get out of that school for a bit of a break. That woman's one of life's abiding comforts and as fond of you as I am—except, that is, when you forget as how I likes two sugars in me tea along of a ginger nut on the saucer. You get her on the phone."

It was a moment to break down and weep, only to be nixed by our almost colliding with Mrs. Mossop when we entered the hall. Seen up close, she was a small elderly woman with a pug face, wearing an overall of no particular color and the expression of one braced to get trodden upon unless she stood stockstill and stopped breathing. The timid eyes darted to Mrs. Malloy's oversized handbag in expectation of having it chucked at her for daring to remain upright instead of getting down on her knees.

"Hello." Mrs. Malloy and I spoke one on top of the other.

Stepping backward, she apologetically informed us that she was Mrs. Mossop. "And I'll not be staying underfoot. Off back to the school I am. Always get in and out quick when doing the Chaplain's House. Half an hour with the mop and duster is all. No need dragging out the Hoover when there's a perfectly good carpet sweeper and you ladies are here for peace and quiet."

"It's nice to meet you." I was afraid of scaring her up the stairs. "I understand your husband works in the grounds."

"That's him. Groundskeeper and odd-jobs man."

"I've had several hubbies," observed Mrs. Malloy chattily.

"Married forty-seven years to Mossop. He's got his ways, but don't we all? A man can't be blamed for not wanting trouble on his doorstep. This business of the retired teacher, Ms. Chips, getting herself killed has him all worked up. I keep hoping he won't go speaking out of turn." Mrs. Mossop's left eye began to twitch. "Saying to others what he's been saying to me—that like as not the woman'd been drinking. And her not being a one for it, from what I've heard. Got a terrible down on drink has Mossop. Any other time he'd have said them steps was put there to kill people. One of the girls took a fall on them just the other day. But like I've said, he's upset. Everyone is. She was a nice lady. You'll excuse me talking. I don't as a rule. Mossop doesn't like it, he always thinks I'm hiding something if I rattle on, but it's my nerves, you see; they've been all on edge."

"I *am* sorry." Under other circumstances, I would have asked her if she was sure she had locked the trophy case on the afternoon the Loverly Cup was taken and if she remembered noticing any suspiciously lurking figures. As it was, I stood thinking how lucky I was to be married to a man who didn't make my eyes twitch when talking about him.

"You and me should have a lot in common, Mrs. Mossop, seeing as how I'm in the same line of work as yourself," Mrs. Malloy said in a gratified voice, "or was, that is, before me health started to fail. Ellie here never did think much of her Aunt Petal going out cleaning. But like I told her, it's God's work, isn't it—doing for others what they don't want to do for themselves? See life from a different perspective when you're kneeling on a floor with a bucket, is what I always say."

Mrs. Mossop's expression changed subtly. It couldn't be said that she brightened or that her voice took on a chirp, but I sensed that she warmed to the opportunity of airing professional grievances. Mr. Mossop could be shoved in the background for a few minutes.

"One of the women staying here—her with the Roman nose—she looked at me like I was dirt when I came in. I don't know if that's better or worse than the ones that look right through you like you're not there. To some of the teachers and that toffee-nosed Matron—she's the worst—you'd think I was no more than a rag on the floor to be walked over. The things we get to hear by way of being invisible!"

Mrs. Malloy nodded sagely.

"I could write a book. Then again, it's likely different working at a school instead of doing houses where there's a divorce in the works or the mother-in-law moving in just when the drains is acting up again—and then should the smallest thing get broken or go missing. . . ."

She paused effectively.

"I've been worried sick that I'll be blamed for that silver cup going missing. I'm just glad Luanne wasn't around here to get looked at funny. She's gone up to the Hall to help Mrs. Brown. Poor woman! Luanne says she has dreadful nightmares. Wakes up screaming."

"Oh, dear," I said.

"Tells you everything, does Luanne. Not one to keep her mouth shut. That's what got her out of here. Stuck out her tongue at Mr. Bumbleton."

"Sounds like you're fond of her," said Mrs. Malloy, in her most companionable voice.

"Like a daughter." Mrs. Mossop's sad little pug face scrunched up even tighter. "Mossop and me wasn't blessed with children. A heartache at the time, but I see now it was for the best. He wouldn't have liked them, however they turned out. Can't stand the little bit of family he's got, let alone my poor sis—"

She was interrupted by Rosemary's raucous voice from the sitting room. "Who's out there jabbering in the hall?"

"I'll be off." Mrs. Mossop shrank back into a mouse with a squeak for a voice before scuttling out the door.

"It's us!" I shouted sideways. "Ellie and Aunt Petal. We'll be with you in a moment."

Mrs. Malloy's eyebrows arched way above her iridescent lids. "Leave it to me, Mrs. H, to find out what that poor woman knows about the Loverly Cup."

"That's what we're about," I said, "gathering up a probably useless amount of information." I was like a child who'd had enough of the party and wanted to go home.

The sitting room door bounced open, and Rosemary cast her shadow.

"Hello, there!" I said. "Did the police return with any more questions about Ms. Chips?"

"No, and please don't get us talking about her again," Rosemary snapped. "I'm sorry about what happened to her—it's awful, no doubt about it—but going on about her good points won't bring her back. Let's move on."

"Isn't she a ray of sunshine at the North Pole?" Tosca chirruped from within. "She's still in the snits because her husband, the oh so wonderful Gerald, has not yet rung up. I ask why she does not phone him and get slashed to shreds because I smile."

"Oh, God! Why can't you hole up in the potting shed and smoke yourself to death?" Rosemary charged back into the sitting room with Mrs. Malloy and me at her heels. We found Phil seated on the sofa, leafing through a magazine.

"How did the lunch go with Ariel Hopkins and Carolyn Fisher-Jones? I'm just back from the school. I saw Gillian in one of the corridors, but she brushed right past me. I really don't think she saw me. I nearly said something to Matron, but didn't, because she's already got enough on her plate."

"Are you planning on becoming Matron's permanent second-in-command? Is that why you're reading a medical journal?" Rosemary sloshed gin into a glass, ignoring the bottle of tonic.

"I prefer it to the fashion magazines in the rack," Phil replied mildly.

"Not a sudden desire to play doctor? Or should I say, play *with* one if you can get him out of Tosca's clutches?"

"I don't think this bickering is good for me in my frail condition." Mrs. Malloy tottered over to the sofa and held out her hand for a drink, which I duly presented.

"If it upsets Phil, I will cancel my dinner date with the handsome and kind Dr. Roberts," Tosca offered from her chair. "I am not a man snatcher . . . although I might be tempted down that path if your Gerald should show up and prove to be all you say, Rosemary."

"You are a pernicious woman!"

"You have had a bad day. Did you get word that your little dog lost its bathing cap or refused to take a shower before getting into the pool? Never mind, Rosie! Perhaps it is better suited for the long distances—swimming the channel, for instance."

"You!" The furiously vibrating finger pointed at me. "I saw that smile!"

"I'm sorry," I said, and meant it. "I've also made the occasional joke at Howard Hound's expense, and it wasn't kind."

"Laurence! His name is Laurence!"

"Do not get the fancy French knickers—which I didn't steal—in a twist!" Tosca purred.

"I will not be ridiculed!" Sobbing noisily—*grotesquely* was the word used later by Mrs. Malloy—Rosemary fled the room.

"What now, girls?" Tosca's lips curved into a cat smile. "Do we get out the ark?"

Phil set aside the magazine. "Why not give the woman a break? This has been a dreadful day, and she probably minds more about Ms. Chips than she's saying. I'm going to my room. I offered to go back to the school in a couple of hours so Matron can get out for a break this evening." She stood up, facing Mrs. Malloy and me. "Do either of you have plans?"

Mrs. Malloy said she was all set on a lazy evening, and I explained that I was visiting a casual acquaintance.

Tosca had once again arranged her legs in a weirdly contorted pyramid. "Sorry! I forgot to tell you, Ellie, that Ms. Critchley telephoned to ask you to meet her at seven where her car is parked if you would like to go out for some driving. She is nice-sounding, and I told her you would be in squeals of delight. Perhaps we should all stay in and be sad for Ms. Chips. But for me the dinner date is as the doctor orders."

"I'll phone Dorcas back," I said.

"No need." Tosca rearranged a foot on her shoulder. "She said if you do not meet her at seven she will know you do not feel up to it and go back inside the school."

We divided up, only Tosca remaining where she was. Mrs. Malloy admitted to being ready for a lie-down after the events of the previous night. When she went into the study and Phil to her bedroom, I telephoned Ben and had a comforting talk with him, followed by merry conversations with the children.

Returning the receiver to its cradle, I thought about going to see how Rosemary was doing but decided she wouldn't thank me for finding her with a tear-sodden face. Phil's charitable view that her awfulness was the result of deep unhappiness was all very well, but I was getting a little tired of human nature. Lying down on my bed, I willed the soothing colors of the room to calm me and closed my eyes. There was plenty of time for a nap before getting ready for the evening, and I did feel sleepy; even so, I was convinced I'd have trouble dozing off with my mind jumping from one thought to another. Wrong! I conked out as if hit on the head with a blunt object.

My dreams were the usual hodgepodge but nothing nightmarish. I was seated at Matron's desk while Carolyn confided that her parents were set on her achieving a great musical career and refused to accept that she didn't have the talent so she was going to be a veterinary assistant instead. At which point she turned into Deirdre Dawson, who said she hated Gillian because that was her job as dorm prefect. I was explaining that only bad people get what's coming to them when a tap on the door woke me and Phil poked in her head.

"I thought you might need rousing, Ellie, if you're going to meet your friend at seven. It's a little after six. The bathroom's free if you need it and I made some sandwiches, although perhaps you are going out for a meal."

"Thanks, I'm not sure what Dorcas has in mind." I smoothed a hand over my face and sat up.

"See you tomorrow if not before."

"Phil?"

"Yes?"

"Mrs. Rushbridge told the Home Skills class that one of the guests staying at the Chaplain's House is an actress. Is that you?"

She hesitated, her hand on the doorknob. "It was silly of me to hide it. I did tell Gillian when she was here yesterday. There's something just too awful about misleading a girl of her age. She said you'd told her I'd worked as a veterinary assistant . . . which is true, after a fashion; I played the part in my most recent play. I do stage work mainly: provincial theaters."

"A TV shampoo advert rang a bell"—I shifted on the bed—"with Aunt Petal."

"I did one last year."

"That was it."

She laughed. "And occasionally for breakfast cereal and furniture polish. They pay well for someone in my league—fairly steady work but nothing that's come near to making me famous."

"Did you always want to act?"

"Always. My parents were horrified; they're dears but quite Victorian in their ideas."

"It seems an exciting life."

"It has been; it was the one I wanted. I wouldn't trade the times of waiting tables till all hours of the morning or selling cosmetics door-to-door to pay the rent." She came farther into the room, and I saw she was wearing a simple but elegant black dress and high heels. "The reason I decided not to say anything was because—"

"You didn't want half the school begging for your autograph."

She laughed. "Even mediocre actresses get that sort of reaction sometimes; it comes with the territory, and much of the time I'm flattered and sincerely appreciative. I came here, though, because I wanted to reconnect with my past, and that seemed easier to do if I left my present behind. But as I said, I did tell Gillian, and given her hope of making musical performance her career I hoped it forged the beginning of a bond between us. That's why it worried me when she looked right through me when we came upon each other in the school corridor this afternoon."

"Yesterday in the kitchen she looked almost happy." I sat looking up at Philippa.

"We'd talked about the risks and rewards of putting what talent one has in front of an audience. I've a feeling, however, that she and I aren't quite in the same category—that where I have a small gift, hers is enormous. That didn't come from any boasting on her part. It"—Phil spread her hands—"just came through. And now, having cleared my conscience to some small degree, I'd best let you get ready."

She slipped out the door, leaving me to slump back on the bed. Why hadn't I grabbed the opportunity to confess my sin of omission toward her when I was Gillian's age and she only a year older? I would have continued to sit, pondering my cowardice, if my watch hadn't shown me it was time to scuttle, were I to have any hope of meeting Dorcas in the parking area by seven. No time to do much with my face and hair. But if I intended on following through with my plan of showing up on Lady Loverly's doorstep and dragging Dorcas along, it behooved me to put my best foot forward. I wasted no time agonizing about deficiencies. Shrugging into a brown sheath dress and stepping into matching sandals, I called the job done and was about to head out onto the landing when Mrs. Malloy called "Cooee!" and came into the room.

"Had a good nap?" she wanted to know.

"Fine. You too, I hope. And that's enough about the Land of Nod. There's something I have to tell you. Nothing to do with the case, but interesting." I proceeded to impart the news about what Philippa did for a living, with gratifying results. Mrs. Malloy swayed like a ship caught in a storm on the high seas.

"Well, who'd have thought it! And what put you on to it was my saying she looked familiar and mentioning that shampoo advert? Well, let's call me clever dick and leave it at that! A real live actress under this roof! Breathing the very same air as you and me! Sharing the loo with us, drinking from the same bottle of milk. We have to get her autograph! The looks I'll get when I tell them at the Chitterton Fells Charwomen's Association! Eyeballs rolling all over the place is what it'll be."

"Not a word to Rosemary and Tosca. It's for Phil to tell them, not us."

"What do you take me for, Mrs. H?"

"Someone I shouldn't be chatting with when I've got to run."

" 'Course she'll have just been modest, saying as how she isn't famous." The eyes beneath the neon-coated lids took on a dreamy glow. "I'm sure, now I come to think of it, that I've seen her other times on the telly." Perceiving the futility of trying to bring her back to earth, I bade adieu to deaf ears and made my escape.

Alas, the world is overly full of people desperate to touch the hem of celebrity. Seated beside Dorcas some five minutes later on the drive to the green, I forgot my demand for discretion from Mrs. Malloy. I provided the facts—without embellishments, assured of their raw captivating charm. "We mustn't spread this around," I belatedly instructed.

Dorcas emerged onto the main road at a crawl. "Decent of Miss Boswell to come clean. And jolly kind of her to take an interest in Gillian. Mrs. Rushbridge, who's up and about now, told me she'd had a word with Mr. Middleton about how ill the girl looked, so she's going to be staying with him and his sister for a few days. Mrs. Battle approved the arrangement, of course. Had a word with her before leaving the school. Said I'd stop by the Middletons' during our drive and report back on how Gillian is doing. Hope you don't mind, Ellie."

"Of course not."

"Still can't come to grips with Chippy's death. Poor old Rushbridge feels terrible. Says if she'd taken better care of her teeth she might have done her own dorm duty. Heart broke for her. Would feel the same in her place. Know Mrs. Frenton feels bad. Had a date and couldn't fill in."

During the remainder of the drive, I filled Dorcas in on what I had gleaned since my arrival. Even to my own ears it sounded a lot of hodgepodge. There was, however, one thing I left out, a crucial one at that—my finding the Loverly Cup in the niche behind the clock. Had I done so, Dorcas's code of honor would have required me to inform Mrs. Battle immediately, and that I was not ready to do.

I fell silent when we came to a standstill alongside Ms. Chips's house. Dorcas briefly bowed her head over hands that clenched the wheel. Then, climbing out of the car, we beheld Mr. Middleton descending the last few rungs of his ladder, propped up against the apple tree. He had the ubiquitous Harpsichord in his arms and a markedly disturbed expression on his face. Surprise at seeing us staring at him, perhaps, or had it dawned on him that, despite all the meows to the contrary, his cat was never going to change? Was he facing the sad truth that he would continue to put up with stress to life and limb because theirs was a codependent relationship? Were such thoughts preferable to the heartache of thinking about the woman who had been his longtime friend and more recent neighbor?

"Are you here to collect Ariel Hopkins?" He waved his furry orange bundle by way of greeting, his kindly smile rimmed with sadness.

"We didn't know she was here," I said, looking at Dorcas, who shook her head.

"She came with Wilma Johnson some fifteen minutes ago, hoping to see Gillian, which Ruth and I thought very kind but better left for another day. We felt awkward making this suggestion to Wilma as well, but she seemed to accept that Gillian needs to hibernate for a little while."

This seemed unusual of Matron. "Where is Ariel?" I asked him.

"Wilma took her into Marilyn's house, although"—Mr. Middleton cleared his throat—"I suppose it must be said it's hers—Wilma's—now. Apparently Mrs. Battle let slip to her this afternoon that Marilyn had left her the house and its contents."

"We'll collect Ariel," Dorcas told him gruffly. "Shouldn't be left to Matron to take her back. Woman may want to linger with her memories. . . . So sorry, mustn't become emotional. Good old Chippy! Know she wouldn't want that. Condolences on your loss, Mr. Middleton. Bound to miss her abominably."

"Indeed, indeed, as will my sister. Ruth would like to see you both—but another time, if you understand—about Gillian. As I just said, she wasn't up to a visit from her great-aunt." He continued to stand holding Harpsichord, his manner as kindly and courteous as always, but there was a pensive look in his eyes that suggested he was thinking of something else.

Dorcas and I proceeded up Ms. Chips's path, to be greeted by a surprised Ariel opening the front door before we rang the bell.

"I saw you through the glass panel." She adjusted her specs as if doubting the evidence of her eyes. "Have you come to fetch me because you were cross that I came to see Gillian? When we were having lunch, I suddenly got this goose-bumpy feeling and decided I just had to talk to her, but first I need a word or two with Elizabeth Anderson. Anyway"—Ariel paused to suck in a breath—"by the time I went looking for Gillian, I heard she'd gone to stay with the Middletons. But luckily, as I was going disconsolately up to the common room after supper, I ran into Matron; and when she said she was going to visit Gillian, I wheedled a lift."

I explained that we hadn't known of her whereabouts but that Dorcas had promised Mrs. Battle to make inquiries and report back to her on how Gillian was doing. Seeing that Ariel was dying to spill the beans or whatever else she had up her sleeve, I told her about our upcoming visit to Lady Loverly and suggested we wait to compare notes until we saw how that went.

"Goodness! If I'd known I'd have washed my face twice before leaving school. You'll have to take me with you!" It was more a demand than a request. "It would be too cruel not to let me be in on this; besides, it should be harder for her ladyship to turn you away if you have an impressionable child in tow!"

"Has a point there!" Dorcas clapped me on the shoulder as we all stepped inside. Chippy's house was a replica of the Middletons'—understandably so, given that the properties were semidetached. Also, the furnishings were similar: pleasantly old-fashioned without too much fuss. This stair carpet was moss green rather than russet, and the linen-and-white striped wallpaper different from the amber paint. Fewer paintings hung on the walls, but they invoked the mood of a home created from well-loved pieces passed down from previous generations along with newer ones tastefully chosen. Ms. Chips had done a great job with the Chaplain's House, but this one had the feel of being lived in and known like an old friend.

"Matron's upstairs," Ariel informed us, in the voice of a parlormaid who took her duties extremely seriously. "She said she wanted to look for something for Ms. Chips to wear for the funeral. She's been up there quite a while, but it wouldn't do to rush the selection, would it? I'm sure we will all want to look our very best. When our time comes."

"Don't like to call her down to tell her we're taking Ariel. Could be having a bit of a weep." Dorcas herself sounded choked with tears as she groped for my hand. "What say we wait for her in the sitting room?"

We did, and found it a place of comfortably worn sofas and chairs, nestling up to lamp tables with plenty of room to hold teacups or magazines. Unlike the Middletons' counterpart, there was no grand piano, but a number of well-lined bookcases topped with framed photographs made up for this lack. I had the pleasant feeling that Ms. Chips would walk in and offer us cups of tea. In any case, we were about to sit down when Matron walked into the room.

Dorcas and I began explaining between us that we'd decided on taking a drive, and—

"And Mrs. Battle will have asked you to make a detour, Ms. Critchley, and inquire after Gillian." Matron began fussing with sofa cushions that had looked perfectly fine to me. "I am not allowing myself to feel hurt that she has chosen to be with them in what is *my* hour of need, not hers. She was never taught by Marilyn, nor did she ever show the slightest interest in sports, to my knowledge."

"She's quite good at table tennis," Ariel offered.

"And that's supposed to make her a soulmate of dear Marilyn?" Matron sat down on the sofa, her hand stroking the material at her side—rather, I found myself thinking, as I would have stroked my cat, Tobias. "Really, it was too bad of Mrs. Battle to give in to Gillian, but as you will understand I have enough else on my mind. I'll need to arrange with Mrs. Mossop to come out and give the furniture here a good polish, so the place will look its very best when people come back after the service. That would have been important to Marilyn, and who's to think of her feelings if I don't?"

"Had a lot of good friends . . ." Dorcas began staunchly but, perhaps noting the glint in Matron's eyes and realizing this was not what she wanted to hear, her voice petered out.

My offer to take Ariel with us went down well, but we were not hustled on our way; we were urged with a surprising enthusiasm to stay and have tea and cake—a chocolate one that Matron said she had brought with her. It would have been unkind to refuse. Also, as we sat watching her bustle about with plates and cups, I realized she was enjoying playing hostess in her friend's house. It was hers now, of course, but she hadn't discovered that until this very afternoon, when Mrs. Battle in her dazed state had let the information slip. Matron could hardly be blamed if in the midst of her grief she was pleased at last to have a home of her own . . . just as Mr. Middleton was bound to rejoice, however sorrowfully, in the knowledge that St. Roberta's could now provide scholarships for gifted students . . . such as Gillian.

15

With Ariel seated behind us, Dorcas drove cautiously in the direction of the Hall, which she had visited this spring on a staff outing. It was by now nearly eight o'clock and, though not yet dark, the night was thickened with cloud. Was the good weather of the past few days on the way out? Were we in for sighing winds and weeping rain?

"Friendship is so important," Ariel said suddenly. "You can tell a friend things you wouldn't even bring up with your own family. I'm talking about the really special ones, Ellie."

"Anything you want to tell me?"

"No, but I could . . . so why isn't Gillian confiding in Carolyn? That's the question I've been asking myself. What can be so bad that she has to keep it all to herself?"

"If she did take the Loverly Cup, she would have to anticipate that her ladyship's goddaughter would take a pretty dim view."

"I'm not so sure. Carolyn has always struck me as unusually understanding. Anything you want to tell *me*, Ellie?"

"I'm wondering if we turned the wrong way at that fork in the road back there. This lane's awfully bumpy, Dorcas."

"Remember thinking that the last time."

"Ellie!" Ariel leaned forward to grab the back of my seat.

"Later."

We turned onto a gravel drive, and from the pleased—if faintly surprised—look on Dorcas's face I was reasonably confident we had arrived at the Hall. With rain now coming down, there wasn't much to be seen beyond ivy-clad walls set with latticed windows and a massive door that sprang open as we mounted the broad semicircle of steps.

"Come inside out of the wet," urged a cheerful voice, as we entered a dimly lit hall, chilly with stone and heavy in timber, to be further greeted by a girl with corkscrew curls and a mischievous face.

"I'm Luanne Wyles. Usually Mrs. Brown gets the door, but she went up to bed the minute Lady Loverly finished her dinner. The poor old duck has been looking poorly all day. She gets the most terrible headaches, so I don't in the least mind taking over for her. Let her have her rest, I said to myself. I didn't go up even when Mr. Aiden arrived, though I know how Mrs. Brown always likes to see him. Awfully kind to her as well as his grandmother, he is. But who wouldn't love her ladyship, is what I say! Working here's the treat of my life after St. Roberta's."

"I hope Lady Loverly won't mind seeing us. I'm Ellie Haskell, and—"

" 'Course not. She's a love, her ladyship is! As for Mr. Aiden, he's a proper dreamboat!"

Luanne was leading us across a heavily wainscoted hall hung with enough armory and ancestral portraits to establish at a glance that visitors should count themselves lucky not to be charged ten pounds for the privilege of breathing the rather musty air. I could sense that Dorcas was fiercely awed and Ariel was fighting off a fit of the giggles.

"Won't Mrs. Frenton have won the pools if he asks her to marry him?" Luanne went on. "It's just so romantic, isn't it? The two of them being so gorgeous, and him inheriting his grandfather's title but being all modern and choosing not to use it, just like he's made his own way in the world, even though Mrs. Brown told me Lady Loverly wanted to help finance his business so he could set up in a better area than Tingwell. Well, enough of my mouth. I just can't get used to working here. It's like being in one of them lovely old-fashioned plays my mum likes to watch on the telly." She turned to stare at Ariel. "You look nice with that grin of yours, so it can't have rubbed off—being around Miss High and Mighty, that is."

She guided us to a door, opened it without knocking in the trusted-employee manner, and departed with a regretful wave.

Aiden Loverly here! I would have to insist on talking to him. Clearly Luanne had succumbed to his shallow charm. I wasn't sure if I was pleased or sorry that he wasn't present in the vast room we were entering. Dorcas was squaring her shoulders, but Ariel was taking everything in, a blend of the sensibly comfortable and eccentrically exuberant. Big sagging couches and chairs, all within hand's reach of a table on which to put things. Lampshades closely resembling a monstrosity of a hat Lady Loverly had worn at one of the school fetes. There were hassocks for the feet, cushions for the back, tasseled shawls to drape on the shoulders. Ebony elephants, hunting horns, and shellacked fish everywhere you looked. What particularly took my eye was the portrait of a woman over the fireplace. Given the entire absence of clothing, it was difficult to judge the period. The subject might, I thought hopefully, be one of her ladyship's forebears, but my hope was immediately dashed.

"Myself in my glory days!" The speaker rose from her chair and followed my glance. "A healthy attitude to the human body has always seemed to me to be important. Wilma Johnson once told me that there has always been too much sex in this world for her liking."

Ariel stood with her tongue in her cheek while Dorcas blushed a fiery red.

"I do apologize for our intrusion," I began, only to be silenced by a majestic wave of the hand.

"No need for all that. I know who you are—you're the woman Mrs. Battle brought in to recover the Hester Bateman cup. I've been expecting you to show up ever since Aiden told me about snarling at poor, meek Gillian. As if that child didn't have enough to contend with, being Wilma Johnson's great-niece."

Lady Loverly sat down and signaled to us to do likewise.

"And you"—addressing Dorcas—"are the new games mistress. Thought you looked a decent sort last time I saw you. But whether you are worthy to fill Marilyn Chips's shoes waits to be seen. What a loss! One can only hope she finds the happiness she deserves in the great beyond."

Her ladyship was a large woman with even more teeth than I remembered and a sagging face that gave her, particularly at that moment, the look of a mournful bloodhound. She directed her gaze at Ariel.

"Why have you brought this child with you? Not that she isn't welcome—I like children, always have done—but there is a time and a place!"

Ariel beamed at her. "I'm Ellie's cousin, and I'm afraid I foisted myself on her and Ms. Critchley."

"No matter. As responsible adults wishing a serious talk with me they shouldn't have allowed themselves to be foisted on. Why don't you go and browse in the library? You'll find it across the hall if you open enough doors."

"Would it be all right if I went and talked to Luanne instead?"

"You'll be lucky to get a word in! That girl's mouth never lacks for fresh air, but I've always liked strong personalities. Off you go, then."

I was rather surprised that Ariel hadn't balked at being banished from what she would expect to be a fascinating conversation; but I kept my focus on her ladyship, who clearly had a lot in common with her young maid.

"I've always been of the opinion that Wilma Johnson's was not a fulfilling marriage. Neither was mine idyllic." Lady Loverly's bloodhound face sagged even deeper. She had a growly voice. "One always hopes not to be blinded by affection, but then how many relationships would we have if we ferreted too deeply?" She shook herself as if coming out of a thicket and smiled at Dorcas, who was looking desperate.

I gave the conversation a nudge. "Luanne said your grandson is here."

"One of his surprise visits. You could have knocked me down with a feather when I saw him standing in the hall."

"Talking about me, fair heart?" The door opened and Aiden Loverly glided into our midst, looking more reprehensively handsome than I remembered.

"As always, you are at the center of everyone's thoughts," his grandmother informed him affectionately. "Do say hello nicely to my guests—Miss Critchley and Mrs. . . ."

"Haskell." I hoped my smile was short and to the point.

"We all met, didn't we, outside Clive Middleton's on Sunday? You didn't appreciate my treatment of Carolyn's friend Gilly." He prowled languidly around a sofa.

"Beastly scare you gave her," Dorcas fired back.

"Yes, and believe it or not I regret it." For once there was no hint of flippancy or sarcasm in his voice.

"Aiden, dear boy, they are here to talk about the Loverly Cup. Poor Mrs. Battle was so distressed—and of course it is upsetting, although I have another very similar one I'd be happy to present as a replacement. . . . Anyway, she brought these two ladies in as private detectives." Dorcas endeavored to protest, but her ladyship plowed on. "I got this information from Mrs. Battle this afternoon when I went to the school to share her sorrow over dear Marilyn Chips."

"I intended to scare the life out of Gillian."

"Aiden!" Lady Loverly expostulated.

"Darling Granny." He bent down and kissed her cheek before ensconcing himself in a chair across from hers. "I did rather come at her on my bike, but only to put the wind up her because I'd decided she'd taken that brooch of yours. But on second thought, I may have been misled."

"I should hope so. Such nonsense, suspecting that child." Her ladyship shook her head. "Really, Aiden, I love you enormously, but you can be the limit."

"I hate the idea of anyone taking advantage of your kindness." He brushed back his long fair hair in an elegant gesture, but he no longer appeared to me to be posturing. I wondered what Dorcas was thinking of him. I wasn't ready to like the man, but I suspected he was truly fond of his grandmother.

"My boy, as we have seen today, life is too full of real tragedy to get worked up over the small stuff. And as I told you yesterday on the phone, I found the brooch pinned on my purple frock. The one you always say makes me look like an emperor in drag."

"I will make a point of seeing Gillian and apologizing to her."

"Overdue." Dorcas looked him squarely in the eye.

"He's a wonderful grandson." Lady Loverly's voice sank to a ruminating growl. "Notwithstanding he has a nasty temper when he feels himself justified. His father—my son and only child—was so easygoing. His death and that of his dear wife came as a terrible blow. Those small airplanes are never as safe as people want to believe. Aiden was still in his teens and not entirely pleased about having to come and live with an old woman."

"Thank you, Granny, for the defense, but I don't think these ladies want to hear it. They have me pegged as a heartless rogue.

Thank God I have finally found a woman who can separate the substance from the shadow."

The lovely Mrs. Frenton? "You said you were misled about Gillian's stealing the brooch?" My breath caught in my throat as I awaited his answer. It was a long moment coming.

"By Carolyn."

"Go on, please." I was struck by the lack of surprise on Dorcas's face.

"She phoned while the hunt for the brooch was on. I mentioned it, and she said Gillian must have taken it—that she'd just that week discovered Gillian had been chucked out of her last school for stealing."

"She wasn't just repeating what other girls had said?"

"No, she stated it as a fact. She said she was dreadfully upset, felt thoroughly taken in, and was convinced from the way Gillian was behaving that she had also stolen the Loverly Cup."

"Why do you now think she may not have been telling the truth?"

Aiden gave me one of his cynical smiles. "Because I've a nose for phonies—in antiques and in people. It didn't take much time spent around Carolyn to realize that her gentle manner hides a viciously ruthless streak, which explains why she has never kept her friends for long. Last year there was a girl named Elizabeth Anderson she used to bring here on visits."

"Nice red-haired girl." Her ladyship nodded her shaggy head.

"Who got the role Carolyn wanted in the school play. When it came to the missing brooch, I admit to letting my emotions prevail, especially since I'd seen Gillian coming out of Grandmother's bedroom on the weekend before last with an embarrassed look on her face."

"I sent her up to get my watch. She may have been taken aback by that portrait of me as a young woman in the bath. The artist was sparing with the bubbles." Her ladyship chuckled deeply. "And she is clearly a girl from a traditional sort of family."

Dorcas sat uncomfortably silent.

"I phoned Carolyn after my near run-in with Gillian and said I intended on having a word with the Battle-ax about accepting a girl into the school with a propensity for stealing. She immediately said she'd been misinformed, but I knew she was lying. I could hear it in her voice."

"When Carolyn first came to St. Roberta's it seemed such a blessing." Lady Loverly sighed gustily, showing most of her teeth. "I hadn't seen her since she was little, and being short on family I welcomed her coming to stay, sometimes with a friend on weekends or at half term. It seemed to bring this old house back to life. Even Mrs. Brown took on renewed energy, baking special treats. But I soon saw what Aiden has described, the concealed nastiness. Before Gillian and Elizabeth there were other friends who came and went."

"Ariel—the girl we brought with us—is clearly being reeled in as the replacement."

I looked from the grandmother to the grandson.

"About the Loverly Cup." I described where I had found it and said I had also found what I was sure was Gillian's chain and cat charm nearby on the floor. "I then discovered that I'd left a compact mirror on the table under the clock and returned it to my handbag. When I took it out today while having lunch with Carolyn and Ariel, Carolyn commented that it was Marie Chantal. I was surprised she would know that unless she'd had a chance to look at the signature on the back—when she was in the Chaplain's House planting evidence against Gillian. But she told me, your ladyship, that you have a Marie Chantal compact mirror also."

"Untrue." The brevity of the reply revealed her sorrow.

"Have to hope she can be helped." Dorcas endeavored to sound bracing.

"And there's another thing. When Carolyn was leaving the Chaplain's House after visiting yesterday, she said that the clock on the landing was *wrong*. That wasn't so when it came to the time, which is what I thought she meant. I'm sure now she was trying to direct my attention to the fact that it did not fit in with the general décor, with the hope I would look behind it and find the niche. Then, when she hid the cap during the night, she left the clock askew to prompt a second inspection. I wasn't awfully quick on the uptake. But the penny did finally drop. And I also found the charm left to implicate Gillian."

"Marilyn hung the clock there because the niche was chipped around the exterior. Otherwise she would have put a clock on the telephone table," said Lady Loverly. "She was looking around for just the right sort, but thought that the present one, being the right size to cover the opening, would do for the time being. I remember she talked about it when I visited the Chaplain's House to view her changes."

"May I leave Carolyn for you to deal with, from this point on? I think that might be a better alternative than my making an official report to Mrs. Battle, especially at this distressing time." I addressed Aiden as well as her ladyship. "Unless she should decide to move the cup—and I don't see why she would—you will find it where I have told you."

"The poor sad girl." Lady Loverly suddenly looked very old. "Her home life has not been all that happy—parents at constant odds with each other—although unfortunately a lot of children contend with that sort of thing without going off the rails. Carolyn's maternal grandmother was my dearest friend, and for that reason I have done my best for the child, while regrettably never taking to her as I should. She must be made to see she has to face the consequences of her actions, return the cup to Mrs. Battle with full apologies, and take whatever punishment that results."

"I'll see to it, Granny." Aiden crossed to her chair and again kissed her cheek. "But I'm not hopeful Carolyn will change her spots; she likes herself too well the way she is. Is it any consolation, my dear, that Diane Frenton has at last agreed to marry me and wants very much to meet the other woman in my life?"

Lady Loverly patted his shoulder and then said briskly, "Ah, here comes Luanne with the tea tray, and your little friend with her. Ariel, dear child, would you move the magazines on that table so Luanne can set down the tray? I do hope you won't object to joining the old fogies now we are done with our chat."

"As an only child I'm quite used to being the only young person in adult company," Ariel responded primly. "I do, however, appreciate your concern, Lady Loverly."

"The cocoa's in the white pot and the tea should be brewed by now." Luanne stood importantly to attention. "As for the sandwiches, there's some egg and cheese and the rest are tomato and cress."

"Very nice, dear." Lady Loverly drummed her fingers on the arm of her chair. "Have you gone up to Mrs. Brown to see how she's doing? She was even quieter than usual today."

"She made it clear that she wanted an early night."

"I'll go up to her. She won't refuse to see her golden boy." Aiden moved to the door. "Long may I continue to flatter myself."

"Ooh, he is an imp, your ladyship!" Luanne giggled delightedly to an accompaniment from Ariel. Dorcas was eyeing the sandwiches hopefully.

Her ladyship and Dorcas chose tea and I joined Ariel in taking the cocoa. The sandwiches were passed and agreed to be most welcome. There was also a plate of chocolate biscuits that could not be ignored; neither could the silence. A feeling of unease I'd felt earlier in the evening was back in full force, and I had a strong sense that I was not the only one affected. It was our hostess who picked up the thread of conversation.

"Perhaps some of you would be interested in seeing the ancestral portraits. In recent times the Loverly family members have behaved themselves for the most part and have not been above polishing their image. The story of the Gray Nun and her sacrificial death is the stuff of legend and over the centuries has been encouraged in preference to the truth."

"Which was?" Ariel sat forward eagerly, spectacles shining.

"Human nature without the heroics. King Henry the Eighth's soldiers did strip the convent of its treasures, and the girl did flee with the gold chalice, but as the willing partner of the bridegroom from whom she had been wrenched at the altar by her parents. A man of humble birth by the name of Lubcock."

"Not to be ashamed of," said Dorcas.

Ariel considered this. "The name would be all right for a butler."

"He aimed higher." Lady Loverly spread a tasseled lap rug over her knees. "His bride came from the landed gentry, and they had money with which to set up in style—after selling the jewel-encrusted chalice. The couple went to London, where they won royal favor by becoming pillars of the new Protestant church, and in due course he received a knighthood from Queen Elizabeth the First. As the story goes, she was enchanted on hearing of his reunion with his nun bride (although one supposes he kept mum about the theft of the chalice), saying, *You are a lover to charm the heart of a queen, and so it shall be recognized. Kneel, Aiden Lubcock. Arise, Sir Aiden Loverly*. Nearly twenty years later the family—there were numerous children—returned to this area and made the Hall their country estate. By then the legend was fully established, and Lord and Lady Loverly found it in their best interests not to disavow it."

"How thrillingly romantic!" Ariel helped herself to a tomato and cress sandwich, the better to absorb the essence of the story.

"Fascinating lives they led years ago!" Dorcas thumped a fist on her knee. "Real story would make the better play."

"The Gray Nun's parents sound a real pair of fuddy-duddies," Ariel grumbled through the sandwich. "I'd like to see Dad and Betty try and stick me in a convent because I was keen on a boy they didn't like."

I consoled her. "Today you'd be taken to a therapist."

"We've been quite open about the story for a long time now," said her ladyship, "but most people cleave to the fictional version. There have been any number of Aidens since the first one. Several of whom have also been adventurers, but"—she reached for her teacup and smiled—"not necessarily wicked, I hope."

Aiden returned to the room and gracefully resettled himself on the chair he had vacated.

"Lady Loverly's been telling us the real story of the Gray Nun," Ariel informed him.

"For goodness' sake." He helped himself to a biscuit. "Don't spill the beans to Mrs. Frenton until I've have had the chance to tell her myself that no one around here remembers that our name was once Lubcock. It does rather take the gilt off the gingerbread." He turned to his grandmother. "I found Mrs. Brown awake but in an odd mood."

"Tense?"

"Less than usual, but she said that she may have to go away for a while. Has she said anything to you?"

Lady Loverly seemed to be fighting back tears. "That woman has been my constant companion for years. She saw me through my difficulties when your grandfather's drinking grew worse, but I have never managed to discover her hidden sorrow." Her ladyship reached into the side of her skirt but couldn't find a pocket, let alone a handkerchief.

I opened my bag and handed her a tissue. She really seemed a dear. Dorcas twitched an eyebrow in my direction, indicating that it might be time to return to St. Roberta's. Looking at my watch, I decided she was right. There was little time to be lost if Ariel was to make curfew without panting up the stairs and skating along the parquet floor to her dorm.

Our parting from the Loverly grandmother and grandson was affable. Aiden, I had to admit, had improved on acquaintance.

Seeing that Dorcas looked tired, I offered to drive and proceeded cautiously out onto the road. It was still raining, although not quite as hard as on our arrival. I checked with Ariel that she was wearing her seat belt.

"Yes, Mother," Ariel chirruped from behind me, then added soberly, "Lady Loverly is a lamb, isn't she? It was sweet of her to tell us her family history. The reason I was glad to go in search of Luanne was that I wanted to ask if she had made—as Carolyn claimed—the comment about Gillian being vindictive and sly or however it went. And guess what? Luanne said she had been talking about Carolyn, whom she'd decided early on was a little witch. Apparently Carolyn was in a foul mood on one weekend visit, because her ladyship wouldn't take her to a movie, and went into the kitchen, picked up a quite valuable milk jug, and dropped it—splat—on the quarry tiles, and then said Luanne had done it in a fit of temper. Luckily, her ladyship believed Luanne's version, having sized up Carolyn long before."

"Have to hope she can be brought round." Dorcas sighed. "Regret to say I suspected Mrs. Mossop of taking the Loverly Cup. Saw her in the corridor the afternoon it was taken. Poor woman looked like she was afraid the hand of the law would clamp down on her shoulder at any minute."

"Really?" I kept my eyes steadfastly on the road. "I thought you were afraid Gillian was the thief."

"Thought crossed my mind later on. Never bought it."

"I wonder if Carolyn planned it or acted on impulse."

"Oh, bother!" said Ariel. "I hoped I'd got in ahead of you. It struck me when we were at lunch that the more Carolyn stuck up for Gillian, the guiltier she made her seem. When I got back to school, I sought out Elizabeth Anderson and got her take as a former best friend. And she explained what had brought about the end of their friendship."

"Her getting the role in the school play."

"Exactly! So I'm sure you've twigged why Carolyn turned on Gillian."

"Help me out." I was navigating a corner.

"That once again—as she will have seen it—she was robbed of her place in the spotlight because Mr. Middleton chose Elizabeth to sing the school song at the celebration of the new gymnasium. But in this case it was Gillian she blamed . . . for not getting Mr. Middleton to choose her. I'm just guessing about this part, Ellie, but it seems to fit, doesn't it?"

"My guess," I said, "it's that Carolyn was more emotionally invested in Gillian than she may have been in Elizabeth—that this time it was more of a schoolgirl crush than a regular friendship. Therefore, the sense of betrayal and subsequent bitterness was greater and more requiring of punishment." I thought of Rosemary and the resentment that had lingered all these years as a result of her schoolgirl crush on Ms. Chips.

We drove past a tall bristling hedge that looked as though its purpose was to keep the inmates from getting out. It would be a relief to get back to the Chaplain's House. Mrs. Malloy might be in bed after her previous late night, but I hoped not. It would be good to talk to her about poor Mrs. Brown.

"Her ladyship does have a gift for making the past come alive. And there is nothing like a good story for taking the mind off other things."

"It was finishing *False Friend at Falcon Abbey.* That opened my eyes," Ariel said loftily. "The main character is a girl named Zoë. She's twelve, which of course is an impressionable age. But I found it far-fetched, the more I got into the story, that she was so stuck on this girl she thought was her best friend that she absolutely refused to believe all the evidence of villainy staring her in the face."

"Who'd believe Carolyn was so mixed up?" Dorcas sighed heavily. "Can't climb a rope to save her life, but nothing in that."

"Yes," I said. "And here we are, back safe and sound at St.

Roberta's." Having parked the car as close to the building as possible, I got out, head bent against the rain, and waited for the other two to join me. "Let's make a dash for it before we all get soaked to the skin."

Despite our speed, we were decidedly damp when we entered the reception hall. Rising from a chair by the staircase was a woman who identified herself as Mrs. Battle's secretary.

"You're five minutes late." Her admonishing voice coordinated well with her stern features. She ignored Dorcas entirely, but she did thrust an umbrella at me with the admonition not to forget to return it. Receiving a huffy look from my young relative, who had undoubtedly hoped I would stay for a chat, I headed out the door with the umbrella and hurried down the soggy slope of lawn to the Chaplain's House. The wind, which had picked up while I was inside, grappled at my clothing and would have made off with the brolly had I not hung on to it for dear life. It also made a snatch at the front door when I tugged at it. Again I narrowly came off as the victor, stepping into the hall to stand shivering and dripping puddles on the floor Mrs. Mossop had cleaned that afternoon.

"Come on up and get yourself dry," ordered Mrs. Malloy from the landing.

Stowing the brolly in the stand, I headed up the stairs. "I've a lot to tell you," I told her, as I followed her into my bedroom. Her head was crowned with purple rollers, but she hadn't removed her makeup. For this I was glad; right now—given the way my mind was working, I needed the blessedly familiar. It hadn't been easy to tell Lady Loverly that she had harbored a serpent in her bosom.

"Into your bedroom, Mrs. H, and pop on your nice warm dressing gown." Mrs. Malloy sounded like the beloved nanny I'd never had.

"I only have this skimpy thing!" I plucked it from the hook behind the door. "This is summer, remember?"

"Well, it'll have to do, won't it?" Nanny didn't appreciate backchat. "I can't turn the seasons round to please meself or you. There's no need to be awkward, whatever you've been through. Let's have it, Mrs. H. What went down with Lady Loverly at the Hall?"

I began telling her as I stood stripping off.

"Left me in the dark all day about that compact mirror, didn't you?" She sounded justifiably annoyed, while pleased with herself at the same time.

"I wasn't sure of my ground. Was I just looking for a way to avoid Gillian's being the guilty party?"

"Some people learn quicker than others that it don't do to let the emotions take over when you're a private detective. Sit yourself down and continue spilling the beans while I pour us both a stiff thimbleful of the brandy I had the sense to bring with me." She pointed at the bottle on the bedside table.

Meekly I did as I was told, ending with my request that Lady Loverly and her not-quite-as-detestable-as-I-had-thought grandson deal with Carolyn and the return of the cup.

"Well, then, now we know that Carolyn's a right little bugger, let's hope she gets turned around, although somehow I doubt it. With that sort, everyone is always wrong but them, and that's a hard thing to change because they just don't get it. There's more I can tell you roundabout the subject." Mrs. Malloy poured brandy for herself into the rose-patterned teacup set out on the dresser as a decorative accessory.

"Go on!" I handed her the floor, along with a good part of the bed.

"I went over to see Mrs. Mossop when I thought she and the hubby would be done with supper. Now, I'm not one to flatter meself that I can charm the birds off the trees, but I got the feeling soon as I met that poor downtrodden woman that I could get her to open up to me. She asked me if I'd like to sit out in her little garden."

"Out of earshot of you-know-who?"

"I speak as I find, Mrs. H. I've got to say as there was nothing about the grunt he gave me when Mrs. Mossop introduced us that a reasonable person could take offense to, and don't you go saying there's always two ways of taking a grunt because it will distract me this late in the evening. Point is, it was clear from the word *go* as how Mrs. Mossop has been needing someone to confide in for a donkey's age. And recent events has brought her to the boiling point. She told me she's got a sister that's had a problem with drink most of her life. There was a husband once upon a time, but he left her and the children don't want to know. As a result, she ended up homeless, living on the streets in Tingwell these past few months."

"How very sad!"

"Mrs. Mossop wanted to take her in, just until she could look around for an alternative home, but the hubby wouldn't hear of it. Said Mrs. Battle and the Board of Governors wouldn't approve, and he was probably right. Anyway, on the Monday afternoon when the Loverly Cup went missing, Mrs. Mossop had been cleaning inside the trophy cabinet."

I nodded. "So Mrs. Battle told me."

Mrs. Malloy bridled at the interruption. "Well, what you won't have been told is that Mrs. Mossop looked out the window and saw her sister crossing the school grounds dressed practically in rags with a shawl over her head."

"Sightings of the Gray Nun," I said. "The girls who were caught by Mr. Mossop on the Dribbly Drop on Sunday afternoon claimed to have seen a veiled figure lurking in the ruins."

"Whose story is this?"

"Sorry."

"Scared of what the hubby would do if he caught sight of her sister, Mrs. Mossop rushed outside the building, clear forgetting to close the cabinet, let alone lock it. After some panicked talking, she thought she'd persuaded Alice—I think that's her name—to go to a shelter and get back in touch. All of a tremble, as she put it, she went back inside to find the Loverly Cup gone. She wanted to tell Mrs. Battle the truth but was terrified of Mr. Mossop's reaction."

"As for the sister, did she really leave as agreed or hide out in the ruins?"

"That's where she's been, all right. Lucky the weather was good until this evening. Mrs. Mossop didn't realize till she heard what those girls had been saying about seeing the Gray Nun down below the Dribbly Drop. Since then she's been taking food down to her on the sly and praying he won't find out. Now she's talking about leaving him and getting a little flat with her sister if she promises to get help for her problem. And here's to hoping it works out." Mrs. Malloy took a look at my glass, saw I'd hardly touched my brandy, poured herself another shot, and plonked down again on the bed beside me.

"We mustn't lose our optimism because Carolyn turned into another False Friend at Falcon Abbey," I told her. "Perhaps if I hadn't been so worried about Gillian, I might have considered the realities sooner. Ariel talked about the great friendship between the two girls, but I saw no signs of it. In fact, I don't think I've heard Gillian say more than a mumbled word or two to Carolyn. She had to have been heartsick when her one friend turned on her. She must have realized when Aiden Loverly came at her the way he did—accusing her of being a thief—that Carolyn was intent on getting her blamed for stealing the Loverly Cup. Who would have believed she was innocent? Not even her great-aunt. She had been made to look immature when Deirdre unearthed the binky from under the mattress. The more worried Gillian became, the more neurotic she would appear. I was surprised to see her talking quite cheerfully to Phil yesterday in the kitchen."

Mrs. Malloy nodded sagely. "It did strike me at the time, now

I come to think of it, as how Carolyn's speaking about Gillian's binky made that piece of old shawl sound particularly babyish. Then again, Matron referred to it the same way."

"Carolyn may have used the juvenile term in telling her how upset poor dear Gilly had been when Deirdre dragged the thing out from under the mattress—after Carolyn, I'll bet, had made it easier to find by moving it from the far side of the bed to the front. And there was another thing. Dorcas mentioned to me that Ms. Chips wasn't particularly gung ho about the friendship between Gillian and Carolyn. There was something about *clinging vines*, which I took as applying to Gillian because she was the new girl, and a very unsettled homesick one at that. But what if Ms. Chips was referring to Carolyn, having noted a pattern of her latching onto other girls because she saw something special in them and liked to bask in their reflected glory? Especially where, as with Gillian, she came off as the protector?"

"Okay." Mrs. Malloy settled more comfortably on the bed, which meant taking up most of it. "Gillian's a musical prodigy, but what's this Elizabeth's claim to fame?"

"She got the lead in the school play. Perhaps, like Philippa, she has aspirations to become a professional actress. And we have another case in point."

"Our Ariel?"

"Exactly. The new best friend, who might be thought to need taking under a kindly wing because she's a bit of an oddity on account of her peculiarly advanced vocabulary, quaint manner, and the fact that her parents acquired their wealth by winning the lottery. But it's all right. Ariel knows what's going on. If Carolyn stays on at St. Roberta's, Ariel won't be beastly to her, but she'll stay clear as much as possible. As for Gillian, I think I'll go talk to the Middletons tomorrow morning—or as soon as I can haul myself out of bed." I yawned hugely. Unfortunately Mrs. Malloy didn't take the hint. She repositioned one of her purple rollers and then got up and poured herself another brandy.

"Whether Gillian said squeak or not, you can bet your bubblegum her manner toward Carolyn changed, causing Carolyn in her turn to have her revenge with the binky. What's put that look on your, face Mrs. H?"

"Thinking about Ms. Chips and feeling certain she would feel achingly sorry for Gillian and Carolyn. Perhaps particularly the latter."

Mrs. Malloy was back to being the kindly nanny with a tipple in her hand. "What you need is a good night's rest."

"Yes, Nanny."

"I thought as I was your Aunt Petal."

I laughed shakily. "You see how confused I am?"

"So will Mr. Mossop be when he wakes up one morning and finds his wife's walked out on him."

"My head is spinning, Nanny."

"Oh, all right! Nighty-night."

She had been gone no more than a couple of minutes when I heard footsteps crossing the landing from the direction of the stairs. Opening the door, I saw Phil, looking charmingly vibrant in her black dress, coming toward me.

"Am I disturbing you? I haven't been able to sleep and heard voices in here. Brian came up to the school when I was up there this evening. He'd had dinner, as you know, with Tosca, but they didn't linger. He wanted to see how Matron was doing after the shock of losing her best friend, but she wasn't there. She'd gone over to Ms. Chips's fairly early in the evening and wasn't back when I left—with Brian."

"Oh!" I sat up straighter.

"We went for a drive in his car. Nothing like going for a spin in the driving rain!" Smiling, she came into my bedroom. "He made no attempt to talk about the old days, but—selfishly or not—I had to explain and apologize. Discovering that he was living in the area was the reason I came back. I've always felt guilty, knowing he'd deserved better."

I sat back down on the bed and looked up at her inquiringly.

"That day there was such a rumpus about my leaving the San to meet him in Lilypad Lane? I didn't—"

"I know." I was knotting my fingers together. "But I didn't speak up on your behalf because I was too much of a coward."

It was her turn to stare at me, so I explained.

"My word," she said. "It's hard for me to understand anyone hating lacrosse so much that they'd hide out week after week. I loved it!"

"I know! And when I think of how you lost out not only on becoming head girl but being captain of the team, I'm consumed with remorse."

"Well, don't be." She sat down on the bed beside me and placed an arm around my shoulders. "It would have made everything so much worse if you'd spoken up, because that would have put my friend Sally Brodstock in hot water. If we're talking about cowardice, I would have won the prize. I didn't have the courage to tell Brian out loud that I wanted to break up with him because I didn't want any distractions from my goal of becoming an actress. Things were hard enough, I felt, with my parents being so against the idea. So I wrote a letter and then phoned and asked him to meet me before he caught the train back to London on that Friday afternoon. He couldn't take a later one because there was a lecture he couldn't miss, but I didn't see that as a problem because I had a free period I would normally have spent in the library. But the stress got to me. I hated hurting him, and I came down with a blinding headache, and when I realized I'd have to go to the San and lie down, Sally said she would take the letter for me. It was she that Mr. Bumbleton saw, and Sally was quite prepared to go to Mrs. Battle and tell her so, but I finally got her to see that wouldn't have spared me. We would both have been punished and I would have felt far worse. I admit I was sorry not to become lacrosse captain; it was a blow. But on the positive side, I got to embark on my stage career earlier than I had planned."

"None of that alters the fact that I was a wretched weakling."

"Shall we form a club?"

I had to laugh. "Did it go well—your talk with Dr. Roberts?"

"Oh, yes." There was a dreamy note to her voice. "I had no thoughts of romance blooming anew; that sort of thing doesn't happen. We were both young and unformed then. But the moment we started talking this evening, it was as though the part of me that had been missing was back in place. And he told me when we were driving that it had taken him that way too."

"I wondered if you were upset when Tosca said she was going out for dinner with him."

"No. If I acted bothered it was because hearing him mentioned brought my feelings of guilt to the fore."

"Before the close of confession," I said, "there's something else I should tell you. I don't have an Aunt Petal. Mrs. Battle learned from my friend Dorcas Critchley that Mrs. Malloy and I have had some experience as private detectives, and she requested our help in discovering who took the Loverly Cup."

"I guessed something of the sort. Are you afraid Gillian took it? Because, if so, I think you're wrong. That girl is so transparent one aches for her."

"I'm absolutely sure she didn't." I did not add to this. It wouldn't have been right, after leaving the matter to Lady Loverly and Aiden.

Phil said good night and went along to her own room, leaving me to mull over our conversation until I fell back on the bed, too exhausted to crawl under the covers. Sleep grabbed me by the throat, and I might not have woken till morning had I been warm enough. As it was, I surfaced to the realization that, even though I was still wearing my wrap, I was chilled to the bone and that something . . . or someone . . . was tapping at the window. Another wee-hours visit from Ariel or Dorcas? Or a ghost, not of the Gray Nun but of Ms. Chips, with a message from beyond the grave?

16

It was only a tree branch. Morning and I, never the best of chums, got off to an unfriendly start the next day. Straggling downstairs around nine-thirty, I found the place empty except for Mrs. Malloy, looking resplendent as always despite the one purple roller still in her hair. I decided against pointing this out and gratefully accepted the cup of tea she handed me.

"I've only been down a short while meself." She sat back on the kitchen stool that she had vacated with the reluctance of a queen abdicating her throne. "Talk about feeling washed out, Mrs. H, I can't do the late nights like I used to. When a woman hits fifty, it's harder to leap out of bed the morning after with a song in the heart." We both knew she had encountered this speed bump in the road of life a good decade before, but I didn't bring it up.

"Where are the others?" It had become my first question of the day, a routine part of living at the Chaplain's House.

"Haven't seen any of them. A good thing too, when it comes

to that Rosemary. That voice of hers would knock the head off a bull, and even Tosca's a bit too bright and breezy before I've had me Weetabix. Phil's a different matter, of course, but my guess is she's off having another word with that doctor of hers."

"I hope he *is* hers, and they end up getting married and having lots of children," I said. "Did you get any sleep? Have you managed a bite of breakfast?" It was written all over Mrs. Malloy's face that she was exhausted.

"Who can remember anything at this indecent hour of the morning? I'll take a slice of toast if you're offering, but don't bother with marmalade. It don't seem right to be enjoying ourselves after all that's been happening at St. Roberta's"

"I'm surprised Rosemary didn't come in to tell us to be quiet last night."

"Oh, I don't know! She said in her snotty way when she was going up to bed last night as how she'd got herself some industrial earplugs and was going to shove them well in. As for Tosca"—Mrs. Malloy took the plate of toast I handed her—"she said she'd bought a sedative when she was at the chemist's and planned on taking a dose and dreaming all night that she was smoking her head off. Ms. Critchley rang just as I came downstairs, and when I said as how you was still sleeping, she said not to wake you."

"I never heard the phone."

"It rang again, right after I'd hung up the receiver. That time it was Ruth Middleton, hoping to have a word with you. She said, if it wasn't asking too much, would you come by her house when you could manage it. Her brother was up at the school teaching this morning—classes are going on much as usual—and he phoned to ask after Gillian. After they talked, he went home. It was clear from her voice something has happened."

"I'll go now," I said, getting off my stool. "Do you want to come with me?"

"Thanks, but I don't think I will. I'm not looking me best.

And like I always tell me sister Melody, meeting a single man for the first time deserves two hours before the mirror. Not that I suppose he'd take that good a look, with his heart still set on his deceased wife. But I have me standards and won't budge from them." Hand pressed to her majestic bosom, she went on. "When a woman starts letting herself go there's no end to it. The next will be going out with rollers in me hair."

"If you're not coming I think you should go back to bed with a book. I brought one with me that I haven't so much as opened yet; help yourself if you like. It's sitting on the top of my suitcase."

Some twenty minutes later I left the Chaplain's House with Dorcas's car keys in my handbag—I'd forgotten to return them to her last night—and the umbrella lent to me by Mrs. Battle's secretary held aloft. It was not raining hard, but there was a brisk wind and the ground had a lot of suction. Halfway across the lawn, I encountered the wiry Mr. Mossop trudging toward the school.

"Hello," I said. "Nasty day, isn't it?"

He glowered at me from under the limp brim of his dirt-colored cap. "It is that! My wife's up and left me! Found a note on the mantelpiece and no breakfast in the oven. It's a crying shame what a man has to put up with these days."

"Oh, dear!"

"Like as not, with her gone I'll be given the shove."

"Oh, surely not!"

His currant eyes raked me over, daring me to present a bright side. "What is the world coming to? is what I ask. First that silver cup stolen, then Ms. Chips killed, and now this! Could get a man down if he let it."

"Mustn't give way." I was desperate to press on before one of us drowned.

Away he trounced and I made haste to reach the car before the umbrella took sail for the Americas. With the wipers going full speed as I drove through the now-sheeting rain, I should have had one thought, to get to the Middletons' house, but my mind kept darting around the question of whether St. Roberta's would be forced to close down as a result of unsavory publicity. Much to my surprise, I hoped such would not be the case, not only because Dorcas was already devoted to the school's interests but because it was a really good school, with a sound academic and—give credit where due—sports tradition. Besides which, it was . . . *my* school.

The windows had started to fog, something that always makes me nervous, as I pulled up outside the Middleton house. I had barely pressed the bell when Ruth opened the door. She ushered me eagerly into the hall, where she took my soggy raincoat and umbrella, stowed them away, and led me into the comfortable sitting room.

"How about a cup of tea?" She looked pale and shaken.

"Thank you, but I'm fine . . . although that doesn't sound quite right after what happened to Ms. Chips."

"Remember how we saw her and Mrs. Brown Monday in the restaurant where we were having lunch?" Ruth watched me take a seat before positioning herself in a chair across from me. "Clive's back from St. Roberta's but he's gone for a walk . . . to the place just a few streets away where Anya was run down. And I've been sitting staring into space for a good fifteen minutes; I'd just got up to pace when I saw you from the window coming down the path."

"What's wrong, Ruth?"

"A letter came this morning, and I just had to confide in someone. I don't understand why, seeing that we don't know each other well, but you were the person who came to mind. Clive won't object. . . ." She pressed a hand to her forehead, and again I took in her drained face.

"Letter?"

"Addressed to Clive, from Mrs. Brown. My telling him about it over the phone brought him home. He read the contents through to himself first and then out loud to me. It was a confession and a plea for forgiveness. Ellie, Mrs. Brown was the driver who knocked Anya down and drove off without summoning help."

"Oh, my goodness!" I crossed over to Ruth's chair and knelt down beside her.

"She said she'd had one of her dreadful migraines that night and was lying down when the phone rang. It was someone from the pub saying that Sir Henry needed to be picked up because he wasn't sufficiently sober to make his own way home. Lady Loverly had taken Aiden to the opera in London that evening, and they would not be returning until the next day. Mrs. Brown was alone in the house. She wrote that she should have asked for Sir Henry to be sent home in a taxi, but she was afraid that if she failed to do her duty she would be let go—foolish, but she's always been a compulsive worrier." Ruth reached down for my hand. "Lady Loverly would never have sent her packing, though there'd never be any convincing Mrs. Brown of that. She got into the car provided for her use—completely groggy, from what she writes—and admits to careening up onto the pavement and feeling a mind-numbing thud when she hit Anya. Unable to think, let alone reason, she backed up and continued to the pub, where she collected Sir Henry. The next morning, she checked the car for signs of damage but could see none. When she learned shortly afterward that Anya was dead, she knew she should go to the police but was petrified that she would be sent to prison."

"Oh, Ruth!"

"She wrote she had never told anyone until the other day, when Marilyn invited her out for lunch and asked if some worry might be causing her dreadful headaches."

"What will your brother do?"

"Nothing. By that I mean he won't go to the police. But he said straightaway that he *will* go and see Mrs. Brown, to tell her she has suffered long enough. It was an accident, and there's no point in anguishing about should-haves-but-didn't. Thank God for Marilyn. Finally, after all these years, I think Clive can come to terms with Anya's death. At the moment he's in shock. That would have been the case at any time, but this comes right on top of Marilyn's death and our very deep concern about Gillian. I have to say I feel sorry for Mrs. Brown. Living with guilt of that magnitude must have been intolerable." She patted my hand. "Thank you for coming. I really would like us to be friends. Any word on the Loverly Cup?"

"Yes, and it affects Gillian." I told her, adding that I had left it to Lady Loverly as donor of the cup and Carolyn Fisher-Jones's godmother, with the support of her grandson, to decide how best to proceed. She sat in silence for several moments. I offered to make her a cup of tea, but she refused. Thinking her brother was unlikely to want company when he returned from his walk, I said that I probably should get back to the Chaplain's House. We were in the hall and I was putting my raincoat back on when she said there was something else she wanted to tell me.

"Clive was concerned that he must have struck you as distracted when talking to you yesterday evening."

I smiled. "He had just come down the apple tree after rescuing Harpsichord."

"Yet again." She returned my smile, but it did not reach her eyes. "He saw something when he was at the top that bothered him. It shouldn't have . . . and he wasn't quite sure why it did. But he said he felt a prickly feeling go down his spine, and that's not like my brother."

"Tell me."

"It's going to sound petty and spiteful. And do bear in mind that neither Clive nor I are overly fond of Wilma Johnson. We never have been since hearing via the grapevine that she accidentally—as she claims—informed Marilyn's bridegroom's mother that there were family mental problems and thereby ensured the end of the marriage. Anyway, this time Harpsichord had climbed almost to the top of the tree, and when Clive reached for her he saw Wilma prowling around the landing next door, adjusting pictures on the wall, shifting ornaments on a table, stroking a bench cushion. Of course these small actions could have been her way of expressing affection for Marilyn, coupled with grief at her loss, but Clive said she turned around so that she faced his way for a moment and he saw this look of—sounds awful to repeat—horrible complacency on her face."

I had seen her stroking the sofa too, and a feeling of revulsion had seized me, along with an inexplicable unease.

"Is there something else, Ruth?"

She stood rubbing her folded arms. "Gillian came down half an hour ago and said she was going to school to see *Matron*—she didn't say *Aunt Wilma*. Naturally, I said I would take her in the car, but I felt I should wait until Clive got back from his walk, in case he wanted to go and see Mrs. Brown immediately. Gillian said she understood. I went into the kitchen to get her some breakfast but when I came to tell her it was ready she was gone."

"She would have taken the bus."

"It leaves from the other side of the green and will take her to the stop just beyond the ruins, across from Lilypad Lane on the main road. Ellie, I know it's silly to be worried—"

"Why?"

"Gillian said that for once in her life she had to stop being a coward and confront the truth; if she didn't she'd regret it for the rest of her life. I thought she meant she was going to have it out with Wilma about never having wanted to come to St. Roberta, but as the minutes tick by I'm not so sure that's all there is to it."

"I'll go after her," I said.

"And I'll come with you." She followed me to the door.

"It shouldn't take two of us. I think you need to be here when your brother returns."

"Yes, but—"

"I promise you I'll find Gillian and make sure Matron doesn't give her a bad time."

Once in the car, I struggled to relax. Ruth was understandably on edge after Mrs. Brown's letter and leaping ahead to the worst of scenarios. But the last thing Gillian needed was a seriously unpleasant encounter with her great-aunt, during which she would find herself labeled self-centered and ungrateful. I liked both Middletons. Ben would too. Perhaps we could persuade them to visit us at Merlin's Court one weekend, bringing Gillian with them. . . .

The car was on its best behavior as I drove to the bus stop where Gillian would disembark. My hope was to catch up with her before she reached the school, let alone Matron's office. I would explain how concerned Ruth was on her behalf and—but I didn't get much further with these thoughts. Deciding to park in Lilypad Lane and check the time listings on the bus stop, I climbed out, tossed the keys in my handbag, and was about to turn in the direction of the main road when I heard a muffled cry coming from the ruins. I'm not much of a runner, but I must have broken a world record reaching the roofless refectory. Belatedly, I was remembering Mrs. Malloy repeating the words I had striven to catch during Ms. Chips's final moments. "Will . . . my." This filled the situation But what if she had been trying to say Wilma?

On entering I saw no one; rain and heavy cloud cover had darkened the refectory to an unearthly gloom. The cry came again, and I located the source of the sound—the corner giving onto the steps leading down into the crypt—and I heard Matron's voice.

"Very well, you miserable child, we'll take a breather before I drag you below and leave you to rot. No one goes there, and certainly not to look for *you*. They'll decide you ran away: hitchhiked and ended up like other runaway girls, buried in some ditch or woodland."

"I *did* run away—or was going to, the night before last. I was talking to Philippa Boswell at the Chaplain's House when I suddenly made up my mind. Mrs. Haskell advised me to phone Mum and Dad, but I knew they'd try to talk me into staying, whereas if I showed up on the doorstep and explained how miserable I've been since Carolyn turned on me, they wouldn't make me go back. I've still got my birthday money for train fare, and if I left early I'd have time to walk to the station."

"How resourceful you sound for a girl who can't sleep without the remnant of her baby blanket!"

"I thought it only fair to leave a note in your office," Gillian continued, in a voice that sounded as though it had been recorded. "I'd written it earlier. But just when I was ready to go, I saw a shadow cross the dorm and climb into bed. It was Carolyn. I had to wait until I felt sure she was back asleep before I could get up."

"I wish you'd broken your ankle in the dark, the way I did out on the moor all those years ago." What chilled me was how matter-of-factly this was said, a woman completley absorbed by self. It clicked that she had relished talking to me about her relationship with Ms. Chips. I had been an unexpected audience, one who would hopefully see she was the one who had been hard done by and misjudged.

"When I opened your office door, I could hear you and Ms. Chips talking in the San. She was telling you that she had left most of her money for scholarships for St. Roberta's students with special abilities. I didn't hear your reply, but I caught a glimpse of your face. You looked so angry it made me feel sick, so I left, taking the note with me."

"Marilyn got up and looked out the window." Matron laughed unpleasantly. "I expect she couldn't face me. Turning back, she said someone was outside, crossing the grounds, and she would go after whoever it was. I said I wouldn't think of letting my lifelong friend go out alone. What if it were some lowlife, perhaps the person Shirley and Miriam had twittered about seeing near the ruins? Unthinkable to let dear Marilyn take such a risk. Was I hoping she would head toward the Dribbly Drop? I really can't be sure what I was thinking. I was deeply hurt, more so even than when she first came into her legacy and I was so sure she would want me to have the house I had rented in Cygnet's Way and buy it outright for me. But she didn't. She offered to let me have what she obviously considered a sizable down payment, but there would still have been a mortgage. How could she be so selfish?"

"I saw you both—just two people, really—coming after me, so I hid in the bushes close to the Dribbly Drop. Then the moon came out and I saw Ms. Chips standing at the top, and you"—Gillian's voice quivered—"I saw you push her and then go down the steps."

"I had to check on her condition. It was the least a friend could do. I felt for a pulse and couldn't find one. I was sure she was dead. Which I imagine was also your assumption."

"Yes."

"But as she wasn't when found by that Ellie Haskell and her vulgar crony, I suppose I wanted it so much I convinced myself. This is why it doesn't do to trust friends or relatives. These pearls of wisdom would stand you in good stead if you lived to absorb them, but I knew, the moment you got off that bus, that you had to die without further loss of time. I've been worried in case you did see what happened and might decide to talk. Even though it's doubtful you'd be believed, given your unbalanced state, my new-found happiness is being impinged upon. Had you already confided in the meddlesome Middletons, you wouldn't be here alone. So no need to bother about them. And if you'd spilled the beans to anyone before going to them, the police would already have questioned me. How fortunate I'd come out for a stroll, so I could think about my new house! Perhaps if Marilyn had told me she had left it to me, I might not have been so upset, but she didn't, so there—or, I should say *here*—we are. And it is now time to make our descent to the crypt. There's no point in fighting me. I am far stronger than you—at least that's one advantage of having a stocky build."

"You were only able to drag me in here because you caught me by surprise. I'll scream. Someone's bound to hear."

"Remember, you already did and no one has rushed to the rescue."

"That's where you're wrong," I said conversationally.

Either Matron or Gillian gasped. They emerged from the gloom, the older woman's hand around the young girl's throat.

"Oh, it's you!" Her voice was loaded with contempt, the pebble eyes blackly visible in the gloom. "Before you can get to us, I'll have dragged her backward and hurled her down the stairs. They're three times the length of the Dribbly Drop, and with luck she'll bounce the best part of the way. To think I wanted to help her, to give her the chance at a fine education, and this is the thanks I get. But let's look on the bright side. She finally has good reason to be miserable."

I stood there with something in my hands. While listening to the distressing conversation, I had remembered the lacrosse ball in my handbag, the one Elizabeth Anderson had asked me and the other residents of the Chaplain's House to sign in remembrance of Ms. Chips. Could I, who had hidden out in the little sewing room above the San because I was so miserably inept at games, throw that ball at Matron without felling Gillian instead? I raised my arm and let it fly—and amazingly I made contact, hitting the right place on the right face. I heard a scream, Matron toppled, and Gillian raced to my side.

Later I was informed by a member of Her Majesty's police that I was being considered for a citation. Breaking an assailant's nose is satisfactory in itself, but breaking it in three places was a triumph.

17

The next day, Dorcas, Mrs. Malloy, and I were to return to Merlin's Court. I was waiting for them in the parking area when I saw Rosemary stowing a suitcase in the boot of her Mercedes. Her scowl on noticing me was hardly complimentary.

"Oh, God, it's you. And I was hoping to get away without further goodbyes. Not that seeing the last of Tosca wasn't one of the highlights of my life. Mark my words, she'll be back to smoking again the minute someone blows a puff in her face. I expect that's why our country doctor dumped her after half a date." Slamming the boot shut, she had the grace to look awkward. "There's no need to look at me that way! I admit it was a sad way for Ms. Chips to go, and I'm sorry. Really sorry. She was a good egg. Deep down I've always known that. But I've a lot on my mind, if you haven't noticed."

"Do you think you should be taking off?"

"Why shouldn't I?" She straightened up to loom over me.

"The police may want to talk with us some more."

"I wasn't a witness to anything, remember. So with or without your blessing, I'm off."

"I'm sure your family and Laurence will be glad to have you home." My attempt at sounding soothing won me no points. She stood with arms folded, her feet shifting as if eager to kick something, preferably a wheel of the Mercedes.

"Do you want to hear something that will make you smirk, Ellie? Well, here goes! I didn't come to the Chaplain's House worn out from my wonderful life. The truth is, Gerald lost his job due to downsizing, we're faced with selling the house and taking Nichola and Sheridan out of private school, and to make everything even more perfect, my marriage is on the rocks!"

"Rosemary, I'm so sorry."

"That makes two of us. I went to see that acquaintance in Tingwell, before you arrived Sunday, because Gerald's been offered a job there at a pittance of his former salary. I wanted to take a look at the place and see if I could survive in a similar house—the size of a box, all mod cons excluded. After seeing the grim reality and picturing drug dealers and drunks on every corner, I thought there was no chance in hell! But now I know that murder can happen anywhere, maybe I'll reconsider."

"Good luck," I said, as she climbed into her car.

"I'll need it." She stuck her head out the window. "Gerald's furious with me for what he calls my *lack of emotional support.* I thought he'd get over it if I went away, but he hasn't phoned. Guess I'll have to turn on the wifely charm."

"Do that!" I encouraged. It was starting to rain again.

She started the engine. "One more thing."

"Yes?"

"Want a laugh? It was Mrs. Mossop's vagrant sister who pinched my blue silk knickers. Well, at least she preferred mine to yours or Tosca's, and who can begrudge the woman for creeping into the house when no one was around and helping herself to a change of underwear, without coming off like an ogress.

Take care, Ellie. You're not such a bad old stick, and neither for that matter is your Aunt Petal." With a nonchalant wave, she went off down the drive, and feeling surprisingly lighter in heart I looked toward the Chaplain's House, to see Dorcas and Mrs. Malloy coming toward me.

The luggage was already stowed in the boot. I was going home to Ben and the children. Dorcas would drive, with me seated beside her. Mrs. Malloy and Ariel, who'd been given permission by Tom and Betty to stay with us for a week or so, would ride in the rear.

The plan was to return with Ariel for the ceremonial opening of the new gymnasium. Gillian, who had also gone home to her family, would be back to play a recital in honor of Ms. Chips. Earlier that day, the Loverly Cup would be handed over to this year's lacrosse champions; her ladyship had cheerfully agreed to continue the tradition of making the presentation. Aiden Loverly was officially engaged to Diane Frenton. And Mrs. Brown had gathered the housekeeping reins back into her hands, while conceding that Luanne might one day successfully take over. The Middletons I fully hoped and expected to see again. As for Mrs. Battle, she had made an announcement that pleased me very much: in honor of a hope that Ms. Chips had voiced, the little mending room was to be designated in future as a retreat for any girl who felt the need to snuggle down by herself for a few hours.

Getting everything right every time might have been beyond the likes of Saint Roberta, had she ever existed—which according to Ariel's research was seriously in doubt. My return to my old school had brought home to me that I didn't want to be a saint or experience the heights of adventure, as the Gray Nun had done, but instead face up to past failures; that was my way to get out from under my dark cloud of guilt. Gillian had already faced the most frightening adversity of all: herself.

As Dorcas drove through the countryside with her usual

sensitivity to other drivers and her car's idiosyncrasies, I longed to be seated in the garden at Merlin's Court, listening to the sparrow ensemble trilling away on a branch above my head, while Ben lay on the grass tossing daisies at me and the children occupied themselves in being healthily naughty one minute and reasonably good the next.

Without saying anything, Dorcas stopped in front of Miss Chips's house. In the past few days, I had faced the fact that some exteriors don't accurately reveal what is going on inside. Ms. Chips's house was an exception: a dwelling whose outside was an honest reflection of its interior. A house that had seen happiness and sorrow and was the more real because of that.

The first thing the children would ask me when I arrived home was what I learned by going back to school. The answer would be simple and wonderfully consoling. I'd tell them I now knew what I wanted to be when I was fully grown up: someone who did not let heartache prevent her from living and loving to the full. A woman who touched other lives and made a difference without fanfare . . . so that it might be years before those affected truly realized her impact.

When Dorcas slowly pulled away from the curb, Mrs. Malloy offered Ariel a toffee, which was graciously accepted. I leaned out of the window for one last look at the house and whispered, "Goodbye, Ms. Chips."